LGBT FICTION

THE LEONARDO CHRONICLES

LGBT Fiction
The Leonardo Chronicles
Erotic Historical Romance
by Rose Anderson
Published by Indie Artist Press
Eagle Mountain, Utah
www.indieartistpress.com
First Edition
Loving Leonardo by Rose Anderson
Loving Leonardo – The Quest by Rose Anderson
copyright © 2012-2015
All rights reserved.
ISBN-10: 1-62522-038-3
ISBN-13: 978-1-62522-038-7
June 2015

Loving Leonardo is an OKRWA International Digital Awards Winner; a CataRomance Sensual Reads Reviewer's Choice Winner in Historical Romance; a Two Lips Reviews Recommended Read; an Erotic Ménage Romances Fans' Choice Nominee.

ACKNOWLEDGMENTS

My heartfelt appreciation goes to my family and friends who routinely offer encouragement, laughter, suggestions, and yes, character study. It's true. Everyone I love shows up in the small details of my stories. I suppose this is my way of having you live forever. Trite to say, but you are the wind in my sails.

My appreciation to Karen Adams, the best editor an author could work with. I suspect her head is as full of details as mine for she understands my thoughts in this creative process. More than that, she holds my feet to fire where anachronisms are concerned. It might have been said somewhere, but it had better be in the vernacular of the time if I use it. Wordie that I am, I admit I *love* this.

My thanks to artist extraordinaire Kim Van Meter for a fabulous cover, as seen inset on this edition. And thanks to my friend and fellow author Jane Leopold Quinn who convinced me to travel uncharted territory, and who, upon reading Loving Leonardo's first draft, responded with wonderful words of encouragement. She put a smile on my face that lasted for days when she said she'd "kill me" if I sent this anywhere that didn't "deserve a well written, literate, sophisticated story like this." It still makes me smile. Here it is Jane, may the world be as kind.

You do ill if you praise, but worse if you censure, what you do not understand.

    — Leonardo da Vinci

Book One

LOVING LEONARDO

PROLOGUE

Carlo Posateri shrugged his cloak back on his shoulders, the thin wool gone heavy from absorbing the September fog. He peered into the night then checked his pocket watch under the misty gaslight. Few people would be out in an evening fog like this and there was a word to describe many who were — *Ladro*. It was a perfect night to make deals with a thief.

The acquisition ritual played in his mind. To start: a warm bath and a brandy, followed by an excursion into the most brilliant and salacious mind ever produced by the Renaissance. He envisioned the sinful eroticism the book was certain to contain; the impression settled heavy in his loins. Salivating in anticipation, he swallowed. He wasn't a sinner. His disdain for the sodomite artists didn't mean he couldn't enjoy their unique and compelling art. But he wasn't *one* of *them*. He simply appreciated their artistic technique.

Born and raised in Rome, he'd planned to return after his

Silvia died. But her older brother Pietro encouraged him to stay because without other family, they were all each of them had in the world. Though he liked Pietro well enough, familial ties weren't incentive to remain. Rather, being his wealthy brother-in-law's sole heir was. Beyond that, he had other reasons to stay in Venice. Outside Florence, old Venice drew deviants like a candle flame attracted moths. Then and now, the world had no place for such debauchery. The most depraved artworks could be found in the ports and once purchased, he'd destroyed many of them for the filth they were. A few pieces he'd keep to study.

His collection grew in the seat of Renaissance decadence; how fitting. Carlo often imagined living during that artistic age. Had he lived exactly four hundred years ago, he would have helped Girolamo Savonarola build the pyre for the Bonfire of the Vanities. Carlo licked his lips, seeing it in his mind's eye: the pair of them feeding the flames with art and artist alike. A small lantern light maneuvered along the Grand Canal. Looking around him once more, he moved closer to the water.

Curiously, tonight's meeting had been arranged by a different man. He'd received a note from one E. Fortuna describing several antique books in his employer's possession, including one of homoerotic art reminiscent of Leonardo da Vinci's work. Quoting a price, Fortuna added he'd also contacted other potential buyers, no doubt to spur him to act quickly. But in the span of a day, a second note arrived. This one from Signore Falconetti, saying the book changed hands and was still for sale. What happened to E. Fortuna?

Carlo didn't like dealing with Falconetti, though he had twice before. Both times he felt fortunate to leave with his life. The prospect of owning such a work, however, was too tempting to ignore. He looked around again to be sure this meeting was private, as Falconetti demanded. Falconetti had a reputation, and it wasn't a good one. Men like this often found themselves employed by multiple clients, who would occasionally be at cross purposes with one another.

The small gondola bumped in the darkness and Carlo heard rather than saw the removal of the remo pulled from the forcola. The oar wouldn't be in *his* way, for he had no intention of stepping into the man's boat.

***

Without a doubt, Carlo Posateri knew the Heavenly Father watched over him. He ran his trembling fingers over the precious book's leather and brass bindings. Beyond a doubt this was the pinnacle of his private collection. As soon as he had laid eyes upon Falconetti's amazing offering, Carlo was driven to pay any price. Unfortunately the price had quadrupled, from E. Fortuna's initial quote. He'd somehow managed to convince Falconetti to take what money he had with him by swearing he was good for the rest, and more. The dangerous man told him his life depended on that being true.

Doing the church's work had made him as poor as a beggar in St. Peter's Square — he simply didn't *have* more money to give the man. As it was, his last maid would only be working until the end of the month. Carlo poured himself a brandy, his shaking hands sloshing the amber liquid onto his sleeve. It took both hands to hold the snifter still long enough to allow a fortifying sip. He must persuade his brother-in-law to lend him more money. He glowered into his glass. Experience told him this would prove difficult. Pietro frowned on Carlo's sacred mission even though he knew the last Pope himself approved.

And now there'd be no time to ask him. Pietro was inopportunely traveling to London, England for an appointment with an American diplomat regarding selling his raw fibers to the American textile markets. Awash in a mixture of elation and hopelessness, Carlo raked a hand over his sparse head of hair.

With no other option, he took up a pen and scribbled a quick note to his brother-in-law to say he wanted to go with him. Pietro had made the offer weeks ago; he'd no doubt be pleased. Carlo rang for the maid then wrote another note to Falconetti promising the money by mid-October at the latest. He hoped the delay wouldn't matter, but just in case, *this* note would be delivered *after* he and Pietro sailed.

***

Calmer from his bath and double-shot brandy, Carlo Posateri fully appreciated his purchase. He couldn't have imagined better; the sinful sketches in the book were enhanced by shockingly seductive prose. In full appreciation of the art, he found his release in the first four pages. Deciding he wouldn't turn another page until his return, he sought a latch behind several leather-bound volumes on his shelf. The false front sprung open to reveal a secret recess with a stack of paintings and several old books. Compelling erotic vignettes lingering in his mind, Carlo placed da Vinci's book with the rest.

~1~

Hearing the urgent knock, I wrapped my dressing gown around my damp person, tying the sash on the way to the door. The smell of baking bread hit me hard the instant I opened it, to discover a flour-dusted Mrs. Fletcher, obviously pulled from her Tuesday baking, standing with an envelope in her hand. She gave me a brief once over.

"Excuse me dear, I'm sorry to be interrupting your... uh... visit. A courier brought this to the door just now."

Seeing the discomfort written on her face, I gave my housekeeper a light scold. "Dear heart, I would have come down, why didn't you ring the bell for me? You know you shouldn't be taking the stairs with that bad hip of yours. What will Dr. Compton say?"

She smiled. "He won't be saying anything dear boy, because you won't tattle. You know I feel funny about that bell. Whoever heard of a service bell rigged the other way around?"

I chuckled. "It's more important to me that you're not in pain, dear. No one outside this house needs know of it." She'd been in service since the age of twelve – some fifty odd years. Such ingrained habit was difficult to ignore.

The splash from behind me spurred her to peer over my shoulder. Her cheeks pinkened and passing the envelope, she said, "I wouldn't have brought it upstairs, save the man said his lady would be calling within the hour and I didn't think you'd want Thomas up here when she arrived."

Wiping the water from my face with my sleeve, I spared the housekeeper a reassuring smile. "I so appreciate your diplomacy. It warms me that you always look out for us."

"Someone has to, and I'd rather see you both here and safe then off who knows where. Please send my nephew down, I'll see him fed before he leaves." She smiled and turned to go.

"I'll do that. Thank you, dear."

"*And* I'll bring a tea tray to the library when the lady arrives."

"I can fetch it myself."

She scoffed, "And *make* me look the useless old woman I am?" She smiled. "No, I'll be bringing it up."

"You're a stubborn woman, Merry Fletcher."

Brooking no further argument from me, she laughed, turned on her heel, and made her way down the stairs. I could tell it pained her. An obvious afterthought, she tossed from the lower landing, "The bread is almost done."

"It smells *wonderful*," I called after her. With that, I closed the door behind me. The woman was a marvel. Not only was she discreet regarding what she once referred to as a "harmless and temporary" interest, she was at once both understanding and loving toward me as well as her orphaned nephew, Thomas. He'd been born to her late husband's brother, and as they never had children of their own, she took to motherhood like a duck to water. A fact I benefited from as well, for I too had been orphaned at a tender age. She was, in every way that mattered, a mother to me. In her eyes Thomas could do no wrong, and neither could I. Not that she openly approved of our relationship, but loving as she did, she didn't condemn.

So when the tenth anniversary of our "temporary" interest drew near, it was she who suggested I procure the townhouse away from my dowager grandmother's potential disapproval. Grannie knew I'd bonded with her housekeeper when I was just a frightened young boy. She knew too that I loved Merriam Fletcher and she loved me in return. Loving in her own way, Grannie turned a blind eye to the fact I'd stolen her housekeeper for myself.

Thomas briskly rubbed his wet hair with a towel. "I should be getting back; your grandmother will be finishing her tea by now. I hope she don't wonder why my hair's wet! I'll have to tell her a raincloud followed me, which is better than someone tossed a pot, I suppose." He grinned. "Then again, a tossed pot is better than admitting I shared bed and bath with her grandson."

My grandmother's coachman Thomas always made me laugh. Wry wit was one of several talents the man possessed and I was extremely fond of him. I watched Thomas dress, remembering how I'd come upon him and the farrier's boy that summer of my second year at Eton. Up to that moment, I thought my unnatural desire to be a singularly unique condition. Just three years my senior, he begged me not to tell. I asked him to teach me all he knew. These twelve years, we'd stolen many moments while Grannie was otherwise occupied with her cards or social teas.

Needless to say, I'd learned a great deal from our trysts.

"Grannie's eyesight isn't what it used to be when we were younger, Thom."

"No it's not, Lord bless her."

Taking his face between my hands, I kissed him. Lips parted and his tongue met mine with obvious need, a need that would unfortunately go unsated this day. I helped him button the drop fall of his livery trousers. Caressing the unrequited bulge I said, "Come to me Friday when she's playing cribbage at Lady Ashford's."

He gave me a playful cupping under my robe. "We'll finish what we've begun, and next time *I'll* be first."

I leaned into it. "In case we're interrupted again?"

"No, just because."

"That's hardly reason." I chuckled as the sensual grip demanded I concede to the idea. "Alright, alright, you'll be first."

He grinned and gave me a sweet peck on the cheek. "So long, Nic."

"See you soon. Now go. If you don't have time to eat that lunch your aunt set aside for you, I'll never hear the end of it."

"She's a sweetheart."

"Indeed she is."

Alone now, I tore the seal and read:

Miss Elenora Schwaab
May 2, 1896

My Dear Sir Nicolas, Earl of Halstead,
    I do hope you remember me. We met at Lady Margaret Eastlake's garden party a year ago this coming

June. I believe our common thread is my sister Luise Marie
and her husband, art historian Jean-Paul Richter. I wish to
speak with you about a most exciting discovery. My
imagination is piqued and I'm fairly beside myself with
possibility. I believe we might be able to work together on an
extraordinary venture. I've sent this message ahead because I
am in the area and would visit if you're at home. I'll come
round at two and hope it's no imposition.
    Yours,
    ES

Yes, I recalled the details of the meeting as written. I quickly
dressed then read it again. I remembered the attractive and petite
young woman — a bold-as-brass American with ready wit and
sensible opinions, the daughter of the American Consul. Her
sister had married Jean-Paul Richter, a fellow scholar and art
historian devoted, like me, to the Renaissance — specifically the
works of Leonardo da Vinci.

While our careers ran on parallel tracks, I had to admit my
interests were far more personal than academic. When I was
hardly more than a school boy, I found myself confused by a
world of black and white, while I was nothing less than grey. My
classmates were consumed by seamstresses and barmaids, and
while I found these fair women fine enough to occasionally turn
my head, my eye was consistently drawn to the corded arm of the
smithy or the flanks and mouth of my grandmother's coachman.

One afternoon while studying in the university library, I
chanced upon a book describing the aberrant homoerotic
tendencies of famous artists of the Renaissance. I studied the
forbidden sketches and my cock got hard, because behind the

artwork I understood the minds of the men. This made sense to me. These great men were no more or less than I. They loved no better or deeper than I. That day my fascination began and my feet set upon a path of art history. After Eton, I'd taken my training at Oxford, and from there did my internship. I recently became a fellow at the Ashmolean.

Initially the Dowager frowned upon my employment. With roots deep in the peerage, our family didn't *work*. But after I'd helped acquire several choice artworks for the museum and that effort brought praise from her Majesty, Grannie found my profession worthwhile. Royal accolades were all that was needed to throw off centuries of this inherited idle. In the past two years, I'd caught her in more than one conversation with peers saying, "Certainly Nicolas spends his free time at the museum. Halsteads are known famously for patroning the arts."

That was enough for me. At eighty-one, Grannie was one sweet old bird.

Marriage is like putting your hand into a bag of snakes in the hope of pulling out an eel.

– Leonardo da Vinci

~2~

The clock below stairs chimed once, then twice. Miss Elenora Schwaab would arrive at any moment. Sure enough, the bell rang in the front hall and shortly after, I met the woman in my library where Mrs. Fletcher had deposited her.

In a color scheme that would have inspired Pierre-Auguste Renoir to fetch a blank canvas, she wore a cream-and-blue cotton confection accented by a blue-and-cream rose-bedecked bonnet, reticule, and parasol. Excitement shone brightly in eyes the pale turquoise-blue of a clear autumn sky. Ripping off her cream lace gloves, she jumped from her chair to thrust her hand at me. "Sir Nicolas! Thank you for receiving me on such short notice."

Americans. Chuckling to myself, I bowed over her smaller hand. "Miss Schwaab, what a pleasure to see you again." They had the oddest mannerisms. Not rude, exactly; rather forthright without the stodgier affectations of the Empire. On the whole, Americans reminded me of impressionist artists. The artists violated the rules of academic painting, and Americans violated the rules of conventionality. As a student of nuance, I very much liked it.

Mrs. Fletcher entered with the tea. Addressing my guest she said, "I wasn't sure if you'd like lemon or milk, Miss, so I've set the tray with both."

"Why, thank you ma'am."

The housekeeper turned to me with a smile sparkling in her eyes. I could tell the sparkle came from being addressed formally when she considered herself only a housekeeper. She said, "And *that* bread is warm from the oven as you like it, *and* the butter's fresh from the dairyman this morning. Is there anything else, Master Nicolas?"

"No dear, this is quite fine. Thank you."

Alone now, I buttered my bread and addressed the lady busily adjusting her tea to taste. "So Miss Schwaab, you say you've a venture in mind…"

"Please, Sir Nicolas. Call me Ellie as all my friends do."

I smiled at what she implied. I could certainly see us as friends. "Very well, how can I be of service, Ellie?" I took a bite and nearly choked at her next words.

"To be blunt Sir, I'm in need of a mandrake. I need *you*."

My mind raced. The chit was declaring me homosexual. "I *beg* your pardon?"

She smiled a rather unsettling sentient smile. And in those pale intelligent eyes, I could see her thoughts forming like clouds before a rainstorm. In fact, I could almost smell the ozone in the burning machinery of her mind. When she spoke, her thoughts were perfectly ordered.

"I'm not one to beat around the bush, Sir Nicolas. Not being forthright wastes time, and time may very well be short. Last June, I overheard a rather intimate verbal exchange between you and another man. I didn't see who he was exactly, but I *did* see *you*."

I felt a hollow sensation in my chest. In it, I could hear the echo of my up-tempo heartbeat. "Miss Schwaab, I—"

She held up a hand to interrupt me. "Please, hear me out. I consider myself to be a progressive. You see, I don't care what adults do behind closed doors. An individual's nature and sexuality form the most intrinsic core of their person. And who are we to take issue with another's nature? Only a fool would see one path to human intimacy. We *are* naked apes after all, and apes have no issue with homosexuality."

I couldn't fault her logic. "So, what do you propose Miss Schwaab? *Blackmail?*" Though my obvious concern wasn't humorous in the least, she laughed merrily.

"Please, call me Ellie."

"Ellie. I believe that was a reasonable question."

The same smile was back and with it, sparkling eyes. "I want you to marry me."

Completely dumbfounded, I just looked at her. "You can't be serious Miss…"

"Ellie."

"You can't be serious, *Ellie.*"

Her laugh was filled with mirth. "Oh, but I am!"

Finding that impish gleam in her eye irritating in that moment, I set my plate aside. In my mind, this meeting could go one of two ways — she'd out me for a sodomite if I didn't do as she asked, or I'd be saddled with an insane wife. While Parliament abolished the death penalty for deviants like me years before I was born, my truth wasn't fodder for the masses. "You have me at a disadvantage, madam. What madness would spur you to make such an outlandish proposal?"

She set her cup down and leaned forward as a man might when sharing an inside stock tip. I found myself oddly attracted to her forthright and almost mannish American attitudes. Looking me square in the eye, she said, "You are an authority on Leonardo da Vinci, correct?"

"On his artworks, I am."

"Then I assume you are familiar with Gian Giacomo Caprotti da Oreno?"

I suppressed a smile at her halting Italian. Gian Giacomo Caprotti was da Vinci's protégé. Affectionately called *Salai* or the *little devil* by the master himself, it was said when Leonardo painted nudes and phalluses, they were modeled by his young lover Salai. The most telling of these — the sketch called *Angelo-Incarnato* or Angel Incarnate, which depicts the little devil himself with a substantial erection. On the back, da Vinci wrote out his turbulent feelings for the young man in Greek: *astrapen, bronten,* and *ceraunobolian.* His metaphoric choices literally translated: lightning, storms, and thunderbolts. I nodded.

She smiled. "And I assume, although not in your field of expertise, you must also be aware of such erotic artworks as Japanese pillow books and the *Kama Sutra.* One chapter of which was so recently translated by your celebrated orientalist, what's the fellow's name?"

Field of expertise? I took her question to mean I was unaccustomed to erotic works depicting *women.* Beyond my proclivity and given profession, of course I knew of these ancient works of erotica. I named the man for her, "Sir Richard Francis

16

Burton—"

She cut in, "Yes, that's the man!"

"And yes, I *am* aware of such books." It was obvious when her pretty smile widened that she could see she'd hooked me like a trout. In fact, I had the impression this woman had somehow studied me at length. Though my interest was piqued, I couldn't fathom what she was driving at, nor could I see a connection between ancient Asian renderings and da Vinci's longtime lover... *let alone* a connection to a proposal of marriage to *me*. "And what does Salai have to do with these works?"

She smiled that smile again and this time I was met with a sense of familiarity I couldn't quite identify, like there was more to it than what was seen upon the surface. My focus redirected when she explained, "My father is in the American Consul, you see. And now with my elder sister Luise Marie wed to Jean-Paul, I've become my father's hostess when he entertains here. I don't mind it, though listening to men talk trade and commerce mostly bores me. Anyway, enough about that." She waved her hand and shook her head, as if determined not to go off point. "The other night my sister and her husband joined us when we entertained an Italian merchant and his relation by marriage. The former, a Signore Ambrosini, deals in raw fibers such as cotton and jute from India and is seeking business relations in the New York textile industry. I found him a likeable man. The latter... well, there was just something not quite right about him. His name is Carlo Posateri. He..."

My mind could barely keep up with the twists and turns Miss Schwaab's mind was wont to take. Then too, I was somewhat surprised that this conversation was being piloted by a woman at all. Women of my acquaintance steered clear of most sexual topics, though every one of them would perk if the focus of conversation leaned in that direction. Sifting through her rambling recount of that night, I learned this Signore Posateri hated all things homosexual in nature, including the works of the masters. Apparently the man took pride in influencing Pope Pius IX to castrate the statues in the Vatican for the homosexual thoughts they provoked. Out of sight out of mind, I'd say, or a gloss on the phrase Shakespeare wrote in Hamlet: *The man doth protest too much, methinks.* In my experience, them that had the most to say against a thing often coveted that very thing. Her next words pulled me from my contemplation.

"To put it simply, I plan to steal it."

I stared at her dumbly having not fully listened to what preceded that statement. Eyeing me suspiciously, her pretty bowed lips took on a frown when she reproached, "Oh fiddlesticks. You *weren't* even listening. Have you no concept how *important* this work is to humanity?"

Chastened that her winding road of a tale had lulled my mind, I ate the crow. "Forgive me Miss… " — her eyes narrowed, causing me to amend — "Ellie. My mind was lost on the man's contribution to the Vatican's defiled statues. Please, if you would, back up a bit and explain it again."

She took a breath. I was struck by the curious glint of sympathy shining in her pale blue eyes and the faint blush that signaled ire or embarrassment. Unacquainted with her as I was, I stabbed in the dark and took the blush for the latter. My thought was proved right when she said sincerely, "I *know* I ramble when my head is so full of details, and I apologize. I really do. But please, bear with me if you will."

"You'll have my undivided attention, I assure you."

Ellie brightened and launched into it again. "Alright then. Signore Posateri boasted of his measures to rid the world of artworks created by the greatest artists of the Renaissance. Jean-Paul got him to admit he buys them from private collections and destroys them, you see. When asked about pieces that were not purchasable, he said he 'has his methods,' which I take to mean he *steals* them or has thieves in his employ, the sanctimonious cur... " Her words trailed off.

I stared at her expectantly.

Exhaling sharply in what could only be annoyance, she continued, "At this very moment in Venice, *somewhere* in his palazzo, he has in his possession a previously undiscovered book written and illustrated by Leonardo da Vinci's own hand."

Of all the things I thought she'd say, *that* was not one of them. "Oh?"

She nodded. "Yes, created by da Vinci for Salai. It's a book of love, Sir Nicolas — a pillow book that managed to remain hidden for four hundred years!"

Knowing the mind and desire of the artist like I did, I could almost see this book. "Such a thing is entirely possible."

My words brought about her effervescent smile. She asked, "Wasn't Salai with him a long time?"

"At least twenty-five years. Salai inherited many of da Vinci's works. How did you come upon this information? Surely they didn't discuss this topic in your presence?"

She dug through her reticule and scoffed, "As if they would. No, when I left the men to their brandy last night, I stood just outside the door adjusting the strap on my shoe under the pretense I'd lost a button, you see. I chanced to hear Signore Posateri speaking of this book." Pulling a folded paper from her bag, she read, "And I quote, 'Although unsigned, in breadth and scope, there is no question this was Leonardo da Vinci's book. It is clearly the work of a sodomite. The disgusting words of his twisted affection made more foul by the accompanying sketches.' Galling, his hatred."

Needing more to fully comprehend, I urged, "Go on. What else did you overhear?"

"In the conversation that followed I could tell Signore Ambrosini was put aback by his companion's rabid fanaticism. Then I heard Jean-Paul ask him what he intended to do with it." She read from her notes, "He said, 'After I study it to better know the minds of these repugnant artists, I will burn it with the rest, of course.'"

She met my eyes, her fair cheeks flushed in her pique. For reasons unclear, John Opie's oil painting of *Boadicea Haranguing the Britons* came to mind. She said, "Burn it! Can you just imagine the loss, Sir Nicolas? Jean-Paul was beside himself over the idea; he even offered to buy it. But the man said he'd never sell it at any cost."

After I study it... The man's words confirmed my earlier opinion. Signore Posateri was himself a homosexual — if not in deed, then certainly in desire. I nodded, "I agree. It *would* be terrible loss."

"*That* is why I have plans to *steal* it."

I stared at her and she suddenly laughed. "Oh you think me mad, don't you? *You do.* I can see it in your eyes!" She leaned forward and looked at me with interest, as if she half expected me to admit that I did indeed question her stability. How quickly she went from John Opie's warrior queen to James Tissot's *Young Woman in a Boat*. The astute little imp made me smile despite myself. "I admit I do. And where exactly do I fit into this insanity?"

"I've come here because time is of the essence. Signore Posateri will be leaving for Venice at the end of the week. And if we leave tomorrow, the day after, at the latest—"

"I still don't see my presence in this scheme of yours."

Ellie sighed. Her earlier words about wasting time came back to me. I wasn't trying to be obtuse but for the life of me I just didn't see it. I asked her to explain how she figured I fit her plan.

She said, "You have your influence, being an Earl and all. You're in the House of Lords. We can use your academic standing and income to save these precious artworks from being destroyed by this fanatic, for surely he is in possession of more than one. You know Leonardo da Vinci's works. You'll know at a glance if Signore Posateri is correct in his assumption that this is indeed Salai's pillow book." When I didn't comment she added, "Look, I know you barely know me, but I know you, and I'm completely alright with it."

"Alright with *it?*"

"Yes."

She reached across the distance between us to briefly place a small warm hand over mine in a comfortable gesture which I recognized as sincerity. I had an idea of what she meant, but needed clarification. It wouldn't do to guess wrongly. "You're referring to my particular predilection?"

"Yes."

I rubbed the point between my eyes.

She asked, "As a friend, may I leave your title aside and call you Nicolas?" At my nod she continued. "Nicolas, I'm no fool. For all that I'm a progressive woman: I live in a man's world. And while society may change in the future, I'm hindered in the here and now. It would be difficult to travel on my own, and certainly tracking down homoerotic artworks would be next to impossible for a woman. I wouldn't even know how to *ask* about them; trained proficient I'm not. Were we to marry, I see advantage for the both of us outside this venture."

"Advantage?"

"Yes, you'll be free to love who you will without society casting rude speculations your way. And aside from my being free to be who *I* am, I'll benefit by a social standing that will allow me to affect change from *within* society."

I considered her a moment. Miss Elenora Schwaab was an extremely pleasant-looking young woman with her wise blue eyes and cinnamon hair. She was fit and fashionable, and without a doubt a highly-educated and intelligent person. Her ready humor and matter-of-factness were also quite appealing. Yes, I could see myself enjoying this woman's companionship if nothing else.

Running down a list of potential advantages of marrying someone not shocked or repulsed by my nature, I surprised myself by finding her proposal no less than brilliant. Many marriages started with far less. Still, there was one bit that must be addressed. It had always been my understanding that one day I'd be pressed to marry and sire children. When one inherits the title of Earl, especially a Halstead Earl, there are responsibilities one must naturally live up to. But until that hourglass ran out, I considered myself free to love and enjoy whom I would. To be fair she'd have to be told. "I must tell you that I have obligations to my title and estate. These obligations would necessitate my producing an heir in the future."

My wording was met by a brief frown. I could see she hadn't

considered such an intimacy between us were we to marry as she proposed. This was confirmed by her next words. "But wouldn't that be imposs… that is to say… I mean… oh *fiddlesticks*. But *you* don't *enjoy* women *that* way."

Summoning my straight-faced composure, I said, "We British are nothing if not dutiful. Perhaps with the lights off." Her expression priceless, I laughed. "I'm teasing you, my dear. Actually, I've never attempted to make love to a woman. And truth be told, I don't see that happening for a good many years yet."

Something akin to relief shown in her eyes, suggesting if she had say in the matter it would be a long ways into the far-distant future. I wasn't sure how I felt about it but didn't have too much time to contemplate my curious reaction to her relief, for next she blurted, "Then lights on or off, we'll cross that bridge as it comes. Let's marry straightaway."

My earlier opinion fortified. The unflappable Ellie Schwaab, late of America, was indeed bold-as-brass. There was no denying this outrageous proposition made sense. For one, it negated the need for an awkward conversation with a future wife, for surely Ellie was one of a kind. I'd be, as she said, *Free to love whom I will.* I found myself liking the idea very much. If nothing else it would stop the parade of marriageable young women thrust my way at every social gathering. I nodded. "It does make good sense, doesn't it?"

"It does, and I assure you I've come to this opinion from every angle." She gave me a brilliant smile and laid her hand back on mine. This time she left it there. I covered it with my own. And that's exactly how Grannie found us when she walked into the room.

"You've obviously something to tell me, Nicolas," my grandmother said without preamble, an unmistakable glint of joy in her albescent eyes.

Rising, I brought Ellie to stand beside me, hooking her arm in mine in what I hoped would be a convincing display of affection. I said, "Grannie, may I introduce my fiancée, Miss Elenora Schwaab, daughter of Mitchel Schwaab, the American Consul to her Majesty. Ellie, may I introduce you to Countess Lady Augusta Halstead, my grandmother."

Her hand thrust forward in that very American gesture and had my grandmother bubbling with charmed delight. To my surprise, Ellie not only had a fair working knowledge of me, she knew about my family. When my Grannie incorrectly deduced our love began at Lady Margaret Eastlake's garden party a year ago, neither of us dissuaded her. The cover was brilliant, and I was once more taken with Ellie's quick intelligence. In short order I'd become quite fond of her. This might work out well after all.

Somewhat surprised to see an expression that was at once both delighted and relieved, I met Grannie's eyes over my recently acquired fiancé's head and winked at her. I could almost see the visions of babies forming above the dear old woman's very large hat.

~3~

The following afternoon, after the business aspects of marriage were secured in London, we sidestepped the need to procure a special dispensation for our marriage certificate by heading off to Gretna Green. The Scots took no issue with impulsive lovers and their quick weddings. We'd leave first thing in the morning.

Though Grannie and Ellie's family threw us a small celebratory dinner, none had been pleased to hear of our plan to circumvent the waiting due a traditional courtship. In the end it was the Dowager Lady herself who spoke on our behalf, announcing she was content with what she referred to as "the impetuous romance of it all." I'd bet my last penny any misgivings she might have had over our haste had been soothed by the notion I'd soon produce her great-grandchild.

As for my new in-laws, except the haste they were undeniably pleased. Detecting a strange impression of relief that Ellie would finally be settled, I tucked the notion away with the other tidbits so recently learned about the Yankee enigma I'd soon take to wife.

***

Having heard of my pending nuptials from his aunt, Thomas came to me just before midnight to wish me well or to commiserate if need be, and found me eating more of Mrs. Fletcher's fresh bread and butter. Pointing to the plate, he said, "Oh, that looks good. Mind?"

Knowing he loved the hard heel of the loaf, I waved to the plate. "Of course not, help yourself." I poured him a sherry to wash it down.

We chatted over the day's happenings awhile. Pleased that I was content with my life's upcoming readjustment, he took my soon-to-be marriage in stride. But then I expected he would. The fellow was a free spirit that way. In good humor, he said, "Well we knew you'd have to do the *deed* eventually, Earl that you are. High time, too!"

I chuckled. "High time?"

He laughed with his mouth full, "You know as well as I do. Since the day you turned thirty, Halstead great-grandbabies are all your Grannie talks about. It's driving me batty!"

The laugh was infectious. I ran my hand down his arm. "We can still be lovers, Thom."

Setting the heel of bread aside, he took my hand in his. "Oh Nic, as much as I'd hunger to, and God help me you know I would, I wouldn't do that to your Lady."

I went on to explain Ellie's unique perspective, adding, "She said I'd be free to love who I pleased. I don't see why things need to—"

Thomas put a hand up to stop me. "She sounds like a remarkable woman Nic, truly she does. But don't you know that women are a breed apart? Ofttimes what they *say* is tolerable isn't, in the end. You wouldn't believe the stories below stairs at the Ashford's. I don't think there's a man alive in that family who doesn't dream of doing himself in for the daily hell his woman puts him through."

I laughed lightly. The family produced women with balls and eunuch males and all of them married their opposite. Grannie said her visits were better than going to the theater. "From what I've heard, the Ashfords are legend. But I don't think Ellie has it in her nature to be judgmental. Remember, she came to me *knowing* I was homosexual and proposed regardless."

"That's unique, I'll give you that. But it's one thing for a husband to say he likes fucking blokes; it's another to have the proof stare the wife in the face. She'd come to hate me for buggering her husband, and then she'd come to hate you for allowing it. I love you far too much to hasten such a circumstance."

I hadn't thought of that possibility. Would my inclination turn Ellie's mind eventually? Considering the concept, I couldn't see it happening. She and I had talked more after Grannie left and I found her refreshingly sincere. As such, I took her views to be as she said — progressive.

I watched Thom coat his bread with the sweet cream butter. He licked the side of his hand where the butter had smeared. I was so comfortable with his salt-of-the-earth mannerisms. I'd miss him, I truly would. We'd been together for more than a decade. From our first union, I'd had a regular lover in dear Thomas. Largely, our love life had been exclusive to one another.

Of course, like other animals in the wild, the pair of us were opportunistic feeders. Men had their chums, and occasionally some had similar predilections. Yet Mrs. Fletcher's continual words of caution inspired us to take very few lovers into our collective bed. Yes, he had the occasional liaison with the farrier's son. That relationship had been going on far longer than had his and mine, but opportunity was scarce since the family moved to the countryside these eight years past.

By comparison, my own encounters with other lovers were few, transient, and only when abroad. I'd had several brief dalliances on my grand tour, but sucking and fondling only; never anything as intimate as what Thom and I shared. I was aware there was a new footman at Lady Ashford's who'd caught his eye. Perhaps he'd grow to love him and be loved in return. I'd miss his strong arms around me and the way he made my body sing. I told him so.

"I'll always be here if you need me Nic, you know I will." He undressed.

I wiped my tears. I knew he felt the same because I could see the unshed truth of it glistening in his eyes. My clothing followed his to the floor. "I know Thom, and it's the same for me."

We held each other close while the clock on the mantelpiece ticked away the seconds. Wordlessly, our eyes met before we kissed. If this was to be our last loving between us, then we were determined to make it our best. The match struck, and we lavished attention everywhere our hands, lips, and tongue could reach, over paths familiar and affectionate. When he scooped the soft butter off the plate, I knew what he wanted our lovemaking to be. I stood while he slathered my cock. The rest he smoothed into my hand before he turned his back to me. My fingers buttered him like a bun as I kissed along his shoulder.

Oiled and ready, he lay on my bed invitingly. Kneeling against him, I took him in my buttered hand and stroked him slowly. Gripping my own cock as well, I traced his slippery opening with my tip. Pressing forward, each circling pass eased into the tightness until his body surrendered to me fully.

In the end we slept in each other's arms. My last kiss came when the clock chimed four times. Before he left in the predawn, he whispered, "Make yourself a happy life. Never forget I love you, Nic."

I smiled wistfully. "Never Thom. I love you too."

I have been impressed with the urgency of doing. Knowing is not enough; we must apply. Being willing is not enough; we must do.

– Leonardo da Vinci

~4~

The steward handed me the key after opening the posh stateroom door. "Your luggage is inside, sir." To my wife, he asked, "Should I send round a maid to help you unpack, ma'am?"

"No, thank you," she said, covering her yawn with her gloved hand.

Once inside our ship's quarters, Ellie went to our small bit of starboard balcony and opened the double doors to the noise of passengers and crew getting ready to depart. "Good Lord, it smells ghastly out here."

Indeed, the air smelled of seal shit, burning coal, and the breath and bodies of the steerage class.

Our last minute steamship passage on the Great Eastern gained us smaller quarters than I would have liked. Ideally we would have had adjoining rooms and the privacy that arrangement provided. I opened the door to our single bedroom. The bed was nice enough but the loveseat in here, as well as the one in the outer room, were both far too small for me to sleep on. I sighed inwardly. We'd work out something later. Coming in, Ellie ripped off her hat and stuffed the long pins in it, then set it upon the smaller settee. Falling back on the bed, she pulled her hands from her gloves one finger at a time. "I'm *exhausted*."

I was pretty done in myself. Our days and nights confined to bumpy coaches afforded us a condensed courtship, giving us an opportunity to become acquainted with one another. But the whirlwind of legalities and travel in our attempt to have details ironed out and still remain ahead of Signore Posateri was positively draining. We'd gone hundreds of miles from London to Gretna Green, and on, to reach the Liverpool dock. I chided, "You *did* ignore my suggestion that you sleep on the coach as I did."

She stretched and moaned. "*Fiddlesticks.* Is that what you British call *sleep?* I'm still sore all over from those terrible Scottish roads, and besides my mind was running over with details. It was too active to sleep. How ever you managed it, I still don't know."

"What would you have me do? We've gone non-stop since that brazen marriage proposal of yours." Her laugh made me smile. She really was delightful company.

"I don't see it coming easy when my mind is so full." Impossible to contain by the hand before her mouth, she let out a not-so-dainty yawn, then hastily apologized. "Oh, excuse me."

"We'll have at least ten days to go over details, my dear. You'll have to sleep eventually." We'd be on the ocean for the better part of a fortnight. Before our voyage ended, we'd have a ready scheme, one that would be both successful and void of scandal. If nothing went amiss — namely the sea didn't fling us to Calypso's island to lose seven years like Odysseus — we'd arrive in Venice two full days before Posateri.

Finding my way to the bathroom, I pressed my hand to the warm copper water tank. Calling to the other room, I said, "Why not have a soak before we go down to dinner? We haven't stopped long enough to bathe, it might refresh you." I'd no sooner said the words when three blasts from the ship's horns filled the air. An instant later, a vibration traveled the full length of the ship as the massive gears engaged the propeller. I knew we'd launched when the slight tug swayed me where I stood.

Figuring she'd missed my suggestion in the din, I returned to the bedroom to discover Ellie sound asleep. *Poor little Yank.* To have slept through that, she *must* be tired. Chuckling, I drew the coverlet over her. I undid my tie and cuffs and proceeded to undress. I'd make good use of the water now and see the tank refilled for her use later.

***

I found my thoughts upon my wife while I bathed. Ellie was unlike any woman of my acquaintance. I hadn't met many Americans in my life but the few I'd had were not quite as straightforward. What I saw in her was something far more. In our journey to Scotland and back, I'd learned that she and her sister lost their mother early in their childhood and that they were raised exclusively by their father and their governess. I'd recently read an article in the *Times* regarding the work of Sir Francis Galton and his "nature versus nurture" philosophy. Could this early, predominately male, nurturing be the source of her liberal attitudes?

I had just stepped from the tub when Ellie came into the bath calling my name.

"Nicolas, I'm so sorry, I drifted off…Oh!"

Accustomed to servants seeing me unclothed since I was a boy, I didn't give her interruption a second thought. Ellie, on the other hand, appeared positively dumbstruck and I had no idea why. I took a dry towel and rubbed it briskly over my head. I couldn't see her watching me, but curiously, I could feel her eyes. Sure enough when I lowered the towel she was still standing there with pinkening cheeks. *You're embarrassed?* Formally trained as I was to look for distinction in art, I couldn't help but notice this was a slightly different hue than when I'd last seen her embarrassed. Knowing her to be bold-as-brass, I couldn't credit this emotion in her. I said, "Ah you're awake. Feel rested, do you?"

Self-declared progressive or not, I had the distinct impression my new wife had never seen a man in the flesh; a curious notion in light of the customary boldness I'd come to anticipate. I dropped the hand that held the towel to my side and let her look. That she didn't excuse herself was telling, though I wondered if she tested me or herself.

I found utterly fascinating her brassy determination to prove she was unfazed to see me thus. Her eyes traveled my person from head to toe and lingered half-way. In some unanticipated biological response, I felt my cock swell. In that instant I knew with certainty that some time in our future I'd be able to do the deed without hesitation or impotence. Although the foreign concept made me extremely nervous, the notion of loving this compelling creature pooled in my loins.

Those blue eyes grew wide then flew to my face. Prattling excuses, she left the room. Did she think I lied about my sexual appetites? I followed her.

"Ellie wait... Ellie?"

She stopped in her tracks, her back to me. I could only assume she was finding resolve. In what must be an attempt to prove she had no qualms being married to a homosexual man who'd just gotten hard for her, she turned to me. Her mask of calm indifference was hardly believable, given the flushed cheeks. I took her by the hand and led her to the settee. "Sit a moment... "

I sat and she didn't.

"I should get dressed for dinner. I didn't mean to sleep as long as I did, or to interrupt your bath." Her eyes darted uncomfortably.

"A moment, Ellie." I gave her hand a small tug and she sat beside me. With her eyes looking this way and that, it was obvious she was struggling to keep her gaze from wandering to my crotch. My cock found that fact fascinating. Leaning forward, I blocked my loins from view and wondered what possessed me to come out here nearly full-staffed and without the damned towel.

She worried her bottom lip in uncertainty and fidgeted with invisible lint on her skirt. My fleeting arousal dimmed and I realized I was drawn to her boldness more than shy female attitude. I gave her a reassuring smile and squeezed her fingers encouragingly. "Listen to me. You are my *wife,* but more than that, we've become friends. One day, we must address how we shall come together to start a family. This can be as soon or as distant an event as you'd like it to be."

She finally met my eye.

Grinning, I teased, "With the lights on or off."

Her mouth twitched. She offered, "Seeing you unclothed

brought about an unexpected—" she searched for the word, and not finding one, she let out a breath. The next moment, having found the resolve she'd been searching for, she said matter-of-factly, "Look, Nicolas. I know it is impossible for you to desire me, woman that I am. Knowing that fact like I do, it surprised me to see that rise." She briefly dropped her gaze to my lap before returning to my face, "I can only assume it to be a causal effect of a hot bath?" When she looked there again, I felt my heart start to pound with the truth as presented. I rather fancied this boldness of hers. She finished, "What's more, I find myself desiring you. I was unprepared for that, is all."

Causal. Yes, and she was the cause. The bold-as-brass American was back and with her my growing erection. And unaccountably, so was my case of nerves. In fact, I hadn't been this nervous since Thomas first instructed me in male loving. This would bear some reflection, as my body's reaction to this woman suggested that I was compatible to both women and men just as playwright Oscar Wilde and illustrious emperor Julius Caesar had been. *Was I?* Had I been all along or was it simply her?

Just as I considered putting that theory to a test with a kiss, the first bell rang. We had only fifteen minutes to ready for dinner. I gave her a smile. "We can revisit our discussion after dinner, if you like."

The look in her eyes was inscrutable.

***

With its fine linen and velvet upholstered chairs, heavy dishes and thick-bottomed water glasses, the dining room was as opulent as one might expect of such an ocean liner. The dinner tables sat eight so we found ourselves sharing the meal with two other couples: the Ormonts, the Brookses, and a Danish brother and sister on tour. They were following Byron's path, and would begin in Portugal like the poet did in the early part of the century.

Young and blond, the brother stole regular glances in my direction over our courses. All through dinner, I could feel him. I'd never had to look for lovers with Thomas so handy and agreeable but that didn't mean I turned every offer away. My suspicion rang true when he slowly inserted his fingertip into his mouth while his eyes held mine — an invitation if ever there was. It was brief and no one noticed, but I knew the look, indeed I did.

Given my station, I'd put much care into reading such signs; taking things for granted was a dangerous proposition. Arrows pointed to an incident I'd witnessed the year I'd turned nineteen. Just before the Christmas holiday, I took my dinner at an inn on the Thames where I'd planned to meet Robert Markham, a fellow deviant. I was more than eager to sow my wild oats. Until then, I'd never had a lover other than Thomas, and Robert was quite appealing with his large brown eyes, soft full lips, and ready invitation.

Arriving early for my meal, I chanced upon a conversation between the innkeeper and the butcher from the shop several doors down. A fellow had been beaten to death upstairs in the last hour. He'd been a young Lord in his second year at Eton. Apparently the man often procured a room upstairs to study undisturbed, and he'd often had fellow students come share the space for the same reason.

Then the innkeeper relayed to the butcher in disgust how surprised he was that the Lord turned out to be a sod who'd been using the room for his foul pursuits. This time, however, the Lord invited the wrong man upstairs. He no sooner spoke the words when the police carried the body down the staircase on a litter. I recognized the signet ring on the blood-streaked hand that hung over the side. It was Sir Robert Markham — the man I was to meet. I'd been extremely cautious ever since.

As a result of that day, I'd become a keen observer of body language — a survival instinct, no doubt. My instinct evolved to know when sexual currents existed between people and when they didn't. It served me well and moreover kept the family name from scandal.

Involved in a rather philosophical discussion regarding women voting in the American west, specifically in the state of Wyoming, Ellie detailed how that right had been revoked when the territory became a state in the union. The other men at the table looked on indulgently, for she was by far the loveliest woman there. They may not have agreed with her politics, but they certainly enjoyed this reason to focus their attention on her in the presence of their wives. The wives on the other hand seemed unable to countenance the topic. I couldn't help but compare and found myself quite proud of her keen intellect and superlative company. My life with her would never be dull.

The ladies took their sherry as ladies do, and the men headed to the lounge for cigars and port. Of course wherever men congregate, politics and finances are on everyone's mind; that, and the Queen's upcoming Jubilee. The century would be turning shortly and industry and modernization were keen topics alongside investments and instability in South Africa. Queen Victoria's bellicose grandson Wilhelm had recently alienated public opinion by his interest in the Cape Colony of South Africa.

More than one man in the room felt the foreseeable future held a second Boer war. I found I didn't have much to say, my thoughts otherwise occupied by my body's surprising reaction to my wife, and the way the blond Dutchman rolled the end of his cigar between his lips.

I was certain Ellie would retire when she'd had enough small talk. From the little I knew of her progressive attitudes, small talk of hats and fashion weren't topics to hold her interest for long. I was unversed in American politics but I doubted half the men in my own House of Lords were as well versed in Britannia's policies as she was in the politics of her country. My wife wanted the vote. As wise and learned as she was, America was wrong to deny her. In quick order, I found myself lost in thoughts of her. Under a newlywed's pretense, I downed my port, made my goodnights, and took my thoughts to the deck where I became momentarily captivated by the moonlight sparking upon the water. It was an image that brought to mind the dappled water of Pierre-Auguste Renoir, coupled with the hazy quality of Ivan Aivazovsky's *Moonlit Night*.

Although his invitation had been crystal clear, I was nevertheless surprised when the Dutchman walked up and stood beside me. We talked about sea voyages, Lord Byron, and the feel of a fine Cuban cigar over your tongue. His description was such that I asked him to show me what he meant. He "just happened to have one in his cabin," he said, "a fine hand-rolled Havana, the same sort that Britain's own Prince Edward enjoyed." Primed with innuendo, needless to say, I followed.

The cabin was dimly lit and private from his sister. After he closed the door behind us, he made no move to light the lamp. In a flash he was on his knees before me. It wasn't a Havana he wanted rolling over his tongue, but then I never thought it was. He kissed his way up my thighs, switching from one to the other as his fingers deftly undid my trousers. Pulling them down to my knees, he closed his hand around my now hard cock, while his other hand freed his own. This would be no long coupling. It would be short and hard and infinitely satisfying.

My eyes closed and I held my breath as his warm mouth enveloped me. A man knows what feels good, and my Dutchman treated me as if he sucked himself. He laved my shaft until I was sloppy wet. I couldn't help but sink my hands into his golden hair to guide him, and my fingers coated with his spicy Makassar oil. He gagged, he slobbered, and he sucked me hard. All the while, the whapping sound of his hard-handed abandon filled the quiet space. I knew his delicious act drove him over the edge, and he made little sounds of surrender as I held him fast and fucked into his mouth; plummeting along tongue and teeth, while my balls slapped against his chin. The groan was unmistakable and I knew he shot his spunk by the feral scent in the air. I gave him the rest in quick short jabs. An instant later my floodgates opened and I pumped into him, thrilling to the carnal duet of his muted gags and straining gulps. He was glorious.

***

I'd just returned when Ellie entered our stateroom and informed me she wanted to take that bath she'd missed earlier. I watched her gather this and that and close the door behind her. That I experienced a sudden wash of guilt over my romp with the fair Dutchman came as a surprise. I didn't like that feeling, nor did I care for it overlaying my angst associated with my newly-realized sexual nature. Pulling the cord, I waited for the steward.

The man arrived several minutes later. "How may I help you, sir?"

"Please send 'round a decanter of brandy and two glasses if you would."

"Yes sir, I'll get that straightaway."

I used the time to dress for bed. I had only the dressing gown as I usually slept in the nude, but decided for our first shared bed, it was better to be clothed. We'd been together round the clock for three days but this was our official first night. Thankfully, we had a lifetime to become accustomed to one another. And this was a good thing. My nerves were strung taut. I hoped the brandy might help.

By the time she entered the sitting room smelling of jasmine, I was pouring her a brandy and having myself a third. I'd always enjoyed the scent of jasmine.

For the first time I took notice of the little things about her, things that I'd found pleasant enough as we traveled but now found strikingly beautiful. Ellie had delicately arched eyebrows and her pink bottom lip was fuller than the top. Unpinned, her riot of cinnamon curls fell like a cloud to the small of her back and damp ringlets framed her fresh-washed face. I'd only seen her hair up in pins these past few days. I had no idea she possessed a lovely mane that would bring about the desire to bury my fingers in the mass. Art historian I, she reminded me of William-Adolphe Bouguereau's *Venus*. She smiled prettily and that Venus transformed into Renoir's *Little Irene* so completely, it made me blink. I'd found her high-styled and attractive that day she breezed into my home. I found her no less than a work of art now. Port and brandy loosening my tongue, I told her so.

She smiled and it lit her eyes. It wasn't quite the bold smile she treated me to in my townhome, but it had that quality I found so appealing. In what could only be described as having the minds of two men inside my head, I felt my cock thicken, the sensation instantly squelched by that returning rush of guilt. We had to talk, and god help me, I didn't know where to begin. I handed her the glass, took another for myself, and swept my hand to the settee. "Come sit with me, Ellie."

She sipped her brandy and sat beside me on the small settee. She said, "We don't have to revisit our conversation, you know. We can talk of other things."

I nodded. I had *other things* on my mind at the moment. So we chatted about the meal, the dinner company, the voyage in general. Then, she suddenly thrust at me a point of no return. "He was quite handsome, don't you think?"

I blinked. "Who?"

"Our dinner companion, Jerone Some-such. I don't remember his last name — you know, the Dutch brother to the sister sitting with us tonight?"

My heart started to pound. "Pleasant enough. Why do you ask?" Draining my snifter in one overlarge sip that nearly choked me, I let the alcohol flame run like a burning fuse down my gullet.

Eyeing me sharply, she smiled that knowing smile of hers; a smile that caused me to feel a heavy presence between my legs. It was everything I could do to keep my robe from rising like P.T. Barnum's circus tent.

I couldn't help but feel she led the conversation when she said offhandedly, "I assume there will be men in your life. I might be wrong, yet I'm certain the man is attracted to you."

Refilling my glass for the fifth time, I reached for hers as an afterthought. "You bring up a point I wish to discuss."

Realization dawning in her wise ocean-blue eyes, she drained her brandy in one astounding swallow. Those same eyes watering, she handed me her glass. I saw the dawning transformation a split second before she burst into a delighted squeal. "You *didn't!*"

I opened my mouth to speak and absolutely nothing came forth. I couldn't think of what to say for myself. My silence condemned me.

"You *did!*"

Ellie's eyes were bright and her color high, either from spirits or the request forming in her mind. "Will you tell me about it?"

Her assertiveness appealed to me, no question about it. However, I wasn't sure this was a topic one *had* with a wife. "I don't think… "

"*Fiddlesticks.* If my *own* husband can't talk to me about his lovemaking, then *who* can?"

My quickly-downed libations were affecting me. I didn't know what words to use, where to begin, or even *what* to say. But that didn't stop her interrogation.

"I'm assuming the two of you had some sort of encounter… "

Seeing the blushing excitement before me, my heart fluttered unexpectedly. My Yank was desperate to know the act. The thought she'd want me to describe it left a heavy presence between my legs. In for a penny, in for a pound, I asked, "And what would your feelings be if I had?"

My eyes searched the whole of her for clues as to what she was thinking in that moment. My god, she was a lovely thing. Free of her blousy clothing, she also had small pert breasts in the gossamer folds of her dressing gown. Her nipples were hard. Wondering why, I reached for the decanter.

Her hand on my arm stopped me. Inserting the glass stopper in the bottle, she set it and snifters aside. "Nicolas, we've only recently met. And while I grow fonder of you by the day I'm not feeling jealousy, if that's your concern. I do understand that you have needs that must be seen to. Homosexuality exists in the natural world, therefore is a natural chapter in the book of life. Don't you agree?"

I nodded. In my inebriation, she might have said Father Christmas was a hedgehog who took tea with the Queen and I would have agreed.

I watched her absently twirl a cinnamon curl around her finger as if she saw what had occurred between the Dutchman and me. Her next words should have surprised me, but they didn't. "I find the idea of my husband having male lovers a fascinating concept. And besides, how else will I learn about *you* if *you* don't tell me?" Dropping her curl, she laid her hand on my knee. Her touch was warm through the brocade of my dressing gown. I could see the sincerity in her pale eyes when she added, "Please Nicolas, trust me with this aspect of your life. You're *safe* with me."

After three days of non-stop companionship I found myself thoroughly loving how her sharp mind rationalized things. What's more, an assurance of safety struck a chord in me. I felt myself relaxing, or perhaps this was the work of the liquor. The latter proofed when I heard my own words come out in a slur, "What would you like to know, my dear?"

That gamine smile widened and seeing it, my cock started to thrum to my heartbeat again.

"All of it, of course. I've never had a man in my bed, but the mechanics of man and woman are down well enough in my mind. Though try as I might, I can't fathom how two men come together."

Bold-as-brass, I said to myself. My Yank was consumed with questions and responsible for a rather stiff cock to boot. I felt a sticky dribble soaking into my robe front. What an astounding notion my attraction was.

Covering her hand with my own, and taking her at her word, I explained my encounter in the young man's cabin.

Her brows went together as she worked a maiden's piecemeal imaginings into information. "Wouldn't he choke? I mean it's rather large, isn't it?" Her eyes went to my crotch while my heart pounded loud enough for me to hear. The fabric of the big top began to rise as the center pole lifted. Sure enough the small hand slipped from under mine in a tentative climb. Pausing, she met my eyes. "May I see?"

I couldn't fully comprehend my case of anxiety. In many ways, I too, was as untried as she. I might have had my male lover since the age of seventeen, but I'd never shared an intimate exchange with a woman before this moment. It wasn't the lesson in futility I'd always assumed such a chance meeting would be either. I eyed the decanter again but decided I'd had more than enough and was likely sound asleep and dreaming the encounter anyway. Untying the sash, I experienced a peculiar disconnect between my sotted brain and the quavering hands at the ends of my arms. Swallowing nervously, I folded back the sides of my robe and exposed myself to her.

"That's amazing." She looked from my cock to my face as if expecting me to concur. Clearly deliberating how to proceed, she worried her bottom lip as questions filled her mind. "It *is* fully engorged, isn't it? I mean, you're *much* larger now than when you finished your bath." Her eyes met mine. "Are you thinking of him now?"

Damn me if her unabashed words didn't fill the last inch. Seeing that, she drew a sharp breath. The strange thing is, I wasn't thinking of the Dutchman in the least. Noticing the unconscious flexing of her fingers in a tentative itch to feel my length, I heard a voice come out of my mouth. My drunken brain could scarcely credit it was I who suggested, "Touch me if you'd like."

Though her reaction to my words rivaled finding the lucky bean in her Twelfth Night cake, her reach was at once hesitant yet curiously eager. Her fingertips found me first. They traced the knots of veins just under my skin.

"Oh, you're much warmer than I imagined, and unbelievably firm. I never imagined that, nor did I think I'd be able to feel your pulse down here."

My breath caught as small soft fingers closed around me then eased my foreskin down until the crown of my cock lay fully exposed. She released it and my sheaf resumed its natural position. Like a child with a new wind-up toy or a scientist on the verge of discovery, she tested my flesh again. Over and over she plied me until her comfort in touching me grew. I imagined her picturing the Dutchman and me; and I half expected her to try to swallow me like he had. The heady thought brought about a shiver that raced through me from head to toe.

Apparently she hadn't missed the sexual tremor that seized me. Her exploration halted, those eyes met mine but her hand stayed put. Somewhere in my haze I recalled I'd found them pretty just that morning, but good god they were lovely. For the first time I noticed her irises had dark olive green rings around the blue and small gold flecks in a corona around the black center.

Holding her gaze, I covered her little hand with my own and

slowly stroked the length with her. To my surprised delight her slight grip tightened on its own. For all the sensation was different, I enjoyed this soft intimate caress as much as I enjoyed Thomas' rough and firm hand.

She moistened her lips with her tongue and her left knee began to swing to and fro with tensile energy. Even in my inebriated state I recognized these small gestures as those normally reserved for when her focus was piqued by some thought. Whatever that mind of hers was thinking, it was evident my wife very much liked this imagery of hers. Her next words broke my trance, "I find myself envious."

The slow soft stroking and my over-indulgence of spirits were muddying the waters of my comprehension of the moment. I could only imagine what that detail-hungry mind was thinking, for I was having trouble following the thought. My voice sounded dull to my ears when all I could do was repeat her.

Her next words had a breathy quality. "Yes, envious. I imagine what having a blade like this might feel when sinking into the heat of a lover's body."

For a moment it felt as though my heart had stopped, and I forced a breath to be sure it was still engaged. I'd once seen the marble statue of the androgynous Hermaphroditus: the bisexual offspring of Aphrodite and Hermes, sleeping in the Louvre. Lost in the erotic thought of her having a cock along with the rest of her fair attributes, the breathtaking notion enhanced by her softly stroking hand, I closed my eyes and immersed myself in the fantasy. What glorious imagery it was.

And while visions danced behind my closed lids, the effects of nerve-dousing brandy and travel fatigue coalesced. My new wife gently examined every male detail that made our bodies differ, and damn me if I didn't miss most of it. Done in by drink and her gentle touch, I went off to sleep in the arms of Morpheus.

***

I woke sometime in the night to discover myself half on the settee and under the spare coverlet from the bed. For a moment I didn't know where I was. At last the details of the evening came in from the sides of my mind. I lifted the coverlet. That my cock was glued to my thigh was a mystery. I couldn't remember past Ellie's novice exploration of my privates.

One thing was certain however; the copious brandy to settle my nerves had kicked me right between the eyes as surely as a mule. I felt plain awful. Trying hard not to wake her, I quietly went to the commode where, hugging the throne so to speak, my body expelled the evening's spirits as quickly as I'd taken them in. I poured myself a glass of water to rinse my mouth then hied myself back to the settee where I curled into a miserable ball and promptly fell back to sleep.

***

The next morning when I opened my bleary eyes, I felt a little better thanks to my midnight purge. Experience told me my queasy headache would last for several hours. In the outer room, an ungodly loud rap on the door was answered by the pleasant voice of my new wife. I heard her say, "Thank you. No, I'll take it from here."

A moment later she brought a wait cart into the sitting room. I greeted her groggily. There were covered dishes and carafes, but I could easily determine the menu by the savory scent of bacon and kippers, and sultry aroma of butter and cinnamon. My sour stomach told my nose to ignore it all.

She smiled. "I thought you'd prefer breakfast in here this morning."

Needing to atone for my poor behavior, I offered, "I very much regret last night, Ellie. Please accept my ap—"

She cut me off, "We drank a rather lot last night, you and I. I must say I… "

I listened to her dismiss the fact I'd acted like a dreadful sot by including herself in my solo drunkenness. That she'd seek to protect me from embarrassment by sharing the blame touched me deeply. I gave her an appreciative yet apologetic smile. "You're kind. But it falls on my head, and believe me my head feels my remorse acutely."

Laughing lightly, she handed me a dry biscuit. She tsk-tsked, "You *poor* thing. Here nibble this… slowly."

She poured me a cup of coffee, adding cream and sugar lumps, presumably to her taste. "Coffee helps the morning-after head far better than tea. And this helps even more, believe me." To my surprise, she splashed a tot of brandy in the cup. After my early-morning episode with the commode, I admit the sight of the decanter made my stomach lurch. I found myself wondering how she knew the *hair of the dog* remedy for a drunkard's hangover. I asked her.

Laughing, she confided she'd "learned the hard way," explaining vaguely that progressive Americans much enjoy their leisure, though they occasionally must pay the piper like everyone else. She also asked I please not mention that to my new father-in-law.

I gave a head-splitting laugh and promptly quelled it in an act of self-preservation. That sentient smile played over her lips, and once more the notion of familiarity came to me and then it was gone. Instead, I was reminded of a comment Mrs. Fletcher once made after catching her nephew and I kissing in the buttery. "It is wise to conceal that which cannot be disclosed, and disclose that which cannot be concealed. Now go find yourselves a private place to test the waters or tongues will wag, and Master Nicolas, you *don't* want that, dear."

Handing over the steaming cup, Ellie met my eye, "Trust me."

Damn me if I didn't.

~5~

We had nothing planned for our first full day at sea, and lord knows my substantially pickled brain did *not* have Leonardo da Vinci's book foremost and center. I couldn't think of much other than a nap and perhaps a bath to rid myself of the liquor's remaining affects. So when the invitation came for Ellie to take tea and stroll around the deck with the women of our previous evening's dinner party, I encouraged her to go. She was gone most of the afternoon, and I used the time to nap and later to make myself presentable. It was likely that Jerone's sister took the stroll with the others, so I half expected my young Dutchman to come calling. This would have been an undeniable temptation for me in my bachelorhood, but not today. A powerful and previously uncharted attraction called to me. This was proved by how pleased I was to hear the door open and close. My wife had at last returned from her outing.

She found me in the bathtub, where I'd been soaking for the

better part of an hour. She stood in the doorway with a gaze that raked me from my damp head to my wrinkled toes. I asked her how her day had been.

"Far too long, honestly." As she pulled off her gloves and extracted her hat pins, she rattled off details of her afternoon at sea. "The conversation moved rather slowly at times, well, *much* of the time actually. But we saw dolphins at the prow when we walked the deck. To me, the dolphins appeared to be playing, but the others saw them as simply trying to get out of the way of the ship." She shook her head. "I suppose I just have a bit more fancy in my imagination… "

That image of Hermaphroditus came back to me. I think I had enough fancy for the both of us.

Without pausing to draw a breath in her conversation, she rolled up her sleeves and perched her bottom on the edge of my tub. Grabbing up the sponge, she proceeded to lather it. I allowed her to bathe my back and shoulders and enjoyed the experience in equal measure to the many times Thomas and I shared a bath. *Equal measure.* I wondered about that.

She wrung the sponge over my shoulders. "So I learned something useful from Mrs. Ormont… Oh *fiddlesticks,*" she blurted when the bar of soap fell and splashed her blouse with water, effectively ending what she was about to say. "Excuse me." She stepped from the room to return a moment later wearing only her bloomers and camisole. I drew my legs back to make room and asked if she cared to join me.

A blush pinked her cheeks and she laughed, "Are you serious?"

I challenged her with a teasing grin. "All *progressive* British homosexuals share baths. Don't you know?"

"Oh, you *are* funny."

I considered her. The sheer cotton of the damp camisole clung to her skin and her rosy nipple peaked the cloying fabric. Never in my life did a woman's breasts interest me more than in passing. They did now. I gestured to the water, "Please."

She worried her lip and through her hesitation I was reminded that for all her modern American ways, my wife was as green as a spring sapling. The bloomers went first. I hadn't realized there was an open split to the garment's crotch but seeing it, the construction made sense. The camisole followed. Without her flounces and bustles, Ellie was a petite little thing; trim but shapely enough that no one would ever doubt she was a woman grown — despite her small breasts barely making a shadow on her chest. These were tipped by rosy nipples that stood stiff from chill or perhaps modesty. I was struck by how soft she looked, like Pierre-Paul Proudhon's small-breasted *Standing Nude*.

I often compared life to art and my eye was consistently drawn to the small details and colors of life and the world around me. Had I a natural talent for brush and oil like the artists of the ages, I might have become a great proficient myself. A surprising fancy took me as I imagined her shaved and posed for the brush and canvas of the great masters. My erection grew as my imaginings pictured their hands upon her, turning her this-way and that, to the light. She noticed.

"Are you thinking of him again?" She asked me in a tone somewhere between scientific curiosity and marvel.

I smiled. "Not this time." The tip of my cock rose from the calm like Poseidon.

I knew she took my meaning because the blush came on instantly. The tub was high and her step over the side afforded me with a flash of pink of a different sort. She sat and displaced water sunk my shaft as smoothly as Jules Verne's Nautilus dropping to the ocean floor.

"A little tepid, but nice." She settled back in the water. I reached above and turned the water tank key to allow in more hot water. Grabbing the French-milled jasmine soap, she lathered the sponge again then dragged it back and forth over her face, arms, and breasts. She was like William Etty's *Bather*. I watched her, completely captivated by the feminine detail in her washing. Thomas was always matter-of-fact in the task, as was I, but the sponge had purpose in Ellie's hand. Hard to do, but she managed to turn her back to me. Handing me the sponge over her shoulder she asked, "Would you mind washing my back, please?"

I worked up a thick lather and bathed her — a different experience from washing Thomas' angled planes. I wrung the sponge out over her shoulders several times to rinse long after the suds were gone, just because I liked the sight of water cascading over her skin. Her bones were delicate, the soft wispy hairs at her nape sprung into dark curls, reminding me of the ballerinas of Edgar Degas. I was struck by the desire to kiss the column of her neck. I told her so.

She turned to me in surprise and our eyes met but no words were exchanged. I rose and stepped from the tub. Reaching a hand to her, I helped her out on the rug then took the Turkish towel and patted her dry with trembling hands. It was never the brandy that caused last night's tremor. It was her.

She stood with her back to me covered in gooseflesh. How fine her bone structure was. Christoffer Wilhelm Eckersberg painted a back such as this in his *Woman Standing in Front of a Mirror*. My hands glided up and down her damp warm arms, and the gooseflesh smoothed away. Because Ellie was so slight, I had to bend to kiss her shoulder. She was a swan covered in the finest down, and my lips overjoyed at how soft they found this experience. I kissed her neck, sweeping my lips to her ear where a small gold-and-garnet bob dangled from a tiny hole. I took it between my teeth and lightly pulled, stretching the lobe as it followed. Releasing it, I traveled on to the line of her jaw. With her pulse against my lips, I could almost hear the blood as I passed over her jugular. My hands came around and swept across her pert high breasts and firm yet pliant nipples.

My cock found her as compelling as my mind did, for close as we were it sought familiar ground. I gripped myself with one hand and slowly dragged my spar along the split of her bottom as my other hand ran free upon her.

She turned to me then, the look in her eyes possessing a heat I knew corresponded to my own. Meeting that gaze, I felt the shift inside me. Only suspecting this truth the day before, I knew with a certainty then and there that I wasn't the homosexual I'd always thought myself to be. Like Lord Byron and Hans Christian Andersen, I *was* bisexual — an androgynous epicene who took delight in all. I was immersed in delight.

Taking her in my arms, I slid my cock between her sleek thighs and she tightened her legs around me, effectively trapping me along the warm furrow of her sex. The heat emanating there made me dizzy to discover it. I could do nothing else but press forward. Locked in this intimate embrace, I bent my head to kiss her. I no sooner had my lips upon her when the first bell rang, signaling our fifteen minutes to dress for dinner. Her lust-dilated eyes became huge and her hands went to my chest as her upper body arched away from mine. "We have to dress!"

Reluctant to lose this moment of self-discovery, I drew her back and nuzzled the side of her neck. "Why?"

"For dinner."

"*You're* my dinner." I drew her close once more and lightly bit her ear. She made a little noise halfway between a squeak and a gasp. It was adorable.

Her hands pressed against my chest again. "Today on the deck, Mrs. Ormont told us that her husband had invited an Italian historian to join us for dinner tonight. We *have* to go to dinner."

I pressed my lower half forward, hoping to remind her of what she held trapped between those silken thighs and found the groove a slick passing. "We're on a ship, my sweet. Surely we'd encounter him again."

She paused, and holding her like this, I could feel the machine of her mind processing. I very much liked that the decision to stop was as difficult for her as it was for me. Apparently coming to a judgment, she shook her head. "Nicolas, he has a palazzo in *Venice*. He can help us navigate."

I searched her face and saw the logic of meeting the man tonight. If we were to successfully pull off the theft of a priceless artwork and avoid the scandal of failure, we needed to use our time aboard ship to plan. I let her slip from my arms, but not before saying, "I would revisit this moment."

Her smile was beauteous. "I'd like that."

~6~

Ellie and I weren't the only passengers to arrive as the last bell struck. People filed through the dining room's double doors to take their seats. This congestion would lessen as people became accustomed to how long it took them to ready themselves between the ring of the first and last bell.

More so than the other meals aboard, dinners were often a mingling affair. We sat with the Ormonts and the Brookses again while the Dutch brother and sister took their seats at the table next to us, the sister involved in a rather animated conversation with a new friend. Jerone did smile when I looked his way. His eye jerked toward the door in open invitation. Despite the twinge that silent proposal sent to my loins, my smile widened as my eye jerked to my wife. He gave me a pretty moue, his brief pout good-natured. It was a long voyage after all.

I sat Ellie and pulled a chair for Mrs. Ormont as she waited for her husband. A moment later, Colonel Ormont brought the historian to our table and made introductions. Luca Franco, late of Florence, was a Professor of Antiquities returning from London. I found the Italian quite the attractive fellow, impeccably dressed as he was. When in the presence of true beauty, my mind often imagines the person unclothed as the artists of the ages might have seen him. Sitting at my table was a statue carved in marble by Gian Lorenzo Bernini; an artist known for his remarkable ability to capture the essence of a narrative moment. And I found Luca Franco to be exactly that — a moment indelibly captured in time — a moment of meeting the mind could revisit in its entirety.

From every angle, he was beautifully made: black-haired, of medium build, and physically fit. He possessed a warm hue to his skin, his lineage no doubt stamped centuries past by the darker Moors or Turks. In startling contrast, and quite handsomely framed by black lashes, he had striking eyes the color one might see in a shadow falling across snow — not quite sky blue nor exactly steel gray, but a blending of the two in gradated rings.

I rose to shake his hand and felt the unmistakable current of compatibility. If this man weren't forward in his mutual attraction, it was there nonetheless. I watched him bow over the ladies' hands and found it curious that he lingered over Ellie's fingers a tad longer. It made me smile. I had the distinct impression I was in the presence of a fellow dual-nature like myself.

The regular chit-chat occurring over the courses was quite enjoyable. There was a part of me, however, that would have been content to take my wife back to our stateroom and lose myself in the wonder of my newfound truth. Like the great navigators in ages past, the thought of uncharted lands titillated my imagination. I was anxious to explore her body, anxious to immerse in her heated places and scent, and smell and taste every part of her. I wanted to lose myself in the hedonistic feast of the senses I knew I'd find.

Ellie's question pulled me from my imaginative foray. "Professor Franco, it's my understanding that you are an authority on Leonardo da Vinci."

Chuckling, he shook his head and replied in softly accented English, "You flatter me, Lady Halstead. As a professor of antiquities my work takes me into the far corners of the world's history. The museum I work for sends me to procure various historical treasures. But where da Vinci is concerned, I wouldn't say I'm an authority *per se*. You see, my interest is personal."

Ellie's eyes lit. "May I ask then, what is it you find so interesting about the man to spur a *personal* pursuit?"

He gave her a genuine smile that crinkled the corners of his eyes. It was a very handsome smile indeed. As he appeared to be of an age with me, the crinkles had me wondering if he often worked in the sun.

"Da Vinci was a universal genius."

Reaching for the buttered peas, Mrs. Ormont repeated dully, "A *universal* genius? My goodness."

The Colonel followed, "I say dear fellow, what is that title, exactly? I've never heard of such a thing."

Even the blind could see that Luca Franco possessed an innate animal magnetism, but when he smiled the world tilted on its axis. My gaze went to my wife and knew she concurred by the distinctive tint upon her cheeks — the sexual tint I'd so recently come to recognize. I couldn't help but wonder what brewed in the cauldron of her mind. As for myself, I harbored an

undeniable attraction for the both of them. It was all I could do
to keep the stallion of my imagination in the paddock.

Luca explained, "Da Vinci wasn't simply an artist. His range of
accomplished study went far beyond producing memorable
artworks. He was an inventor and a scientist who never
developed his ideas systematically, because he didn't need to. He
intuited their success, because he simply understood processes."

Brooks wiped the crumbs from his curled mustache, "How's
that?"

"If one already knows it's been proven that lead melts at a
lower temperature than iron, one needn't employ a bellows to test
it."

Brooks nodded like a walrus. "Makes sense, makes sense. That
would be useful knowledge, eh?"

"Precisely. He understood numerous systems — the series of
actions needed to arrive at a particular place in his inventions.
This knowledge was implemented whether his inventions
remained preliminary sketches or were actually created. Scholars
believe that were his drawings implemented today as plans, and
those same inventions built, they'd do exactly what he theorized
they'd do."

"Hmm." Satisfied with the answer, Brooks nodded again then
busied himself with his meal. I watched the Bordelaise sauce
deposit a greasy gleam where the crumbs had been a moment
ago. The sight brought a brief recall of my head in the commode.

The Colonel said loudly, "The man sounds like an Italian
Faust!"

Mrs. Ormont laughed lightly, "Oh my! Given his gifts by the
devil! And here I only ever understood him to be a simple artist."

I offered, "Oh, da Vinci was far more than a *simple* artist, Mrs.

Ormont. Aside from being the most complex genius of the Renaissance, and perhaps of all time, his artistic skill was enhanced by a working knowledge of mathematics."

"Well said, Sir Nicolas." Luca smiled at me and I felt it like static in the air prior to a thunderstorm. I returned it.

I would have rather continued our mutual adoration of the man in private, but Mrs. Ormont drew my attention once more. Her silver brows knitted in confusion, and she looked at me over the rim of her bejeweled spectacles. There was self-critical humor in her voice when she said, "Sir Nicolas, I'm afraid you'll think me quite silly, but what do you mean? What has mathematics to do with it?"

Brooks chuckled, and taking a drink, dipped his mustache in his water glass. He came up for air looking very much like the Emperor Tamarin Monkey I'd once seen in the London Zoo.

I set down my fork and knife and helped myself to the heel of dry bread to calm my stomach, then explained, "Were a trained eye to look upon da Vinci's Vitruvian Man with his arms and legs spread wide in the illusion of movement, it would see an image based on the much older writings of the Roman architect Vitruvius. Many of the sacred geometry principles of the human body as well as ancient architecture have been compiled into art by Leonardo da Vinci. His perspectives are considered perfect and balanced."

Mrs. Ormont, either lost or disinterested, said, "Oh."

That was the way of it for most of my academic career. A certain curiosity went part and parcel with being an art historian, and not everyone shared it. Luca Franco however, had found one of his own. I could read the truth of his discovery upon his face when he added, "That is quite fascinating about his art. It's my understanding that da Vinci was a philosopher and dreamer unhindered by the opinions of others. For example, he had little interest in things that would cloud his own personal discovery such as literature, history, or religion for that matter, much to the great annoyance of the church. Because the church was a determined hindrance to his pursuits, he eschewed religious doctrine."

My bold-as-brass Yankee progressive harrumphed and all eyes went to her. I chuckled, knowing what had irked her. Yes the church hindered the poor man, and hindered was a poor word at that to describe it. They repeatedly condemned the artist for sodomy. Perhaps the Anglicans and Catholics at the table didn't find the artist's lack of faith all that amusing. The Professor of Antiquities smiled at her and she returned it in her sparkling blue eyes. I felt the current of attraction pass between them, and by default through me as well. A fleeting image of Édouard-Henri Avril's erotic sketches came to mind and I pictured myself sandwiched between my wife and this sensually charismatic man. The thought made my balls ache.

Rather than be lost to my own imaginings, I added to the conversation at hand, "From my own field of expertise I would agree with you, Professor Franco. The ideas of other men muddied the waters of da Vinci's personal immersion in discovery. He concerned himself with what the eye could see, rather than with purely abstract concepts. To him it didn't necessarily matter what had come before his personal observation. He was a most excellent observer." My smile was for Luca when I added, "A dreamer, as you say."

He returned it and this time I caught the nearly imperceptible scent of our mutual chemistry.

Ellie addressed our dinner party with a winsome grin, "If you haven't already guessed, my husband finds da Vinci, the man, fascinating. I admit his life and works have captured my fancy as well though I gravitate toward his reasoning rather than his art."

Mrs. Brooks announced that she knew little of the man, but was stunned to discover the *Mona Lisa* to be the small a painting it was. I looked at Ellie. *That* was the smile I found so similar in hers but had yet to identify — a smile that hinted there was more than met the eye. The mention of the *Mona Lisa* put our dinner conversation on far simpler ground — a ground void of invention, theology and speculation on genius. The conversation around the table went to galleries we'd seen and we came to speculate on the artistry of the Renaissance in general. I filled them in as far as their interest held. I could feel both Ellie and the historian's disappointment over abandoning our interesting topic. It echoed my own.

Our Italian dinner companion reached for his glass, the action raising his cuff slightly. He had fine strong wrists, a jagged scar run up the side and I briefly wondered what he'd done to have gotten such a wound. Drawn to artistry as I was, bone structure often caught my eye when I looked at people and this wrist drew my attention. Michelangelo's *David* came to mind — David with his corded forearms and finely-detailed hands slightly larger than they should be. A hint to the size of the full erection the artist had in mind, were it made of flesh and not flaccid stone. I wondered who had been his model, for like his contemporary and rival da Vinci, he had a male muse among his models. Lost in thoughts of anatomy, I watched Luca raise his glass to his lips and licked my own before I was aware I'd done so.

He leveled me a snow-shadow glance over the rim of his wine

glass, before saying, "If you have the inclination Sir Nicolas, I would enjoy conversing about da Vinci's life with you. It's my good fortune to find a man of your knowledge and kindred interest on board." Grinning, he lowered his voice conspiratorially as if he confessed to the others there, "You see I'm considered quite the bore at home."

The throng laughed, and Ellie met my eyes with excitement burning in her own. I read her mind. Luca Franco was approachable after all, and perhaps in more ways than one. The laughter continued after I pulled my wife's hand to my lips and kissed her knuckles in sympathy, "As am I."

When the sexes divided for the requisite sherry, and port and cigars, I used the opportunity to continue the conversation with Professor Franco, who now insisted I address him by his given name. He'd come round to visit at two o'clock the next day. As I was still in no physical condition for port, and the cigar smoke was reanimating my earlier headache, I took my leave and hied myself back toward our stateroom.

Given our recent personal and academic discoveries, it was no wonder I met my wife on the deck. We debriefed ourselves of the evening's conversation and then stood at the rail enjoying the gibbous moon. The captain found us while taking his stroll and Ellie asked where we were on the ocean. He answered, "We've made good time, ma'am. We'll likely reach the Strait of Gibraltar the day after next."

She smiled at me. Yes, we were making good time.

***

Back in our stateroom, Ellie put away her jewelry then went to change out of her formal attire. In the meantime, I rang for champagne. After tipping the steward for his impressive uncorking, I closed the door behind him and saw to replacing my own dinner garments with my more comfortable dressing gown.

My wife came out of the bedroom looking absolutely beautiful wearing a gauzy gown with a low yoke of fine lace. With the pink tint of her skin visible through the lacework, it brought to mind the little light-filled windows for which Johannes Vermeer was noted. The view being enhanced by her cloud of undone cinnamon curls, I found it all rather enticing. Who would have thought? I handed her a glass and she raised a brow.

"Champagne?"

I chuckled. "When I thought about an after-dinner drink, I found it far less obnoxious than the idea of brandy."

I loved it that she laughed. In truth I wasn't sure how to recapture our earlier encounter and thought a milder drink might relax us and open us to any eventuality, whether we came together again tonight or not. But to her, I said, "I thought we'd toast to our new beginnings as man and wife."

The blush pinked her cheeks. Ah, the green sapling. We clinked our glasses and sipped. I could see a question forming in the blue depths of her eyes. But it wasn't there for long. She refilled our champagne, then in her typical fashion launched right to it.

"I must admit, I'm confused by what occurred between us earlier. I know you'd made it clear that afternoon in your townhome that one day we'd have to figure something out. You know, procuring an heir for your family and all... but am I wrong to believe your desire was for me today... desire for me, a woman... and not because you'd remembered fondly Jerone's actions of the night before?"

Not in all my years did I meet such a forthright woman as this intriguing wife of mine. I thought how to answer this question, the answer for which contradicted a decade of my sexual practice. Meeting her eyes, I couldn't help but notice she had the slightest worry in her brow. She *wanted* me to want her. And I did. I wanted her more than anything in that moment. I took her empty glass and set it with mine. Leading her to our bed, I sat with her there, holding her hands for a time; more to steady mine than hers, truth be told.

Seeing she needed an answer from me, I brushed back her curls and took her face between my hands. Drawing close, I kissed her. It began as a tentative touch of my lips to hers. But her mouth was soft and pliant and, unlike my male lovers, her chin and upper lip were void of rasping whiskers. This discovery alone caused my kiss to firm. I pressed into it wanting it all. Slanting over her, I dragged my kiss back and forth forcing her mouth to open to me. Her sweet champagne tongue coiled with mine hesitantly at first, but this grew bolder the more familiar our lips and tongues became.

For all our restrained beginnings, I could tell in her return that kissing wasn't new to her. She knew how to kiss a man, god yes, she did. I craved to know this enigma, craved to comprehend this contradiction I was fastly discovering Ellie to be. She was both neophyte and temptress. It was her shyness that confused me. It came and went like waves lapping on the shore. Her hands covered mine as her body melted against me, the leverage gained deepened her kiss as she plunged her tongue and forced mine to chase it.

I loved this audacious attempt to dominate the moment, so I

gave over to it and allowed her to press me back on the bed. I was anxious to see exactly how far she'd take this imperious loving. Straddling my thighs, she opened my robe and pulled and yanked until it was completely off and tossed to the floor. I hiked her gown, gathering the material in my hands until I had enough of the flounces gripped to pull it over her head. Naked now, we rolled over one another like eels in a barrel. Her mouth on my nipple was more than I could bear. Flipping her to her back, I took charge. Pressing belly to belly, I went back to the sweet lips and satin-smooth face.

When she tried again to have the upper hand by dipping her head and suckling my other nipple, I pinned her arms over her head. Starting at her elbows, I kissed my way down her body and sniffed the jasmine on her now-fevered skin. The shadow of my beard grazed her armpit and elicited a twisting giggle. Not one to miss such advantage, I lingered one side to the other, until she begged me to stop. My mouth found her nipples one at a time and I leisurely explored them with lips and tongue. They were larger than Thomas's and firm, and I lingered there enjoying the fact there was so much more flesh to suckle. My god, she was so soft. By the time I worked my way to the sparse cinnamon thatch, she was writhing.

I had a unique advantage as I coaxed her legs apart. With my body effectively blocking her, her legs would remain spread for me. Turnabout was fair play, and while I might not have remembered how her exploration ended the night before, I certainly recalled how it began. I told her all the things I planned to do. Her upper body lifted as she braced on her elbows. She looked down at me and I could see in her eyes that she wanted to watch this new experience of mine.

I hadn't noticed when we shared our bath, but now I realized the cinnamon curls before me had been trimmed short and I wondered why. I pictured her with scissors, her mirror held by a cherub like Diego Velazquez's *Venus at Her Mirror*. The musing brought a singular heaviness to my balls and I pressed to the mattress seeking some sensation.

Propped on my forearms, I used my fingertips to spread her cleft. My wife lay before me in all her glorious color like the hand-tinted lithographed botanicals hanging in Grannie's sitting room. Indeed, this dewy flower beckoned me on as if I were a lust-drunk bee. I felt her lips, warm, soft, and pouting. I ran my fingertip between to spread them like butterfly wings. She was amazingly crimson at her core, and moist, very moist.

Where the scent of a man's balls was feral and hungry, her perfume was evocative and heady. Trembling now, I touched a tentative tongue and her essence exploded over me in a wash of scent and taste. It did things to my mind — created a lightness of being that could only be described as intoxication. I dipped my head and feasted, my tongue finding every ridge and valley. At the top of these lust-swollen, dew-soaked petals I found her tiny version of a cock. I knew what to do with a cock in my mouth and latched there as if I'd be swept out to sea if I didn't. I worked it over, sucking and swirling my tongue.

I slipped my finger just inside. My god she was tight and slick and hotter than a blast furnace. Parts of her were smooth and parts ridged, and I was beside myself; my senses lost in discovery. On the underside of her thighs, my hands, moving of their own accord, spread apart and widened her even more than she was — a conscious act done for no reason but to allow me to lap at her in pure unimpeded depravity.

Her legs began to tremble and her hands covered mine. Small helpless whimpers filled the room, and an instant later her back arched at the same time her curling fingers dug into the back of my hands. Never before had I witnessed such primal beauty. The compass needle of my cock pointing me home, I left her panting after her release and rose to kneel between those slender wide-spread thighs. I jacked my cock to the glistening splendor of this ebbing tide. Moving closer, I rubbed her rubbery swollen lips to and fro, dragging my cock head over her soft sloppy-wet sex, circling her clitoris like a lightheaded bee dancing over a flower.

Despite her release, my bewitching wife wasn't ready to surrender the game. My bold beauty lifted her hips in blatant invitation. I pressed forward, inch by amazingly-tight inch. I'd never been met with muscle all along the route before and relished my slippery entry. There was no need for spit or butter, for she was slick and ready, indeed she was. Eyes closed in bliss, I felt rather than saw the moment I breached her. Along with that exquisite grip came a moment of tension that quickly faded as her body stretched around me like a glove on hand.

Lifting her legs, I set them over my shoulders until my balls rested warm along the split of her rear. Palms on either side of her head, I began to pump into her, each slice deep and immensely satisfying. Sweating now from exertion and restraint, I very much wanted to see the orgasm as I'd missed her last. But letting it build was exacting a toll. My balls ached to empty into her, my cock driven to seek out all the friction it could find on her magnificent griping ridges. Her small breasts jiggled with each thrust. Utterly amazed I watched an invisible hand paint her with color right before my eyes as our crescendo drew near. My body fastly surrendering, I ground out between the thrusts, "Come darling, I can't hold back any longer. Come, I can't... hold... "

She moaned. "Mmm... fuck me hard... yes fuck me... "

I could scarcely believe I'd heard what I had, and my mind quickly filed the words away as American slang. I met sultry eyes fathomless with mindless abandon and wondered briefly if I'd heard her speak the words at all or they'd come from me. But the seductively sentient smile confirmed it and that's what lit the fuse. Who would have thought brazen words coming from a woman would command such power over me? I fucked into her hard to chase it down, hard enough for my balls to slap loud and wet against her ass. Her feral cry gave sound to the convulsing tremor of heat that suddenly wrapped around me. Like a tight fist that heat milked me, forcing me to give all I had. She touched that zenith amid her cry and found release the very instant I reached my own. I sunk to my root, spewing my mettle with a volcano's force.

With her body doubled beneath me, I laid there with my head tucked between her neck and shoulder trying like hell to catch my breath. I'd had amazing sexual encounters before — rough, wild, infinitely satisfying. But I'd never felt this. Rolling over, I pulled her damp body close and spooned with her, my arm wound around her protectively as she snuggled against my back. Lost in wonder for a time, I pressed through the mass of curls and kissed her temple.

I attributed my rapid development of feelings for her to the fact I enjoyed her company in so many ways. Our whirlwind preparations for this trip had given us ample opportunity to become accustomed to one another as companions, and I confess she was unparalleled good company. She was kind and considerate, and intelligent beyond measure. I enjoyed conversing on any and all topics with her. I enjoyed her wit and the laughter we shared. There was no doubt I found artistry in her beauty. What's more, my desire for her was unchallenged — and me an avowed homosexual of thirteen years.

It hit me then, and I suddenly recognized the reason I'd never felt like this, for all my sexual abandon through the years. I was head over heels for my bold-as-brass Yankee wife. I had fallen in love. I told her so.

I'd expected some response to my heartfelt sentiment, but my words were met by her regular breathing. Her completely relaxed body confirmed it — she'd fallen to sleep. French poets called orgasm *la petite mort,* the little death. I couldn't help but smile at how adorable she was and kissed her again. Reaching for the coverlet, I tucked us in as much as one hand would allow, and closed my eyes as well. I know I went to sleep with a smile on my face.

***

The next morning I was met with a moment of surprise at finding a woman in my bed. Lying on her back with one arm tossed devil-may-care over her head like Jules Joseph Lefebvre's *Magdalene in the Cave,* my wife was a vision of loveliness. Sometime in the night, we'd discarded our blanket. Indeed, I'd found her body very warm to lie next to. I propped on my elbow and drank her in. That wild cinnamon mane was tousled and her lips were noticeably kiss-swollen.

In what could only be called compressed time, in our unanticipated courtship, we'd been together for less than a week. She drew me in with her outrageous plan to stop a crime against one of humanity's treasures. A week ago, I saw marriage as a thing of duty — some far-distant future with a brood-hen of a wife, from whom I'd have to hide my true nature. Then this little tempest came blowing into my home to propose marriage, and for the life of me I don't know how it was that I agreed. In short order she charmed me. That same charm captivated both Mrs. Fletcher and Grannie. And on top of that, Ellie turned my world upside down and made me question my awareness of my own self.

Consequently, our intense coupling had been transcendent for me, as had the emotion that followed. I wondered if she'd felt what I had. I wanted to ask but didn't know how. While my emotional epiphany came quickly, she might find me nothing more than a friend in our life's journey together. I sincerely hoped that not the case. Yes, I'd have a life companion in Ellie, and that in itself was priceless. But I found I wanted a full loving life with her as well. I was in love.

My typical morning erection exceeded itself while my mind replayed some of the finer moments of our first night together. There was something about her, and for no reason in particular I had the distinct impression that like da Vinci's *Mona Lisa*, my Lady Elenora Halstead was far more than met the eye.

And as far as what the eye *could* see, I was quite aware of her small breasts and sleep-soft nipples, as well as the downy cleft between her thighs. In contrast to the night before, her skin tone was now muted in sleep, a far different palette than when she was aroused. Following an impulse, I eased myself down the bed and gently parted her legs. The musky scent of her was wildly masculine, beyond the feminine note I'd so recently come to crave. Resting on my arms as I was, the tip of my tongue was my only point of contact. This I ran up and down along her slit. I knew this taste and slowly dragged my tongue over our mingled musk until she began to rouse. She murmured something I couldn't quite make out, and I licked again to see if she'd repeat herself. She did, and the words surprised the hell out of me.

"Mmm, Felicia... that feels very nice. Mmm." Waking suddenly, her head popped up and she looked at me wide-eyed and alert. A cat was out of the bag.

I finally understood Ellie's dichotomy; the reason she was at once both shy yet sexually perceptive — neophyte and temptress. My progressive Yank was only new to the desires of *men*.

My eyes held no condemnation, nor did my heart.

Smiling that bold, cock-stirring, sentient smile, she said, "And now you know."

I pulled her back to her position of a moment ago and spread her with my hands. I kissed the inside of her thighs then buried my face in our blended scent. I pictured her and the extrapolated Felicia — two identical nymphs John William Waterhouse might have painted. I saw them in the dappled sunlight of the glade, lying belly-to-belly, their glossy manes wild and their silken arms and legs a sensual tangle. And in my mind's eye I saw them lapping each other's nectar like this. I slid my fingers inside her heat, my words forming between delving licks. "And now I know."

Birds of a feather. I think I actually loved her more.

Learning never exhausts the mind.

– Leonardo da Vinci

~7~

Both ravenous from our morning of complete hedonism, we managed to leave our stateroom for lunch. After, we strolled on deck and whispered the physical attributes we were each drawn to in both men and women. I thoroughly enjoyed my intimate peek inside this fascinating creature. The object lesson and surprising commonality did much to broaden our understanding of one another. The one o'clock bell rang, so we took ourselves back to eagerly await our guest. It turned out we were *both* attracted to Luca Franco.

In anticipation of the afternoon ahead, we'd ordered an early tea. Luca arrived with a steward on his heels.

After politely kissing my wife's hand and shaking my own, sincerity lit his eyes when he said, "I'm very pleased we'll have an opportunity to share our common interests. I've thought of nothing else since dinner, and that should tell you how starved I am to converse with kindred spirits!"

Student of nuance I, I found Luca noticeably tense. I took this for his respect for our friendship at odds with the understandable allure of another man's wife. He was obviously drawn to Ellie's unorthodox American manner and I wondered if that magnetism was the same for him as it was for me. As we got acquainted over our tea and biscuits, we learned Luca was born and raised in Florence and since becoming head of the family he lived between his family's holdings in both Florence and Venice.

Ellie said, "I'm very much looking forward to Venice. I'd read it was once a cluster of islands with much of it built upon stilts."

Luca nodded. "I've read such descriptions too. One hundred and eighteen islands comprise Venice as we know it. But when such descriptions say Venice is built upon stilts, they inaccurately describe the engineering process."

I could see the wheels of her mind turning. Luca was offering information, and my wife was wont to harvest it. "However did they manage to build Venice in the marshlands without the benefit of steam? London's Tower Bridge took all manner of steam machines to construct."

Obviously recognizing this was a woman who craved factual information, Luca explained in detail how massive posts were sunk into the mud and platforms built upon them. The city was built upon that. He said, "Our canals and bridges link the islands together. To my knowledge, it was all done by hands already familiar with canal digging. Not quite as awe-inspiring as the building of Pharos's pyramids, but a marvel of ingenuity nonetheless. You see, the lagoon dwellers had their reasons and so made the best of the unwanted marshlands."

She nodded. "That people would leave the mainland to dwell

in the lagoon... It certainly explains how intolerable the waves of invasions were to expend that degree of effort."

Luca looked at her in surprise, before the smile crinkled his eyes. He complimented her, "Ah, so much more than a pretty face. My Lady, you impress."

I toasted her with my teacup. "Luca, that Yankee mind is sharper than a tack."

The blush on her cheeks came in reply. That fair tint brought other colors to mind.

Luca fed her need to know. I found myself quite enthralled by him. "The invasions certainly were reason to move from the mainland, and many who did were refugees from such wars. In the early days Venetians traded fish and salt from the lagoon, but trade being the fluid industry it is, they soon expanded to include cargos of silk, rice, and spices from the Near East and the Orient and before long other goods from across Europe passed through our Venetian ports. They still do."

It was clear our like minds enjoyed the intellectual discourse of fellow enthusiasts. Our conversation budded like a many-headed hydra and we'd stop and laugh at our individual tangents that ranged far off topic. We chatted a while longer on trade routes and the Silk Road. Given our common interests, we soon returned to the topic of the Renaissance. The epicenter of this movement was in Florence, and discussing the building marvels of the ages, we touched upon the fact da Vinci himself was an architect and engineer.

Luca explained that da Vinci's insatiable desire to learn was a direct result of his illegitimacy. "Many scholars today cite this lack of conventional schooling as the source of his genius. But the stigma of bastardy in those days was small and illegitimate offspring were quite common. Even the Pope fathered several bastards. Still, because of his illegitimacy, da Vinci wasn't allowed the traditional Latin and Greek education of his legitimate peers."

Ellie frowned. "I had no idea. How terrible for society to limit a mind like his."

I shook my head. "I wouldn't view it as hindered. If anything it helped him become the genius he was. I know his insatiable drive to know contributed greatly to his art."

Luca said, "This is true. Without the preconceived thought built upon the observations of others, he would come to test his own ingenuity against the methods and materials of the age. This way, he discovered the world of knowledge for himself."

Refilling our teacups, Ellie said, "From what I've read, he immersed himself only as long as processes fascinated him. After he'd learned all he could, he'd move on to greener pastures in his quest for knowledge. At time even leaving things unfinished because he'd learned all he cared to."

Luca nodded, "That's accurate. He was a searcher of *unfathomable* things. Like many Renaissance figures he was a true polymath in that he was proficient across many intellectual pursuits."

"Yes." I ran them off on my fingers, "Geology, botany, medicine, anatomy, and geometry among them."

Luca offered, "As you say, his insatiable drive to know contributed to his work as an illustrator. But it went beyond the art. He possessed an *incredible* knowledge of how individual components of mechanical processes worked."

Indeed. The man was able to draw his ideas with such detail that hundreds of years later, these very sketches were essentially blueprints for the models he fabricated in his mind. Many of his fantastical inventions and ideas were hundreds of years ahead of their time, equal in scope and imagination to the fictional inventions cited in Jules Verne's literary worlds.

I described several paintings which clearly underscored his humanist values — the belief that the Greek and Latin classics contained all the lessons one needed to lead a moral and effective life.

Ellie said, "But outside of Florence, humanism wasn't a popular belief."

Luca agreed. "No it wasn't."

I said, "Most people don't realize the mind behind the artwork. His works of art weren't only beautiful: he painted disquieting smiles and gesturing hands that suggest the mysteries of human personality. His works were filled with symbolism representing his deep philosophical beliefs. Some of the most curious held meanings and references that only the trained eye might recognize." I mentioned some of the more glaring pagan symbolism that flew in the face of the church — a church he was at odds with, and as a result, with himself as well.

Luca looked surprised. "I didn't know this about his art."

"I would think that difficult." Ellie commented as she reached for the dish of biscuits. "The church often provided the butter for his bread."

Our guest answered, "I do believe had he lived another seventy years, the Inquisition would have seen him put to death for heresy. He was without question, a man of his time."

Indeed. Observation rather than faith was the order of the day. Renaissance humanists didn't just write about new ideas, they lived them. It was their willingness to go beyond prescribed dogma to actually *study* nature to gain knowledge. Coming to know her mind like I was, I felt Ellie's next words dripped with innuendo when she said them. "People in Renaissance Italy specifically were quite explicit in their reliance on empiricism, weren't they? That all knowledge was derived from their senses… a concept that truth could be discovered by human effort? From what I know of him, da Vinci regularly engaged in sensory experience. I've heard that some of the paths he took were very much at odds with the moral code of the day."

Luca raised a brow but his eyes sparkled, and I wondered what connection was made in his mind. I wasn't to find out, unfortunately. When the dinner bell sounded, we knew our pleasant afternoon had passed too quickly. Still, before we scattered to prepare for dinner, we agreed this voyage would be far more enjoyable if we met here again the following afternoon.

***

Coming in late like we did, the three of us weren't able to sit with our usual dinner company, but there were chairs available with the Dutch siblings. For the duration of the meal, the blond Dutchman dropped his invitation on the table like so many gold coins. In times past I'd have had a little war with myself over such an invitation, as he had an amazing mouth. But Ellie and I were newlyweds and I'd recently experienced the glorious magnitude of our joining. Simply put, our trip to Venice had become our honeymoon. Until we'd discovered all the joy to be found in the opposite sex, hers was the only field I wished to plow. At least for the time being.

I must say that Jerone was good about my declining his tempting offer. By the time the group of us parted sexes for sherry, port, and cigars, he'd turned his eye to our Florentine friend. I watched as they took their leave first one, then the other. If ever I had doubt of Luca's inclination, it evaporated in light of their subtle exchange. I found myself fantasizing, and the ménage à trois called forward in my mind rivaled any erotic hedonism ever depicted on a Grecian urn.

I encountered Ellie on her way to our stateroom, and as my blood was high, I closed the door behind us, spun her around, and pinned her to the door with my body. Bold-as-brass, her hand slid inside the front of my trousers and she purred at my lips. "I saw them."

She closed around my now-straining cock and attempted to stroke me in tight confines. I stripped her clothes away until she stood in a puddle of silk and tulle, dressed only in her white stockings and shoes. Pulling the pins from her hair, the cinnamon cascade fell over her like a cape that allowed her nipples to poke through the strands. My teeth lightly pulled her bottom lip. "Whom did you see, my love?"

Having decided she needed more room, she stopped only long enough to undress me. The object of her fondling now free and at full staff, she immediately returned to her bewitching caress. She stroked slowly and flicked her tongue over my lips before finding my tongue with a taste of sherry upon hers. "Luca and Jerone. I saw them meet at the deck behind the lifeboats. They were kissing. Oh! You *like* that picture, do you?"

"Very much." I kicked my shoes and socks aside to step from my trousers. In my haste to feel all of her with every inch of my skin, I forgot to attend to my cufflinks. To my great annoyance, I found both hands trapped inside my sleeves. My struggle to be free only made it worse. I looked at Ellie helplessly, and attempted to raise my hands ensnared by the body of the shirt around my back. The devilish gleam in her eye caught my breath.

"You want to be free, do you?" she asked, while running her fingernail down the side of my neck, to my chest, where it circled my nipple.

"Yes." Her touch made me lightheaded.

"I'll help you, but there will be a price had for it, you understand." She tweaked the firm little nub.

Thomas and I often played rough; one of us would take charge over the other. His brown eyes often held the very same gleam that I now saw reflected in her blue. My breathing became shallow. "Oh?"

"Tell me what they might be doing in this very moment."

I played dumb. "Who?" My breath drew sharply as her tweak turned into a double pinch. The identical Waterhouse nymphs in my earlier imaginings of Ellie and Felicia danced before my eyes. They were treating one another's nipples this very way, as one took the reins over the other in their lovemaking. The fancy was followed by a heady thought of turnabout.

She purred again, "Luca and Jerone."

My wife was a minx — a boldly sensual cocktease. "What would you like to know, that I found myself wanting to join them?"

She palmed me from balls to tip. Leaning close she drew my nipple into her mouth and worried it with her teeth while she suckled. I longed to bury my hands in those cinnamon curls, but I couldn't touch her with my hands trapped as they were. I told her so. Looking up at me, she let go with a little pop. Her lips met mine as she murmured against me, "And if you had joined them, what would be happening right about now?"

Where once was lit a gleam, a full flame now shone in her eyes. Mesmerized, I spoke the words, husky even to my own ears. Each punctuated by my returning kisses, "Kissing... stroking... sucking... fucking... "

Her brows drew together slightly in confusion, then those blue orbs of hers grew wide as the last puzzle piece of my duo sexuality fell into place. Breath shuddering as she inhaled, I felt a twinge of fear that she might condemn me for the beast I was. Searching her face, I looked for a clue to where her mind was in that moment, but I couldn't discern a bloody thing. Then that sentient sexual smile of hers played upon her lips. It left me dizzy with want when my body responded by funneling every last drop of blood to my cock.

She picked up my trapped hands one at a time, and folding back the cuffs to expose the links, freed me from my bonds. Taking me by the hand, she led me to our bedroom and I followed blindly. In a voice sounding more sultry than hesitant, she said simply, "Show me."

I thought of da Vinci, who himself once said, "Only observation and experience is the key to understanding."

Only observation and experience is the key to understanding.
— Leonardo da Vinci

~8~

Sharing our secrets not only brought Ellie and I to complete understanding of our dual natures, but the nature of one another as well. As a result, we spent our intimate moments like the epicures of ancient Rome — engaged in complete sensorial experience of our mating and the contemplative wonder that came after.

It had become our custom after these sublime engagements to talk while still wrapped in each other's arms, for it was then that our minds harmonized best. Immersed in her as I was, words of love formed in my mind and this time she was awake to hear them. She'd yet to verbally acknowledge her feelings for me, but I couldn't deny the change in her touch or the noticeable lover's daydream in her eyes when she looked at me. What began as curiosity transformed into loving. I was sure of it. Still, I *wanted* the words.

Cutting short this cerebral harmony as well as the declaration forming on my tongue, a steward brought a surprise breakfast cart to our door — apparently an arrangement made by Luca the day before. There was a note among the trays:

> *My Dear New Friends,*
> *Last night at dinner, I'd overheard that today would mark your one week anniversary. I've taken it upon myself to order a champagne breakfast in celebration. Newlyweds should enjoy such simple pleasures on their honeymoon. I am looking forward to our one PM discussion.*
> *Yours, L*

A tousled Ellie came from the bedroom shrugging into her dressing gown. I handed her the note. Reading it, her eyes lit happily. "How *sweet* of him."

"Yes, it's a thoughtful gesture."

Ellie didn't bother tying her robe closed. It made her appear poised to enact whatever sensual fancy that might arise. What was it about this ethereal creature that captivated me so? I'd known her for mere days yet I'd swear my soul knew her far longer. Never could I have imagined I'd be so welcomed to be who I was. She was my match, intellectually and in appetite, and I trusted her completely. In fact, there wasn't a part of me I wouldn't hand over to her safekeeping. Seeing opportunity to bare my heart as fully as I'd bared my soul, I filled our glasses. Handing one to her, I raised mine. "My dear Lady Halstead, you blew into my life as surely as Prospero's tempest. How is it you've completely stolen my heart?"

She sipped her champagne. Laughing lightly, she repeated, "You believe I've stolen your heart?"

Her lighthearted reaction felt unsettling. Questions filled my mind. Did I declare too much too soon? Had I read her gaze and touch wrongly? Was Thomas correct that she was a breed apart and I'd never *truly* know her mind? Setting my glass aside first, I took hers and set it on the cart beside mine. Gathering her close, my head bent to rest against hers. I poured my thoughts into her mind, silently willing her to understand how I felt. Having gone this far, I confessed, "Completely."

She pressed her small hands against my chest and drawing back, searched my eyes before saying, "You mean it, don't you?"

I didn't trust myself to speak. Instead I nodded.

She said, "I'd never expected more than friendship between us. When I proposed, I didn't *want* more than a marriage of convenience." Her soft hand came to caress my cheek. "That changed for me after we came to know one another. I *do* want more, Nicolas. I've fallen in love with you."

Crushing her to me, I swayed with her as my words came, "I love you; I've loved you for days and wanted to tell you but I feared you'd think me fickle."

That got a merry laugh. "I guess I'm far more traditional than I thought!"

She was anything but. Even *unconventional* was by far too tame a descriptor for Ellie. I laughed, "You can't be serious."

Her mirth-sparkled eyes met mine. "Please don't speak a *word* of it to my father and sister."

It made me smile inside. "Your secret's safe with me, my little traditional progressive bisexual Yankee wife."

That brought her *Mona Lisa* smile forward. I might have reminded her that traditional views didn't normally include being accepting of a bisexual husband or that she'd had a female lover, or the fact she now openly lusted for *two* men. The last bit made me pause. Truth be told, it was more than lust that *I* felt.

Our friendship and comfort with Luca had grown through our common interests. But there was much more between us. We both wanted him in what could only be described as a tangible desire for deeper intimacy with a kindred spirit. Finding Luca sensually compelling the way we did, he unknowingly came to play an intermittent role during our intimate explorations of one another. The fantasy of him was shared between our kisses and caresses of the night before.

By their manner together, it was obvious that my wife and Luca shared a mutual attraction, and that he found her as uniquely compelling as I. On his part I detected an awkward note in his worldliness — an attitude one expected to see in an untried youth. Perhaps this was simply his guard. If that were the case, I understood such a demeanor. The world was unkind to those who lived beyond societal dictates, and his relationship with us was still rather new.

Early on I could tell Luca didn't know what to think of Ellie. It was completely understandable. I believe most Europeans, no matter their country of origin, would find Americans somewhat unusual. His comfort with me and shyness toward her made me wonder. Was his attraction to this woman or *any* woman as new for him as it had been for me until recently? The thought of he and I exploring this unique possibility together was heady indeed.

Observing Ellie in Luca's presence, and privy to the workings of her mind as I was, made my study rather fascinating. I'd come to learn every element of Ellie was imbued with nuance, however innocent or intentional. What I'd once taken for unconventional American mannerism in her was something else entirely. Such a refreshing little nymph she was. Her sharp intellect and insatiable curiosity combined like a turbine to turn the gears in her mind. When she told me several days past that she was "not one to beat around the bush," she meant it. And I understood now. Anything else slowed this insatiable desire to understand and experience all.

Aided by my engaging Yank's winning ways, by the second afternoon with us, Luca was mostly at ease. More than once I was reminded of fly fishing in Scotland. Ellie would toss out a lure of innocent innuendo, he'd nibble then relax. She'd reel in her lure and he'd venture just a little bit closer. There was an obvious current passing between the three of us now — a lingering glance, a glint in the eye, and surprise at how quickly our time together passed. Not to mention disappointment that we must end our visit, to see to mundane details like meals in the dining room.

Ellie laughed.

I looked at her dumbly. She'd said something but as I'd been so engrossed in the image of the three of us, I'd completely missed it. I apologized.

Her sparkling eyes belying her words, she lightly admonished, "You really should tell me when your mind flies to the moon. Then I won't prattle on like I do. Whatever are you thinking about?"

I ran my hands down and around her sides to cup her bottom. Pulling her to me with a smile, I said, "I will only say the images dancing through my mind were very captivating. So tell me, what did I miss in my delightful imaginings?"

She laughed again. "I *said*... we've come to this venture from every angle and I only now realized our hands are tied in many ways. We don't know the land... nor do we know the people."

For two mornings running, we'd discussed the plan ahead

including several ways we might gain entry to Carlo Posateri's home. Unfortunately, every single one of these ideas was a knife-edge of potential ruin. I suggested, "We have several days yet. Let's share our tale with Luca when opportunity presents itself. Perhaps he'll have insight."

***

Luca arrived just seconds before the steward today, and we sat over tea and cakes to share Leonardo da Vinci as only true enthusiasts might. Da Vinci was a product of his time — himself a flesh-and-blood marvel in an age of inventiveness and discovery. Today we discussed how human potential achieved greatness in the Renaissance, and all concurred that da Vinci's contribution was notable.

This golden period between the fourteenth and seventeenth centuries lead to development in arts, literature, culture, and science. It broke from the stranglehold of fear so insidious in the Dark Ages and set a solid groundwork for our modern thinking and perspective. Despite the regression and suppression of knowledge under the Holy Inquisition, humanity returned to thrive in the Enlightenment.

I listened while my companions shared their cosmopolitan views and realized this was not mainstream thought even by the standards of this modern age. People take much for granted in our amazing mechanized world of today, perched as we are on the cusp of a new millennium. Who gives thought to the achievements of the past in relation to how we live our lives today?

As we mused on the life and times of Leonardo da Vinci, we

had no doubts that without the progressive attitudes of forward thinking individuals, individuals who so thoroughly enhanced our human condition, we'd still be living in a state of superstitious ignorance. Their attitudes literally gave us permission to evolve. Perhaps one day, those same attitudes would lead us to tolerance.

Time stays long enough for anyone who will use it.
– Leonardo da Vinci

~9~

We'd passed through the Strait of Gibraltar, and our ship stopped long enough at Portugal's port of Cascais to drop several passengers, the Danish siblings among them. Onward to Spain, we picked up a few more passengers at Valencia. That night, our dinner table was graced by Colonel, Sir Robert Beaumont, who not only got himself decorated after being wounded in the Anglo-Burmese War but to my surprise had also been an old school chum of my grandfather. To my greater surprise, I learned the man was still close to Grannie through their regular correspondence.

At some point over our after-dinner cigars, the Colonel took me aside and told me pointedly that he found my wife "enchanting" and was "relieved" to find me married. Apparently, Grannie confided in the strongest, most capable man of her acquaintance that she had "concerns over her fatherless grandson's lack of a strong male figure." I couldn't help but chuckle. She'd certainly tried to compensate — manly fencing lessons, boxing instruction, and of course the many hunting excursions on the estate with the husbands of her friends. And all these years I thought I'd kept the wool pulled over the dear old woman's eyes.

***

Our days were warm and sunny upon entering the blue Mediterranean. The sky and water were exact mirror opposites of one another and brought to mind the artwork of American luminist George Caleb Bingham. The following day we'd have the coastline of Italy in sight as we rounded the toe of the boot to the Ionian Sea. Then we'd pass the Strait of Ortronto into the sandy waters of the Adriatic. Autumn often came with changeable weather. If it held, we'd be in Venice before long. I'd been there before, on my grand tour, but this was a new experience for Ellie. I found myself eagerly anticipating sharing it with her, beyond our goal.

At breakfast one morning, she'd charmed the captain into lending her a spyglass that she might use it on our private deck. I wasn't surprised he'd said yes, of course. After all, she did manage to convince me to accept her marriage proposal, and I believing myself an actively homocentric bachelor at the time. There wasn't a man alive who could say no to this little nymph. Knowing this daughter of Sappho like I now did, I suspected many a woman would acquiesce too.

Ellie was fascinated by the white houses and villas perched like sea birds among the coastal rocks. I found her childlike wonder over the sights in the spyglass to be most endearing. Then and there I decided when this pending intrigue of ours was behind us,

I'd take my Yank on a proper tour of Europe's mainland. I'd show her the artworks that so compelled me, and together we'd find the works that celebrated the natural duality in all life. I told her so and gained a beautiful smile for myself before she turned back to the eyepiece.

I stood against the rail watching her. She'd yet to tame the riot of curls with her hairpins and the sunlight gave fiery highlights to the cinnamon, and streamed through the diaphanous flounces of her white dressing gown to reveal lithe limbs and every sensual peak and valley of her slight body. It brought to mind the veiled goddess statues of ancient Rome.

I knelt before this goddess of flesh and blood. She left her view to look down upon me. Wordlessly, I lifted her hem and crawled beneath the gossamer folds. She drew me in with the primal musk that lingered from our coupling several hours before. Parting her with my fingers, I paid homage in my own way.

For once you have tasted flight you will walk the earth with your eyes turned skywards, for there you have been and there you will long to return.

– Leonardo da Vinci

~10~

Our ten days at sea passed quickly. Today when Luca came for our visit, we learned he'd made changes to our customary tea. The steward followed him in with a dish of fruit and cheese and a bottle of wine. Our charismatic guest explained that the Venetian version of afternoon tea was called *merenda* and it didn't necessarily have tea and cakes on the menu. He felt that since we were so near our mutual destination – and in the spirit of the Renaissance's experiential immersion — we'd enjoy a native experience.

How right he was. We were hungry to experience life through complete abandon to the senses in the way of da Vinci himself, and if that meant wine at tea, then we'd happily partake.

Very much like the three of us, da Vinci was extremely curious with an insatiable desire to learn. He tested knowledge through experience and sensorial intake. In this he went so far as to implement the removal of senses such as sight, that the other senses might be enlivened, and included ambidexterity as a method to experience all. One of the most intriguing things about him was his eye for beauty; an eye where others were blind. His sketches of grotesquely deformed faces and bodies clearly proved it. This gift and his genius enabled him to go beyond conventional thought. I was coming to see Ellie and I as being very much like our friend Leonardo, for we too were a paradox to convention.

Enjoying our continental *merenda*, we picked up the conversation where we'd left it the day before — discussing the ideals of classical antiquity that inspired the Renaissance and made da Vinci the man he was. I described to my companions how the artists of the time yearned for perfection in their work — the same perfect beauty Homer and Virgil strived to achieve in their verse. Artists looked to those clean lines of Ancient Greece and Rome and saw the natural splendor there. And with this ideal in mind, sought to recapture that simple truth in everything they did. If nothing else, the Renaissance was an age of idealism.

Regarding the aftermath of the Black Death, Luca and I schooled as we were by our separate but similar pursuits, explained to Ellie in detail how a public of shaken faith had been reduced by half and struggled to make sense of a situation beyond comprehension.

Luca said, "While *we*, in this wondrously modern age of ours, understand microorganisms and the potential harm they could do, *they* were told by their church that the plague was an occurrence of sin. But how could this be? Priest and serf had fallen in equal measure."

Ellie commented thoughtfully, "That terrifying realization must have shaken their entire world of belief."

I said, "Can you just imagine?"

She sipped her wine then went on to describe belief constructs of the age. Since I'd taken her as a remarkable woman from the start, it had come as little surprise to learn my wife was a student of philosophy in her higher education.

By Luca's nod, I could tell he was impressed as well. He said, "How could it not have turned their world upside down? The one thing they were sure of was the intervention of religious mediators had done nothing to save them. And given so, it was wiser to invest in independent scholarship than feed the coffers of an impotent church. Self-education became tantamount to personal advance in the world. And this was easier now. Knowledge was freed at last."

Ellie's brows drew in question, "Do you mean the people who'd been holding knowledge from the masses had died, so that knowledge was out in the open?"

"Yes. Ecclesiastic control held humanity's ancient knowledge hostage for centuries. The uneducated masses were easier to govern, you see. But the plague had done away with the keepers and their books became available to anyone wishing to read them. Of course, over the ensuing centuries, the church would scramble to regain their control with the help of zealot monarchies. But the tide had turned. The common man became educated and there was no going back."

This was a true observation. With the advent of the Gutenberg printing press, books once confined to monastic reproduction were now available to a self-educating populace. Agreeing, I said, "Absolutely so. And when these doors were suddenly thrust open, opportunity for knowledge was let loose on a new Europe desperate to understand the world and redefine herself."

Ellie suddenly treated us to a beauteous smile. Seeing it, I could only assume the machine of her mind had deduced some compelling philosophic correlation from the conversation. Refilling our glasses, she raised hers in a toast. "Gentlemen, if I may quote our good friend Leonardo, 'The noblest pleasure is the joy of understanding.' To redefinition!"

Raising our glasses with hers, Luca and I joyfully repeated at once, "To redefinition!"

To feed his own curiosity, Luca studied da Vinci's world and his place in history. Ellie was drawn to the philosophy of the man long considered the personification of the Renaissance. I studied the mind behind man's unique artworks — an interest formed from my personal affinity. What a trio we were.

We called for another bottle and the conversation flowed with the wine. Comfortable and relaxed, and fortified by grapes and cheese, we decided to forgo dinner and continue our conversation unhindered.

With the wine inspiring a languorous attitude, Luca sat back on the settee in complete ease. Crossing his well-muscled legs before him, he put a question to me, "Nicolas, isn't it said by some, that da Vinci's *Mona Lisa* is actually a self-portrait?"

I smiled thinking of my wife's own enigmatic smile. Had she lived then, I'd swear it had been she who'd modeled for the artist. "There is speculation of that sort, yes. Other theory suggests the portrait is one Lisa del Giocondo. But I don't believe that to be the case."

"No?" Luca sipped his wine, clear interest on his handsome countenance.

I shook my head and explained my opinion, "For fifteen years the *Mona Lisa* went everywhere with him, it was even with him when he died. That's hardly the action of a man who'd painted that portrait as a commission, is it? No, I see the work as a riddle. Her face compels us to try to read her character. Leonardo challenges us to interpret her thoughts, 'to capture,' as he said in his own words, 'the motion of her mind and the passion of her soul.' Then he draws a veil of ambiguity across her features and creates a riddle of her smile. On top of that, there is nuance to the form and shadow… something deliberate in the smoky quality akin to a magician's trick."

Luca asked, "The *sfumato?*"

That he knew the proficient's term for the shadowy quality found in da Vinci's oils surprised me. Nodding, I sipped my wine and continued, "The *sfumato* plays a role none of us knows, unless we learn the reason behind it from Leonardo's own words. As I interpret it, the background and the subject are one and the same. In the *Mona Lisa*, I can see the artist's face in the work. That's clear when you see the man's self-portrait and compare the two. But beyond the deliberate ethereal quality to the piece, there's a part of me that believes the painting is a blending."

I could tell Ellie was intrigued by the idea when she sat forward. "A blending, how so?"

"A blending of the artist himself, and Gian Giacomo Caprotti. This was the person for whom Leonardo held passionate love."

Luca nodded. "Ah yes, Salai, the 'little devil.' I can certainly see that, now that you've mentioned it."

In that moment I had the distinct impression Luca too was drawn to homoerotic art, led perhaps by his own sexual proclivity to identify with artists who walked a very different path in both love and life. Knowing how compatible Luca had been with our blond Dutchman, I was certain he'd find it interesting that Salai's face and body could be found in several da Vinci artworks from sketches to oils to frescos. In for a penny in for a pound, I threw my seeds to the furrow and voiced it, "He wasn't free in society to love whom he wished. So he used his lover's face and form in many works he created. What he didn't reveal blatantly, he concealed in symbolism. But it was there; his lovers were there."

Pausing with her grape in mid-air, Ellie said, "I find this topic utterly fascinating." Then, in her bold-as-brass fashion, she turned to our guest and asked, "You're not put off by the topic of Leonardo's homosexuality, are you Luca?"

In Great Britain the topic on the table was not usually discussed in a lady's presence. Not that my nymph of a wife minded, indeed, she voiced it plain enough. Luca didn't answer right away, instead he sipped his wine. I wished in that moment I could read his thoughts for he appeared nervous. I wished for a lot in that moment.

Luca met her eye. "Did you know the ancient Greeks didn't consider sexual proclivity to be a social characteristic? They didn't distinguish a person's sexual desire by biological sex, only by the role that he or she played in the act."

Ellie took on her lovely blush, and for the first time I realized both desire and discomfiture lie within the hue. She asked plainly, "Do you mean to say all that mattered in ancient society was whether someone played the active penetrator or the passively penetrated?"

Bold-as-brass. I chuckled.

Luca's smile widened and his shadow-blue eyes sparkled. "Yes."

I believe we were all aware of a sexual tension growing in the intellectual-rich loam. There were little things at play now: the way Ellie moistened her lips and looked at us with eyes that lingered from one to the other. The way Luca's irises had darkened from snow shadow to moon shadow as he looked upon her. The way I'd catch myself with a reminder to breathe as my eye was drawn to these small distinctions. Like da Vinci's *sfumato*, our mutual attraction hung in the air, and I was struck by the notion that the smoky quality depicted in his art was *desire*. Desire like this.

"Ah." Ellie nodded in understanding and circled the rim of her wine glass with her fingertip. I could feel the gears turning in the perfect machine of her mind. She proved my estimation right when she laughed suddenly, "Why Signore Franco, I *do* believe you've evaded my *original* question."

He touched his heart with mock surprise. "Would *I* do that?"

That made Ellie laugh just as she was about to sip her red wine, causing her to slosh it on her white silk blouse. "*Fiddlesticks!* Please excuse me gentlemen, I must see to this before it sets." Giving us an adorable self-deprecating smile, she quickly excused herself. We watched her go and shortly after the tap ran in the bathroom.

To a man such as I who'd lived on the same side of the fence for so many years, Luca's answer had been plain enough. There was a silent language men like us used in public that only those of the same persuasion might guess what lie below the surface. Society might speculate all it wished, but unless the intent was blatant, no one knew of it for certain. In a world of unfounded prejudice, discretion might save one's life. Our eyes met. *We* knew.

He told me sincerely, "She's a treasure. Your Ellie is unlike any woman of my acquaintance."

I smiled. "Indeed. My good fortune is beyond measure because she's my match in all ways that matter."

He set his glass aside to rest his hand beside mine on the settee. "She seems an open-minded woman. I confess other than with my sisters, I've never found myself so comfortable in the presence of the fairer sex. She makes this easy."

My little finger stretched slightly, I swear by its own accord. "She does, at that. She declares herself a progressive in her world view. Ellie is extremely open-minded, and this is a truer fact than many know."

He raised his hand to the side of my face, and there his thumb traced along my bottom lip. My heart started to pound and my cock swelled. The hand slid around to the back of my skull and pulled me close for a kiss. A kiss I very much wanted.

I could taste him under the sweet tang of grapes and wine. I fed my tongue into his mouth and found his. The small whiskers trimmed so close to his upper lip and chin were sharp exclamation points along my heady exploration. I've no clear image of how exactly it happened, so absorbed was I in the sensorial bliss of the moment, but shirts and flies opened as magically as if Ali Baba himself called "open sesame" to the cave.

Lean-ribbed and fit, he had a raven thatching over his chest that was slightly thicker than my own, and I petted him as though he were a sleek jungle cat. We freed each other's cocks as we kissed and caressed and I soon learned that chest hair wasn't all that was thick on Luca. Da Vinci himself couldn't have sketched a finer image than this bold firm cock. His kiss deepened and he stroked me slowly with an expert hand while I closed my fingers around a shaft a few inches shy of the length of my forearm. Driven to make free with all he offered, I broke from our kiss. It was then I saw her.

Assessing her attitude quickly, I detected no condemnation. However, my years of secrecy and constant vigilance made me pause. Luca followed my gaze. Appraising the scene she'd walked in on, Ellie stood quietly, her breathing erratic and her cheeks quite pink. This time I knew why. Naturally, Luca was unable to discern what passed between my wife and I. Wary, no doubt from a lifetime of similar conditioning and secrecy, his eyes went to us from one to the other. And he very much looked like the cat that ate the canary.

The sensually-charged static in the air was palpable. No one said a word. Standing, I stripped from my shoes and clothing, all the while my eyes upon her. Naked now with my full-staffed erection jutting before me, I held a hand to our guest, wordlessly asking him to follow. Luca read the scene and relaxed. The cock I thought large a moment ago surged to its true fullness when he stripped for my wife's heated gaze. It was just as I suspected early on. Luca *was* one of us.

Ellie walked to the bedroom settee and we followed. She licked her lips when her eyes met mine and I could see our carnally-charged conversations of evenings past mirrored in her lust-dilated eyes. She wanted to see firsthand what it was like when two men loved. I put my hand on Luca's back and led him to lie upon the bed. There, I crawled over him until we lay side by side. Taking his face in my hands, I kissed him long and slow, as much for her as for him and I.

I could feel her watching us, feel her heat emanating in waves. I wanted the blast of that heat to burn me, to reduce me to ash that I might know myself. Truly know. I'd rise like a phoenix — a bird plumed and painted in fire. The art in the loving would be mine at last, the art I'd always known existed but had yet to find for myself. I wanted the both of them because this was who I really was. I wanted this rebirth. I wanted *my* renaissance.

Our legs entwined as hands slipped between our bodies to find the other man's wet-tipped steel. It didn't take much to turn around, but turn we did. I nuzzled his balls but his obvious hunger drove him without preamble to pull my cock into the furnace of his mouth. He was hot, so very hot. Compelled, I drew my tongue along the full length and found him pulsing. Like a python, I swallowed him. Men know things that women only guess. We're wild stallions driven to hard and fast satisfaction. Our teeth and tongue work with measured restraint only to make the encounter last, for we want nothing so much as to lose ourselves in fast primordial fucking.

When we'd worked ourselves to near madness, I sought my wife. She was naked now with one leg drawn upon the settee. Watching us with unabashed hunger burning bright in her smoldering eyes, she was lit by the incandescent light above. I could see clearly the sexual tint painting a swath across her upper chest — a tint that exactly matched the blush between her legs.

I felt her mind. Several nights past I'd demonstrated my technique by implementing everything our differing physiologies allowed to make my point. Her intimate knowledge enhanced by that loving, she now wanted the animalistic *homme à homme* coupling her imagination craved. I'd give this woman anything.

Rising from the bed, I met his eye and assumed the passive role he'd politely described for us earlier. And like a stallion his nostrils flared, and I heard the shuddering breath of desire as he moved behind me and made me ready. Minutes passed as he took his time, the luxurious effect made all the better by the heated gaze of my wife. I could feel his hot body standing behind me as I waited at the edge of the bed and knew he'd gripped his cock to work up his spunk because I felt it wetly run up and down between my cheeks. A dizzying sparkle of lights danced before my eyes as he slowly pressed into me, sinking until his balls rested like heavy embers against mine. I had no doubt that Luca had danced this dance before in either role or both, for he expertly remained still as I grew accustomed to his presence and my body fully surrendered to his intoxicating filling.

Ellie drew near to admire the art of us as we posed like the marble wrestlers of antiquity. One small soft hand ran down my back and across my ribs. I felt the other slide between us to grip him in his mooring. His stance widened and her hand stilled. Luca's body began to tremble. Wondering why, I looked over my shoulder to see my wife kissing my lover, *our* lover, passionately. On the move again, her hand caressed our sacks as they lay draped slightly one above the other before coming around to find my cock. Where her other hand lingered at that point I didn't know, but the trembling eased. I knew her nymph's mind, yes I did. I knew she craved a cock of her own with which to enter the fray, for she'd told me as much the night I instructed her how men love one another. Gliding into her hand driven by that heady thought, I induced Luca to come with me and heard, as well as felt, his moan from behind.

She came to me then and kissed me wildly. But it wasn't enough. Climbing upon the bed she spread her legs to me. Intent to taste, I moved forward but my breath caught when lust-driven Luca grabbed my hips. He held me firm as his body arched and gave me his last magnificent inch. It was our dance now.

I could do nothing but rest upon my forearms, mere inches

from her sex. I spread her orchid petals and fingered her slowly for him and he filled me for her. She was soft like butter, swollen and scented, and I knew she loved our experiential tryst as much as I, as much as he. Dipping my head I found her steaming hot, sopping wet, and salty-sweet. Helpless to do aught but feed on her arousal, I devoured her. But again it wasn't enough.

I rose with straight arms to lift my chest from the bed, my movement causing Luca's heavy furred balls to buffet my sack. Spying a way to sate her hunger, Ellie shimmied beneath me. Luca took her by the ankles and held her legs while I buried my cock into her tight lust-swollen heat. Linked to my wife and Luca, the sensations were such it was all I could do not to weep. We fit together like an Oriental puzzle box — each erotic piece precisely fitting into the next.

Now that that we three were fully joined, Luca pulled Ellie close to trap me between them and began to move in earnest. His every full-measured thrust sunk me into the lava below. I fucked back and he fucked forth in a seesaw of orgiastic delight. Our animalistic coupling brought our groans and grunts to harmonize with passionate mewls and feminine whimpers — a concerto of sexual bliss. Tempo up, I could feel him reaching his peak as he ravaged and rode me. I in turn glided out in full arcs only to be slammed back again by a sledgehammer cock wielded by a master smithy forging iron into cherry-red steel.

In our sensual storm, Ellie had gathered all the lightning she could hold. When her back suddenly arched, the rolling shudder of her orgasm thundered over and through me and strong muscles intent on wresting my last drop gripped me hard. By reflex my body tightened and a deep male groan was gained from behind. Luca pummeled me now as she rode her climax. Milked and filled I wholly surrendered to the both of them; my seed spilling into her as his spunk flooded into me. Tied like mating wolves, we all rolled to the bed breathless and sated.

Lost in the wondrous release, our breathing calmed and our bodies cooled and minutes passed before any of us moved. Pinned as I was, I waited on Luca, and Ellie waited on me with the weight of two spent men pressing her into the mattress. She started to giggle, the merry sound breaking our silent enchantment. Luca and I couldn't help but join in with joyous laughter. Easing from me, he went to wash.

Ellie whispered in awe, "I can't believe the power of what just passed between us."

Her forehead was damp and half of her hair pins undone. Not quite ready for speech, I freed the last of her curls and kissed her. Luca found us thus entwined upon his return. He'd brought with him a damp towel, a fist full of wine glass stems, and a bottle tucked under his arm. Pouring and passing the wine first, he followed by busying himself with wiping us both down as one might dry a prized thoroughbred who'd just won the race. That completely sensuous act brought my cock back to life. Seeing it, he chuckled and pulled my semi-flaccid cock into his mouth for a quick suck. "Mmm," he said, smacking his Ellie-flavored lips before sprawling out beside us. Ellie giggled happily. Chilled by our washing, but too warm for the coverlet, we three snuggled under the sheet with our wine.

Luca took Ellie's hand and kissing it, told her in his native tongue, *"Bella Signora, voi mi avete onorato con la condivisione di questo speciale legame che hai con tuo marito. Grazie."*

Looking at us from one to the other, she replied, "That's lovely, what does it mean?"

I shook my head. "Don't look to me, love. I'm afraid my Italian isn't *that* well developed."

Chuckling, Luca repeated in English, "I said, beautiful Lady, you have honored me by sharing this special bond you have with your husband. Thank you." He reached across her chest and touched my cheek. "And thank *you*. Never have I felt such loving acceptance."

Echoing what she'd said to me just moment before, Ellie said, "I can't believe the power of it."

I said, "That surpassed anything I've ever experienced."

Luca smiled. "You're very right, *I miei amori*. I believe this is because the expression of love itself is *perfection*. Such was the power Leonardo found with his Salai."

It was fitting that Luca referred to us as *his loves*. The pair of them were certainly mine.

~11~

Involved in world trade and commerce for centuries, Venice was well-suited as a merchant's city. Then as now, its ports were filled with goods coming from and going to destinations all around the world. As a consequence, from the moment we rounded Sicily, the waters took on a bustling air. After my bath, I donned my dressing gown and went to join Ellie on the starboard balcony where she dried her damp curls in the warm Adriatic sun and peered through her borrowed spyglass. It hit me then how quickly she went from Waterhouse nymph to Knut Ekwall's *Siren*. My arms circled around her. She set her spyglass aside and leaning back against me, remarked, "It's so busy here. I swear I've seen more ships in the last hour than on our entire voyage."

"Ships? What ships?" My nuzzling at her neck brought forth a giggle.

Twisting away, she tipped her head, "*Those* ships, you salacious man."

This was an instance of the pot calling the kettle black if ever there was one. I grabbed her and pulled her back against my chest again. It felt better that way. Cupping her pert little breasts and pressing my lower half against hers, I whispered at her ear, "Perhaps like mine, your attentions have been elsewhere." Indeed, it had been hard to concentrate on anything but our insatiable desire to fill our new definitions. I nuzzled her again. Whatever might come today, above all, this was to be a day of planning.

As far as we knew, Signore Posateri sailed at the least two days behind us. Ellie said that Signore Ambrosini lived on the Grand Canal in a *fondaco*. He'd explained upon her asking that the *fondaco* was both his residence and warehouse for his raw cotton, jute, and occasionally silk. It was then she'd discovered his wife's brother, Signore Posateri, lived nearby. With this information to guide us, we knew that we needed to find Signore Ambrosini's warehouse. We hoped we'd not have to travel the entire Grand Canal to do it.

Being new to the region, there was no doubt we'd need to find agreeable assistance once we came into port, and that fact spurred us to create fictitious names for ourselves so as not to leave a trail back to London. After a few hilarious attempts, we settled on personas that would work well enough. Once we set foot on land, we'd be the newly-wedded Mr. and Mrs. Pendergast having a stop in Venice as part of our honeymoon tour of the continent. Beyond that, we knew this venture would unfold hour by hour as it came.

There was no way of knowing what or whom we might encounter, but figuring money would smooth the path wherever we went, I'd had my London banker convert half our notes to coin for ease of use. Deciding upon which essentials were to be left out for the next day, we'd packed our trunks and valises and stacked them at the door for the porters. The smaller portmanteau would hold what remained to be packed in the morning.

Somewhere on deck the hour was struck and I felt a rush of heat run through my veins. Luca would be here any moment. Having promised to come to us the next day, he'd returned to his stateroom last night to pack his belongings because he too didn't want to waste our precious last hours together. After our week of coming to know the man — and especially after our rousing evening of sensual camaraderie that sealed what could only be called a transcendent friendship — I felt confident that were we to reveal our venture to Luca, he'd offer his assistance navigating this country of his. But Ellie and I had completely forgotten to bring it up the day before. Small wonder that.

With his compelling charm and abundant magnetism, we'd been completely surprised to learn last night that Luca had never been in a woman's bed before, for all he found them lovely to look upon and for all they found him quite the same. Conversely, he was surprised to discover he and I shared this condition until recently — yet another tie between us. He explained that a gentle induction by an older man came at a time when beautiful women made him exceedingly apprehensive. Despite all that passed between us, he gave Ellie a shy smile and confessed they still did.

Another woman might have laughed at a shy man's confession, but not my astute and compassionate wife. Rolling into his arms, she kissed his lips. Meeting his eyes, she assured him with conviction, "All that women want is to be treated as the thinking human beings they are. You already do that Luca, and that's all any man need ever do."

Never so proud was I that I'd accepted her marriage proposal than in that moment. I turned to them to share their next kiss. Our three tongues met and I found the dichotomy between their kisses to be absolute heaven. Then, with Ellie's permission, Luca and I explored her feminine mystique together. By the enchanting little sounds she made, I don't think the nymph minded in the least.

***

We discussed our tryst over breakfast and confessed our deep and unabashed feelings for Luca. Unknown to one another until that moment, she and I had made an independent decision last night — as glorious as it might be to have Luca fully, we had an obligation to my family name. Any offspring that might come of our loving must be a Halstead without conjecture. Hearing her profess love for Luca, I admit my mind sought alternatives — rubbers, perhaps. Of course such protection of various materials had been around for ages and this latest iteration of the condom made of vulcanized India rubber no doubt sufficiently did what was intended, without sensation or comfort. Still, it was something to think about.

The rap at the door broke me from my musing. Giving Ellie's temple a kiss, I said, "He's here, love. Stay on the balcony for the moment. The steward needn't see you are entertaining in your dressing gown." Her lips turned at the corners. I chuckled and went to the door contemplating the power of that *Mona Lisa* smile of hers.

"Luca, how nice to see you."

"Good afternoon, Nicolas. How are you this fine day?"

Happiness sparkled in his snow-shadow eyes; more so than I'd ever seen. An image of Thomas Waldo Story's marble bust of Flavius Honorius flashed before my eyes. And like that patrician emperor of Rome, Lucas too was exceedingly handsome. I badly wanted to kiss him.

"I'm well, thank you, and yes it *is* a fine day."

Luca stepped aside for the steward. Laden with fruit and cheese and two bottles of wine, the man stayed only long enough to pull a cork. Alone now, our lips met and his tongue danced with mine as our hands cupped one another in unabashed longing, making it a kiss worthy of a sigh.

Her slender curves backlit by sunlight, Ellie came in from the balcony appearing to be wrapped in a diaphanous veil sculpted by Giovanni Maria Benzoni's own hand. Between the pair, I stood in the presence of living art. She, the artist's muse, and he with a face and physique that would make Michelangelo himself weep, as well as cause Richard Payne Knight, dilettante he was, to abandon his worship of Priapus.

Remembering to breathe, I said, "There she is."

The static of Luca's appreciation went through me like lightning. He smiled and said, *"Buon giorno bella Signora."*

The smile she gave us was beauteous. Laughing happily, she said, "I do believe I understood that! Good day lovely lady?"

Notably less shy than a day before, Luca beamed. "That is correct." They kissed their hello as had he and I.

Watching them, I wondered how to proceed. My sensual recount prior to Luca's arrival had primed my desire. True we had Venice to discuss, but we also had precious few hours to freely immerse ourselves in one another one last time. Last night I'd felt steeped in love and I longed to have it again. In just two short weeks I'd come to love Ellie with a ferocity I could never have anticipated or even deemed possible. And what I felt for this tender, intelligent man was far more than the fondness I'd felt for other lovers in my lifetime, even different than what I felt for Thomas. Impossible to deny, I also loved Luca. We had bonded through our common interests, beliefs, and temperaments, and through our demonstrative affection for each other and for this amazing woman. I wanted nothing better in that moment than to express that love.

I could scarcely believe the routes we'd traveled coming to know one another — scarcely imagined the truths we'd come to share, nor the uncharted ground we'd joyfully claim in our self-exploration. Having literally redefined ourselves, we'd come to this position of complete understanding in the very way Leonardo da Vinci had — through sensorial experience. This was superlative empiricism at its best. Who knew where it might lead?

I poured our wine and handing them their glasses, confessed my sentiment, "On this, our last day together, I must tell you something. I feel my heart and soul enriched for knowing you both. Never before have I felt such harmony and peace than I have these past several days, and especially so after yesterday. My life has been one of subterfuge, my nature repressed, my love bound by societal limitation... " My throat constricted with the sad hard truth of it, but rather than be voiced, the emotion demanded its release by pooling in my eyes. I blinked it away.

When I met their glistening eyes, it was like looking in a mirror. They understood perhaps better than anyone else in the world because this too had been *their* lives. And seeing it was enough. Heart full to the brim, I smiled, seeking to lighten the emotion of the moment. "If I told you both that my mind cannot cease seeing our bodies entwined, would you think me callow after my tender confession just now?"

They both laughed and echoed my sentiment.

Ellie took the glasses from our hands and set them aside. Standing on her toes between us, she kissed me, her grape-sweet tongue swirling into my mouth as she extended a hand to Luca. He joined our kiss adding his own tongue to play with ours. I don't know how long we stood thus sharing soft lips and breath, but it brought upon a heavenly delirium akin to drinking many glasses of champagne.

We freed Ellie's mane and untied her dressing gown; the diaphanous veil fell in a puddle at her feet as if she were Aphrodite on the foam. Standing in all her feminine glory caped by her riot of cinnamon curls, she met our eyes with a look that was boldly expectant. Understanding it, Luca and I undressed to her silent command.

She moved to our lover and he reached for her, but she took both of his hands and stilled them at his sides. I gripped myself, loving the upper hand she took with this fine stallion of a man — loving the bold-as-brass manner in which she experienced all she desired. I knew the effort it took for him to remain still to her kisses and wandering hands. I'd been in such position myself.

His visible head-to-toe tremor rolled over him in waves but Luca stood like a bronze statue while she caressed every dark-skinned angle and plane; critically examining him as though he were a prospective acquisition on the Turkish auction block. To procure him for our own — a heady imagery that. We'd discussed such imaginative play in our midnight embraces. That flight of fancy and the scene before me made me fiercely hard and compelled me to stroke my cock. She raised a brow at me. Her gesture quickened my hand, and my action gained me her knowing smile.

Her petite form disappeared behind him but her roaming hands transformed Luca into a many-armed Hindu god. Thumbs circled his small nipples. His mouth opened as he inhaled raggedly. I licked my lips and watched the sweeping caress of the slight and delicate hands running down the midnight fleece on his belly. That is when his eyes met mine, and I saw the fire behind the smolder was blatant and hungry. She hefted those full balls, gently pulling and rolling them in her palm. His hands closed in fists when her fingers curled around his magnificent cock. She came round to his side, and meeting my eyes, she stroked him slowly.

Between the two, their heated gaze was akin to standing near a blast furnace. I had the distinct impression she was calculatedly provoking my arousal. It was working. I slowed my hand; each slow and deliberate pass intent to entice. Two could play that game.

Leading her stallion by his cock, she brought him to stand face to face with me. She took mine and his and stroked us together, forcing our cockheads to rub against one another like fire sticks. Impossible to contain, we slicked her fingers with premature excitement. By god, if the fact didn't redouble her efforts. Helpless to it, the pressure of impending orgasm filled us, and we got a seductive shushing for our husky groans. Having recently become a proficient in ways of loving men, Ellie stilled her hands and tightly gripped us at the root until the premature splendor passed. The minx would have her day and by the smolder in her pale blue eyes, I was certain it would be filled with more sensual torment for Luca and me.

***

The setting sun cast long shadows into our stateroom by the time the steward came with our dinner cart. Since discretion was in order, Luca and I dressed and Ellie and her wine glass hied away on our starboard balcony. Sure enough, the man's eyes darted here and there, no doubt expecting to see my wife. He removed the covers from two plates and I had him leave the third to stay warm for my wife's *return*.

We took our plates and hers and joined her for the sunset. Our favorite topic was revisited and given our intimacy, we traveled new ground with it.

Explaining the land of his birth, Luca said, "In the Florence of da Vinci's time, it was common for young men to be involved in intimate relationships with older men. They embraced an interest in the classical studies of ancient Greece, and such expressions of love were in keeping with that. But the church took exception, and life took on a secret, dangerous air."

Early on in my own pursuit of sexual identity, I'd heard a derogatory term for homosexuals directed at other men, *Florenzer*. The German slang for homosexual was coined to denigrate the free-loving men of Florence and anyone like them across Europe. I wondered if a slang term existed for men and women like Luca, Ellie and I, those who expressed love to both sexes. Then again, I had to wonder why it mattered to anyone, for who was harmed by such expression of love?

I voiced my thought.

My wife threaded her arm through mine. "What we are doesn't harm anyone."

Versed as he was, Luca explained the historical view through time. "No it doesn't. Through the centuries it was thought to enhance rather than harm. For some, male love was a chaste religious practice… "

Ellie cocked her head, "Oh?"

"Yes, for example, simply to gaze upon the beauty of a boy brings the Sufi closer to God. At the other end of the spectrum, homosexual acts were seen as conquest — an act of power over the unwilling man."

I relayed several abridged incidents along those lines, including a tale Thomas had heard involving a gang buggering aboard a navy vessel. Though he didn't elaborate, I noticed Luca's brows draw down briefly. I felt a shift in emotion from him when he spoke of acts of rape as conquest. It made me wonder.

He continued, "But in ancient Greece as it was in my Florence, such relationships were bonds between men. It was felt that the younger man was enriched by the friendship of his older experienced lover. Then as now, men often strive to be worthy of one another and this allowed bonds to grow stronger. To the ancients, such partnership was thought to make them undefeatable in battle and therefore it was encouraged — a passion of a *different* sort you might say."

Nodding, Ellie said, "From the philosophical view, the ancients loved men and women equally. Love was one of the key purposes of existence. Even Zeus, king and husband though he was, loved Ganymede. I forget his father's name — the Trojan king, but his son was beautiful. So deeply did Zeus love him, he spirited him away to be his cup bearer among the gods."

I said, "Unfortunately, the mediators for the new god were less tolerant of such affections."

Voices from below signaled we no longer had privacy for what

Ellie termed *our progressive topics,* so we took ourselves inside to continue privately over wine. Luca and I sat upon the settee, and Ellie stretching out between us leaned against me with my arm around her, while Luca massaged her dainty little feet. In the natural course of conversation fueled by our common interests in art, history, and philosophy, we found ourselves examining the thought behind various Renaissance artworks from the Florentine perspective.

I said, "Florence had its prized artists in da Vinci and Michelangelo and a new style of painting in perspective was born there. But *all* of Italy teemed with creativity." I rattled them off on my fingers, "Donatello, Brunelleschi, Masaccio, Bellini, Titian, Botticelli, Caravaggio, Raphael, Bernini... I could go on."

Ellie mused, "Isn't that odd, that a country would have so many? The United States has its artists too — Mary Cassatt comes to mind. Nowhere comparable to that list of yours, though." Her sharp mind was rationalizing. I could feel it.

Luca offered, "It would seem curious. To understand art in my country, you must understand the time. New exploration and trade agreements brought wealth to Italy. The affluent wanted to show the world just how well-off they were. To do this, they decorated their homes, choosing artists celebrated as particularly talented to help them best display their fortune. These men became patrons to the artists and provided all they'd need to live on while they worked. Artists flocked to this opportunity to create without worrying from where their next meal would come."

I added, "That's true. They soon became bound to this support but considered themselves fortunate. There was little choice in their world. The artists often chafed at the patronage, as some arrangements neared exploitation. For example, Michelangelo was imprisoned for months to force him to paint the Sistine Chapel."

My Yank couldn't fathom it, and expressed her colorful disbelief.

I chuckled. "Yes, indeed. His preferred medium was stone, not paint, and certainly not fresco. He *loathed* fresco. The paint was applied to wet plaster and set quickly, too quickly for fine artistry. Working upon it was a race against the clock before nuance of light and shadow was lost."

Luca added, "I've read several disparaging accounts in his own hand regarding the work on the ceiling. He was miserable in the working… I believe that misery lasted four long years.

I explained what I knew of Michelangelo. "Four years, yes. What a marvelous work despite it all. His Sistine Chapel ceiling is a triumph of the Renaissance. What's more, despite the religious purpose of the artwork, it is in fact an advertisement for the humanist ideal."

Stretching across Ellie's legs for the bottle, Luca refilled my empty glass and then his own. He said, "I agree."

"Thank you." I took a sip then continued, "Do you know there are no less than twenty *ignudi* on the corners of the biblical scene?"

Ellie shook her head, her curls tickling my nose. "I'm not familiar with the word."

Brushing the silky poof aside with my hand, I caught Luca's wide smile over her head. Chuckling, my eyes held his as I explained quite suggestively, "They're beautiful naked men with sexually overt accents, twisting in poses allusive of intimate acts." Luca licked his lips. I wanted him again. Anchoring myself, I slipped my hand inside Ellie's robe to cup her bare breast.

She covered my hand with hers and held me there. "Ooh. But wasn't the Sistine Chapel commissioned by a pope?"

I smiled. "That's what I find most intriguing — well-muscled bodies, blatant frontal views, muscular backsides, sheaves of wheat and acorns... "

Her confusion evident, Ellie asked, "Sheaves and acorns?"

Luca grinned, pressing her dainty foot against his crotch suggestively. "*Testa di cazzo.*"

"Ah," she said.

Luca then placed Ellie's other foot over the back of the settee. Her slender legs opened to him, he caressed her inner thighs while we talked.

I couldn't see for myself, but I imagined her cheeks took on the alluring blush.

I'd heard Luca's term before in my studies. The acorns were thought to represent dozens of little cockheads added to the abundant penises dangling like stalactites from the chapel ceiling — the artist's symbolic message to the powers that be. It was rumored there were even more under layers of painted loincloths that inexcusably defaced the work years after Michelangelo's death. Turning to Luca, I asked, "Have you seen the chapel celling?"

"I regret to say I have not; reproductions only."

"Nor have I, but I'd like to."

His fingers absently swept up and down. Higher now, they brushed along her rosy core. Seeing it, there was nothing to be done except for me to toy with her nipple.

She made that adorable little sound of hers

A handsome smile lit his eyes and he said in good humor, "But

I will have to go there now."

Ellie squirmed, "Yes, to look for acorns."

We laughed.

Our conversation touched upon other art forms from that famous fresco to sculptures and from there to poetry. It turned out that both my wife and Luca were avid lovers of the written word. Ellie told us of a book of Sappho's poetry belonging to a friend in New York, herself a scholar at Vassar, my wife's alma mater.

I caressed both small breasts and teased her nipples. Seeing it, Luca's fingers plucked my wife like a harp. Predictably, Ellie began to lose the thread of concentration as our wanton hands made free. Lamenting that her mind was drawing a blank when she tried to remember a few favorite lines from the book, she promised to share as they came to her. Turing her head, she met my eye. That familiar sparkle was there and I knew she spoke of Felicia.

Luca surprised us with a recital of Michelangelo's poem to his lover Tommaso Cavalieri, "May I burn if I do not love thee with all my heart, and lose my soul, if I feel for any other. Lovely, no?"

I offered, "I find the artistic breadth and scope of that remarkable era quite astounding really. Like Michelangelo, several prominent artists of the day literally painted and sculpted in prose, as well as pigment and stone."

Luca nodded. "This is true. And poetically said! I have several books of Renaissance poetry in my collection. There is something there in the words of love that I find particularly poignant, especially between men, in that transitional time. There were arranged marriages then, and marriages without love in them produced few love stories. These poems between men, forbidden as they were, are nothing but pure unbridled emotion."

This was true. There had been many homoerotic odes written across cultures and throughout time. In Europe, the narrow-mindedness seeping from Rome went on to change the world, and the flowers of this beautiful sentiment choked in the weeds of organized xenophobia.

They shared more and I thoroughly enjoyed my wife and my lover regaling me with snippets of favored poetry. All this was enhanced by our hands coaxing and kneading Ellie's flesh while she stroked my cock at her side and amorously caressed Luca with her bare foot.

Stopping all action, Luca straightened excitedly, then said something that Ellie and I could scarcely believe.

"You both might find this interesting, given our mutual interest in the life and loves of Leonardo. Several months ago, my work brought me to a private collection of Renaissance books in a library in Florence. The owner had died and as the collection was purported to contain historical volumes, the university sent me to acquire a portion of the works. I came upon a book of poems and sketches that could only have been created by da Vinci himself, though not one page bore his name. It wasn't something the university would want. Given the content, the disdaining proprietor of the estate saw no purpose to it either. So I bought it myself. The images are pure da Vinci in their heavily-detailed eroticism. The prose is sensually explicit. I suspect it was written for Salai. To me there is no doubt, but I'd love if you were to confirm it, Nicolas.

Ellie sat up. We stared at each other, our faces mirroring how thunderstruck we were to discover the book in our quest belonged to *Luca*.

Misinterpreting our odd behavior, he laughed, "Yes it is astounding to find never before seen works of a famous artist. Would you be able to stop at my home and examine… "

My mind awhirl, I cut in, "Luca, how long have you been away from home?"

Unfazed by my interruption, he laughed and went on to explain that as eldest son and heir he'd recently found himself at odds between his life's work and the shoulder of family responsibility. His family held four properties. The three in the Vento and Tuscany regions produced wines and grew olives for oil. The *fandaco* in Venice was the launching point for their oil exports. Because he traveled as frequently as he did, he took up residence there for the access to the ports.

His married sisters and two younger brothers were invested in the family operations. He, on the other hand, preferred his scholarly pursuits. Several months ago he'd been offered employment in London's Ashmolean Museum to help build their collections. I filed away that bit of happy news. Oxford was my alma mater.

He went on, "Subsequently, I'll take on the role of advisor only. My youngest brother has a head for business, he's brilliant really. More importantly, he loves the work as our father and grandfather did. As they are all willing and compatible, I'm confident my family can manage without my daily presence. If necessary I can return in under two weeks' time by ship."

Reaching across the settee, I put my hand on his shoulder. "Luca, Ellie and I would like to explain our venture. There is a reason we are going to Venice."

Over the next quarter hour, Ellie and I explained our marriage and the reason behind our unorthodox honeymoon, including her meeting Signore Posateri and learning what the man intended to do with a certain precious book.

Luca jumped to his feet amid a slew of emotion-riddled Italian. He added in English. "This is unbelievable! *He has my book?*"

Ellie nodded sadly, "I'm sure of it, Luca."

Looking staggered and clearly not knowing what to do next, he raked his fingers through his black hair. "When *was* this? *When* did you meet him?"

Ellie stammered trying to count the days in her head. "Eleven… no, thirteen, today. Yes, thirteen days ago. From a comment he made, I figure he's two days behind us. That's why we rushed to marry. We needed to travel quickly because he said he planned to destroy it."

"Destroy it?" Fingers clenched in fury, Luca muttered a curse under his breath, *"Figlio di troia. Cazzo!"* Despite his obvious distress, he caught himself and apologized to my wife sheepishly. "Please, Ellie, forgive my outburst and my ill-mannered tongue. Even in my unfamiliar language, those words are not suited for a lady such as you."

"Luca, I understand."

I asked, "Do you know of him, this Signore Posateri?"

I saw a range of emotion on Luca's face, from disbelief to rage. He flopped back down on the settee. "Yes, I know of this deranged man. I know what he does with precious masterpieces. This… this *dog* plundered my property while I was away."

Sitting on either side of him, we both covered his clenched fists with our hands. I assured him, "And *we* will take it back."

A well-spent day brings happy sleep.
– Leonardo da Vinci

~12~

The gondoliers were lined up in the water like so many wheel-less, horseless hansom cabs on London's Piccadilly Street. Luca hired three: two for our trunks and parcels, and one for us. We took the swiftest route to Luca's home. Curiosity burned in Ellie's eyes and I wanted nothing better than to show her the Venice I'd seen on my tour years before, but helping our dear friend came first. There would be time for an expedition when this venture was behind us.

It was July when last I'd been here. I remembered the muggy air and the flies. Now in the first days of October, Venice was void of insects and we were treated to a vivid blue sky of vaulted clouds and a pleasant breeze of moderate temperature that thankfully was neither fishy nor foul.

We found ourselves at Luca's *fondaco* before a quarter hour had passed. The centuries-old building was three stories tall and possessed a curious hodgepodge of architectural elements. From arabesque Corinthian columns, trefoil embellishments, and roofline finials on the upper floor façade to the long stone arches in the Gothic-Byzantine style found at ground level, each line and flourish reflected Venice's imported influences through history.

Our gondoliers punted us into the main portico and we, and our cargo, were unloaded. All around us were large glazed terracotta olive oil jars stacked on wood pallets. A faint green aroma lingered in the air, left no doubt by the oily spill under a cracked jar now attended by a man with a barrow of sawdust. Seeing us, his face broke into a wide smile. Luca greeted him warmly, and a flurry of cheerful Italian echoed in the warehouse. The man hurried away only to return an instant later with a small plump woman quickly wiping her hands on her apron. The pleasant couple shared a striking family resemblance down to the sparse mustache, and left no doubt that we were meeting siblings.

Luca introduced us first, in his native tongue, then said, "My friends, I'd like you to meet Vittorio and Martina Renaldi. Their family has taken care of my home and the warehouse for more than a century."

They nodded and greeted their welcome in broken English.

Turning to his man, Luca asked in Italian, "Where is Enzio?"

Vittorio looked at his sister, who met his eye with a worried frown. Their silent communication prompted Luca to ask again. Vittorio started to speak then stopped. His hesitation spurred Luca to turn to us, "Please, excuse me a moment. Martina will take you upstairs."

He said something to his housekeeper and she smiled widely and motioned for us to follow her up the winding marble staircase. Glancing down upon the talking men, I couldn't help but notice the expression on Luca's face. I assumed he was being told about the theft. This was born out several minutes later when Luca relayed his news.

"I'm told while my household staff prepared to pack my shipment to London, my foreman caught sight of an antique book among my belongings. Vittorio tells me Enzio's unusual interest put Martina on edge. Sure enough, the Renaldis discovered the same crate opened the next day, the book gone, and Enzio hasn't been back since. Martina is certain he took it, as am I. Vittorio tells me Enzio has a fondness for gambling and loses far more than he wins. He believes Enzio saw my book as a means to settle a debt."

Ellie said, "That's terrible Luca. Then he must have sold it to Signore Posateri."

Luca nodded, "That's my guess, yes. Come, let me show you my home while Martina prepares your rooms on the third floor." He smiled engagingly, "The rooms are the nicest and they're next to mine. They've also been vacant for a while so Martina won't see you settled until they're perfect to receive guests."

Luca's home above the warehouse, as old as it was, was quite grand. I couldn't help but think of Grannie feeling perfectly at home here. The high scalloped ceilings were adorned with paintings in gilded frames. I couldn't identify the artists, but whoever painted the scenes did so in an incongruent blending of Greek gods in idyllic settings and billowing sailing ships coming and going from bounty-laden ports — an obvious nod to industrious Venetian commerce. The library was impressive with its floor-to-ceiling shelves of books and large Queen Ann furnishings dominating the room.

The ballroom had a French flair with its delicate Louis XIV chairs and tables on three walls around the perimeter and a massive chandelier shrouded in a dust cloth in the center. Luca explained this room was seldom used, in fact in his lifetime he only had one recollection of a ball. The formal dining hall suffered the same disuse.

Luca explained his mother preferred the family to take their meals in a small dining room off the drawing room, as was her family's habit.

The flooring on the second level was geometric marble and on it sat French Aubusson and thick Turkish carpets. Built upon centuries of cultural exchange found in maritime lands, the interior furnishings reflected the same exterior hodgepodge of styles. Curiously, it all worked together to make a lavishly comfortable home.

Ellie voiced my opinion, "Your home is extraordinary, Luca."

He smiled. "Thank you. I had very little to do with the décor, only my books and a few odds and ends. My family's lived here for the last two hundred and ninety years, and my needs are simple. I saw no reason to change any of it when I moved in. I'm leaving for London after my younger brother Paolo arrives. I've mentioned he's the intelligence behind the family exports. He'll live here where it makes sense for him to be, and perhaps bring the family home into the new century, too."

Ellie said, "I wouldn't change a thing. I think we lose ourselves when we discard the past. Who we are is in direct correlation to who we've been."

He smiled. "That is exactly so, Ellie. My family's history is here more so than in the orchards and vineyards. I'll request he keep changes to a minimum."

He ushered us into the large drawing room. There we sat and drank glasses of refreshing watered wine and talked about the care of such a grand place. As Luca was hardly ever there, the number of household staff was small. This would change after his brother Paolo took residence. We learned that Martina was in the process of reviewing letters of recommendation from the previous employers of several servants answering her advertisement. For the time being, Vittorio and Martina Renaldi did most of the upkeep here, as well as directed several workers who cleaned and laundered weekly.

Grannie employed no less than a brigade of staff from scullery maids to footmen. My household staff consisted of Mrs. Fletcher and twin sisters who came once a week to clean and launder under her direction. I found it more than adequate despite the Dowager's regular protest that my staff was too meager. In my mind, I didn't ever see me returning to live in the Halstead mansion, but as heir I'd have to address that one day.

Luca explained that his mother's people were simple farmers who employed labor only for those tasks that needed extra hands, adding, "Personally, I'm grateful my parents taught us self-sufficiency, doubly so that they both felt workers were necessary for growing and producing our wines and oils!" Grinning, he showed us his hands and joked, "Though they aren't stained purple with grape and green with olive anymore, I always knew *these* hands belonged to a scholar."

Indeed, his hands had the lightly hardened softness of the sort that knew work, and I loved how they felt. I was just about to voice it when Martina joined us with her sunny mustachioed smile. She conversed with Luca in their native tongue, and after she left us, Luca translated, "Martina will see to a light meal for us shortly. Perhaps over dinner we can determine just how we'll go about regaining that book of mine. Venice is not so large. A few coin placed in certain hands will help our search."

***

As unanticipated as our arrival had been, Martina did a credible job producing a late dinner out of thin air. As we had a mild October night, Luca suggested we go alfresco and eat outdoors in the walled piazza. The tranquil space was lovely, especially the pink stone illuminated by dying rays of sunlight. Ellie herself a canvas of pinks and roses, she never looked more beautiful than in this setting. I could tell Luca felt the same, for his eyes also tended to linger.

The courtyard's garden was filled with occasional vines and vestigial summer blooms, all accented by a water-spitting grotesque whose distorted face brought to mind the sketches of Arthur Rackham. Such architectural elements were adopted during the baroque period and underlined the church's involvement in art. After the rampant decadence of the Renaissance, the twisted and contorted bodies of the baroque period were indicative of the torments of hell — ready reminders at a glance to stay on the straight and narrow.

While we ate, Vittorio made some discreet inquiries to a friend "who knew people." Just as we were about to retire some two hours later, he returned with several pieces of information. The first was that Enzio had been found floating face-down in one of the nearby canals. By Vittorio's pantomime with an invisible oar, his informant described an injury to the head. The second bit of news was far more disturbing. Pietro Ambrosini, the raw textiles merchant, returned home this afternoon, and with him was Carlo Posateri. Luca thanked Vittorio and sent him on his way. We cleared our own dishes before taking ourselves up the long winding stone stairway to the topmost floor.

Her tone reflecting how disturbed she was by the news, Ellie said, "They told us they were leaving at week's end… but now he's back. *What do we do?* What if he destroys da Vinci's book as he said he would?"

She stopped suddenly and whirled around, and as I was behind her I nearly tumbled backward. The staircase was dimly lit but I could still see the excitement on her face. "I've met him!"

That fact began this venture. "Yes?"

"Don't you see? I can call on him and introduce my *new* husband." She smiled then turned and continued up the stairs.

Three steps above us, Luca called down, "That is a *brilliant* entrée, Ellie."

I nodded. "I agree. Given my profession, I might be able to open a dialogue with him." A recollection came to me. "That afternoon in my townhome, you mentioned Signore Ambrosini being taken aback by his in-law… "

She said over her shoulder, "Yes, he seemed embarrassed. His eyes darted and he showed his glass of port a little too much attention. What are you suggesting? Remember, Jean-Paul didn't get very far playing the cards in *his* hand, Nicolas. The man was very closed-minded from the little I overheard of their conversation. My brother-in-law was quite beside himself, and Jean-Paul *isn't* a man of few words."

Knowing him like I did, I had to chuckle. That was most aptly put. "I imagine he *would* be beside himself. To art historians such as us, destroying art is nothing less than a sin. But da Vinci's art? Now *that* is tantamount to *mortal* sin."

"We might call upon *him*. If we can entice Posateri from his home, Luca can retrieve what is his."

Luca offered, "That might work. I'll take Vittorio with me." He took us down a hall that was opened on one side to the two floors below. Pausing at a door embellished with handles in the form of bronze horses, he opened both to lead us to our rooms. Were he a married man of the Renaissance, this room would have belonged to his wife. Plush and extravagant, the room sported gilded trim, and the draperies, walls, and antique upholstery were done in reds and purples. Given the cost of such dyes, this was yet another nod to the wealth of his merchant family.

"I had him put your belongings in here before he left. They don't live in the main house, you see. Nearby yes, in the quarters adjacent to the kitchen. We are left to our own devices until morning."

Luca's invitation made me smile.

The large rococo tester bed was fit for the queen, with its stylized silk-lined wooden crown for a canopy. Massive yet delicately carved curlicues decorated both the head and footboards. Running her hand over a particularly impressive mahogany curl, Ellie said, "Luca, how beautiful!"

He smiled genuinely. "And made more so by the caress of your hand."

Ellie caught my eye to let me know she'd warmed to that compliment. She wanted to make love with us tonight. I wasn't surprised. Our three-way desire started rising in the air as night enveloped us. Loving Luca together was as addicting as opium. And by the silent signals he'd been sending me all day long, I knew the sentiment was returned. I raised a questioning brow to her and she treated me to a smile. I still marveled that such a simple thing could make my heart race in anticipation.

As he was head of the family, I'd expected Luca's bedroom to be opulent. This room left me speechless. Richly appointed in a stunning timeline of furnishings, the master suite depicted centuries of the Franco family merchant history in microcosm. The centerpiece: his *massive* bed. Four alabaster caryatids nearly as large as my wife stood as posts at the corners; each carved female suggestively posed and draped in robes that weren't intended to be modest.

On one wall stood an ornate fireplace, as tall as the bed was wide. Here, two more caryatids flanked the flickering hearth and supported the mantelpiece on their heads. Incongruous to the caryatids but in keeping with a merchant's eclectic patchwork of styles, marble baroque lions sat at their sandaled feet.

Taking up an entire corner at the far end of the room, an enormous square tiled tub sat three quarters enclosed by a giant Moroccan latticework screen. Beside it a very large copper tank with an iron brazier burning below. The tub in the other room paled by comparison.

Luca's snow-shadow eyes lit in anticipation. "I asked Martina to anticipate our needs shortly after we arrived, and she's done so. It would please me if you'd both share my bath."

My bold-as-brass Yank answered by unbuttoning her blouse.

The water was by no means hot, but quite pleasant nonetheless. We spent an hour discovering swell-and-swale, learning how one another's textures and tight places were enhanced or made breachable with the slippery addition of fine castile soap. Never in my life had I enjoyed a bath so much and I determined to have such a tub made for our townhouse.

Luca rose like a bronze Neptune with his cock now standing hard and thick. Reaching for Ellie's hand, he helped her to step over the high side then wrapped her in a large Turkish towel before offering his hand to me. He didn't offer me a towel though. Instead he walked me to stand before the hearth. His mouth closed over a droplet, then licked another. I knew what he was about; he planned to lick me dry. Over and over his tongue chased rivulets from my neck to my ankles. I placed my hands on his shoulders and led him to his knees. There, he licked my cock like a cat licking its paws. I met Ellie's eyes and saw that naked hunger pooling there.

Dropping her towel to the chair, she came to us bedecked in jewels of firelight glinting off the occasional water droplet. Leaving my cock throbbing, Luca turned to treat Ellie the same. I petted his silky ebony hair while she and I kissed. In turn, her hand closed around my length and fed him.

I don't know how it was we found ourselves on the massive bed, but bodies maneuvered head to crotch like a child's daisy chain with room to spare. Luca laved Ellie's velvet folds while I licked and sucked him. She in turn ran her sweet tongue over my cockhead several times before swallowing me whole. Who knew how much time passed in our sensual adoration of one another?

Needing more, Luca broke from us to press me to my back and then took command of our lovemaking. He had Ellie straddle my hips and with his hand to guide me, ran my cock all along her slick entry. Seating her fully, he then pressed her down to kiss me. I felt him then as he moved down the bed and nudged my thighs apart. There his warm breath and moist tongue plied the point of our joining. He licked my balls and root and wet my passing with each lift of my hips. When Ellie moaned into my mouth, I knew his tongue had ventured to new ground.

I felt her body tighten then relax. An instant later I felt his finger slowly run the length of my cock by moving gently in and out. My balls started to ache and I wished I'd had eyes to witness this introduction. A while passed in slow exploration. Then I heard him ask something in a husky, out-of-body voice. Ellie nodded against my kiss, her voice a soft whimper, "Yes."

Luca rose on his knees between our thighs. The firebrand heat of his cock traced wetly around my root then disappeared. A moment later Ellie's breath came in quick little shuddering pants and I knew where he had gone. I could hear the rumble of his voice but not his words. She gasped against my mouth as his blade seated itself along mine. His tender consideration stilled him, but it didn't keep me from moving.

I loved his husky moan and the weight of both lovers upon me. When she'd relaxed and he began to fuck, my fingers slid between her body and mine to find her completely stretched around my girth. The flint-hard nub stood firm and my fingers dallied there. He and I moved within our human pyre with measured, though slightly out of sequence glides. Filled completely and intimately caressed, it didn't take long to make her tremble with pending release. Her hips rocking forward and back, she was riding us now and Luca and I didn't stand a chance.

Ellie's kisses and bites ran along my neck like a firebrand. Oh, how I loved her. I could see Luca's handsome face above us and watched him close his moon-shadow eyes to fully absorb our generated bliss. His look of pure ecstasy might have inspired Giuseppe Bazzani. And how I loved him.

Luca was the first to cry out as he poured himself into her. The climax transforming his fine features would make angels weep to witness it. Ellie arched her back and clenched with her belly full of heat. Her shuddering orgasm washed over me in cascading waves that rolled on for several magnificent milking seconds.

Minutes passed before we came down from the clouds and extracted ourselves from our oriental puzzle box. Luca left us for a moment. The sound of running water came from behind the Moroccan latticework screen. Presumably, he emptied what was left in the copper tank.

Rolling to my side, I brushed the damp ringlets from Ellie's face. Her look was dreamy yet inscrutable. I asked about it. "Wool gathering, love?"

She traced a finger over my lips. "I'm just wondering how warm the bathwater is in the other room."

"Oh?"

She grinned, and leaping from the bed, glibly tossed over her shoulder, "I had no idea loving men was such a *messy* proposition."

I couldn't help but laugh.

We used the tub in the adjoining suite and didn't linger longer than necessary. This time it was all about the washing.

***

Unless Martina or Vittorio walked in on us in this very moment to discover we hadn't actually *slept* in both beds, Luca's privacy was intact. Having adequately rumpled the bedding in the master suite, we adjourned to our bed where we slept in a loving tangle. Comfortably pressed front to back; my arms held Ellie close while Luca wrapped around me with his cock nestled like a sausage on a bun. Sandwiched between love like this, I could die in my sleep a happy and contented man.

As I lay drifting off, I had visions of the three of us living and loving together in London and wondered what my dear liberal-viewed Mrs. Fletcher might say about it. No sooner had the thought come to me when Grannie's disapproving visage danced under my closed eyelids. I pushed the responsibility of my birth and station aside. Perhaps it was enough for the three of us to share our love when opportunity arose.

The greatest deception men suffer is from their own opinions.
– Leonardo da Vinci

~13~

Ellie's idea to seek an audience with Signore Ambrosini as his recent acquaintance was indeed brilliant. He sent a reply to our request via his servant saying he'd be delighted to see her and meet her new husband. He also asked that we come to dine with him and his brother-in-law so they might return the hospitality Ellie and her father had shown them.

We spent the day in preparation. Martina helped Ellie attend the wrinkles in her unpacked dress, while Luca, Vittorio, and I took a gondola past Signore Posateri's palazzo to determine his route that evening.

Like most of the surrounding dwellings, Posateri's home was modest and from what I could tell at a glance by the architecture, at least four hundred years old. The only difference between his palazzo and those around it was the array of saints that stood across his roofline — a miniature version of St. Peter's Basilica. It declared to all of Venice that here dwelled a pious man.

There was another telling feature that stood next to the front door — a smaller copy of the original *Bocca della Verità*, or mouth of truth. The only one I'd ever seen was in Rome, and that had been taken from a first-century Roman bath. The large disk with a wild-haired face of a man had an opened mouth for a water spout and was thought to be the pagan god Oceanus. The image was appropriated by the church sometime during the Middle Ages, and it was believed if a sinner's hand was put in the open mouth during questioning, it would be bitten off if he told a lie.

I didn't know much about Carlo Posateri, but had definite opinions built upon the body of information I'd learned from Ellie and Luca. Add this pretentious presentation before us, and Posateri wasn't simply a religious fanatic, he was a bloody righteous bugger.

I listened as Luca and Vittorio discussed the plan as they saw it. After he left us the night before, Vittorio put questions to several people he thought might know more about the silk merchant's brother-in-law. Apparently, from the four corners of Venice, this man was disliked. He was known for paying large sums of money for the items he destroyed in a public display reminiscent of the Bonfire of the Vanities. We also learned the cost of this habit had come dear. Posateri no longer had servants in his employ because he couldn't afford to pay them. This was good news. It meant the house would be empty tonight.

***

The hired gondolier punted us up the Grand Canal and assured us in broken English that we'd make our dinner engagement by eight PM. Luca had specifically picked this man, a friend of Vittorio, to ferry us to the Ambrosini *fandaco* for the historic tour he knew we'd receive. I hadn't expected to see much, but a nearly full moon had risen in the cold cloudless sky and lit our way.

Indeed, the centuries of architecture came alive for us as our guide identified every grand structure on our route. Several palazzos were dark but dozens more were richly lit by torches. Including the Ambrosini *fandaco*. A liveried servant met us with a lantern held high and offered Ellie his hand as she stepped from the gondola. A grinning Pietro Ambrosini welcomed us at the door with a kiss on both cheeks. "Ah Signora Schwaab... oh forgive me, *Lady Halstead*, I am so happy you've come. And this must be your husband, no?"

Ellie smiled brightly, "It's so good to see you again Signore Ambrosini, and please, call me Ellie. Yes, this is my husband, Sir Nicolas Halstead. Nicolas, may I introduce you to Signore Ambrosini."

I shook the man's hand warmly. "Pleased to make your acquaintance, Signore Ambrosini. My wife has had nothing but good things to say since you met in her father's home."

He beamed. "She is being kind, Sir Nicolas. I hope to make amends."

Ellie laughed, "Signore Ambrosini, whatever would you need to make amends for?"

He smiled at her indulgently. "Please, before we travel the evening further, I must insist you both call me Pietro." At our nods, he continued, "My brother-in-law shared some inappropriate views over dinner when last we met. It hasn't set right with me, and I assure you, it won't happen again." Turning to me, he said, "My brother-in-law Carlo is a man of deep conviction and unwavering views, and because of this, he can be a hard man with whom to converse."

I told him he could hardly be held responsible for the thoughts and views of a family member.

He said, "Thank you for that, Sir Nicolas. If you don't mind, I wish to explain him before he arrives. This knowledge might persuade a favorable opinion of him far better than he would be able to do on his own. You see, Carlo is a devout man, a pious man. At times he feels so passionately for his convictions, he leaves a bad taste in people's mouths. I admit there are times where he puts me off as well. But my late sister Silvia saw the good in him. And good or bad, he and I are the only family either of us has left in this world. I've cautioned him to remember we dine with a lady tonight and he has promised me his best behavior."

Ellie wasn't one to hold a person responsible for another's action or lack of decorum either. She placed a hand on his arm to convey her sincerity. "I took no affront Pietro, I assure you."

"That pleases me, Ellie. Carlo should be arriving shortly. He said he had business to see to and asked that we not hold our dinner. He will be joining us for our dessert." With that, he led us up the stairs.

Like Luca's *fandaco*, the bottom floor was devoted to business. Muslin- and burlap-wrapped bales sat on pallets to one side of the stairway and the whole of it smelled like damp hemp rope. The stairway was unique in that it stood at the corner of the building like a turret and reminded me of the cathedral bell tower in Pisa that leaned so perilously.

The upper living quarters were as curiously decorated as the Franco house — it too a mismatch of elements and styles particular to various periods of history. But here the tapestries and furnishing lacked the lushness of old wealth. Where Luca's ancestors had centuries of their merchant history lavishly depicted on every available surface, the Ambrosini home was inundated with gold-painted plaster cherubs. In fact, every spare corner sported a fat, winged baby boy — some of these repainted time and again as their faux gilt peeled. We learned Pietro inherited the textile business from his mother's only brother and he himself was a musician who once planned to live in Genoa. He explained, "And so I abandoned one dream and made for myself another."

Without preamble, we were seated and before long had worked our way through several courses while Pietro regaled us with stories of his youth and travels after he inherited a textile business on the verge of financial collapse. When dinner had finished and dessert was left waiting on Carlo, we took ourselves to the topmost floor where a large grand piano sat amid a throng of empty chairs. This musician-turned-textile merchant apparently gave regular performances for guests. He played lovely. At one point we joined him for some light-hearted singing. Pietro Ambrosini was a delightful man and I could tell Ellie enjoyed him as much as I.

After an hour, he rang for our dessert, saying it wasn't like Carlo to be so late. I could see the worry in his eyes. Ellie caught my eye as the cherub-bedecked mantle clock struck eleven. I hoped there was nothing amiss.

As we'd planned a signal between ourselves should it become time to leave, Ellie forced a dainty yawn and seeing it, Pietro humbly apologized for his brother-in-law again. Shortly afterward we said our goodbye, and made the offer to please call on us should he ever find himself in London or New York. To our surprise, our gondolier was nowhere in sight but rather we found Vittorio waiting nervously in Luca's gondola. Luca wasn't with him. I asked him where Luca was.

A string of whispered Italian burst from the man's lips. Seeing we didn't understand, he tried again in very broken English, "Uh… Luca not."

"Luca not what… *here?* Is he there? Is Luca still there?"

He nodded, "Si… eh… *morti.*"

"Dead?" Ellie gasped and covered her mouth with both hands.

My eyes flew from her to him. It couldn't be. My stomach clenched. "Luca *morti?*"

His eyes grew wide in the lantern light and he shook his head vehemently. "Oh, no no no. Uh… Signore *Posateri* e morto. Luca uh…Luca venire a lui…uh…pronto."

Ellie said, "I think he wants us to go to Luca."

Vittorio must have seen light at the end of this dark tunnel of broken communication. His head bobbed. "Si! Luca uh… say… uh… *come.* Si, *you* come."

Our life is made by the death of others.
– Leonardo da Vinci

7

~14~

Sound tends to carry across water. Dousing his lantern some distance from our destination, Vittorio quietly maneuvered his way up the side canal guided by the occasional shaft of moonlight through the now-cloudy sky. Only two neighboring palazzos were still alight at this hour, the rest in darkness, their owners retired for the evening. He carefully docked then looked at us expectantly. I guessed Luca had given orders to leave us.

I turned to my wife and whispered, "You should remain here. I have no idea what we're facing inside."

With the same softness, she said, "Fiddlesticks. That's the very reason I *won't* stay behind."

Figuring that's what I got for marrying a stubborn American, I said, "Then I insist you listen to me once we're inside. By necessity I've learned to read situations quickly. If I say run, you'll run. If I say hide, you'll hide. Do we understand one another?"

She nodded, "Fair enough."

A thought came to me. "Take note of where we are. Should things go awry, look for Vittorio and return to Luca's home… "

"But—"

I reassuringly squeezed her hand in the darkness. "Don't worry, love. Luca and I will manage to find our way back."

Vittorio pointed to the Posateri courtyard and we silently headed there. We found Luca waiting in the shadows. Putting a finger to his lips, he motioned for us to follow him inside.

"I've closed the curtains. We don't want to be seen here." He struck a match and lit a lamp. "Ellie, I would prefer you allow Vittorio to take you home. This scene is not for a woman's eyes."

She shook her head. "I understand you both would prefer I leave, but I'm staying. I come from New York. Nearly every corner of that city is populated by gangs seeking to control power in their area. What's more, murders and violence in the streets are common sights among the immigrants."

Luca and I exchanged glances. Resigned, I tipped my head. Nodding, he said, "What you are about to see is exactly that — violence and murder." He went on to explain that he'd entered the home and found Posateri dead, adding that he'd given the house a preliminary search and found nothing — not even so much as one of the sketches Posateri was known to have acquired.

Perhaps it was too late. Perhaps Luca's book had already been destroyed.

Leading us to the library, Luca pointed out the mostly bare shelves and the dozens of books scattered over the floor. I saw Posateri's stockinged foot sticking out from behind the settee, its shoe lying nearby. Reaching out, I tucked Ellie behind me. This *wasn't* a sight for a woman's eyes, no matter how accustomed those eyes were to seeing violent scenes in New York.

Naked from the waist down, Posateri was curled over an ottoman with his hands tied behind his back. Even from here I could see the frozen mask of terror on his gagged face. The conclusion was most disturbing. Carlo Posateri, the would-be homosexual who decried the act yet collected homoerotic art, had been forcibly sodomized.

I felt Ellie peering from behind me and heard the soft gasp. Accustomed or not, this gruesome display shocked her. She said, "Why do I smell almonds?"

Luca and I said at once, "Cyanide."

"He was *poisoned?*"

"Forced to drink at his violation, I'd say." I pointed to the vial on the floor near his head.

"Oh my god. What about Pietro? He'll be *crushed* to see this." She pulled my sleeve. "We have to right this somehow."

I looked at her dumbly, not understanding what she wanted us to do.

She clarified, "Nicolas, it is one thing to find his family member robbed and murdered. It's quite another for Pietro to find this... this... *terrible* scene. He'll be beside himself over the death naturally, but this indignity will *haunt* him. Please, can we at least put his trousers on?"

Luca said, "I see no harm in that."

We left Posateri on the floor with hands tied but fully dressed. The body wasn't warm but neither had rigor mortis fully set in, giving proof this deed happened very recently. Then, we searched the house for the book. Luca explained that he and Vittorio had seen a very identifiable gondola parked before Posateri's home, so they'd made several passes and returned when it had gone.

I asked, "So you recognized the gondola?"

Ellie followed, "You *know* who did this?"

Luca was noticeably uncomfortable. He nodded. "The gondola was unmistakable. I believe Posateri was murdered by Conte Acario Bruno."

"Conte? A Count of some importance?"

"Yes, from a very old family in Italy. He's known for three things: Being openly homosexual to the point of loathing women, being ruthless, and acquiring anything he fancies at any cost within or outside the law, including artworks." Luca let out a breath. "*He* undoubtedly has my book now. After you've both left Venice, I will see about retrieving it."

I was about to ask exactly what he meant by that when one of the bare shelves caught my eye. It was noticeably shallower than the rest, a slight trick of nuance that I detected but perhaps the murderer missed. Close examination revealed a latch. I pulled it and the shallow shelf lurched forward. Peering inside a recess, I said, "*Hello,* what do we have here?" I pointed to the latch. "I think I've found Posateri's collection. Luca, help me shove this panel aside, if you would."

Stacked against the back of the hidden alcove was an amazing array of homoerotic oils. The first was obviously a Bouguereau; the scene an erotic ménage of men. Next, an oil that could only have been painted by Guglielmo Fiammingo depicting a young man in adoration of an ebony-haired angel's cock. Another must be the unsigned work of Lord Frederick Leighton. In this oil Hercules mounted his love Alcestis. The next oil had to be Julius Kronberg in an erotic version of his *David and Saul.* The look of bliss on David's face gave me a twinge. Perhaps they were authentic or perhaps creative inspiration taken from original paintings. Whichever they were, these forbidden works of masters or their forgers was a fine collection indeed. I was overwhelmed by the treasure before me.

Ellie spoke from behind, "May I see one of those books, please?"

Luca passed a Persian pillow book to her waiting hands. I heard her say, "Oh my. I shudder to think what dear old Pietro will think of all this."

An idea came to me. "He doesn't have to know."

She reasoned, "But you've found them, he will too."

"Not if we take them with us."

"Take them?"

"These are precious works of art and Conte Bruno might be interested in a trade," I suggested. I noticed Luca's frown but didn't give it more thought in light of our haste to leave this incriminating scenario behind us.

***

We wrapped the oils and books in linens and drapery cords found upstairs, and quietly loaded them into Luca's gondola. Vittorio was obviously relieved to leave the premises and so were we. Luca asked his man to learn all he could the next day, thanked him for his faithful help, and then sent him home.

We carried our precious cargo upstairs. Deciding tomorrow was soon enough to form a plan to meet Conte Acario Bruno, Luca poured wine to settle our nerves. After examining each oil and sketch in some detail, the three of us found ourselves rightly aroused. With new positions and poses in mind, we put the events of the evening aside and became living art.

~15~

Ellie sat on our bed, a crease forming between her bows. "Couldn't I dress as a man?"

I inwardly chuckled at the image her words painted. "Suppose we could adequately conceal your sex, do you think I'd put you in front of a murdering misogynist? No, we must trust Luca in this. His opinion is you'd be in danger from the start. Remember, Conte Bruno has strong opinions regarding women."

Her frown deepened. "Yes, you're both right. But I'll have you know, I'll be beside myself with worry the entire time you're there."

I kissed her forehead, then lightly chucked her under the chin. "We'll be alright."

Luca had sent a dinner invitation to the Conte that morning, and in response gained for us instead an invitation to a small gathering the man was having the next evening. It made me even more curious when Luca went on to explain while he'd never attended one of these notably decadent affairs, to people in the know, in other words homosexuals, they were legendary. He then said we should abandon this until Ellie and I were safely on our ship and bound for home. When Ellie asked why, his only reply was "This is a dangerous man we deal with."

I answered the knock at the door. It was Luca looking quite finely dressed in black with an ascot that exactly matched the blue of his snow-shadow eyes. I had nothing so fine with me, so wore clothes borrowed from Luca's wardrobe. It was a close enough fit for all he was broader than I. The color was such in the green brocade waistcoat that wearing it turned my hazel eyes green enough for Ellie to comment about "the magic of it."

Showing a black silk ascot in his hand, Luca motioned for me to turn around and face the mirror. I watched him tie it around my neck. Lord, he was a handsome fellow. All my years of art study had done much to teach me to read emotional distinction. There was something around his eyes, slight, but there. Perhaps because he felt Conte Bruno was a dangerous man. He seemed worried and determined not to let us see it.

When the neckpiece was properly done, he helped me into the black morning coat before kissing my cheek. His eyes met mine in the glass and I felt his breath hot at my ear. "You're a most beautiful man, *mi amore*." Suspecting dressing me in the mirror had done for him what it had done for me, I reached behind and caressed the bulge. With that he pressed himself against me. The simple act brought about that flutter in my belly again. For an instant, the worry around his eyes disappeared.

***

Come evening, Conte Bruno had sent round a gondola for us, but Luca declined. Vittorio would punt us there. The man was a murderer. As far as we knew two men had already died by his hand — Posateri and Enzio Fortuna, Luca's former dockhand. We'd have our own craft so we could leave if need be. Luca advised Vittorio to linger a short distance away to be sure he was there when needed. I couldn't quite put my finger on it, but Luca seemed to carry himself stiffly in a high-strung sort of way. Behavior very much at odds with the man I knew him to be.

Even from a quarter-mile upstream, I could see our destination. Up close it was impressive indeed. Lit with tall torchiers from dockside and along a path to the formal garden, the large Venetian manor house was a yellow-bricked Renaissance beauty fit for the Doge himself. A man who I could only assume was the head butler met us at the garden gate.

A moment later we were announced loudly, "Signore Luca Franco and Lord Sir Nicolas Halstead!"

The formal garden took one's breath away with its sculptured hedges and bricked paths. Nude Greek and Roman statuary stood here and there, nary a female among them. Despite the cool evening air, the setting was made warm by dozens of blazing fire urns. First count revealed at least twenty-five guests besides Luca and me. I could feel eyes appraising us as we walked among fellow deviants, several of whom were involved in lascivious behavior. I did my best to appear unfazed and uninterested. Never before had I encountered public displays such as this though I'd read about secret fraternities where such was common.

Liveried footmen in scandalously snug uniform carried trays of food and drink. I made to grab two flutes of champagne for us on our way to our host, but Luca stayed my hand. I thought it odd, then remembered Carlo Posateri's run-in with potassium cyanide.

We were led to a white-columned pergola. Summer must have seen the structure festooned in bougainvillea. Now void of blooms, it sported a canopy of silk leaves in an array of autumn color among the remaining greenery. There on a silk divan amid an assortment of cushions, and between two pedestaled fire urns, sat our host. He possessed thinning hair the color of murky water. Notably, his features had been stamped by some blooded patrician sire that gave his family their noble standing back in the day.

Visible under a caking of greasepaint, Conte Bruno had a six-inch scar down one cheek like he'd been cut. His dun yellow clothing was form-fitting yet crisply creased and immaculate. He possessed the routine over-embellishment one often found in vain individuals. He broke into a handsome smile when he saw us. Rising, he held out his ring-studded hand. "Ah, Luca, I cannot express what it means to me that after all my invitations you've finally come. And this must be your friend the British Earl… " He raised a brow in question.

Luca curiously didn't take the hand but instead bowed his head slightly. "Yes Conte, may I—"

The Conte interrupted, "Please Luca, call me Acario. There is no need for formality between *us*."

Luca drew a deep breath. Ignoring the man's request, he said, "Conte, may I introduce my dear friend Sir Nicolas Halstead."

Our host eyed me from head to toe. Without offering me his hand, he said, "Sir Nicolas Halstead, how good of you to come with my dear Luca."

I bowed.

To Luca, he said, "I found myself intrigued to have been asked to dine at your home after all this time. It warms me, Luca. Dare I believe your feelings toward me have softened?"

"Sir Nicolas is an art historian," Luca said and took me by the hand in an obvious declaration. He gave my fingers a squeeze. Sensing I should not show the surprise I felt, I merely smiled. The show had begun.

Bruno's eyes went to our clasped hands, before lighting on me in renewed interest. I felt weighed and measured. He motioned for us to sit. "Is that so?"

I gave what I hoped was my most engaging smile. "Yes, I trained at Oxford and did my internship in the Ashmolean Museum there." I felt a slight jolt run through Luca and into my hand. Had I forgotten to mention to him that my training occurred at his new place of employment? I smiled inwardly at all we shared in common.

Conte Bruno exclaimed, "Brava! I've been there you know, *marvelous* place. What a stunning assortment of pre-Raphaelite paintings…"

I nodded. "One of the finest collections outside the Louvre."

Luca said, "Nicolas has bought several compelling works since he's been my guest."

"Really? It's my understanding you only just arrived these two days past. I trust your visit is on a schedule?"

I didn't much care for his knowing anything about me. Asking about my schedule was obviously a veiled inquiry about when I'd be leaving. I hedged, "I'm simply an emissary for the university. I'd made arrangements in London to acquire several pieces for them and perhaps one or two for me. The transaction went more smoothly than anticipated."

"Ah, the best transactions go smoothly." The Conte's lips turned. He was a handsome older fellow for all he had a crocodile smile and blood on his hands.

In for a penny in for a pound. I returned the smile and offered, "I'd love for you to see them before I depart. Collectors like us have much in common." I left the provocative statement hanging in the air.

"I'd enjoy that, Sir Nicolas. An expert such as you might be able to answer a question I have regarding a recent acquisition." The Conte turned to Luca, "I presume he's staying with you."

"Of course." Luca slightly raised his fingers laced with mine and drew attention to the fact he held my hand — a declaration that said, *yes, and in my bed.*

The Conte looked at our hands and his jaw tightened. He then looked me up and down before turning back to Luca. "Yes, of course he'd share your bed. A man such as you… so virile… so *insatiable…*" Decorum flown out the window, he prattled on in a stream of husky Italian. I couldn't follow it all but knew enough Latin to piece together its suggestive meaning. The fact was proved by a substantial erection inching down his dun-yellow pant leg.

I could tell Luca was about to land the bastard a retort when a footman dropped a tray somewhere near. All heads turned in that direction. The young man looked uncomfortable. Conte Bruno flicked his hand and the footman came forward and rattled off his apology in rapid Italian. The Conte said something I couldn't understand. The man quickly unfastened his trousers while a large padded ottoman was dragged to the center of the floor.

I watched the footman kneel upon it on hands and knees. When I turned back to the Conte, charming or not, handsome or not, the carnivorous look on the man's face made my throat go suddenly dry. I swallowed. This was the face of a ruthless murdering rapist. He rose and began unbuttoning his trousers, all the while priming himself by unloading more suggestive verbiage on Luca.

Luca's hand tightened around my own and he suddenly said to our host, "We're leaving now, Conte. Do let us know when you can view Nicolas's artworks."

He stroked himself suggestively, and spoke as a lover might, "*Acario,* Luca. I repeat, there is no need for formality between *us*."

Ignoring him, Luca said plainly, "Do let us know, Conte."

To this I added, "Yes, I'm looking forward to appraising your recent acquisition."

Ignoring me, Bruno frowned. "I was hoping you'd both stay, Luca. You've never come to my home before tonight. I've much planned in preparation… "

"The family business allows no rest." Luca gave him his charming smile but knowing him as intimately as I did, I could tell it was forced. By the look on the Conte's face, I could see it completely disarmed him. Even if he wasn't stroking his length in a slow and deliberate display meant to entice Luca, the naked desire in the man's eyes was more than obvious. Conte Bruno was infatuated. I found his blatant interest in my lover irritating.

His eyes never leaving the object of his desire, the Conte cocked his head to the side as if contemplating. He nodded to himself, apparently coming to some twisted conclusion. He said, "I will call upon you tomorrow."

Luca bowed his head.

With that Bruno shifted his attention to his clumsy footman.

We turned to leave and I found myself startled to see every

eager-faced man under the pergola was busy fetching his cock. As a young man I'd heard more than one sailor tale from Thomas. Of the service class, he rubbed elbows with other servants wherever he chanced to go and always came back with thrilling tales of this or that. One came to mind about sharks circling when blood was in the water. They were circling now. I could only guess how this evening would unfold.

Animated by firelight against the yellow-bricked garden wall were the silhouettes of the footman with his ass in the air, and the Conte fucking him for all he was worth. Given the sharks waiting to feed, I could just imagine how that poor footman's bum would feel come morning.

Seeing it, Luca doubled his pace, literally pulling me along. We swiftly headed to the dock and it struck me suddenly that he believed they'd come after us and force us to be part of Bruno's "preparations." Indeed, I heard footfalls quickly following behind us.

Fortunately Vittorio had just made his third pass. We jumped in the gondola and punted away. Luca held a finger to his lips as two men on the dock missed their chance and returned to the garden festivities.

***

We remained silent even after entering the *fandaco*. I followed him as he rushed to the topmost floor. Having heard our return in the library, Ellie came running up the stairs after us. In the master suite, Luca poured brandy and downed one fast before pouring two for us.

Somewhat out of breath, Ellie searched our faces. "What happened? Did you meet with the Conte?"

Luca pounded back his brandy and took another. I couldn't fathom why he was so upset. Abandoning my evening attire, I reached for my robe. "Yes, we've met him and planted a seed. He's interested in meeting again to see the artworks."

"That's good, no?"

Luca was silent.

Ellie turned to me with more than one question burning in her eyes.

I took Luca's glass and temporarily set it aside. Within moments, I had him undressed and wrapped in his dressing gown. With his mind elsewhere he moved machine-like, like a carnival automation. I handed him his snifter and walked him to the settee before the hearth. Sitting to one side of him, I motioned for Ellie to sit on the other side. I said softly, "Luca, help us understand what's amiss."

Ellie placed her hand on his arm.

He ground out the words. "That man is despicable. And yet his money and title keep him above the law." Taking a large gulp, Luca drained his brandy. When he made to rise for another, I stayed him and handed him my half-drank glass instead. Eyes pooling from emotion and alcohol, he stared into the flames without saying a word. Suddenly, he flung the glass into the flames then doubling forward, he sobbed into his hands. We both enfolded him and let his perplexing misery take its course. When enough had drained way, he patted both our hands and said, "I'm sorry. That footman brought back disturbing memories."

Meeting my eye, Ellie gave me a silent request for information. I explained the footman's blunder and the dues he paid for it, adding that homosexual men would not stay in that type of employ if they found such abuse unappealing. She looked horrified. I didn't want to see Luca pained, but if he needed this venting of emotion, I would listen. I asked, "You've seen this before?"

He nodded sadly. "I wish it weren't so, but yes." He took a deep ragged breath and let it out slowly. "I've mentioned my first lover. I was sixteen when I met Cesare D'Ovidio. He was eleven years older than I, a gentle man, wise, and learned, a loving and generous soul. He was my sisters' dancing master and fencing instructor to my brothers and me. I'd often watch him with the girls while I waited on my lesson. The way he moved — so confident he was — as though the music were inside of him with or without his foil in his hand. A year went by… and then their instruction and mine came to an end. Cesare moved to another village to tutor another family."

Luca sipped his brandy. "Several years later, I met him again when my father sent me to Tuscany to arrange business with the cork cutters there. I didn't know my way around. He took me to dinner and after I stayed with him. It didn't take us long to fall in love." Luca shook his head as though inner dialogue continued on after his words had ceased.

I had a gut-wrenching feeling I knew where this tale was headed.

Luca gave a small smile and clasped our hands. "Not since Cesare have I given my heart. Not until now."

Ellie assured him, "We love you too, Luca."

I smoothed his hair back. "We do."

It brought a small smile to his eyes. Needing to voice it, he explained the rest, "I stayed with him while my father's transaction was completed. One evening we dined at his favorite *locanda,* a private inn where he preferred to dine. And there we met Conte Bruno. Taking a fancy to me, the man took a seat at our table though he wasn't asked to join us. Before our meal had ended, he'd propositioned me. Cesare said I wasn't interested, that I was here on my father's business. The Conte replied that he'd watched me for some time, and wondered just what business put me in Cesare's bed. I was sick inside. My father would never understand my love for another man."

Luca continued, "The next day, the man sent his footman with a note clearly stating he and I would meet that day, or my father would receive a letter. Cesare had told me this man was no good and to steer clear of him. But Cesare was with one of his pupils; I couldn't seek his counsel on what I should do. I told the footman I would only meet with the Conte in Cesare's home. I thought I'd be safe talking with him there. I thought I could reason with him. I was wrong."

Ellie asked, "What happened?"

"He arrived an hour later. He tried to seduce me, and when that didn't work, he tried force. I fought with everything I had, but his two men were with him. They did his bidding and were preparing me for his assault when Cesare came home. He still had with him the *scherma fiorett,* the fencing foil. It wasn't sharp. You've noticed that scar on the Conte's face? That was Cesare's doing — a dull blade, no less. He fought them… my hands were tied behind my back and my trousers were down to my knees. I *couldn't* help him. I threw myself at one of them and was knocked to the floor. Cesare told me to run…" Luca's voice trailed off as the scene played in his mind. Several minutes passed in silence, then he spoke, "I don't know how I got to my feet, but I did run. I ran until I found a shed with a window… I broke the glass and used a piece of it to free myself."

Luca held up his hand to show the jagged scar there, across the side of his hand and up his wrist. I'd noticed it before. An inch to the right and he might have bled to death while cutting his bonds. A tear ran down Luca's cheek as he relived the event. "I ran back there. Cesare was tied like Posateri and positioned like that footman tonight, and the Conte was exacting a price for his bleeding wound. I flew at them and one of the men struck me unconscious. When I woke, the sun was down and Cesare... "

Luca swallowed hard. "For seven days, Cesare suffered agony. I tended him. He'd have no one else know what happened. He said there was nothing a doctor could do, and I'd be implicated and my family shamed. The Conte was a powerful man; he'd see to it. Cesare had been brutalized... it wasn't enough that they'd taken him by force. He'd cut the Conte's face, so they savaged him." Luca's voice lowered to a grief-stricken whisper, "They took him for their pleasure, then... took him again with a broken... they used... used a... oh *Dio... mio Dio.*"

The rest of the grisly scene came out in sobs — an emotion-riddled amalgamation of English and Italian. Luca needed to say it far more than he needed us to know the words, though my mind knew enough of his language to piece together an unbelievably heinous crime. As fresh and raw as it was, I felt certain he'd never shared this secret pain with another soul. It broke my heart to hear it and I couldn't help but extrapolate the last minutes of Posateri's death as well. We'd done right to keep that horror from gentle Pietro.

Ellie and I rocked Luca gently until all of the festering recollection had drained. When his composure returned, he went on to explain that his plan to leave Italy was a direct result of Conte Bruno's harassment. Luca's work for the museum had begun in March. "He's courted me relentlessly since that day," Luca said. "When I lived in Florence and Rome, he lived in Florence and Rome. When the monster learned I'd come to Venice, he came here as well. I am only glad my father is no longer alive to be hurt and shamed. My brothers and sisters know my nature. They don't approve or condone, but they know. He can't hurt me with disclosure any longer, and I'm leaving the family business. He can't ruin that either."

Ellie said, "The book isn't that important Luca. Let's leave for London as soon as possible."

Luca nodded. "Soon Ellie, soon. Leonardo's book gives me an unforeseen opportunity — of which I *must* take advantage."

She squeaked, "*Advantage?* Luca, you know better than anyone that he's a madman! *Please,* reconsider this meeting."

I said, "She's right, Luca."

Luca chuckled but it was void of his natural good humor. He kissed her cheek, then mine. "He is at that, *I miei amori.* As I've told you, I've been Bruno's obsession for a dozen years. For some of this time, I've managed to keep him at bay with my schooling and my travels. But now *I* seek *him.* I'm no longer a boy to bend to his will. He can't hurt me, and he won't abuse and murder another soul. Before I leave for London, I swear on my dear Cesare's life, I'll see him brought to justice." The last words held a slight slur. The rapidly-downed brandy was having its effect.

We sat in silence for a time, then I rose and held my hands out to them. Together we walked arm-in-arm to the massive nymph-guarded bed and snuggled into our embrace. Luca lay between Ellie and I and we poured our love into him in hopes of chasing the demons away. Overcome by melancholy and brandy, Luca drifted off to sleep with Ellie wrapped tightly in his arms. I rolled to my side with my belly pressed against his back. I caressed them both, reveling in the differing physiologies under my hand — he, firm and smooth, and she, downy and slight.

I petted them absently as I found myself replaying the Conte's garden party in my mind. After what I'd heard and seen these last two days, I wondered what became of the footman. As I'd explained to Ellie, the man wouldn't be in Bruno's employ if he objected to such. Perhaps such transgressions by that household staff were treated by a good group fuck, an excuse as it were. Such deviant practices had been around for ages, most recently in the old Hellfire clubs of London and Ireland where serving maids and footmen were deliberately made to stumble and pay the *consequence* for their clumsiness.

The footman had looked uncomfortably embarrassed tonight, but certainly not frightened. After all, he'd only dropped a tray. It didn't involve theft, as it had for Posateri, who'd undoubtedly put up a fight to keep what he erroneously thought was his. Nor was it payment for a scar that disfigured a handsome and vain homosexual for a lifetime. I extrapolated the faceless Cesare D'Ovidio, who no doubt had died from sepsis brought about by his impaling. Poor Cesare. He must have been a special man for this dear soul to have loved him.

I understood now why Luca had taken my hand in an open display of affection. He wanted the Conte to know neither of us would be found alone. I kissed Luca's warm shoulder. Whatever foul obsession the man possessed where Luca was concerned, my lover had drawn a line in the sand. And he wasn't alone. I was right by his side.

Nothing can be loved or hated unless it is first known.
– Leonardo da Vinci

~16~

Luca sent a note to the Conte stating two things: the time to arrive and insistence the Conte come alone. A reply arrived an hour later. Luca crushed the paper in his hand, a slew of vulgar Italian under his breath.

Peeling it from his fingers, I smoothed the note and read aloud:

> *My Dearest,*
>
> *If you only knew what seeing you the other night has done to me. Even now imagining your beautiful eyes and your lips makes me swoon. I will come to you as you wish, grateful that you've invited me to your home. It is my sincere hope this begins a new chapter for us. Counting the hours, I am.*
>
> *Yours Always,*
>
> *Acario*

Tossing the note in the hearth, I echoed Luca's sentiment,

"Bloody *turd*."

Having dressed, Ellie joined us. "I still don't see why I must remain out of sight. *I* certainly have nothing the man wants."

Luca looked at her indulgently. "That I love you, *mio amore,* is enough to put you in harm's way. I couldn't bear it if I unwittingly brought harm to either of you. Please understand. This is a cruel and dangerous man with people paid to do his bidding. Nicolas at least can fight if need be."

She squeaked. *"Fight?"*

I pulled her into my arms and hugged her close. She smelled like violets. "I've had years to learn how to look after myself. And yes, if anyone could give that man a run for his money it would be you, my sweet. But you know Luca is right. And *I* know that sharp mind of yours sees the reasoning."

Ellie let out a sigh and wrapped her little body around me. *"Fiddlesticks.* Yes, I do."

Luca joined our hug. "Thank you for your understanding. I'd rather you weren't here when he comes. I've arranged with Martina to take you to pick out a pattern of glassware from the very craftsmen who make it. Venice is known for our glass, you know. This will be my wedding gift to you."

Breaking the hug, she smiled up into his eyes. "Thank you, Luca. You're saying I'll be able to see how it's made?"

He returned the smile. "Yes."

I could feel the gears of her mind turning. Her smile became radiant. "I'd love that."

I laughed. "Oh ho! Something interesting for that inquisitive mind of yours, love. Luca, I don't think you could have planned a better outing."

For the first time since Bruno's garden and the painful release that followed, Luca seemed truly happy.

***

Alone now, Luca and I sorted the paintings and the pillow books. Knowing the Conte's depraved nature, we chose the most blatant erotic works to catch his eye. I was struck again by the masterpieces before me. There was no true way of determining their authenticity of course, for none were signed works. Three of the lot struck me as absolute forgeries because I knew for a fact the supposed artists were devoted to the female sex in their regular depiction of nude women. Still, I had a dual nature, as did Luca. It was entirely possible these men did as well.

Luca absently flipped through the Persian pillow book, the scenes within by far the most graphic of the lot. He showed me a page depicting in full erotic detail one woman and two men physically engaged. The acrobatics depicted were next to remarkable. We'd sampled it ourselves three nights ago, much to Ellie's delight. A twinkle lit his eyes when he said, "I'll keep this book. When this business is over, we'll begin at page one."

It had to contain a hundred sensual illustrations of various poses. My body reacted to Luca's suggestion as I turned pages. Lost in the heady imagery, I was just about to say *why wait* when the moment evaporated with a knock at the door. Suddenly Luca crushed me to him and kissed me soundly. Holding my face between his hands, he looked me square in the eye but didn't say a word. He didn't need to. His mixed emotions were plainly written in the snow-shadow blue. I saw unease and trepidation among the love reflected there. He vowed, "I'll never let him hurt you. I *promise*."

Clasping his hands, I assured him, "He won't hurt me. Come, love, let's get this detestable meeting over with."

He sighed. I followed behind as he went to the door. Upon seeing Luca, Conte Bruno was positively beside himself. Dressed as impeccably as the night before but this time in blue, he also had on a careful application of theatrical make up designed to conceal the facial scar. I had the feeling he took pains to look good for Luca. He had with him with a large flat box under his arm.

Luca tipped his head, once more avoiding the hand the Conte offered.

Bruno smiled at us and chided, "I must tell you, the longer I waited for you to open the door, the more delicious the imaginings filling my mind at what could possibly cause your delay."

Bloody sod. To him I said, "I can't wait to see your acquisition, Conte Bruno."

He took his over-large cigar box to the table and opened it. "Yes, this is something with which an art historian such as you is sure to be familiar." With that, he withdrew da Vinci's book to Salai. He said, "I've only recently acquired it. It's believed to be an unknown work of Leonardo da Vinci."

Luca showed only mild interest but I could feel his mind working hard to keep righteous rage at bay.

"Do tell." I looked it over with a critical eye and I too waged a war within me. My excitement felt like champagne bubbles in my veins but this man could not see my interest. I coolly and slowly flipped through several pages and it was all I could do to steady my unabashed reverence. It was beyond what I'd imagined. The images were rich and highly provocative, and I was certain the foreign prose was just as lyric and sensual, some of it written in a mirror image in the classic da Vinci idiosyncrasy. With my best mask of disappointment showing, I met Bruno's expectant face and shook my head sadly, "Alas Conte, it grieves me to tell you this is a forgery."

"*What?* That's… that's *not* possible!"

Showing him elements on several pages, I explained they were common to such reproductions. I lied smoothly, "And see here? This curl? There was a counterfeiter in the 1860s known for innocuously inserting his initials into his copies."

"I don't see it."

Nodding, I pointed, "It's there, see? It looks like letter script; see the T and the F here? His name was Thomas Fletcher. A well-known chap — a master in his own right." I met Bruno's eyes again. "I do hope you didn't pay very much. It's an interesting and well-executed facsimile, but quite worthless."

Luca knew about Thomas. That I'd made Grannie's coachman a forger made him smile. He turned away to hide it and presumably to gloat over this foul man's disappointment.

The Conte's mouth was a grim line. He said, "Then it's worthless to me." He took a moment to flip through da Vinci's pages then slammed the book closed.

Opening the book again, I turned a few pages. "I wouldn't say worthless, exactly. It *is* amusing after all. And I suppose it might be useful as a teaching aid, were you to donate it to a university. Other than that, I see no value."

Coming to the table, Luca leafed through the pages. His voice laced with mockery, he said, "How unfortunate for you, Conte."

Bruno looked at Luca. I'm sure the sarcasm wasn't missed. I added more fuel to the fire, "I feel badly for your loss, Conte

Bruno, but what can one do? You're not the only connoisseur duped into believing they have an authentic masterpiece."

Clearly annoyed, Bruno said, "I'd very much like to see those artworks of yours, Sir Nicolas. Perhaps you have a piece that might offset my disappointment?"

He could have them all, as far as I was concerned. Twisting the knife I wished were real, I said, "Most are not mine to deal Conte, but I'm agreeable to considering an offer on several that are."

Luca led us to the salon, where the artworks stood propped against the wall.

Bruno hurried to kneel beside them. Whipping a monocle from his waistcoat, he examined each in turn. *"Bello! Eccellente. Ahh… stupendo… magnifico."*

Within moments, the full length of his erection was visible under the cloth of his trousers. Luca and I exchanged glances. We'd picked our bait well.

Bruno adoringly ran his finger down the painting by Fiammingo in which a young man and an angel were involved in a rousing depiction of fellatio. He lingered before it. "Such *perfection*." Turning to me, he said, "I want this. Name your price."

I looked from him to the oil. For the first time I saw what Bruno saw: the angel was dark-skinned, his hair black and flowing. But it was the eyes. Gazing up toward heaven in rapturous ecstasy, his eyes were blue — the same moon-shadow blue hue Luca's eyes took when he was deep in passion. The same eyes I'd seen the other night when the three of us made love. The thought disturbed me. "I'm sorry, Conte, I was drawn to this one myself—"

The man cut in, "Yes, that's perfectly understandable. But I want *this*, and I'm willing to pay your price, whatever the price."

Luca spoke from behind, "Is this one a forgery, Nicolas?"

"No, this is a genuine piece." I turned to look at him. He raised his brows as if to ask why I would keep it. He wasn't aware of the resemblance to him.

That fact changed a moment later when the Conte said, "This one speaks to me. These eyes are exactly *yours*, Luca. Name your price, Sir Nicolas."

The eyes in question grew large and flew to the oil. In an instant, Luca's face was transformed by seething hatred. He turned away.

Seeing my lover's discomfort, I refused Bruno's request. "I'd planned to keep it."

"I shall double the price paid, triple it."

I wanted him gone. I told myself it wasn't Luca, it was only a likeness. Letting out a sigh, I played along. "Very well."

Bruno rose and turned to me with a very handsome smile and a very noticeable erection in his tight trousers. He surprised me by extracting a substantial purse of coin from his coat's inner pocket. We discussed the price of the transaction for a time. When it was settled, I went upstairs to retrieve some canvas and cord unwrapped from the artworks the night we brought them home. I caught a bit of their heated conversation upon my return.

Bruno tried wooing Luca. "I can't get you from my mind. Please come to me, I know I can make you happy. Nicolas will be leaving, you'll be alone again. Come to me. Let *me* love you. Anything you wish, and I will do it for you. I will give you anything… "

In the doorway now, I watched the scene unfold.

Luca had yet to turn. Bruno must have taken the lack of rebuttal as acquiescence, for he came up and ran a hand across

Luca's shoulders in a sweeping caress.

Luca said, "You'd do anything for me?"

"Anything, Luca."

Luca turned and those lovely eyes of his shot arrows at the older man, his words spoken in deadly calm, "*Allora uccidere te stesso, tu figlio di puttana.*"

On Bruno's face, I saw the flicker of pain and disappointment. Then he smiled a very unsettling smile of the sort you'd see on a man very certain of an outcome. He said, "No, *il mio amore*, I shall not kill myself. I will rather make a prediction. I predict you will come to me tonight. And when you do, you will leave your clothing and this attitude outside my bedroom door. You will lie upon my bed, and make yourself mine. Our fates are entwined you see, it can be no other way. Make no mistake."

Before Luca could throttle him, I made my presence known. "Let us complete our transaction, Conte. It's time for you to leave." Luca stormed from the room, his hands clenched in rage.

I could feel Bruno's eyes boring into me as he stood and watched me wrap the painting. I walked him to the door. His gondolier was waiting and he called him to load the artwork. Turning to me, he said, "Go now and soothe his ruffled feathers for the last time. Bed him well, and then consider your relationship ended."

"Whatever are you on about?"

He smiled that same disturbing smile. "Determine your priorities, Sir Nicolas. He's mine, not yours."

***

I found Luca in the library. He stood, arm leaning on the

mantle, staring down into the fire.

I caressed his back. "He is gone and your book is back where it belongs. We'll book passage tomorrow, if you like."

He didn't turn. "Had you not come into the room when you did, I would have killed him with my bare hands. I need to finish this, tomorrow I'll—"

He was interrupted by a door opening and closing below and the echo of cries for help coming from the warehouse.

Running there, we found Martina sobbing hysterically and struggling to carry her seriously injured brother. Vittorio looked to have been beaten. Martina too had been roughed up, her face swollen, her clothing torn. Rapid Italian flew. Martina pulled a note from her pocket.

Luca turned to me with dread and anguish shining wildly in his eyes, "He has Ellie!"

~17~

Momentarily curious as to why the bloody sod had written in English, I determined he expected *me* to read it, and so I did:

> *My Dearest,*
> *Come to me this evening exactly as discussed. If you cannot bring yourself to make this decision, Sir Nicolas will help you. She's a lovely creature, Luca. Know if you do not comply, she will feel my displeasure. I expect to see you alone. Do not disappoint me.*
> *Yours in Love,*
> *Acario*

"We'll get her back, Nicolas. It's a simple thing he wants."

Heartsick, I saw the faceless Cesare ripped open and left to die. *My Ellie, my poor Ellie.* I was completely beside myself. I told him, "We must inform the police—"

He cut in, "We don't know who, or how many, he's bought."

"He's a madman Luca!"

"He'll hurt her if I don't do as he says. You don't know him like I do. There is no other way, Nicolas. *No* other way. I *must* do this."

"I'm going with you."

He took the note from my hand. Reading it again, he shook his head. Before he could open his mouth to say no, I said, *"Fuck him* and his demands. Luca, she is my life. You *both* are my life."

Dropping the crumpled note to the floor, Luca took me by the upper arms and looked me in the eye. He too burned with frustration and fear for her. "Listen to me, find Ellie and leave. Whatever happens, don't concern yourself with me." He lightly shook me to emphasize his point. "Promise me this."

"I promise you, he won't hurt *any* of us."

Patience serves as protection against wrongs as clothes do against cold, for if you put on more clothes as the cold increases, it will have no power to hurt you. So in like manner you must grow in patience when you meet with great wrongs, and they will then be powerless to vex your mind.

– Leonardo da Vinci

~18~

With Vittorio suffering from broken ribs, we punted ourselves to Bruno's palazzo. Upon seeing the place dimly lit, I said, "I expected one of his gatherings."

"He wants us to be alone."

I felt cold inside, cold and sick with dread. What if he'd hurt her already? What if he...? Good God, I felt so helpless.

Conte Bruno met us at the garden gate. The smile in his voice was evident as he said, "Ah, I can't express how pleased I am that you've come to me, Luca." Then his eyes met mine in the lantern light. "But why are *you* here? My note said Luca was to come alone."

I growled, "Where is my wife? If you've hurt her, I swear—"

Ignoring me, he said to Luca, "I was very clear in my note. His presence has changed things."

"Where is my wife?"

Luca stopped me with his extended arm. In a voice dripping

with menace, he said, "Stop this game. Where is Ellie?"

"She is upstairs. A bit ruffled, but otherwise unharmed for now."

Alarmed, I said, "What do you mean?"

The Conte took his sweet time answering. He spoke directly to Luca, as if I weren't standing there. "He knows very well you belong to me now."

I wished I had a revolver or a knife, even an axe would do.

Luca said, "I'm here, aren't I? You will bring her to Nicolas *now*."

Bruno was quiet a moment. Then smiling genially, he said, "I'd initially planned for my guests to make sport with Lady Halstead tomorrow night. But after you and I have loved one another, I will allow him to walk away with his Lady. Unsporting of you to spoil my plans, Sir Nicolas. That pale bottom tempts me—"

I raged, "*God damn you.*"

"Enough!" Luca growled. To me he said, "He knows better Nicolas, he's only taunting you. He knows I'd kill him with my bare hands if he's laid a hand upon her."

That sobered the bastard. His smile absent now, Bruno said, "You will not fight me, Luca. You will allow yourself to enjoy all I have to give you. Is this clear?"

Luca answered in hate-laced Italian.

Shaking his head, Bruno tsk-tsked. "And *that* sentiment will be the last of its kind. Do you understand?"

Luca hissed, "You'll have me, and you *will* release them. That's all I care about. Do *you* understand *me*?"

"You'll love me in time, *il mio amore*. I have every confidence."

Luca spit on the ground.

Bruno led us up the marble staircase to his bedroom. Telling me to wait, he led Luca inside. Through the opened door I heard him say in a voice intentionally loud enough for me to hear, "Kiss me Luca." Followed by, "That was wonderful but I know you're capable of better. It must be your best if they are to leave here safely." A moment later he said, "Mmm. Look what you've caused. How I ache for you. Now make yourself ready for me. I'll return shortly."

Bruno closed the door behind him and ushered me to an alcove with a window that opened onto his bed in the next room. Luca was undressing. Unbelievably, Bruno wanted me to watch them in bed. To him this was akin to twisting a knife into me. I turned to him, but Bruno stood transfixed, watching Luca through the glass. He muttered unintelligible words under his breath. I said with far more reserve than I felt, "You bloody sod, I demand you bring my wife to me *now!*"

He absently fingered his scar as he looked me over slowly. "You're a handsome man, Nicolas. This fact alone is what my Luca responds to. But tonight, you'll watch him respond to *me*. You'll see it's *me* he wants."

"I said *bring* her to me, *damn you.*"

Laughing dementedly, he left me there in the alcove. I watched my friend and lover with a bleeding heart. There had to be a way out of this. There had to be. A minute later I heard Ellie's voice drawing near but I couldn't quite make out what she was saying. Bruno and his man brought her into the alcove. She was naked, her hands tied behind her back, a cloth sack over her head. By the sounds she was making, she'd been gagged. Her arms were covered with bruises of the sort one might obtain from rough handling.

Ripping off my overcoat, I shoved both men away from her

and covered her quickly. She started to scream and struggle. Wrapping her in my arms, I shushed her. "It's alright love, I'm here now." Upon hearing me, my name came muffled through her gag.

The man spoke in rapid-fire Italian. Bruno laughed. "He tells me she's managed to escape twice. Mischievous little thing, she is. Such spirit would have made exciting sport for my gathering." Obviously disappointed, he turned to the window. Seeing a naked Luca waiting faded all thoughts of abusing my wife. Dismissing his man, Bruno then said to Ellie, "I am wondering, Lady Halstead, if you know your husband prefers men in his bed?"

The bastard thought his comment would shatter my marriage. There was a moment of silence, in which I could feel the gears turning in Ellie's head. Playing along, she then pretended to sob under her sack.

He laughed and left us. A moment later he stood next to Luca.

After untying Ellie, I removed the sack and gag. Ruffled she was, with nary a tear. She shrugged into my coat and then threw herself into my arms. I'd been sick with worry. I held her tightly as much for me as for her, and murmured at her ear, "I'm so sorry, so sorry."

"That vile, repulsive, disgusting… Oh Nicolas, I got as far as the water twice. The last time that *bastard* took my clothes and covered my head with that stinking onion sack. As far as I could tell, he only has two inside house servants, *that* one and one other. I've heard no other voices."

I had to ask, "Did they hurt you?"

"Not really. The other cretin made free with his hands but I screamed as loudly as I could. Conte Bruno came and I never saw the man after that. Then I was gagged."

I heard a sound below stairs. I pressed my finger to my lips and looked down the hall. No guard had been left on us here. I crept along the marble balustrade and saw no one. For all intents and purposes, we were quite alone. The hubris of the man led him to believe that without Ellie's clothing, he had us over a barrel. He didn't know my bold-as-brass American wife would walk naked through Trafalgar Square if doing so was a means to an end.

Coming back to the alcove, I looked through the glass to find Bruno undressing. When he'd finished, he went to Luca who stood beside the bed. We watched Bruno say something then Luca bent to kiss him.

Ellie said, "What a horrible man. What can we do to get Luca out of there?"

"*We* aren't doing anything."

Obviously missing my meaning, she said, "We can't leave him there!"

"Ellie, neither of us will chance you being hurt."

"What would you do if I *weren't* here?"

"It never would have gotten this far." I watched the disgusting man walk around Luca as though he were a prize bull at the county fair. He caressed him intimately with one hand while stroking himself with the other. It was all I could do not to knock that fucking door down and beat Bruno into pulp.

Seeing it, she said, "Nicolas, you can't mean to do nothing."

I needed to see her safely tucked away before I helped Luca. I told her so.

"*Fiddlesticks.* I can look after myself."

I said to her, "That you will *not* do, wife. These are dangerous men. Come with me and do exactly as I say."

We crept down the stairs. I grabbed a small porcelain cherub and a bronze figurine of Apollo from a table, moved into a hall, and shoved Ellie behind me. Tossing the cherub across the floor to make a commotion, I readied myself. Sure enough, the man came in to investigate. When his footfalls declared him close enough, I stepped in front of him and swung with all my might to smash the bronze into his face. Teeth and blood splattered across the floor. Without a doubt, the foaming convulsion and stink of bowel that followed confirmed I'd killed him. I'd gladly do it again. Ellie heaved dryly. I felt brief sorrow she had to witness this grisly scene.

I took her by the hand. We ran through the kitchen as quietly as possible and made our way out into the garden and past the walled gate to the dock. The water was calm and the sky cloudy and dark, and as far as I could tell there wasn't a soul in sight. Kissing her hard, I put her in the gondola. Bruno's gondola was parked beside ours and taking his brocade cushions, I covered her in an attempt to conceal and offer a small measure of warmth.

Speaking low, I cautioned, "Stay hidden. Don't come out for any reason. *Please* Ellie, if I have to worry about you too, I won't be able to help him."

"I understand, please be careful." For the first time I could hear fear in her voice.

"I will."

***

I made my way past the corpse on the floor and paused to listen. Somewhere in the house, another servant lurked. There was no time to think on that possibility further, for I was greeted by a blood-curdling scream from the floor above. I took the stairs two at a time with Apollo clutched in my hand, determined as I was to beat Bruno to death if he hurt Luca.

But it was Luca who met me at the top of the stairs. He looked to be favoring his left arm, as he was fastening his trousers with only his right hand. Shoeless and shirtless, swelling and bruises were forming on his face and his hair looked wild. From his chin and running down his chest, he was painted with streaks of blood. The screaming continued behind him. As Luca walked down the stairs, I looked past him, unable to fathom what had happened. He asked in a desperate tone, *"Do you have Ellie? Is she safe?"*

"She is." His relief was instantaneous. I didn't have time to ask what happened, for a screaming Bruno came down the open hallway, his face as white as parchment. Both hands clutched his crotch and blood poured through his fingers to stream down his legs.

On the landing beside me Luca turned and dropping some bloody thing to the floor, said, "Are you looking for *this*?"

I followed his gaze and there, lying at his feet, was a good portion of dismembered cock. Luca kicked it and sent it flying over the balustrade. With that, he took my arm and walked me calmly down the stairs.

Bruno growled; the sound halfway between man and animal. He called for his men but Apollo had seen to it that one of them would never rise again. Enraged, he screamed after us, *"Nicolas, damn you! Damn you. You can't have him!"*

In blind rage, he proceeded to run down the stairs to come after us. But the marble at his feet must have been slick with blood for he slipped and hurtled headlong into a fall, tumbling down two flights of hard stone to the ground floor. He lay motionless at the bottom, one leg lying at a grotesque angle, one hand gripping the stub.

Luca met my eyes when he saw Bruno's henchman lying dead with a smashed face. I shrugged, like such killings were an everyday occurrence in my life. Luca smiled and shook his head in wonder. Flexing his shoulder, he hissed in pain. By the angry swelling at the juncture, I suspected an injury to his collarbone. I pulled a handkerchief from my pocket and dipping it into the foyer's fountain, proceeded to wipe the blood from his face and chest as best I could. I then shrugged out of my waistcoat and carefully helped him into it. It was better than nothing. I winced seeing that his ebony hair had been ripped out by the roots in places, and his shoulders and upper chest would certainly be covered in bruises come morning. I didn't need to ask how he'd come by this abuse. It was clear as day. Compelled to suck, he'd bitten off the man's cock instead. By the obvious battering he'd received over it, it must have been a slow removal.

Cupping his hand into the fountain, Luca rinsed his mouth and spit in the direction of Bruno's lifeless body. Tucking the portrait of the blue-eyed angel under his good arm, he said to me, "Let's go home, *il mio amore*. Cesare can rest in peace now."

It had long since come to my attention that people of accomplishment rarely sat back and let things happen to them. They went out and happened to things.

– Leonardo da Vinci

~19~

Ellie and I stayed to see Luca and Vittorio healed. One morning we extended our condolences to Pietro Ambrosini. Undeserved affection or not, Carlo Posateri was Pietro's only family. He was decidedly upset by the loss of his brother-in-law.

We'd been right to follow Ellie's request the night we tidied Posateri and covered the disturbing circumstance of his death. His brother-in-law believed he'd died at the hand of someone to whom he owed money. As bad as that image was, it *was* better than learning his loved one had been raped first.

As we didn't have much with us to begin with, there wasn't much to pack. Tomorrow we'd send our trunks to the ship and depart the day after.

Initially, my desire was to take Ellie on tour of the continent when this venture was completed. But after the intrigue and excitement of Venice, spring would be soon enough for that. In the meantime, Mrs. Fletcher and Thomas, Grannie, and my in-laws would undoubtedly be glad for our return for the holidays.

In the last two days, Venice had experienced the high autumn tide of the *acqua alta*. Though I hadn't experienced the flooded streets upon my last visit, I'd heard of this phenomenon before. My wife was both fascinated and concerned. Luca did much to set her mind at ease when he explained this was an annual occurrence.

Informed or not, when I found her standing at the balcony rail peering into the twilight, I do believe she was monitoring the situation. I came up behind her with Luca's heavy dressing gown and wrapped it around her shoulders. "Here, love, you'll catch your death."

"Thank you." She leaned back against me. After several moments she said, "I've mixed feelings about returning home."

"As do I." I knew exactly the sentiment.

We'd been free to be ourselves for the last few weeks and were loath to leave that freedom behind. Luca's belongings were shipped on ahead to my home. He'd stay with us while he looked for a townhome of his own nearby. I found myself toying with the idea of simply acquiring a larger home, one with enough rooms that we might all live together without scrutiny. Luca's trunks and crates left on an earlier ship, and with them, I'd sent word to Mrs. Fletcher to expect us sometime within the next three weeks. I hoped my missive wouldn't arrive after the fact. But either way, she was a tolerant soul.

We would have our privacy. Mrs. Fletcher lived below stairs and given her advanced rheumatism, rarely ventured to the upper floor unless absolutely necessary. The two maids that came to launder and clean twice a week wouldn't come up unless she directed them.

Before I'd left, I explained to her that her nephew and I had ended our long time relationship but would remain the lifelong friends we were. I also assured her Ellie and I wished her to stay with us always. I loved her like a mother and was certain she'd been charmed by Ellie in the sliver of time prior to our wedding. I knew they'd get along famously.

Luca's brother Paolo, the new head of the family businesses, should arrive tomorrow afternoon, and with his coming, our sleeping arrangements would change. Sleeping with my two loves was another thing I was loath to leave behind. In the past four days, Luca's facial swelling and general bruising had faded, and the patches on his scalp where Bruno had ripped his hair out by the roots had begun to grow back like fine fuzz on a ripe peach. The local physician confirmed the fracture in his collarbone. Outwardly, only the greenish-yellowish shadow left under his right eye and a small cut on his lip declared he'd been pummeled by the man who'd forced a cock in his mouth and came to regret it.

Since Bruno's inexpert castration and broken neck, Luca's spirits had soared. From Vittorio's contacts there was very little found out about the old sod's death. Apparently the Conte had had his fingers in quite a few official pies and mum was the word. Venice was certainly better off without him. Posateri's art collection had been sold sight unseen to a private collector of Luca's acquaintance. The man was ecstatic to have them and the money for their sale was slated to seed a scholarship in Cesare D'Ovidio's name, once Luca got himself settled in London.

***

With Martina busily looking after her brother, Luca made our dinner. He had a fine hand in the kitchen at that. After, we slipped into our dressing gowns for comfort and their ready potential for discard. Cognizant of his physical discomfort, we'd kept our loving to simple caresses while he healed. Tonight was our last opportunity to love one another fully until we were aboard ship. I poured our wine while Luca retrieved his book. As his work had taken him away shortly after he'd acquired it, Luca had yet to view it in its entirety. To say we three were excited was an understatement.

"Will this do? It's rather small… " Ellie had found a hand mirror among the accoutrements on the dressing table just in case we encountered some backward writing.

I nodded. "That should work well enough." I considered the genius of the ambidextrous mind who routinely wrote and painted with both hands, and who composed in backward text as easily as I could write in my normal hand. It was astounding really.

We took ourselves to the massive bed and propped ourselves on the pile of pillows arranged for us at the headboard. Luca situated himself between Ellie and me. A native, he'd translate da Vinci's words for us. Having seen a few pages the day Bruno returned it, I was beside myself now to be able to view it fully.

The book was a simple thing as far as books went. The cover looked to be horse leather with small brass brads decorating the front in such a way that you were certain the design itself meant more than mere decoration. By the binding, it appeared the pages were created individually and bound together instead of it written and illustrated within an already-bound book. Care had been taken to fit the whole of it together precisely and that fact alone told me da Vinci had been the bookbinder.

Luca opened it carefully, though it was surprisingly flexible. Leonardo da Vinci had been a man of invention. I wondered what process was used on the velum that would allow a book of this age to maintain such structural integrity. The flowing script here was not backward and along the edge of the page the same *sfumato* overlay the sketch of a small rearing stallion displaying a rather substantial erection. I knew da Vinci had spent a great deal of his life drawing horses and had been doing so from the time he was a boy. That familiarity with the detail of muscle, sinew, and vein gave a dynamic power to the animal.

Ellie said, "My goodness, it almost looks as though it could trot off the page."

Luca read the first lines:

> *Who holds the rein upon you?*
> *Not I. I only hold the sweet in the palm of my hand.*
> *Come press your velvet here and taste it.*
> *Allow me to ride with abandon,*
> *Feel my sigh against your neck.*

The allegory wasn't lost upon us. The next page held detailed sketches of masturbation by two notably different men. Luca held the mirror to the backward text:

> *You, my heart, are a virtuoso.*
> *Pluck my string,*
> *I beg for nothing more.*

If not for the addition of fingers and for all that it was an extremely erotic pose, the next image was so anatomically perfect it could have been used in a medical text. My cock started to rise and I wasn't the only one who found the image immensely compelling. Luca's robe had parted as his length inched upward over his belly. My wife had a lovely flush upon her cheeks. Luca read for us:

> *There is a fire burning within my veins.*
> *One touch will bring forth the flame.*
> *Touch me. I will burn for you,*
> *And this fire will light our way.*

The next page took my breath away. Done in oil, an angel and devil lay in a *soixante-neuf,* each mouth lavishing attention in exquisite detail. Ellie said, "That reminds me of our first night together, of the way *we* began."

Indeed. Luca and I had demonstrated how men loved while she watched with heated gaze. This was very similar to our first encounter, though who played the devil and who the angel I couldn't say.

"Yes, it does." Luca set the book aside. He wound his hand in Ellie's curls and pulled her across his chest for a kiss. Seeing opportunity, I opened his robe and copied the depiction as best I could. Before long, we immersed ourselves in Leonardo's amazing declaration of love and recreated the painting exactly as he meant Salai to see it. All the while soft hands and lips added the final artistic flourish. Da Vinci, avowedly uninterested in women, might not have enjoyed Ellie's presence in the loving, but we did. Undeniably so.

***

Having finished our sensually-scripted vignettes for the time being, we lay on our bellies comfortably sated and warm under the coverlet. Heads together, we now examined the book in more academic fashion. Starting at the beginning, something caught my eye just as Ellie turned the page. "Wait, love, turn that back if you please."

She asked, "What is it?"

I studied the edges of the image. Was it a trick of light or of age upon the velum? A smudge perhaps? "Luca, hand me the mirror, if you would."

I held the mirror to the *sfumato*. "Am I seeing something that's not there? No, it appears to be script. Luca, are you able to *read* that?"

He looked closely then shook his head. "I see script in the haze of the *sfumato*, but this is not written in Italian."

Ellie squeezed closer, "You're *both* seeing hidden words? Here, let me look." I handed her the mirror. She angled it on the misty edge then gasped, "I see it! It's in French."

The words rolled off her tongue, seasoned as they were by her decidedly American accent. She repeated in English, "*My dearest love, if you have discovered this message, I know that you will find the rest. Use your mind, my love. I adore it in measure with your body and heart.*"

We looked at one another in complete astonishment.

Luca exclaimed, "Amazing!"

Ellie turned the page, "I don't see anything here… "

I perused the four-fisted cocks. Going by where the last was hidden, my eye sought the *sfumato*. I turned the book sideways, and finding what looked to be a flourish in the mist, I set the mirror against it. Sure enough there was another bit of script — this time in Latin. I handed the mirror to Luca. Of the three of us, the professor of antiquities had the best chance of fluency in the ancient tongue. "It appears to be Latin."

Ellie asked, "Can you read it, Luca?"

"Yes. It says, 'Always in the smoke.'"

"*Always in the smoke?*" Ellie shook her head. "What on earth does it mean?"

I explained my interpretation, "*Sfumato* literally means *up in smoke*. The subtle blending of the smoky quality fools the eye into believing the subject and the surroundings are one and the same. Da Vinci pioneered the technique. It's a brilliant way to add nuance, really. So much more can be said, so much more expressed. It allows us to gain a better understanding of the *emotion* behind the art if not the intent. And *all* art is an expression of emotion."

Luca said, "Then I would say from this point on, his messages are to be found in the smoke."

Ellie twirled a corkscrew of silky cinnamon around her finger; a mannerism I'd come to equate with deep pondering. She turned the page to the fellating angel and devil. I studied the oil but could find nothing. Turning on its side didn't help either.

Ellie squeaked, "Wait! Is *that* it?" She turned the book upside down and tapped her finger to the blur of white at the underside of the angel's wing.

It wasn't mirrored writing. The text was simply created wrong-side-up in the detail on the wing where the *sfumato* blurred the feathers into the surroundings. Luca read in Italian "Go no further my love, lest you read the first. Seek *La Scapigliata*. She will show you the way."

Ellie said, "*La Scapigliata?* I'm not familiar with that piece."

I said, "It's also known as *Head of a Woman*. Many consider it to be incomplete. I've always felt he left it exactly where he wanted it."

Luca asked, "Is that the portrait where only the face has been completed?"

"Yes, done in oil on canvas. It hangs in the Galleria Nazionale di Parma. I saw it on my tour several years ago."

"Where's Parma?" Ellie asked.

Luca and I said at once, "In northern Italy."

She asked Luca, "When do you begin your work at the museum?"

"As my work involves travel and winter draws near, it will be March at the earliest."

Her fingers twirled her hair and her eyes sparkled with possibility. The minx was definitely thinking. Chuckling, I asked, "What goes through that pretty head of yours?"

"Speaking only for myself, I tell you: knowing we have clues to follow and nothing to work with will eat me alive."

Luca and I laughed. I looked at him. Seeing the question upon my face, he nodded. I said to her, "Well, we wouldn't want that."

Ignorance does mislead us. O! Wretched mortals, open your eyes!
– Leonardo da Vinci

AFTERWORD

Salvatore faithfully followed the instructions. An invalid's food was often disgusting, and by the surgeon's recipe, this looked to be a foul combination of ingredients. After combining carefully-strained beef broth and warmed goat milk, he added a good dollop of honey, an egg yolk that had been stirred into a bit of cooked farina, and a little olive oil. Preparing for the worst, he tasted it. All in all, the gruel wasn't bad. It was meant to be nourishing and his employer was eager to regain his strength. Filling the invalid feeder with the thin warm paste, Salvatore set it on the tray, alongside a glass of water with lemon. He headed upstairs.

The wound itself was revolting. Being witness to the daily treatment of it turned his stomach. Given the scene when he'd returned from the market, it boggled the mind the man was still alive. Thank god his master was unconscious when he'd burned him. It was so horrific, six days later the stench of burning flesh still filled his nostrils. Hearing voices, Salvatore stood just outside the door. His stomach lurched at the scent of the sulfur and oil-soaked bandages. He would wait.

***

Dr. Paliano carefully undid the bindings and seeing progress, nodded. The glass tube in the urethra remained where he'd inserted it, to keep the urine away from the skin, and to prevent the urethra from closing up under scar tissue. It needed to be turned several times a day so it wouldn't be grown into the flesh. The solution of morphine for pain was allowing the patient to rest, and sulfur on the bandages had kept inflection at bay thus far. Filling his eye-dropper with solution, Dr. Paliano emptied it around the wound. Gently taking hold of the tube, he cautioned, "Now take a deep breath while I turn this."

Despite the morphine anesthetic, the action produced a sharp hiss of discomfort from the patient. Urine and blood trickled from the tube, though it was much less blood than two days before.

Dr. Paliano didn't ask how this horrible maiming, concussion, and hip dislocation had occurred. His patient wasn't the sort of whom you asked too many questions. As it was, he was sworn to secrecy — threatened, more like. As far as the world knew, this man had died. And he would have died, if not for his servant's quick thinking. The butler had cauterized the torn flesh with a red-hot knife from the kitchen. The burning had unfortunately closed the urethra and by the time he'd come to reset the leg and treat the rest, he'd had his work cut out for him inserting the glass tube.

The patient had lost a good deal of blood. Ideally copious fluids would be given, but not with an injury such as this. It required Dr. Paliano to pore over textbooks, learning what the heathens did when they castrated their slaves. While this injury wasn't a full castration, a man losing the head of his penis was in keeping with some of their castration processes. The urethra must be allowed to heal around a rod. The rest was just the common sense of clean bandages and medicines. The healing urethra had necessitated the patient receive only small sips of water for the last three days. Today they'd see how he handled the special broth. He was in desperate need of fluids and it couldn't be put off any longer.

***

The feral growl filled the room as clotted blood and dark urine squeezed through the narrow tube and into the chamber pot, the last of it coming free of blood. The patient managed the broth well enough. The doctor smiled encouragingly. "You're healing well, Conte. You'll soon be your old self." Realizing the absurdity of his last words, he groaned inside. "I mean…"

Conte Bruno leveled an eye at him. "Doctor, let's not be ridiculous."

Dr. Paliano handed him a glass of laudanum and honey, and stammered, "This will allow you to rest and continue to heal." Then he busied himself, applying new bandages.

Conte Bruno downed the tincture in two swallows. Tipping his head to the uncomfortable gauze-wrapped stub and its glass tube protruding like a goose quill, he asked, "How soon before this atrocity is healed?"

"A week, perhaps another ten days."

"Good. I have a debt to repay."

Dr. Paliano blanched. The look on the Conte's face turned the blood in his veins cold. As the patient succumbed to the heavy dose of laudanum, the doctor gathered his things, then hurried from the room.

Book Two

LOVING LEONARDO-
THE QUEST

This book is dedicated to Mead Friday and the extended family who gives steadfast encouragement each week. I love you all. Thank you.

I have been impressed with the urgency of doing. Knowing is not enough; we must apply. Being willing is not enough; we must do.

– Leonardo da Vinci

~1~

With Vittorio recovered from his beating, he and Martina saw to it that Luca's belongings and our larger trunk were bound for England. We'd sent word to Ellie's father, Granny, and Mrs. Fletcher to inform them our honeymoon would continue a few weeks more. As yet, we didn't know where our hunt for Da Vinci's clues would take us, but the moment we arrived in Parma, we'd begin a journal of our own to map our course.

Though the ride was rough on occasion, the coach was private for much of our travel. We put that time to good use by reviewing the book and discussing points of Da Vinci's life that we might have missed on our trip to Venice. The book's poetry and images proved a heady distraction, however, and twice we found ourselves close to surrendering to the love the artist felt for Salai. It wasn't realized unfortunately, for when we'd passed halfway through Verona, we were treated to the company of a priest. With Luca's help over the language barrier, the conversation proved lively. Father Tioretto knew his region well and explained how several main roads intersected here, a major contributor to the density of the population.

I hadn't been to Verona when I'd taken my tour several years before, and passing through now, I found its Roman architecture fascinating, especially the massive amphitheater and the giant arched aqueducts that continued to bring water into the city. At one point, we found ourselves quoting Shakespeare's Romeo and Juliet. Even Father Tioretto joined in.

Ellie said, "I'd read that he never actually went to Verona prior to writing Romeo and Juliet."

Luca translated for the good father, who looked surprised to learn it.

I confirmed Ellie's comment with a nod. "He created an exotic story backdrop for his audience, one that was, in all probability, both foreign and glamorous to anyone watching his play. He might have said Verona was populated by Veronese circus elephants and his audience would have believed it."

Ellie laughed. How I loved to hear it. I was also delighted to discover she appreciated Shakespeare. Images of a future with quiet evenings over cups of tea and recitations of his plays in Mrs. Fletcher's sitting room took my mind. My dear housekeeper was a huge admirer of the Bard and possessed a complete volume of his works, a gift from my father one Boxing Day. I was raised on the various plays. She'd read them to me on rainy afternoons or occasionally before bed. Many an exciting dream came at the end of Macbeth and Coriolanus.

A full day of travel had gotten us to Parma. Tired and hungry, Father Tioretto led us to a sizable and surprisingly well-appointed inn. Even if he didn't know the area well, by the delicious aroma wafting in the street our noses would have eventually led us there. I paid to have our belongings taken inside and made arrangements for the coachman to come gather us the next morning. We asked for baths and the serving maids hurried up the stairs to ready our rooms. We found a quiet corner and ate our fill of the fabulous cuisine. Father Tioretto explained that Parma was famous for its hard, flavorful cheese. Luca added that the Renaissance Humanist, Boccaccio, praised the cheese of Parma in his literary Decameron. Well-read as she was, Ellie had already made the connection. I once more counted my lucky stars to have found these two who not only stimulated my heart and body, but my mind as well.

As he poured our dessert wine, the sociable innkeeper gave directions to the Galleria Nazionale di Parma. The man just so happened to belong to the Farnese family, the original owners of many of the artworks there. According to our host, his line came from Alessandro Farnese. We showed no recognition at the name, spurring him to explain in detail how the world came to know Alessandro as Pope Paul III, and who, as pope, fathered the innkeeper's grandmother several generations back. Father Tioretto apparently didn't care for the conversation and wolfing down his torta, he wished us well and bid us a hasty good night. The innkeeper's ensuing chuckle made me wonder if he'd elaborated the papal bastardy of his lineage on purpose.

When the maid informed us our rooms were ready, we took our wine and glasses and made our way upstairs to our separate rooms to freshen up. Two steaming copper hipbaths on wheels sat near the stove with a towel-draped folding screen between them. Seeing no need for the screen, I hauled it off to the corner. There wasn't much water in the tubs, but certainly enough with which to wash the travel dust away.

I watched my wife prepare herself, standing before the wall

mirror, her tongue poking in concentration as she arranged the pins in her hair and tightened the curls that were want to spill free. Several cinnamon strands wouldn't cooperate and these she rolled around and around her finger until they were tight curls to be tucked under the rest. I was transfixed by the deliberate feminine processes whose end results were suggestive of the coifs of Degas' ballerinas. Thomas was correct. Women were a breed apart, but as the French said, *Vive La Différence!*

She removed her blouse, skirts, and bustle, and for some reason my mind took a different turn. In my mind's eye I saw her naked and gagged with a burlap sack over her head. For two days now my mind had been intermittently taken by that terrible image, followed by an instantaneous albeit short-lived feeling of dread. I couldn't say why, but for some reason I felt it now. The sensation that Thomas often referred to as "a goose walking over a grave." Kneeling, I helped her from her shoes and stockings. Lifting the hem of her camisole, I pressed my forehead to her bare belly and hugged her to me. How I loved this precious nymph.

I'd felt such panic when Conte Bruno abducted her. Perhaps the image was just residual emotion that hadn't time to drain away. Whatever it was, Ellie seemed unfazed by her experience. She was, without doubt, a most intrepid little thing. She'd taken the kidnapping in stride. I, on the other hand, was privy to information she didn't have. Namely, the gang rape Bruno had planned for her. A shiver ran up my spine. In my mind, I pictured the face of the man I'd killed, the moment of surprise on his face just before I'd hit him with the statue of Apollo. I didn't regret the act, but I couldn't deny that had Bruno had more men there that night, her rescue could have gone terribly wrong.

When I glanced up, she was gazing down upon me. Her soft hands swept back my hair. I'd noticed in the past few weeks that we'd developed an unspoken language between us. This undoubtedly came about from our close contact and soul baring conversation, and the fact we had similar minds. Her next words proved how well she'd come to know me.

"What is it, Nicolas? Something is troubling you, I feel it."

I lied. "No, my sweet, I'm only thinking of tomorrow." Her raised eyebrow declared her doubt. Determined not to let her see the dark cloud in my mind, I sought redirection. I kissed her navel then circled it with the tip of my tongue. Meeting her gaze once more, I could see she believed me. I saw something else as well. Indeed I could, for her nipples had gone hard under the cotton of her camisole and her clear blue eyes had turned sultry. She wanted something. My grey thoughts evaporated when she pulled the camisole over her head, an act that left her wearing only her pantalets.

As a newly-wedded man who'd so recently discovered women, I found myself appreciating the mystery of their fashion. Of course I was aware of the structured framework of their undergarments. The artwork of Lovis Corinth and washday at home and all around London told me of pantalets, bloomers, and corsets. But Ellie didn't corset herself. She was such a petite little thing there was no need to artificially hold her figure.

I ran my hands over her cotton-covered thighs and my cock rose in anticipation of what lay beneath. In my life prior to my bisexual self-discovery, I could never have imagined that going through the flounces of lace and frills of a woman's undergarments would make me as giddy as a small child opening a gift on Christmas morning.

Ellie slightly widened her stance in invitation and my cock grew heavy seeing the utilitarian split at the crotch of her pantalets. I turned her. The sleek lines of her back beckoned me to touch, and so I did. I ran my hands over her arms and legs and along her spine as far up as I could reach from my knees, and then followed a similar path up her bare calves. I peeled both sides apart to expose her rounded bottom and caressed and kneaded the flesh before kissing one satin cheek. I couldn't help myself and I bit her lightly. She made a most delightful little sound.

To my further delight, she bent forward and rested her hands upon the edge of the mattress. From this vantage, I was treated to all of her charms. My finger moved of its own volition along her slit, back and forth until she grew wet and slick. I spread her like a ripe fig, and like that suggestive fruit, she was pink and juicy. My tongue followed in a long leisurely swath.

Only when I had her writhing did I stand. My hands circled her waist to her front and found the small bow at her waist. Pulling the drawstring slowly allowed the pantalets to lower a fraction at a time. I dropped my trousers and spared a moment to gaze upon the succulent invitation that lay spread before me. Slick as she was, I smoothly sheathed my cock into the glorious heat. Grabbing her hips, I fucked hard and fast, distantly aware of the sound the bedpost made as it bucked against the wall. It didn't take long to surrender to her climax, those exquisite clenching muscles wresting my own.

Catching my breath, my body draped over her. Only then did I realize Luca stood watching with his spent cock in one hand and satisfaction burning bright in his snow-shadow eyes. White teeth flashing, he withdrew a handkerchief from his pocket, and with it, proceeded to wipe his own crescendo away. Ellie had not yet seen him but I returned his smile.

Ellie turned and my arms enfolded her. She murmured against my lips, "That was wonderful."

Luca said, "That was beautiful, *i miei amori*."

Surprised, Ellie started. She laughed. "I didn't hear you come in."

"I tried to come earlier, but there were too many people in the hall. Instead I finished my bath and came when I could enter unseen. I'm glad I entered when I did. I felt the power of your coupling as if I were between you."

Ellie smiled coquettishly, "As we're students of empiricism, I believe we'll have to test that theory, won't we Nicolas?"

"Indeed." What a minx she was.

Luca laughed.

Without preamble, she said, "Gentlemen, excuse me if you will. My bath will be brief."

I hurried through my own, in part because the water had gone cold, in part because Luca brought his book with him. Within minutes Ellie and I were ready to plot our course of action for the next day.

Joining Luca at the desk, we huddled over da Vinci's book with mirror and extra lamp. I looked at the text again. It was tucked into the individual angel wing feathers wrong-side-up where the *sfumato* blurred the feathers into the surroundings.

Luca translated the Italian for us again. "Go no further my love, lest you read the first. Seek *La Scapigliata*. She will show you the way."

Ellie's eyes were sparkling. "I can't wait."

We spent the next several hours discussing the extraordinary genius of the subtle gradation of tone found in *sfumato*. Unlike other artists of the age, Leonardo applied his range of earthy greens, blues, and browns in a glaze, each watered-down color precisely laid over a base coat. Adding form and depth to the subject and background, this fine application of color allowed the original layer to show through each subsequent layer.

Knowing technique like I did, I explained how this process of layering wasn't generally used among his contemporaries because it was time consuming, taking days to dry between applications. His system allowed him to create the illusion of depth and distance. As an artist in the truest sense of the gift, Leonardo approached painting and sculpture from the mathematical perspective of sacred geometry. This perfect symmetry was what drew the eye all these centuries later.

Though my gaze was drawn time and again to the *sfumato* on each page, we'd agreed, for the time being, to wait and unravel the mystery one page and one message at a time. My imagination devoured the explicit illustrations on each slowly-turned sheet. Luca's eyes met mine over a particularly arousing scene. Returning to the script, he translated for us a most beautiful expression of love.

> *Were I blind, my ears would hear your breath and heartbeat.*
>
> *Were I deaf as well, my nose would find you by the warm scent of your skin.*
>
> *Were I deprived of sight and sound and scent, I'd seek your taste.*
>
> *Were I unable to see and hear and smell and taste, my hands would reach for you.*
>
> *Were I a husk of a man, my heart would know you.*

Ever the minx, Ellie closed the book and set it, and our theories, aside. She went to her trunk and withdrew three silk scarves. These we tied around our heads like blindfolds. Feeling our way to the canopied bed, she drew the velvet curtains closed and we immersed ourselves in total darkness. Deprived of sight, we gave over to our other senses.

I could see why Leonardo blindfolded himself. Submerged in touch and sound, scent and taste, I understood why he sought this heightened sensitivity. Deprived of sight, it was as if I'd been handed a key to unlock my other senses. The dichotomy of experiencing Luca's firm well-muscled body and Ellie's soft slender curves in complete sightlessness thrilled me beyond comprehension. Their breathy sighs and gasps filled my ears. Even the small hairs on my skin were as whiskers on a cat with which to feel their bodies in the stygian night.

I maneuvered on and around my lovers. The lavender ghost of their soap mingled with their heady musk of desire, and I tasted the salt and clean sweat of exertion upon their skin. All of it: sound, taste, touch, and scent painted a picture in my imagination. They were two exquisite dreams made flesh, and I swear I saw the glow of their souls through my blind eyes. We praised one another's perfection with an eye for detail that da Vinci himself would have surely applauded.

Tomorrow we'd find his *La Scapigliata.*

~2~

The Galleria Nazionale di Parma contained a small but exquisite collection of artworks. It held a number of paintings by the pride of Parma, the renowned Antonio Correggio, but only one work by da Vinci.

That morning over breakfast, as our innkeeper ceremoniously delivered dish after delicious dish, he proceeded to tell us more about the Farnese family and that many of the Galleria's masterpieces belonged to them long ago. Ellie told him she was particularly interested in Leonardo da Vinci's works and had heard there were several she might sit and sketch.

The innkeeper smiled sympathetically and said, "*Signora,* it pains me to tell you there is only one da Vinci there."

The disappointment in her lovely eyes must have moved him because he soon surprised us with a letter to the curator who also happened to be a distant cousin. He explained, "I've asked Giuseppe to allow you a quiet space to do your sketching of *La*

Scapigliata. It would be a shame to travel all this way and be disappointed."

Ellie smiled at me. The ship's captain and his borrowed spyglass came to mind. This little minx could charm the birds from the trees.

***

The letter proved invaluable. In addition to my credentials, it gained us a private viewing. The Galleria had few people that early in the day, so Giuseppe closed the hall and allowed us time with it in private. Of course we were cautioned not to touch it, precious work that it was. The moment we were left alone, we went to work poring over the details with our hovering mirror acting as the proverbial fine-toothed comb.

The woman's head was painted oil upon wood and in places it was clear that Leonardo brushed along the natural pattern of the wood's grain. Having become accustomed to looking for hidden messages in the works, it didn't take us long to find them. The mirror-image words popped out at us from the halo of curls around the woman's head.

Ellie asked, "What does it say?"

Luca read from the page,

> *There are three classes of people: Those who see. Those who see when they are shown. Those who never see. After all this time, I know you are one to see. Look closely, my love. You will discover how you dance through my mind, no matter the subject.*

My wife looked at me. "Do you take subject to mean the

person who modeled each artwork for him?"

"I'm not sure. It could also encompass the topic of each work." I stared at *La Scapigliata*. Art historians and critics alike debated on whether or not this work was complete. I'd always thought so, but I now knew, the proof lay before me. I saw the intent behind Leonardo's carefully hidden text. So deep in thought on the matter was I, my eyes unfocused for a moment. Unbelievably, Salai's grinning smile materialized in the curls of *La Scapigliata*. I knew that smile, for I'd seen it clear enough in his works the *Angel Incarnate* and *St. John the Baptist*, both purported to have been modeled by Salai.

Luca said, "By that look in your eyes, I do believe you've found something."

Ellie chimed in excitedly, "What? What did you find?"

My finger hovered over *La Scapigliata's* hair. "Do you see the smile there? See, just there — a pair of smiling lips. Salai's smile."

Luca said, "*Favoloso!*"

Ellie squinted. "No, I don't see…wait! Yes, I do!" She turned to us, her own smile radiant. "Do you suppose we're the first to see these things?"

I nodded. "I'd like to think so, but we have no way of knowing where the book has been since 1524."

She shook her head. "Why since 1524?"

"Salai was shot in a duel that year. It's known he married six months prior to his death. Given the law of the land then, it's highly improbable that his wife settled his estate. His property no doubt went to his closest living male relative. It's said that Salai was in possession of many da Vinci paintings."

Ellie asked, "Was Salai Leonardo's heir?"

"Curiously, no. Francesco Melzi, another favorite da Vinci

apprentice, was his heir. Leonardo was extremely close to both men. Francesco Melzi's artistic ability is very like da Vinci's artistry. In fact, the style in a few of his oils is so similar it's difficult to differentiate between his work and his master's. It's said that Melzi held onto the da Vinci paintings and saw many placed in safe housing. The *Mona Lisa* and several other pieces were in Salai's possession after Leonardo died. We know the *Mona Lisa* became the property of Louis XIV sometime between 1524 and 1547."

Luca said, "That being the case, whoever settled his estate peddled the works to those equipped to pay well. This book is four hundred years old, yet the condition is very good. Most books I've seen from that era show more wear. I'd say wherever it's been through the centuries, it was well cared for."

Indeed. The book was in remarkable condition for its age. As far as *La Scapigliata* was concerned, it appeared we'd found all we were going to find within it, for nothing else was forthcoming.

As we'd earlier determined a catalogue of any text and illustrations found would be a useful reference, Ellie pulled our new journal from her large embroidered bag and handed it to Luca. He drew a fountain pen from his pocket and quickly wrote out Leonardo's words then handed the journal back to her after blowing on the page to set the ink.

Ellie had offered to reproduce, to the best of her ability, any sketches we found along the way. Her pencil poised to begin sketching, she stopped it mid-air as Giuseppe opened the doors to the hall and interrupted our task. He said the Galleria was filling with art enthusiasts asking to see *La Scapigliata*, and apologized for not being able to give us more time alone. We thanked him for our special admittance and the little time we did have.

Ellie quickly roughed in La Scapigliata's face and hair. A particularly nosy patron brashly looked over her shoulder, and said, "*Ben fatto*," before walking on.

Ellie turned to Luca. "Did she say I've drawn it too fat?"

Chuckling, Luca said, "No, *mia amore*. It was a compliment. *Ben fatto* simply means 'well done.'"

Ellie laughed, and after expressing frustration that she only knew a word here or there, vowed to learn his language if Luca would teach her. He was obviously delighted that she asked. She said, "There are too many visitors now. I'll finish the sketch later."

The Galleria Nazionale di Parma was filled with Italian artists from A to Z, and peppered with the occasional El Greco and Van Dyck, but none held our interest for long. As planned, we also stopped at the Romanesque-style Parma cathedral to see the renowned dome. All morning I'd looked forward to sharing with them this impressive artwork of the Renaissance. Of the three of us, only I had seen it before. By the appreciation in their eyes, it was worth the stop.

The scene in the dome above was the *Assumption of the Virgin*. The fresco was painted by Antonio da Correggio, a master of light and shadow, an artist as skilled at dramatic foreshortening as his contemporary, Michelangelo. This technique fooled the eye of those who stood below to view it, for it wrapped art around a curved ceiling. Were the same composition put to canvas, the bodies would be disproportioned and grotesque instead of the beauty seen overhead. After, we returned to the inn for an early dinner then retired to our rooms to pack and chart our next excursion.

***

Luca came just after his bath to find me still in the tub and Ellie sitting near the hearth in her dressing gown drying those cinnamon curls by the fire. He said, "I believe I've found where we go next."

"Excellent." I was just leaving the tub when a knock came at the door. Luca pulled the dressing screen to hide the tub, and ducked behind it with me. Ellie answered the door. The innkeeper had sent a maid with a bottle of wine and his cousin's apology delivered in hesitant English. Apparently the curator felt remorse for our short interlude with the painting we'd come all this way to see. Ellie thanked her in slightly American-gilded Italian, "*Grazie.*"

After closing the door, Ellie peeked behind the screen and said, "I can't say I feel comfortable with how the maid looked around the room just now. But it was very nice of *Signore* Farnese to send the wine, don't you think?"

Toweling off, I replied, "Indeed it was." The room was chilly and I hurried to dress. Luca's sweeping hand caressed my rear as I passed him.

He said, "Ah, I see we need another glass."

Ellie retrieved a water glass from the carafe at the bedside table and got a kiss on the cheek for her resourcefulness.

We huddled at the table with our wine and Leonardo's book and watched as Ellie's talented hand completed the head of *La Scapigliata*. She really was quite proficient. She added Salaì's smiling mouth as she remembered seeing it in the curls. Luca was amazed, for his surprised eyes met mine over Ellie's head. Having been mesmerized by this woman for the past few weeks and finding her clever across the board, I wasn't surprised to find she possessed a knack for artistry. Indeed, it was my understanding that the education of females leaned heavy on the arts because it was thought they didn't have the minds for stronger stuff. That was laughable. My little Yank could go toe-to-toe with any academician of my acquaintance.

Luca and I complimented her skill and got a beauteous smile for the effort. Finished now, she said, "Just think, no one alive is aware of these messages."

Luca chuckled and shook his head. "It still amazes me. I bought the book on a whim never imagining it held such a secret."

I asked my companions, "So, where do we go next?"

Luca flipped through the pages until he came to the angel and devil lying in a *soixante-neuf*. Here we found the message hidden in the angel's wing. He scribbled the text and then read:

Go no further my love, lest you read the first. Seek La Scapigliata. *She will show you the way.*

Ellie frowned. "We didn't see a clue as to where to go next."

I thought a moment. I knew we must look to the smoky sfumato for there in the subtle blending of hazy edges we'd find delicious snippets of affection tucked away expressly for one person's eyes. Eyes that knew how to see.

Luca turned the page and the obvious neatly tapped me on the forehead. The next page was Salai's face in profile. I'd seen it before — straight nose, strong chin, full lips. Alongside it, a sketch of a much younger Salai, his face in three-quarter profile with large expressive eyes, his notably curly hair wild and unkempt, reminiscent of Heinrich Hoffmann's *Struwwelpeter*. We studied the images a long while. I could see nothing.

Luca shook his head. "I'm sorry, I don't see a thing."

Ellie said, "It must be here. Remember what Leonardo wrote. Those who see. Those who see when they are shown. Those who never see."

Something niggled at the back of my mind. See. There was a recurring theme in the message. I told them, "I do believe we're looking for an eye."

Ellie looked from me to the page, "How did you determine that?"

I explained how I interpreted *La Scapigliata's* hidden message.

Luca nodded, "Ah. The words themselves a clue."

I heard my wife gasp. I asked, "What is it?"

"What would you say if I thought we should fold this page?"

I eyed the four-hundred-year-old vellum and saw what she saw. There were two parallel creases in the page. I ran my finger along the obvious folds. I looked at Luca. It was his book, so whether we folded pages or not was his decision. His snow-shadow eyes widened and he turned the page. He smiled. "Go on, fold it."

Ellie carefully folded back the page along the creases. The image produced by that simple feat appeared instantly. We smiled at one another. There on the page a very large, very detailed, human eye. It was Salai's eye without a doubt.

Noticing scraps of backward script tucked into the patchwork of folds, I handed the mirror to Luca. I directed his gaze with my pointing finger. "There Luca, just there. See it?"

"I do. It says: *Written in stone in the Wilderness.*"

My wife made a pretty moue. "*Fiddlesticks.* What does that

mean? Surely not statuary?"

Luca said, "I take it to mean a painting or sketch of stone."

I repeated the words. *Written in stone in the Wilderness.* Leonardo painted several notable pieces in which grottos figured prominently. I voiced the thought.

Luca nodded. "This makes sense."

She looked at him. "What makes sense?"

"Vinci, the land of his birth, is in the Tuscan hills. There are many rocky visages there."

I thought back to my school days. I'd read Giorgio Vasari's account of da Vinci's life. I knew he had an affinity for animals and did not eat meat. He also loved to explore the mountains. His writings evinced a fascination with caves and grottos and one of his earliest memories involved a cave. Coming upon it, he was both fearful of the great monster that might live within it, and fascinated by the thought that he might actually discover something new. That rocky crag made its appearance in the background of so many of his known works, from the *Mona Lisa* to *Virgin on the Rocks.* Artwork upon artwork flipped through my mind: *Madonna of the Carnation, Madonna Litta, The Virgin and Child with St. Anne.* Even the disputed *Mary Magdalene* had the same rock formations in the background, though my colleagues steadfastly attributed that piece to Giampietrino, a member of Leonardo's studio who regularly painted women of the Bible.

No, I saw it now. The rocks were undoubtedly significant in some personal way. It struck me now though that I couldn't credit from whence my certainty came. I said, "I believe we are to seek his *St. Jerome in the Wilderness.*"

Ellie asked, "And where do we find it?"

"In Rome."

Art is never finished, only abandoned.
– Leonardo da Vinci

~3~

With stops along the route to rest the horses and ourselves, it took us five days to travel from Parma to Florence. Accepting Luca's offer, we stayed in the Franco home at their *vigna*. Within minutes, we were welcomed with opened arms and opened bottles to toast our marriage. It was easy to fall in love with Luca's hospitable family, and the family wines.

We'd previously met Luca's brother Paolo the morning of our departure from Venice. He was a pleasant-looking fellow with the same snow-shadow eyes and black hair as his brother. But Luca was lean, while the younger brother was stocky. Luca also possessed a straight nose while Paolo's nib was decidedly rounded. Like Luca, Paolo had a ready smile. I found the same true for his other siblings. His three sisters and middle brother all had raven hair and those lovely eyes, though on the youngest sister they were a sky blue. They really were a handsome lot, the Francos.

Their expansive villa wasn't the gilded lily of the *fandaco*, but it was by no means spartan. Comfortably appointed and modest by comparison, it was no less a statement that the Francos did well in their various businesses. The house sat on the highest ground, and a glance out any window gave a splendid view of the vineyard. With the last of the grapes cut and the pressing underway, the air was filled with an indescribable sweetness in the morning; however, the scent turned cloying by mid-day. After two days, Luca said he preferred the heavy green scent of the olive presses to this over-sweet perfume.

While true the family was aware of Luca's predilection, I thought it prudent to keep ourselves to our separate bedrooms. Ellie and I felt his absence in our bed, for not a night had not passed in one another's arms since we first came together as lovers aboard ship. By the look on his face the next morning, Luca missed us as well. Sharing one's most vulnerable state — sleep — with others is a most profound declaration of trust. The way we wound comfortably around one another to sleep reminded me of the foxhound pups our stableman reared in the stable. To them, a belly full of milk and warm littermates to sleep against meant all was right with the world.

Once more I was met by questions of how to make our lives fit this world that would keep the three of us from loving fully. To those who knew and loved him best, his doting on Ellie came as a surprise. At one point, his youngest sister took him aside and cautioned that if his attraction to Ellie was obvious to them, it might be to me as well. We learned later that he simply said he was in love with us both, so she shouldn't be concerned. I can only imagine her thoughts after that declaration.

Fortified by breakfast and supplied with wine, fruit, and

cheese, we made our farewells and resumed our travel to Rome. Our first stop: the town of Vinci, a small village perched in the craggy mountains outside of Anchiano.

***

The town of Leonardo's birth was quite picturesque. The red rooftops, shrubby uneven landscape, and arched bridges brought to mind the idyllic sunlight and shadow imagery of Nicolas Poussin's *Cinders of Phocion*. There was surprisingly little here to commemorate Leonardo da Vinci's life, though we did hear, through casual conversation with the hotel's porter, that the city councilmen regularly ruminated over the idea of a museum dedicated to their favorite son.

From Vinci, we headed south. Captivated as we were by the life and times of Leonardo, we forwent the comfort of train travel to cover the route as the artist himself had. We understood from the outset that much of the journey would be a rough ride. During our last four days in the coach, Ellie commented more than once on the condition of the roads. It wasn't a complaint, merely an observation. And understandable, as our coachman literally negotiated over a coach-tossing, rut-riddled goat path to paved stone and back again. When my wife compared the tracks to some of the worst we'd encountered on our whirlwind race to matrimony in Scotland's Gretna Green, there was no argument from me. Indeed. I found myself thankful for the intermittent and remarkably functional tracts laid down by Caesar. Our sore backsides certainly added to our sensorial immersion.

We arrived late in the afternoon and booked our rooms in the long standing Albergo del Sole. Our suite on the second story was small, as one might expect in a fifteenth-century inn, but we couldn't find fault with the view. Our quarters faced the fountain with its Egyptian obelisk in the center, and the ancient Pantheon just beyond. Luca procured a room two doors down.

Rome was a bustling place with beggars and pilgrims packing the streets like so many sardines in a tin. Human nature being what it is, we decided to remove temptation and paid to have Ellie's entire trousseau and my trunk brought into our rooms. There may be pious devotion here, but as we witnessed a half-dozen pickpockets in action, we were certain the counterbalance had a strong footing too.

I stood at the window looking down upon the busy street while Ellie attended to her toilette. I'd been in Rome on my grand tour and this visit, as the last, filled me with the same dichotomy of emotion. My eye was caught by a shriveled slovenly woman begging on the street below who had a babe in arms and no fewer than seven hungry, filthy children in orbit around her skirts. Within a few feet, a rotund cardinal with his bright red robes and matching wide-brimmed *biretta* walked by happily devouring his pastry. He didn't give the starving children a second glance, not even the toddling child who held a beseeching hand out as he walked by. The sad image took my mind as I dug for a handkerchief in the top compartment of my trunk. The entire city was a dichotomy, and I did not like it here.

With a stack of coin tied up in my handkerchief, I returned to the window and whistled for the mother's attention. Waving her closer, I tossed the bundle out the window. The tallest of the lot, I assume her eldest, ran to pick it up, then hurried back to his mother excitedly. She looked up at me tearfully and smiling, called something in a hard-edged language I didn't understand but which I took for *Romani*. I returned the smile and tipped my head to her. I didn't know from whence she'd come, nor why she was here in this city of extremes, but I'd given her enough coin to see her brood fed for the month, at least. If I were able to converse, I would have suggested she use part of the money to leave this place.

I supposed the heart would harden over time to sights so unfortunately common, but I couldn't help but wonder about the papist who walked by without indication he'd seen the hungry children. I determined that for some, the sea of needy humanity was too great and unending. I knew the Carmelites and The Little Sisters of the Poor saw to the needy elsewhere in the world. It seemed to me there must be such helping hands here, of all places on earth.

Threading her arms through mine from behind, Ellie peered over my shoulder. Luca too had come in and stood beside me. Apparently they'd seen my charitable act. She said, "I'm so glad I proposed and you accepted. You're a husband a woman can be proud of."

I chuckled, "Is that so?"

She pressed against me. "Yes. That was very nice of you, Nicolas."

Luca caressed my other shoulder. "Yes, it was." He recited the words of Jesus according to Matthew, "Whatever you did for one of the least of these brothers and sisters of mine, you did for me."

"Ah, well, a drop in a bucket, really." Seeing to their least brothers and sisters had been one memory I still had of my parents. Young as I'd been when they died, I could still recall how active they'd been in several charities, charities Grannie and I still supported in their memory. Now, I watched the woman leave.

She moved like schooner through that sea of humanity with her string of little dinghies following behind. And the place where she'd stood in the square below was soon filled with other beggars and their prosperous counterparts. The sun was going down and the autumn night would be cold. Perhaps that little family would sleep warm tonight. I pictured the ragged poor huddled hungry and shivering in dark corners while fat cardinals dined like kings and slept on their featherbeds. It all made me feel quite low. My companions must have sensed it, for they drew me away from the balcony and closed the doors behind us.

***

Early the next morning, we took our meal in the cramped dining hall before heading to the Vatican Museums. I thought back to my first encounter with the Holy See's collection. I'd just turned twenty when I'd taken my tour of the continent's various galleries, both public and private, peppered throughout many countries and principalities. Books in hand and fresh from the university, the vast Vatican museums were a highlight.

The Musei Vaticani was among the greatest museums in the world. Indeed, the immense collection required several salas to hold it all. These galleries were filled with renowned classical sculptures and notable masterpieces collected by the Roman Catholic Church since its inception. As I couldn't recall what gallery I'd seen it in years before, we had only the vaguest idea of where to look for St. Jerome. It was decided we'd divide our attentions between the two likeliest salas.

The same sad dichotomy that filled my mind the night before returned upon seeing the castrated statues. Following the glory of the Renaissance, the church wielded an edict in the form of a hammer. The Council of Trent met to condemn the principles and doctrines of Protestantism, and as long as they were at it, they decided to clarify the doctrines of the Church. This included banning the representation of genitals, buttocks, and breasts in the art of the church. And they didn't limit this zeal to future acquisitions.

To an art historian, this edict was tantamount to a crime against humanity, for it entailed the mutilation and defacement of countless masterpieces. And here it was all around me: poorly-executed attempts to hide those God-given sexual attributes — a loin cloth here, a robe there, and *castrati* as far as the eye could see — and the butchery covered with plaster fig leaves. I'd read that series of popes had each come to the visually sinful problem with different solutions. While one pope was content to merely deface the oils with modest coverings, another saw the works destroyed outright. Carlo Posateri came to mind.

Other popes saw no reason to destroy such beauty so obviously inspired by god, not when offending backsides could be turned to the wall and cocks hacked off with a simple hammer strike. Then came popes with artistic sensibilities. They brought about the plaster, bronze, and gypsum fig leaves to not only cover the damage but to reflect Adam's shame. And also, I thought, to remove lustful thoughts from the ranks of unnaturally-celibate men, as well as from their own deviled minds.

Ellie broke me from my reverie when she leaned close to ask, "Do you suppose they kept them all?"

I looked at her dumbly then shook my head, unable to determine where the perfect machine of her mind had gone. "Kept what, my dear?"

She whispered for my ears alone. "The penises. Do you suppose they kept them all?"

My laughter echoed through the gallery. Her mouth twitched and she playfully slapped my arm. I told her, "Given the sentiment that led to their removal, I'm certain of it."

I imagined the disembodied cocks — stone and ivory contraband hidden in coffers between layers of church robes to be viewed in private. My mind took a turn and lighted upon the ancient carved ivory, jade, and ebony phalluses of Asia. And just as I was about to give over to headier images as they might relate to this experientially inquisitive creature at my side, Luca found us. He said, "I've found our St. Jerome."

***

The painting hung at the end of the far gallery, between Caravaggio's *Deposition from the Cross* and *Raphael's Liberation of St Peter*. Close examination revealed the fine repair across St. Jerome's torso. I knew the panel had been cut in two and repaired. A story among art enthusiasts held that Napoleon Bonaparte's uncle found the upper portion of the wooden panel being used as a tabletop, and years later came across the bottom portion employed as a shoemaker's bench.

Hanging between completed works, it certainly looked the unfinished painting it was purported to be. It seemed the artist tired of the work and simply walked away. I remembered holding that same opinion of my contemporaries when I'd seen it years ago. But seeing it now, I was of a different opinion. I now knew Leonardo explored his craft as keenly as Livingstone and Stanley explored the Nile. I could envision the hand at work now that I better understood the artist's drive. Perhaps he tested a new formula for tempera on the panel, perhaps an experimental paint of the sort he used on the Last Supper. He might have used more yolks, a different oil, or new mineral pigment. I stared at the fine detail, trying to read the artist's mind.

For the most part, the painting was complete. On the left were da Vinci's rocks, the same craggy hills that appeared in so many paintings and sketches, rocks I now associated with the Tuscan hills. To the right, an unfinished church. Knowing the man's philosophy as I did, this unpainted portion made sense to me. Born and raised in the Catholic doctrine, his scientific works offended church orthodoxy. He based his beliefs on reason and on what he discerned from his senses.

St. Jerome dealt with harsh criticism back in its day, the same way Leonardo dealt with harsh criticism is his day. I wondered if he drew a parallel in his mind when he created this artwork. The few pieces of his art he kept for himself certainly reflected the man he was. Perhaps his St. Jerome had been commissioned like the other religious works he'd done, those paid for by men more adherent to doctrine than him. Perhaps the proverbial well for this painting had run dry, and so was abandoned.

"I see it," Ellie whispered excitedly. "It's backward though."

Luca asked, "Where?"

Her finger traced the air before her. "Just there, along the lion's backbone. A few words only, as far as I can see."

I looked closer. It was there all right, in the unfinished lion which St. Jerome befriended upon removing a thorn from its paw. We'd need to use the mirror, but we weren't alone and the last thing we wanted to do was draw attention to our singular task. Scanning the delicate script, my breath caught as the painting took form before my eyes. The overall design was angular, as St. Jerome's emaciated bones cut sharp angles and planes against the backdrop of vertical lines of stone. These things couldn't be missed. But the lion, unfinished though it was, was curled into a fluid backward "S," for Salai, I knew. Now I understood that this painting was meant to be unfinished, whether or not Leonardo started out with that in mind. It was incomplete in one sense, and whimsically complete in another. It was meant to be seen by those who possessed eyes to see.

Breaking my contemplation, Ellie said, "Well, we don't want people to know what we're up to. How do we get a moment alone…with…" she stopped mid-sentence, that sentient smile of hers turning the corners of her pink lips.

I chuckled. "What's going through that perfect mind of yours?"

The smile widened prettily. She turned to Luca and handed him the small mirror stored inside her reticule. "Move quickly." With that, she turned on her heel and walked to the opposite side of the hall. A moment later she shrieked loudly, "Oh there's a rat, a rat! Nicolas! Oh, I feel…I feel—" she swayed on her feet and three gentlemen rushed forward to catch her before she crumpled to the floor in a feigned faint.

All heads in the gallery turned toward her. On cue, I rushed to her side and the good Samaritans made room. I gathered the actress in my arms as a throng of concerned museum goers closed around us. A well-meaning woman thrust an opened fan in my hand. I loosened my wife's collar and fanned her. "Are you alright, my dear?"

I heard Luca behind me. "Is Ellie unwell?"

Hearing him, her eyes fluttered and she slowly came 'round.

Handing the fan back to its owner with my thanks, I helped Ellie to her feet. She smiled feebly when she told the throng sincerely, "I'm so sorry to have been a bother. I saw a rat." To me she said, "You know how afraid I am of those nasty beasts."

For the final act, I patted her hand. "Well, it's gone now my dear, so ease your fears. Let's get you back to our rooms so you can rest."

***

We'd just returned to our room when the skies opened in a downpour. In anticipation of the storm, the maids had recently stoked the ornate ceramic stove. They'd been so thorough that were the room dark, we'd most likely see the heater's afterglow. Ellie pulled the pins from her hat and hastily opened the top button of her blouse. "My goodness, it's hot in here."

How right she was. I discarded my coat, and immediately saw to my collar and cuffs.

"Ugh, I simply must get out of these heavy skirts. Be a dear and open the terrace door before I melt."

I chuckled. "Please don't. I like your solid form far too much." My words brought laughter from her. I smiled. Her ready appreciation of humor was one of her most endearing traits. Opening the door a crack to let the chilly November air balance the temperature, I was careful to keep my eyes from the theater of humanity below. That morning, two young ragamuffins had tugged at my heart strings and I found myself buying them bread. It was all I could do not to empty my purse.

Lamenting of female discomforts recently appeared, Ellie went to the lavatory to freshen up. If I was ever in the dark regarding such womanly details before my marriage, my bold-as-brass

Yankee wife ensured my education. The poor miss.

In anticipation of Luca and his book, I adjusted the gaslight above the writing table for greater illumination. An instant later, he knocked softly before letting himself in. He no sooner closed the door behind him than a porter with glasses and wine knocked on it. The man cleanly and swiftly dispatched the cork then waited patiently for his coin which Luca paid before seeing him out.

I looked at the wine and raised a brow. "Celebrating, are we?"

Luca set his small stack of books on the desk, and poured three glasses. Ellie joined us in the sitting room. Handing her a glass, he said, "Wine to ease you, *caro*. When my sisters were younger, our mother gave them wine to ease their monthly discomfort."

It made perfect sense to me.

Ellie replied, "Yes, it does help. Thank you for thinking of it."

She pulled out her own chair and sat herself before he or I could react. Though she followed customary decorum in public, one of her more American mannerisms was casually seeing to herself before either of us gentlemen could anticipate her. I was of the opinion this self-sufficient manner was gleaned from her father's single parenting. I found this contrast to other ladies of the peerage singularly refreshing.

Shrugging out of his coat, Luca declared, "*Mio Dio*. And I thought my room too warm."

It was still rather stifling, even with the terrace door opened to the rain. With a wink at Luca, I stripped to my small clothes. He chuckled and did the same. Ellie must have noted the careful manner in which Luca discarded his clothing, for she asked him about it. "Is your collarbone paining you in the dampness?"

"A small amount, yes."

I read his body as he undressed. He was healing well, as one might expect from a strong and virile man, but reading the nuance as I do, I'd watched him grow increasingly uncomfortable as the day wore on. I thought about dear Mrs. Fletcher's rheumatism and determined the storm brought his discomfort. Her condition was certainly a regular barometer to such things; her left knee a veritable Nostradamus of weather forecasts. The patches of Luca's ripped-out hair were filling in nicely, the sparse areas only visible when fingers raked through the silk. Time would heal his broken bone. If only it would heal the rent in his heart left by Cesare's murder.

"We don't need this open to the damp." Ellie made to close the terrace doors but stopped midway when we both asked her not to. The room was still far too warm.

"Just a tad, then." She left it slightly ajar and excused herself, only to return a moment later wearing her bloomers and the camisole with the delicate lacework windows that allowed her skin to glow through the fabric like one of Raphael's Sybils. She said, "There, now we're all more comfortable! So what exactly did we find today?"

I explained the backward S in the curve of the lion's body, and my insights into the possibility that the work was left unfinished because the person who'd commissioned it couldn't pay or quite possibly changed his mind. As an afterthought, I added it was also possible Leonardo redid the work on another panel and the completed piece disappeared like so many other artworks over time.

Luca said, "Prior to my meeting the both of you, my interest mainly encompassed da Vinci's scientific study. I hadn't considered his artworks much beyond the few pieces I'd encountered in Italian galleries or books. Just how many are there?"

I shook my head. "When taken as a whole, there aren't really that many known works to be viewed, a handful only. But there must have been dozens, as he painted for decades. Many artists copied him, however. And some are remarkable forgeries. By last count, fifteen have been confirmed, and a half-dozen remain in dispute."

Frowning, Ellie said, "*Fiddlesticks.* Then we'll never find them all." She sipped her wine.

"This is true. We'll have to be content with what's available." For the first time, I realized our venture could end on the next page. I certainly hoped not. Sharing art with my two loves filled my heart and soul in ways words could barely express.

Pulling our journal from the bottom of his stack, Luca said, "My time to use the mirror there was brief, but I think I have them all, hopefully enough to continue our quest. Before I begin, I'd like to say you were a brilliant actress today, *caro mia.* Your ruse allowed me to check the image unseen."

I smiled. Since her abduction, Luca had taken to addressing Ellie as "my dear" or "sweetheart," just as I did. He generally referred to us both as his loves.

"Thank you." Mirth danced in the sprite's eyes as she caressed his cheek. Her next words made us chuckle. "Come to think, I should have taken a bow, no?"

My Lady Elenora Halstead was really unlike any woman I'd ever known. Her quick study and ready resourcefulness gained us time to find the clue. I watched Luca turn his face to kiss her palm. They were both utterly charming and that charm danced delightfully along my nerves. How I wanted them.

Back to the business at hand, Luca said, "There wasn't much to see. It appeared to me the St. Jerome had been repainted, so I suppose there might have been more words initially."

I explained Bonaparte's uncle and the story of the two panels.

"Ah." Luca translated the few words aloud: *The perspective of disappearance.*

Then he looked up, obviously confused. "I have no idea what this means."

"Nor do I," Ellie said. She too met my eyes, those delicate brows of hers rising expectantly.

But I knew. Through my training I'd learned the term Leonardo da Vinci himself had coined. The "perspective of disappearance," referred to an atmospheric perspective, that is, the visual effect of light passing through the atmosphere. Prior to the artistic renaissance of da Vinci's time, artists conveyed distant objects by painting them higher and smaller on the picture plane. They did so with the same full detail and color saturation of anything depicted in the foreground. It was disconcerting to the eye and confusing to the mind to see things floating in a disembodied way. By contrast, Leonardo was well aware that features and objects appeared lighter with less detail as they receded into the distance. Unlike the artists who preceded him, that was how he painted, and this attention to the obvious gave his drawings depth and reality.

I explained that nuance of color had captivated Leonardo. His many notebooks were filled with observations on the subtle colorings of the world. In his writings, he was especially fascinated by the color blue and especially how it related to his thoughts on the "perspective of disappearance." I told them I'd once read an observation of his in a book from the university library:

Thus if one is to be five times as distant, make it five times bluer.

Ellie asked, "Why blue?"

I revisited the book in my mind. It had been transcribed from Leonardo da Vinci's own words:

> *An object will appear more or less distinct at the same distance, in proportion as the atmosphere existing between the eye and that object is more or less clear. Hence, as I know that the greater or less quantity of the air that lies between the eye and the object makes the outlines of that object more or less indistinct, you must diminish the definiteness of outline of those objects in proportion to their increasing distance from the eye of the spectator.*

I clarified, "Through his experimentation, he found that in order to correctly render objects at a distance, they needed to be painted fainter and bluer as they receded." Seeking to educate, I gave a nod to the window. "Were we to look out that window in the light of day, we'd see a faint blue haze in the distance. We might see buildings or the trees beyond, perhaps sheep and goats in the hills. Whatever we see, the further away they are, the lighter they appear. The objects in the distance fade into the background as the scene disappears, and all would be shrouded by a faint haze. This haze is normally blue, but depending on the time of day and atmospheric conditions, it could also be reddish or golden. This was the effect of atmosphere noted in Leonardo's books — the more distant the objects were, the more their true colors paled, the more they took on the faint blue of the surrounding atmosphere."

Ellie said, "What a fascinating observation. He seems to have focused on creating a haze, wouldn't you agree? The *sfumato* and now this blue 'perspective of disappearance.' One element is smoky and the other hazy. It seems to me they are actually one and the same."

I nodded. "Yes, that belief was held by more than one of my professors. It's mine also."

Her eyes went from Luca's to mine. "I recall what you said about *sfumato* playing a role none of us knows, Nicolas. That da Vinci's intent might have been to blend the subject and the surroundings, to fool the eye of the observer into believing subject and surrounding were one and the same. Michelangelo peppered the ceiling in the Sistine Chapel with sheaves and acorns in defiant symbolism. Perhaps the haze is Leonardo's own stab at metaphor, but symbolism is potent only if understood."

Luca said, "Perhaps that's exactly what it is then. By applying this signature haze to his work, he sought to imbue greater meaning than the subject and surroundings implied."

Ellie added, "I'm fascinated by his reasoning. Suppose the smoke and haze were deliberate clues specifically placed for those whose perceptivity was developed enough to see Leonardo's deeper meaning?"

She had a point. I no sooner voiced the thought when Leonardo's message to his lover came instantly to my mind as if the artist planted had it there himself.

Those who see. Those who see when they are shown. Those who never see.

I saw the understanding take root in the variegated blue of their eyes, as if they too heard the artist whisper in their ear. The three of us blurted at once, "For those who see!"

That got a good chuckle going. How synchronized we were. I looked at their expectant faces, hungry as they were for answers or opinions. I gave them mine. "The haze lends greater meaning to the artwork because it implies exactly that. If we take St. Jerome, for example, the hard stone, much of it phallic in nature, surrounds him. Leonardo's interpretation suggests Saint Jerome fought an internal struggle with celibacy. Or perhaps this struggle lay within the artist himself."

Luca asked suddenly, "What year was this painted?"

"I believe Leonardo began painting it in 1482. Why do you ask?"

"Leonardo was a man often subjected to bouts of melancholy. There are addendums in his writings — scribbles in the margins and so on — showing how he was feeling at certain times in his life. I believe it was 1482 when he wrote in the margin of his *Codex Atlanticus*, 'Why do you suffer so?' He answers just below, 'The greater one is, the greater grows one's capacity for suffering. I thought I was learning to live; I was only learning to die.' This is telling, no?"

We three sat quiet for a time. Leonardo had come to mean much to us, and the thought of that great mind mired in pained turmoil sat heavy in our hearts. Familiar with the temperament of artists as I was, I realized he might have wanted to capture such depth of despair in his art. There were many artists who used their artistic expression as catharsis.

Before I'd left London, I'd dined with one of my mentors, Professor Carlisle, who had recently returned from The Hague, where he'd been on holiday visiting his Dutch wife's family. There he'd been introduced by his in-laws to a promising artist by the name of Vincent Willem van Gogh. The man was in the process of relocating and so wished to sell several of his artworks. After a lengthy discussion with both artist and in-laws, in Carlisle's opinion, the dramatic changes in the man's style paralleled the bouts of severe melancholy the artist was known to have.

As all art begins with emotion, it seemed logical that an artist's state of mind would influence his art. Whilst on my tour, I'd met an Impressionist in Paris who'd been mired in grief over the loss of his wife some years before. Having seen several of his paintings, I could easily discern vast difference in his style and technique before emotional suffering became a daily companion in his life. The man, Claude Monet, once painted life and motion in plein-air impressionism, and now he painted solitude. Edgar Degas too suffered from bouts of melancholy. His *L'Absinthe, The Amateur*, and several other works depicted sad or dejected faces with such intensity that one couldn't help but feel the pain. I explained this to my companions.

Ellie said, "How sad that is. Do you suppose Leonardo painted St. Jerome when in such a state?"

"It's entirely possible." Redirecting, I tapped a finger to the vellum page before us. "So if we go by nothing other than this book, we know Leonardo's art holds more than meets the eye. I'd say the 'perspective of disappearance' will play a role in where we go next."

My wife turned the page. "Then the next clue lies within the blue of the distant landscape."

I looked at the art before me. There, a nude Salai reclined on his pallet, his signature wild hair sketched in such a way as to suggest it moved in a breeze. Posed with one finger near the corner of his mouth and his other hand cupping himself invitingly, he looked as if he slept. Behind him an opened window, and through it, a series of phallic shaped rocks jutted up to the sky reminiscent of a copperplate print I'd once seen of Turkey's chimney stones of Cappadocia.

Ellie's finger hovered over the page. "I don't see anything in the sketch that suggests where we go next. Perhaps a clue lies in the text?"

Luca held the mirror and translated the Italian:

> *I watch you sleep and wonder upon the subject of the dreams that occasionally bring a smile to your lips. Do you dream of me? For I surely dream of you. This is my dream be I awake or asleep.*

My companions looking as perplexed as I. Determined to glean the message I was certain we'd find there, I returned to the page and laid the mirror on the vellum. I turned the book slowly. The image and text reflected in the mirror like bits of colored glass in a kaleidoscope. Finding the hidden message of desire, I chuckled.

Luca laughed. "I know that look. What have you found for us?"

Removing the mirror, I showed them the small curved lines here and there. Unseen without the aid of the mirror to make them whole, there were no less than a dozen stiff phalluses, and four of these had wings!

Seeing the flying cocks, Ellie burst into laughter.

Four winged cocks headed to the window. A clue, perhaps? I studied at the opened window drawn above the sleeping Salai and suddenly knew we were to go to France. I couldn't credit why this next thought came to me. If I were a spiritualist, I'd believe the ghost of Leonardo himself had spoken to my mind. I voiced it.

Still pink-cheeked and smiling, Ellie asked, "What makes you say that?"

"A feeling only. I don't think we're to find any other clues here. Notice the winged phalluses flying to the window? Do you recognize that view in the distance?"

They both leaned forward to peer at the page. Luca said, "The rocks of Tuscany, no?"

"I believe so. That same view can also be seen in the *Virgin of the Rocks.*"

Ellie frowned. "But aren't there two da Vinci paintings by that name?"

"There are." I closed the book and clapped my hands together. "I propose we head to the Louvre first, and then we'll return home for the holidays."

~4~

Shifting the heavy pitcher of lemon water and the goblet to his other hand, Salvatore lightly rapped on the door.

"Entrare," the Conte called from across the room. The luxury of a full bath had only recently been granted by the doctor. He eased himself into the hot water and issued a sharp hiss at the tenderness between his legs. Still fearful of the healed edges opening, he looked down at the stub of his cock to be sure it was okay. The refraction of the water made it look even smaller. Frowning, he turned his attention on the manservant begging his pardon.

"*Scusi*, Conte Bruno. Gino and Celso have finished their meal and have taken the room across the hall should you have need of them."

Bruno nodded. "Good. What have you learned?"

"I've just finished speaking with Tito Farnese, the innkeeper. You were right, my Conte. He said a little better than two weeks ago, a British husband and wife and an Italian man who traveled with them stayed here. They'd come to see The Galleria Nazionale di Parma, specifically *La Scapigliata*. The Lady wished to make a sketch of it. Signore Farnese made arrangements with a relative at the galleria that she would have time alone with the artwork. I believe these people to be Lord and Lady Halstead, and Luca Franco."

"Interesting."

His servant poured yet another glass of lemon water. Intent on preventing an infection in the bladder, the doctor insisted Bruno drink several liters of lemon juice and water a day. Not only was it hard to hold his urine on rough carriage rides, so he'd pissed himself more than once, he'd come to loathe the scent of lemon. He took the offered goblet and sipped it unenthusiastically. "Did you ask to speak with the staff working during their stay here?"

"Uh, no. Conte Bruno."

Bruno cast a disgusted eye.

"I'll see to that immediately, my Conte." With that, the man turned on his heel and left.

For the hundredth time, Conte Bruno gently assessed his headless cock. He could still feel, though nothing so pleasurable as before. Biting back his pooling frustration, he washed his face. Several weeks had passed. The doctor assured him his strength would return but to expect it to come slowly as his injuries had been severe. Noting his fatigue, Bruno washed himself quickly then sat back in the hot water and closed his eyes.

He'd kept his recovery a secret and managed to leave Venice undetected, the façade easily erected as nearly all of Venice thought him dead. Only the doctor, Salvatore, Gino, and Celso, knew the extent of his injury. The handful of wealthy men privy to the truth that he was alive had no idea he'd been emasculated. They had no notion of why he preferred secrecy but they'd kept their lips closed and acted as though he'd died. Deviates all, they had false personas with their wives and children, and to a man they feared him and the information he held. Of course they would keep their silence.

Salvatore returned several minutes later to find the Conte rising from the tub. He hurried to dry him off.

Without preamble, Bruno raised a brow, "And?"

"I've learned Lord and Lady Halstead stayed in this very room, my Conte. I also learned the maid felt they shared their bed with their companion."

The Conte whirled around and met the man's eyes. "What makes her say that?"

"She says Signore Franco's bed was not slept in for the two days they were here."

Bruno waved his hand dismissively. "That means nothing."

"I gave her coin, my Conte. She says she heard lovemaking as she passed the door, lovemaking by three people. That's not a subject usually raised by a woman."

"I suppose not." Bruno pictured himself loving Luca — that beautiful face with his blue angel eyes, that gorgeous body, that cock he so yearned to see hard and ready. He drew a sharp breath and shoved his manservant aside. The brisk toweling had suddenly been too much. He looked down. Raw and tender, the headless cock began to stiffen. Thoughts of Luca caused the stub to swell further. Afraid that the new skin would rupture, Bruno tightly closed his fingers around the balls and let the discomfort quickly put an end to it.

The physical discomfort brought with it an emotional pain.

Luca. Despite his mutilation, despite being left for dead after his fall, he still loved Luca Franco. He stared at the large bed with its brocade coverlet and tasseled pillows. Imagining Luca and Nicolas together in this bed sharing what should have been his alone not only made his heart ache, it filled him with hatred for the Englishman. He should have had the nobleman and his wife killed the very day he learned of them. That they were both in his home when he attempted to make love to Luca had been too much of a distraction for the younger man.

Bruno shrugged into his dressing gown, pondering Nicolas Halstead's American wife. He loathed women in general for the disagreeable sluts they were, but what kind of woman would marry a homosexual and then stand nearby while her husband fucked a man? *Zoccola*. His mind created the sexual scene that had taken place on this bed and his heart ached. The idea Nicolas Halstead would be Luca's lover — when this was something he could no longer be — filled him with rage.

The responsibility for his pitiful physical state rested squarely on Nicolas's shoulders, and nothing would give him greater pleasure than to watch as his men made the Englishman and his *sorca* wife pay. He told Salvatore, "Go back to the innkeeper. I wish to be alone with La Scapigliata tomorrow. Have him see to it."

***

Signore Farnese, curator of the Galleria Nazionale di Parma, deferentially led the Conte to a private viewing of *La Scapigliata*. He said, "I can allow you thirty minutes alone with the piece Conte, and no more.

"Grazie." Conte Bruno stood staring at the incomplete oil

painted upon wood. The completed portions of the woman's head were highly detailed and obviously Leonardo da Vinci's doing. He could have sworn he saw a smiling mouth in the curls. He looked closer. Yes, a mouth. He'd seen that smiling mouth before but couldn't place it. As he turned away, his eye caught something more. Words. Had he seen words? He turned back to the sketch in disbelief. Mirror-image words appeared in the curls around the woman's temple. He called for his servant.

Salvatore hurried to his side. "Yes, my Conte?"

He pointed to La Scapigliata's hairline. "What do you see there?"

Salvatore's eyes grew huge. "Words, my Conte! All around the woman's face. But they appear backward!"

Bruno stepped closer. Whereas he'd seen only three words, close examination revealed what Salvatore saw. There were many more than three. He recalled reading once that Leonardo da Vinci often wrote backward, though for the life of him he didn't know why. He reached into his pocket and withdrew his silver cigar case. Fogging it with his breath, he wiped the case on his sleeve until it gleamed. Handing it to his servant, he said, "Hold the case against the wording and tell me what see."

Salvatore read:

> *There are three classes of people: Those who see. Those who see when they are shown. Those who never see. After all this time, I know you are one to see. Look closely, my love. You will discover how you dance through my mind, no matter the subject.*

Salvatore handed the case back to Conte Bruno and stepped

back from the painting.

As Conte Bruno stared at the words, considering them, he suddenly realized where he'd seen the mouth. He involuntarily squeezed the cigar case so tightly that the lid buckled. He told his man, "I want you to discover where Lord Halstead and his Lady were headed."

"Yes, my Conte, but how?"

Conte Bruno leveled him an irritated look. "Don't be a simpleton. Learn where they stabled their horse for the two days they stayed in Parma. Coachmen converse with one another. Find the people their man spoke with and they will tell you where Lord Halstead and his companions went."

Bruno stared at the backward text of *La Scapigliata,* and the hidden whimsical lips smiling in the curls. *Look closely, my love. You will discover how you dance through my mind, no matter the subject.* It brought to mind the erotic renderings in his book. He let out a breath. Yes, he understood. This very smile belonged to the curly-haired man so regularly featured in the sketches. This backward message implied there were more messages like this hidden in the other artworks. Was that the purpose of da Vinci's book? His jaw tightened. The erotic book hadn't been a forgery, after all. The book was a map to previously unknown words and images from Leonardo da Vinci himself. And Nicolas had stolen it from him with a lie.

***

The coach jostled hard over a rut. Waking upon hitting his head, Salvatore looked to his sleeping master who appeared no worse for wear. It was wise for him to have taken the laudanum. The warm stink of urine caught his attention. He glanced at the

Conte's lap, and sure enough, a telltale wet circle darkened the man's trousers again. Salvatore wrinkled his nose in disgust. The doctor said this uncontrolled urination might continue for the rest of his life or correct itself in time. He tallied the trousers in the Conte's trunk and sighed inwardly. Two pairs were left. He'd have to wash and dry them all at the next inn. He didn't know how he'd manage that, given their rush to get to Rome.

He pulled his pocket watch and checked the time. They'd be there soon. He looked longingly at the small photograph tucked safely behind the glass, then snapped it closed and returned it to his pocket. How he missed his life in Napoli.

***

Waiting on dinner, Bruno sipped his aperitivo and half-listened to his servant inquiring after Luca and Nicolas. After days of uncomfortable travel, they'd been to the three well-known hotels of Rome, and each query had turned up nothing. This was the fourth and final stop, whether anything useful was learned here. They'd spend the night because he simply couldn't sit in the carriage a moment longer. With all that lemon water, it seemed he couldn't hold his piss when he was sitting down. Thinking about his four pairs of pissed trousers brought a dark scowl of humiliation. He'd always prided himself in his appearance but there was no time to find a tailor and he had little patience for ready-made. Salvatore would purchase towels to tuck into his trousers for the coach ride.

Bruno hoped the doctor was right, that this incontinence would eventually end. A flight of fancy took him and he found himself imagining Nicolas pissing himself like a boy. Yes, he fancied seeing the humiliation that would cause. His thoughts of revenge were interrupted when Salvatore returned to gather their things.

"My Conte, I've good news! They were here and I've made arrangements for our rooms." Bruno followed his man. At the top of the stairs, Salvatore opened the door to the suite. "The hotel is so old, my Conte. I'm told the rooms are small but comfortable."

Passing his man in the doorway, Bruno waved his hand. "Yes, yes. But what did you learn about Lord Halstead and Luca?"

"The maid says a sin was committed in their room. They even had nuns come to clear the sin through prayer."

Picturing the scene as if the nuns wielded brooms to chase a bird out the window, Bruno laughed heartily. Intolerant of women anyway, he couldn't stomach nuns.

Nearly two months had passed since Conte Bruno had laughed. Hearing it now made Salvatore jump. Laughter was usually followed by a cruel act.

Bruno wiped his eyes, having thoroughly enjoyed his flight of fancy, which finished with broom-wielding nuns tumbling out the opened window. Sister Mary Patrice had beaten him as a boy. She'd stood him in the corner, made him drop his drawers, and paddled him before his classmates. She'd encouraged the others to laugh at him. Him! The Conte's son, with a title of his own. *Stronzo puttana.* She hadn't laughed when he had her thrown off a bell tower several years later.

He chuckled. For the first time in weeks, his mind was engaged upon something other than his cock. Perhaps it was the influence of the two *aperitivos* upon the several doses of laudanum he'd had today, or perhaps because he was certain he understood what

Luca's travels were all about. It had taken nine uncomfortable days to travel from Parma to Florence. Along the way, he'd learned Luca and the Halsteads had a short stay with the Franco family. Town rumor held the trio headed to Rome and then from there to London.

It had been seven years since he'd been to Rome, eight years since that dance teacher had been eliminated. Bruno absently ran his fingertips over the scar that marred his cheek. The dance teacher had disfigured him with a capped fencing foil. It wasn't until later that he'd learned the man also taught swordplay. He remembered that afternoon so clearly. He'd seen the dance instructor with a young black-haired companion in town. He'd sat across from them as they took their meal, and the instant Luca smiled, it felt like he'd been hit by a thunderbolt.

Since that day, an hour hadn't passed when Luca wasn't on his mind. Such a beautiful boy he was at eighteen, and how luscious he'd grown in manhood. Luca fought at first, as most young men did when Bruno's servants held them down to be fucked. But Luca, with his angelic face, fought with such spirit, a spirit that would have only added to their lovemaking. If not for that meddlesome man's inopportune interruption, he and Luca would have shared such bliss. It was unfortunate that the dance teacher lingered the way he had, and Bruno regretted not killing the man outright for the wound across his cheek. The slow death had unfortunately made Luca view the man's punishment as something unforgivable, but Bruno believed that time would heal his heart and mind.

The room was very warm. Bruno shrugged out of his jacket. He went to the small terrace and looked down on the bustling swarm of people. Priests and cardinals, nuns and beggars crisscrossed the street. A young, lean, and hungry-looking man caught his eye. When he'd lived here last, he'd observed that beggars of all shapes and sizes would do anything for a meal. Setting aside his baser leanings, he looked the young man over one last time and let out a wistful sigh.

Salvatore said, "Your bath is ready, my Conte."

Bruno chuckled to himself, having completely lost track of time and instantly attributed the lapse to the *aperitivos* and the laudanum. He allowed his man to undress him, and then settled in for a hot soak. Tomorrow he'd view the only work of Leonardo da Vinci in Rome, in the Musei Vaticani, to see if it held hidden words or images as the one in Parma had.

Rome held such delicious memories. For a time, Luca was schooled here. Bruno had followed him from region to region while he completed his education, showing up occasionally at the same museum or restaurant to let Luca know he was ever in his thoughts. When Luca had settled in Venice, Bruno had hoped to entice him by purchasing a small palace nearby and creating a showplace for men such as them. Luca Franco filled his senses as no other soul ever had. He'd been so thrilled to have Luca come to his home and prepared a night the younger man would not soon forget. But Nicolas had insinuated his way into the evening. Bruno pushed the unwelcome thought from his mind, and told Salvatore, "I wish to be entertained."

Salvatore blanched, but bowed. "Yes, my Conte." With that he turned on his heel and left. A moment later, he returned with Gino and Celso. The three men shed their clothing and became as entertaining as Conte Bruno wished them to be.

~5~

We'd been at sea for the better part of two weeks, and the weather through the Mediterranean was sunny blue and tranquil. But it wasn't to last. The typical autumn season's strong ocean current flung us through the Strait of Gibraltar and into the arms of a substantial North Atlantic storm. It rivaled Rembrandt's *Storm on the Sea of Galilee.*

My wife had made several Atlantic crossings, and Luca was literally raised on a gondola. Despite my English background, I had no relationship with the sea, and being tossed about on the churning waves made me terribly seasick. Green to the gills, it was all I could do to keep my head out of the commode. During the tempest's first hour I managed to control the urge to regurgitate, but sea dog I'm not. The fact of it transcended any embarrassment I initially had.

Clutching an empty flower urn should I have need to fill it, I took to the settee and watched my overjoyed companions through the open door of our starboard balcony. In my opinion, Prospero himself would have found this passing too much, but they stood at the rail outlined by the pending wrath of Neptune and thoroughly enjoyed the wild wind and roiling waves. Conversely, I clung to my cushion and damp washcloth. Although the balcony possessed a high lattice to keep guests from tumbling into the drink, I felt an honest fear that had nothing whatsoever to do with the storm. I hadn't voiced it to either of them, but I felt an increasing sense of unease, an unaccountable prickling at the nape of my neck as if something terrible was about to happen. I'd had several nightmares since Ellie's abduction and Luca's encounter with the fanatical Bruno. There were disturbing phantoms that jarred me awake and left me unsettled.

I thought about that. Recurring nightmares plagued my youth but tapered off as I matured. Through these bad dreams, I had relived the accident that made me an orphan. I was just a boy when my parents and nanny died during our holiday in Brighton. I don't know what spooked the horses that day, but they ran wildly and my mother screamed as I fell through the tumbling coach door. I also remembered the incredible pain as my small body landed and my arm and leg bones snapped.

That childhood trauma had revisited my dreams over the past several nights, and my adult mind lent an additionally horrific reality each time. In one, I came home to find all I knew and loved gone. Another — all too real — had me savaged at Bruno's palazzo while poor Mrs. Fletcher and Thomas were made to watch. Waking in a sweat, I found myself wondering if Bruno had died in the fall as we supposed. We hadn't checked for a pulse, we had simply assumed. It was getting so I dreaded closing my eyes.

"Nicolas darling, how are you feeling?" Ellie peered under the washcloth covering my eyes and pulled me from my dark musings.

I gave her a feeble smile. "Tolerable."

"It would appear the captain has taken us out of the storm."

I assessed. Yes, the rolling had calmed somewhat. Sitting up slowly, I murmured, "Thank god."

She tsked. "Oh you poor thing, look at you, you're drenched with sweat." Taking up the washcloth, she proceeded to wipe my face and neck as if I were a small boy who'd been in the jam jar. "Luca went back to his room to bathe. How would you like to take a nice hot bath with me? The fishy stink of the storm will only get worse if I don't wash it off now."

I took the cloth from her hand and returned it to my eyes. The room was terribly bright. "Yes. A bath might allow me to feel human again."

I drifted off to the sound of water flowing in the bathroom, then woke to voices at the door. It was Ellie speaking with the steward. Apparently the thoughtful nymph had ordered a tea service, having determined my abused stomach might appreciate the gesture. Naked now, she returned and sat beside me to sweep a caressing hand back from my brow.

"Come sweetheart, you'll feel better."

On that promise I followed like a puppy. She quickly washed herself then saw to me. Her tender care for my sorry state filled my heart, and as she promised, I felt infinitely better.

***

My dignity restored, I rejoined the world of the hale and hearty and enjoyed tea with a biscuit. When Ellie had asked the steward about the state of things, the man informed her that we'd actually made good time in the storm and would be arriving in port the following morning. After the last several hours, I couldn't wait to touch ground. It's funny how the mind decides such things. For the entire uncomfortable coach ride over Italy's rough roads, I longed for the opulent comfort of an ocean liner. Today I felt I'd rather sit bare-assed on a fakir's bed of nails as long as that bed sat on dry land. As it was, we needed to eventually cross the English Channel to Brighton. I pushed the unwelcome eventuality from my mind.

***

Coming directly from his bath, Luca joined us about an hour later as shiny as a new penny and as handsome as always. For the better part of that hour, Ellie stood near the stove fluffing her wild mane in an attempt to get it dry enough to take a brush to. Knowing these two as I did, I counted the seconds until Luca asked her if she needed assistance. He loved her wild curls as much as I did. Sisal rope or Ellie's hair, the man could braid.

We'd learned Luca possessed a fair aptitude for plaits and sailor's knots, a skill learned at his grandfather's knee. After all, the Francos had been sailing the seas for centuries. It also helped that he had younger sisters and regularly helped them set their hair. No small feat that. His sisters each had hair that fell below their knees when unbound. A fact I'd seen for myself when we'd stayed at Luca's family home. With her midnight locks unbound, Carmela, the younger of his two sisters, could have sat as a model for the American Impressionist James Carroll Beckwith.

Sure enough, Ellie handed over the hairbrush. I watched Luca work the boar bristles through the mass with a dreamy look on his face. How could such a simple thing make me stiff? My smile widened. I knew why. Whenever Luca touched Ellie's hair, he transformed into a child with a new toy. From time to time he'd bite his lip in concentration or his tongue would poke out ever so slightly. In our moments of passion, he'd occasionally close his eyes and gather the silken mass in his hands and run the bounty over his bare chest or mine. Within moments, he fashioned for her a cinnamon plait as thick as my wrist and tied up the end in the ribbon she'd handed over her shoulder. Ellie didn't see him raise the braid to his lips. But I did. Sitting there in my loosely-tied robe as I was, my cock made a grand showing.

He'd seen my arousal but Ellie hadn't. Meeting his eye, I silently mouthed, "Come to me." He gave me an engaging wink over the top of her head. Instead of coming to me, the tease moistened his lips with his tongue and shook his head. Then taking Ellie's hands, he bid her rise. He enfolded her in his arms, and wound the braid into his large hand. When he kissed her deeply, he also kissed my mind through her. And heaven help me, I felt it keenly.

When he released her, Ellie said, "Oh my." She turned to me with lovely cheeks painted in that informative blush of hers that declared she wanted loving. Seeing my erection, she cocked a brow at me. I shrugged, pretending I couldn't imagine why I was hard. Her lips twitched when she cast me a dubious eye. Caught like a canary-eating cat, I tipped my head toward Luca. Her delight was instantaneous. She hooked her arm through his and held out her hand to me. "Well, come along then. You might as well be comfortable while you watch us."

I loved her matter-of-fact decisiveness and the way she lived her life without pretense. She wanted me teased, and by god she was going to have it. There was nothing to do but follow. Clothing stripped away among the kisses, I watched my lovers sprawl on the bed side by side and continue what began in the outer room. Seeing open opportunity, I crawled between them. While they busied themselves with hand and lips and dancing tongues, I found other amusements. I nuzzled and tasted, sucked and lapped, just enough to make them want more. Three could play the tease.

Apparently I'd teased enough because Luca said something in husky Italian. Ellie, the budding polyglot replied, "Yes, I think you should."

Next I knew, he grabbed me. Ellie squealed and scrambled to the top of the bed lest she be caught up in the tangle of arms and legs. He pinned me down and kissed me hard. I made a bid for freedom and he flipped me to my belly with one wrist trapped under my weight and the other held by him. His cock positioned itself along the split of my rear as his teeth left sharp exclamation points across my shoulders and neck. He spoke hotly at my ear, "*Non giocare con me mio amore. Otterrai più di questo.*"

I could sense Ellie's delight. I sought her out but she'd left the bed in our fray.

I struggled to turn over under his weight and laughingly huffed, "You have me…at a disadvantage. My Italian…has yet… to refine…itself."

He chuckled and whispered passionately at my cheek. "I said, do not play games with me *carissimi*. You will get more than this." He emphasized this by pressing his hips forward and thus pressing my lower half to the mattress with his own. His balls were hot against mine.

Lord, I wanted him. I laughingly taunted him. This was exactly what I craved in that moment of raw animal power.

I knew my wife enjoyed when he and I wrestled. She often said it reminded her of artworks from ancient Greece. Turning in her direction, I laughed when my eyes found her. Following my gaze, Luca joined me. And what did we see? A most adorable goddess from Mount Olympus had come to watch our game. Having seen potential in our antics, Ellie borrowed the silk leaves from the ship's flower decorations and adorned herself with laurels. It was clear the minx wanted more.

Distracted, I allowed my body to relax. Luca released my pinned wrists. That shift was all I needed. Rolling over, I took him with me. He attempted to regain the upper hand. On Ellie's theme, we wrestled like the Olympians and enacted several of the more athletic poses famously captured in marble. My years of tussling with Thomas gave me advantage over my beautiful opponent, and I soon had him doubled over on his knees. My teasing hand circled his cock and stroked him slowly. I whispered in his ear, "I'll tease you until you beg for more, *mio amore*." That much Italian I was sure of.

He struggled again and I redoubled my efforts. I knew I had him when my pumping hand grew wet with his excitement. To feel him relax in total surrender made my cock so hard I felt every throb of my heart in it. I nearly shot my mettle when he said, "I'm begging now."

I turned to Ellie, who sat hotly observing. "What say you, Goddess?"

Biting back the smile that still danced in her eyes, she ceremoniously gave Luca a downward thumb. Releasing him, I lay back and waited. He treated me to the most exquisite sucking while my fingers ran through ebony strands as soft as ermine. It was I who surrendered. Driven near to madness, my fingers curled roughly into his hair to allow the exquisite glide to chase hard and fast along teeth and tongue. The brief reflexive tightening of his body before he yielded hurled me over the precipice. He must have sensed it, for he redoubled his efforts. My spunk shot like a canon blast, the release made glorious by his throaty moans and muffled swallows. Before my blood cooled and I knew what was happening, I found our positions reversed. I looked to her as he pressed his cock into my mouth. There was no mercy in those pale blue eyes, only heat. When I'd drained him fully, she came to us and lay between. The nymph had her own arousal to see to. For the remaining hour, Luca and I lost ourselves in her secret places. When she writhed, we loved her in tandem. It wasn't long before her climax blazed into being. Unbelievably, when her first crescendo ended, she called for another. It took Herculean effort on our part. The Goddess was insatiable in her amusements.

~6~

The storm had sped us along, so rather than the late morning landing our steward had predicted, we landed at the French port of St. Malo hours ahead of schedule. I for one couldn't wait to set foot on terra firma. With our early morning landing, the day now stretched out ahead of us. Instead of seeking a hotel right from the start, we decided we'd take ourselves to Paris and find lodging there.

After making a detailed study of Leonardo's book on our voyage, we'd come to the conclusion that we wouldn't find all of the man's artworks. There had been so many, far more than the known works I was aware of in galleries, personal collections, and museums. It made better sense to look upon our quest as an adventure and determined we'd make as much of it as possible. I'd be happy anywhere as long as these two were by my side.

The blast of the ship's horn startled Ellie as we made our way down the plank, and her parasol dropped into the drink.

"Oh, *fiddlesticks!* That was a new one." Several would-be heroes made valiant attempts to capture it. But it was upside down, and each lap of the sea against the ship propelled the fancy little sea craft further away from us.

I gave her arm a squeeze. "Paris is full of shops. We'll buy another."

Nodding, her gaze followed her parasol as it floated out to sea. "Tsk. That was such a nice parasol too." Ellie called to her champions in American-accented *le français*, "Thank you, gentlemen. But please, don't trouble yourselves."

Luca met us at the bottom of the ramp. It took a while to have our trunks unloaded from the ship and more time to have them packed aboard our hired coach, but we were soon on our way to the train station in Rennes. From there we'd take the trunk line directly into the heart of Paris.

***

The locomotive belched a stinking coal-fired plume into the air and steam valves hissed and fogged as we hurried along the walkway to the door to our private car. This was had at some expense but well worth the coin, for we were able to recline at our convenience and take in the quaint French countryside. It didn't take long to leave the view behind us. We were just heading to our luncheon in the dining car when Ellie pressed herself to the glass and asked, "That portion of wall in the distance…is that Paris?"

"That wall is what is left of a Roman aqueduct. Paris is some distance yet," the professor of antiquities informed her.

I could feel her hungry mind eagerly searching for more

wonders. She spoke to the window, "I've only ever read about them, but to actually see one for myself… We have nothing so ancient in my country, Indian mounds only, though the southern Americas have their native ruins."

"What would you say, Nicolas, an hour at the most?" Luca had been to Paris before, but never from the west.

I nodded. "About."

Aside from one encounter with a huge flock of slow-crossing sheep and a stop in Chartres to pick up post and parcels, our train kept its steady pace until we rolled into Paris later that afternoon.

***

After seeing our luggage taken from the train, Luca met us at the coach with the stevedore who immediately saw to the loading. Tipping his head toward the gangly porter, he said, "Masseur Renault here suggests we book our rooms at the Grand Hôtel du Louvre for their stellar accommodations."

Undoubtedly compensated for shunting foreigners to various hotels according to their outward display of wealth, the man echoed his assertion that the Grand with its 700 luxurious rooms was the best the city had to offer. After cramped inns and small hotels with minimal privacy for the past several weeks, stellar accommodations sounded quite attractive, indeed.

Upon seeing the tallest manmade structure in the world, Ellie said, "Goodness, I'd read about Mr. Eiffel's marvel, but I had no idea it stood so tall."

The iron girders and impressive stone footings did make a rather grand statement. It had been built for the International Exhibition of Paris in 1889 to commemorate the one hundredth anniversary of the French Revolution. I gave it a critical eye. To me, Eiffel's tower looked like the skeleton of an enormous candlestick. This country had architectural wonders like the cathedral of Notre Dame, the Palace of Versailles, and the Arc de Triomphe with which to compare it, and to my mind it came up lacking. "It's a rather homely thing, don't you think?"

She cocked her head and appraised the looming structure. "The exposed girders do make a modern design, I suppose. Did you know that Mr. Eiffel helped design the framework for our Statue of Liberty?"

Luca said, "I did not. I've seen the statue in stereograph pictures; it's an impressive structure and quite evocative of your country's message." He recited, "Give me your tired, your poor, your huddled masses yearning to breathe free, the wretched refuse of your teeming shore. Send these, the homeless, tempest-tossed to me. I lift my lamp beside the golden door."

We looked at him in surprise.

He chuckled. "What? My mother's brothers immigrated to the United States with their families. That poem was in one of their letters. I found it inspiring. I'd like to see Lady Liberty one day."

Ellie said, "I do believe Paris has a miniature replica of it somewhere."

I nodded. "Yes, on an island in the river Seine."

I listened to my companions discuss the neoclassical Lady Liberty at length and then other structures after we passed the Arc de Triomphe. I'd been to Paris several times through the years. The amalgamation of architectural styles that ranged from Beaux Arts architecture with its obvious nod to Ancient Rome to the long over-embellished lines of the French and Italian Baroque and Rococo styles appealed to me. Everywhere one looked, these elements filled the visual plane, and tucked here and there were the prism-cut bricking of Rustication. Blended styles always caught my fancy, my eye consistently drawn to the contrast of smooth line, curved flourish, and rough accent.

Minutes later, we entered the opulent velvet and crystal-festooned lobby of the renowned Grand Hôtel. Luca saw our luggage brought in, while I took myself to the telegraph room to wire Mrs. Fletcher and my father-in-law to inform them we were in France and would be home shortly. I'd wire Grannie the day we left.

The hotel was bustling. The concierge rang his desk bell and his chasseurs ran hither and yon to escort the guests to their rooms and see to their many needs. I booked us one suite for the three of us. The concierge informed me there was only one bed in the suite, to which I nodded. He briefly looked me over then turned the guest book for me to sign. Perhaps he tried to discern if I had to watch my coin or to determine why I might book a room for three? In my experience, it wasn't that the French were more open to men of my proclivity, no not at all. While it was certainly true lesbians had their discreet salons in which to meet, male deviants such as I were still dealt with harshly if caught in the act. Rather I believe it was the French's *joie de vivre* that had them often turn a blind eye. They simply loved life and oft-times were more tolerant of love in its many forms. On the QT of course.

The street scene beyond the large arched windows was just as active as the lobby, and that's where I found my wife standing at the glass, taking it all in.

"Enjoying Paris, my love?"

She gave me a beauteous smile. "Oh yes, very much so."

I could tell by her wide eyes and flushed cheeks she was ready to immerse herself in all *La Ville-Lumière* had to offer. Paris wasn't called the City of Lights for its electrification. This was where the Enlightenment was born. The great philosophers of the Romantic age were here discussing reason and man's place in the grand scheme of the world — Voltaire, Diderot, Descartes, Rousseau, Montesquieu. Yes, this was a place in which Ellie's intellectual mind could feast. Then and there I determined that as long as we were here, we might as well feed her.

Having seen our luggage safely upstairs, Luca joined us a moment later. I handed him his key, then held my arm out to my wife. "What say you, Luca? Shall we show the lady a tour of the city?"

He treated us both to a most handsome smile. "That's a splendid idea, Nicolas."

There was a wistful moment when I could clearly see he wanted nothing better than to take Ellie's other arm. Our bellboy tipped his head to whisper to another chasseur and I clearly heard the word ménage before the desk bell rang and he trotted off to see to another guest. I was suddenly met with a brief rush of anxiety. This I wrote off as the lingering unease of my recent dreams. Why must our love for one another be judged?

***

The remainder of the afternoon was spent immersed in Parisian marvels, many of which occurred right on the street. We were treated to jugglers and musicians as well as the salacious advance of a rather large marionette dressed as an old-time cobbler. Under the guise of theater, and under the pretense of "looking at shoes," the puppet master's wooden man tried to lift the hem of any woman passing by. After lifting a hem high enough to display one hapless woman's knees, he made a bid for my wife. The look Luca and I leveled him made him back away sheepishly. Apparently finding the prank more humorous than we, Ellie laughed good-naturedly. She raised her own hem, but only enough to show the top-most buttons of her shoes. She told the wooden puppet in softly American-accented *Français*, "Keep your eyes on the shoes, my wooden shoemaker, or my escorts will see you made into matchsticks." Needless to say, the gathering crowd laughed heartily.

On this trip, as my last, I found Paris to be filled with absurdities. All around were signs of blatant eroticism and the occasional disconcerting accent of the morbid. Ellie was wide-eyed. Seeing a sign for a salon that promised a *revue déshabillée*, this daughter of Sappho made a beeline there. Inexplicably, the thought warmed me. Before my new-found sexual identity, I hadn't given much thought to the female form, though in truth I found women pleasant creatures to look upon. Needless to say Luca was confused. Somehow we hadn't conveyed the fact Ellie was as dual-natured as we. I found myself wondering what he'd say about it.

We ordered wine and watched naked beauties on swinging perches as they swooped and displayed with each pass overhead. Ellie leaned close and said, "The one on the left is very similar in appearance to Felicia."

I watched the lovely brunette with interest. Bare save for her black stockings and garters, and the ribbon at her throat, the woman suddenly fell backward from the swing only to catch herself at the knees. The audience, no doubt an amalgamation of regular patrons and newcomers, simultaneously gasped and applauded. Luca asked who Felicia was. Ellie whispered something in his ear and he drew back, his snow-shadow eyes wide in surprise. She nodded and smiled that sentient smile of hers as she lifted a glass to her lips. I got hard. Luca looked at me. I nodded too. His engaging smile widened. I could feel our desire rising but we didn't elaborate further. This conversation was best had back in our suite.

After wine, we moved on to explore the famous Parisian Catacombs. The long-abandoned stone quarry's underground chambers now held an ossuary with the remains of several million people stacked in a freakishly grotesque collage of bone. As dinner was some hours away, we bought ourselves several portable foods from the abundant street vendors and took ourselves to the Eiffel Tower's top viewing platform. High above the city, the early November breeze left little doubt winter was coming. We weren't long up there.

"My goodness, the day has turned cold." Ellie plucked a hot chestnut from the paper cone and passed the nugget of warmth from one kid-gloved hand to the other.

"Would you rather we return to our suite?"

Laughing, she shook her head and swept a hand to the untidy wall of plastered playbills for the various happenings around the city. "And miss all this?"

Luca popped a peeled chestnut into his mouth. His words steamed as he read a bill plastered to a wall, Axël: A drama by Auguste Villiers.

I knew Ellie enjoyed reading of seductive and sexually attractive heroes. While I hadn't attended any Villiers theater pieces myself, I had once read a commentary in the London Times suggesting he created Byronic heroes in his works. I took out my pocket watch and checked the time. "The play begins in approximately twenty minutes. We could warm ourselves there, and then return to the hotel for dinner." I raised a brow to Ellie. "Care to take in a play, love?"

"What a marvelous idea!"

***

We left the theater an hour later. What a mistake that had been. While the play was entertaining and the theme interesting enough, with its occult undertones, the ending had left a bad taste in my mouth. After finding their treasure, Axël the hero and his heroine Sara fall in love, and then decide their dream is far too magnificent to be fulfilled in the unimaginative reality of their lives. With no dream to live for, they killed themselves as the sun rose and the curtain fell.

Apparently unfazed, my companions discussed the story at length as we walked back to the hotel. I couldn't help but draw a parallel to our lives, although I was certain the dark thoughts were mine alone. It didn't help that we passed a mortician's window with the latest embalming on display as a macabre advertisement to the skill to be had there. Beside the door, a glass frame was filled with *memento mori* photographs. In general I found the practice of posing the dead in life-like attitudes a disturbing one. Especially the staring facsimile eyes painted upon closed lids.

Seeking a distraction from my thoughts, I used the tip of Eiffel's tower as a guide and led us across the street and down an alley. We passed a beribboned one-man music show reminiscent of a May Day mummer, a raucous game of Three Card Monte taking place on an upturned dustbin, and Luca received a blatant sexual proposition by a ponce seeking work for his whore. Turning the corner, we chanced upon two women, one young and the other quite old or quite world-worn. Both were obviously Roma, dressed as they were in colorful rustic clothing one might see on country folk. The younger woman rocked a baby. The elder told us in heavily-accented English that her tarot cards held a message for Luca and me.

Unused to gypsies who peddled their wares across Europe, Ellie was enchanted by the idea. She tugged on my sleeve and encouraged a card reading. Luca shrugged and I found myself placing a coin on the scarf-covered folding table.

The elder's smile revealed several missing teeth. She shuffled her worn cards and said, "The cards speak to you first, Englishman." These she handed to me and I cut the deck into three piles as directed. I realized then that this deck of cards was not only quite old, it was hand-painted. Restacking them into her hand, she dealt three cards — the three of cups, the six of swords, and the five of pentacles. I looked at the woman expectantly.

I felt Ellie's eyes on me.

"Well madam, what do the cards say?"

"The cards call for caution, Englishman." She tapped the three of cups with a gnarled finger. "You've gained fortune in love. But this card is your past."

Ellie looped her arm through mine. I could feel her thoughts. As far as she and I were concerned, it was our present and future.

The old woman tapped the six of swords. "Your plans will be postponed and sadly there is nothing to be done for it." She stared at the cards a moment then tsked. She shook her head and tapped the last. "The card sees loss and ruin."

Ellie looked at me with wide skeptical eyes that danced with mirth, the smile tugging at the corners of her lips as she tried to keep a straight face. Luca slapped me on the back in humor, and said, "You'd best watch yourself, Nicolas."

I chuckled, but my unsettled mind absorbed the woman's prophesy.

She gathered the cards again and shuffled them. After Luca cut the deck into three piles, she laid them out as before. The first was the two of cups. "Your recent past shows harmony, man of Venice." Luca nodded, apparently missing the fact the woman knew where he was from. I hadn't missed it. There was nothing in his accent that hinted at a particular region of Italy. She set the next card beside the first. It was the eight of wands. "There is jealousy in your life now," she told him.

He looked at me and then at Ellie. There was no jealousy between us. Proof again these mystic pastimes were nothing more than parlor games. The last card was the king of cups. She looked up into his face and for the first time I realized she had a glass eye that didn't quite move with the other. The real eye looked him up and down, and the perusal made me very uncomfortable. I couldn't say why that was, even if I'd been asked. She suddenly scooped up the cards and declared the reading completed.

Luca chuckled. "Madam, you've not read my last card."

The baby fussed. The older woman turned to the younger and said something in a language I did not recognize but possessed rounded syllables found in the Latin languages. Romanian, perhaps. The young woman nodded and replied, then bared her breast to suckle her babe. She said, "The king of cups tells of a powerful man—"

The old woman voiced something that effectively stopped the younger mid-sentence.

How strange. We looked at one another. Ellie dug into her reticule and set a coin on the table. "I'd like my fortune read too, if you please."

The old woman shook her head.

"Why not? I'll pay."

Chuckling, Luca set another coin on the cloth. Obviously deliberating, the old woman stared at the coins and pursed her lips. In the end, the prospect of more money won out. She shuffled the cards and set the deck on the table. Her one eye moved from person to person, at last settling on Ellie. She told her, "One card only, lady."

Ellie turned over a single card and set it on the scarf. The lovers in reverse. The old woman said, "Separation," and quickly scooped up the deck and scarf and snapped the folding table closed. The card reading was officially over.

"Wait, what does that mean?" Ellie asked obviously confused.

I hooked my arm in hers and said, "It means nothing my dear, it's merely a game."

The gypsy cackled. "A mistake many make."

I tugged Ellie away. "Come love, let's see about our dinner."

***

During the French Revolution, art once commissioned and hoarded by the privileged became the property of the citizenry. The dining hall's vaulted ceiling sported numerous panels undoubtedly taken from the aristocracy. There was no option for intimate dining, with the long tables set to accommodate more than one thousand guests. We found ourselves taking our meal beside a world of nations. Sir Arthur Conan Doyle raved over the Grand's culinary excellence, and the hotel's kitchen staff did not disappoint. Our meal was superb.

To my right sat a rather sallow character whose clothing held a faint note of opium smoke. I introduced myself and for the effort got the salt passed to me. Then I introduced myself and my wife to the English couple directly across the table, a veritable Jack Sprat and his wife. In the din, I couldn't quite make out their names — Anders, Landers, or Flanders — but it didn't matter. The less-than-friendly wife was too absorbed in finding fault with an exemplary meal. Four times did she call for our server to complain about how cold her soup was and how hot her salad was, as well as how fishy the fish tasted, and she asked him to inform the cook that the peas were still in their pods.

Ellie nudged my knee with hers. Mrs. Anders-Landers-Flanders's complaints were laughable because we'd been served a cold soup of potato and leek, an intentionally hot salad of roasted pepper and ham, a pheasant course in cream that was by no means a fish course, and *haricots verts* which were obviously green beans and not unshelled peas. The poor sod of a husband never once raised an eye from his plate while the woman complained; rather, he ate with increased speed. I assume he hoped to cut and run to the men's salon for cards and cigars. The thought was born out a moment later, when he declined the delicious raspberry and chocolate trifle, briefly kissed his wife's cheek, and said, "I'll be playing cards tonight my dear, don't wait up for me." In response the woman tasted the trifle and said, "My word, can I not find one decent morsel to eat in this city?"

***

I had just removed my tie when came a quiet knock at our door. A *chasseur* met me with a silver tray in hand, upon it a telegram. I tipped the man and closed the door behind him. Confused, I turned to my companions. "I can't imagine what this is about."

Luca and Ellie both drew close as I unfolded the paper. It was from Mrs. Fletcher. I read it aloud.

My Dear Boy, Come home. Thomas has been injured and is not expected to survive. Come home. We need you. MF

Ellie laid a hand on my arm. "I'll pack straightaway."

I could barely breathe. My dear Thom not expected to survive. Needing the anchor of her love, I pulled Ellie to me and hugged her fiercely. An instant later, Luca's warm body enfolded me as well. Choking back my misery, I said to him, "I'm leaving now. Bring Ellie."

Winding her arms around my waist, she protested, "No. Nicolas, my place is by your side."

Luca said, "As is mine."

I shook my head. "I'm needed there now." Willing her to understand, I gathered her hands in mine. "I'll not see you travel the channel at night. Wait until morning, the crossing is safer then." I kissed her knuckles then turned to Luca. "I don't know what I'll find at home. I know you understand." I knew he did because I read it in his eyes. Society had a dark underbelly where men of our ilk were concerned. Thom's dire condition might very well have to do with his homosexuality.

303

He nodded and kissed my cheek softly. "I do. We'll follow in the morning."

~7~

After renting a horse and riding rough to Calais, I found myself a small steamer and purchased a ride to Dover. After no little outlay of coin, I convinced the captain to press up the Thames and deposit me in London. From there, I hired a hack and we rode like hell to my townhouse on the outskirts of the city proper. Mrs. Fletcher met me at the door by throwing herself into my arms.

"Oh thank the lord, you received my telegram. Oh my boy, my dear boy...he—" The old dear broke down and sobbed. I held her, my heart breaking more with each tear.

I gently took her arms from me and closed the door behind us. "Where is he?"

She dabbed her nose with her handkerchief and pointed to the ceiling. "The doctor is with him. He's in the guest room at the end of the hall. He's sleeping now."

I kissed her cheek, and then took the stairs two at a time. The doctor met me outside the door. "Dr. Compton, what's happened here?"

He led me away from the door and spoke quietly. "I've never seen such brutality wielded on a man outside the theater of war. You don't need the details, son. Suffice to say it's shocking what was done to him, just shocking. Thomas has sepsis. There's a fever, as expected, and he's drifting in and out of lucidity now." He shook his head. "I know you've been friends a good long time and I'm very sorry there was nothing to do but make him comfortable. If you have anything to say to young Thom, say it now, Lord Nicolas." He turned to go, then turning back to me added, "Merry Fletcher needs you, son."

Mrs. Fletcher's given name was Merriam. Few people called her Merry, and I registered his use of the name with some inward surprise, for it implied that Mrs. Fletcher and the doctor were friends. I sensed he needed reassurance and so I said, "She's been mother to me since I was six years old and I love her as such. Never fear, doctor. I'll always look after her."

Nodding, he gave a small smile of approval then patted my shoulder. With that, he went down the stairs. Seconds later, I heard their voices below.

As I opened the door, the sweet scent of laudanum met my nose, as it overlay the strong smell of sickness and beef broth. The room was dark, save for two small sconces on either side of the headboard and the small candle flame burning under the soup warmer. It was a shock to see him. Even in the dim light, I could make out his bruised and swollen face and the slits of his puffy eyes. I sat carefully on the bed and smoothed his hair back, his soft honey-colored hair now dark and stiff with dried blood. He was so hot to the touch my hand nearly recoiled from him. He must have sensed me there because his eyes fluttered open and he smiled when he saw me. It opened the small tear at the corner of his mouth and a dark dribble slowly worked its way down his chin. I wiped it away with my bare hand. His words were soft and pained, "Nic, you're here. It's good to see you."

I forced a smile I didn't feel, and lightly admonished, "I leave for a moment and look what happens to you."

Those once-expressive eyes were fevered and glassy. He tried to chuckle and sucked his breath in sharply as the action must have caused him great pain. "Don't make me laugh. Fucking hell, it hurts my guts." He gave a hearty try to laugh again. Thom was always so ready to laugh.

Seeing he was both serious and making light, my forced smile widened for his benefit. "What happened to you Thom? Who did this?"

"This?" He drifted off.

Gripped by panic, I held his face, "Thom! No, don't...don't go."

Those eyes opened and were surprised to see me. He smiled again as if he hadn't seen me an instant before. "Nic, you're here."

A knot of fear grew in my belly as the doctor's words came back. Barely lucid, say what I need to say before it is too late. I reached for Thom's hand and though he winced, he didn't pull away. Looking down, I was horrified to see what I held. It appeared there were many broken bones here. I stammered, "I – I'm so sorry Thom. I didn't know...your hand. My god Thom, what happened?"

"Pish. The sod got worse from me, let me tell you." He tried to laugh again, this time the sound wheezed and rattled in his lungs.

My eyes filled with emotion. Trying again, I once more asked what had happened.

"Remember the sailors Lord Walker's footman told me about?"

I nodded. My heart started to pound. My poor Thom had been gang raped. "Oh Thom. Sailors did this to you?"

He shook his head feebly. "No, a toff did this, an Italian toff and his men. Two men." He seemed to drift off again, then coming around, he said, "I was playing cards down at the Crested—" apparently winded, he drew a deep breath and moaned. Mastering his pain, he said, "At the Crested Lark. I overheard these blokes asking after you. I followed them, Nic. Followed them to…to…" His words trailed off in a fit of coughing. Dry bubbles formed on his lips when he whispered hoarsely, "They hurt me, hurt me good, like it was sport, then after the toff took his cane and beat… Bloody sods. Be careful, the toff hates you. Smelled like an old piss pot, he did. I told him that…that's when he beat me, that's when they held me down and he… He wants to hurt you Nic, he's makin' plans to—"

"Plans?"

Thom grew quiet again. I tapped his cheek lightly. "Thom? Thom, what plans? What man is planning to hurt me?"

Thomas half-roused and took another rattling breath, this one I felt as well as heard. He started to cough in a reflexive attempt to clear his lungs. I knew what this was. These final breaths were called a death rattle. My dearest friend was dying. His efforts to breathe released a putrid stink of infection into the air. My tears fell freely now, there was no way to hold them back. He lifted his broken hand to my cheek and repeated as though he hadn't said it but a moment before, "Nic, you're here."

I held his hand gently against my face. "Yes, Thom. I'm here, Nic's here."

He smiled with closed eyes. "You are. I love you Nic, do you know that? Always…have…" The last words were on his lips.

I nodded and sobbed into his palm. "I love you Thom, always have loved you." The arm went slack and the rattle ceased. I gathered him to me, but he was gone.

***

By mid-morning next day, an early winter storm pummeled the coast and roughed the channel. By necessity, Ellie and Luca's departure was delayed. I sent a reply telegram asking that they stay the week, as I had funeral arrangements to attend.

Why does the eye see a thing more clearly in dreams than the imagination when awake?

– Leonardo da Vinci

~8~

Over the past two days, I'd barely eaten a bite nor slept more than a few hours at best. Nightmares seemed to come the moment I closed my eyes. Card-dealing gypsies played a prominent role, as did their cards of doom. Rolling, bone-crushing carriages carrying screaming women or led by screaming horses competed for vividness with the caved-in face of the man I'd killed in Venice. I saw Thomas and Ellie savaged while torches blazed, and books, paintings, and ossuary bones fell from shelves and walls in an avalanche. In one nightmare, Luca emerged from a mangled carriage like a marble nude streaked in blood. In another, Bruno laid dead at the bottom of the staircase with staring facsimile eyes painted on his closed eyelids, which then opened to reveal the pale cold stare of a corpse. Several times I woke in a panic, having dreamt everyone I loved was dead or gone. I missed Ellie and Luca desperately at night. While I'd had several nightmares since leaving Venice, usually I was able to fall back asleep by simply feeling their bodies against mine. Needless to say, I eagerly looked forward to their arrival on Thursday next.

The weight of emotion had aggravated Mrs. Fletcher's rheumatism and sapped her strength. Dr. Compton insisted she not attempt the stairs for the time being. In the emotion-riddled day-to-day, I hadn't given a thought to anything other than comforting this dear woman and taking comfort from her in return. As she repeated several times through her tears, she was thankful she had me, "for you are the only person in the world left for me to love."

I was certainly thankful for her. As we'd both been unable to sleep in our grief, the last two nights found us in the kitchen over glasses of warm milk. We poured our hearts out to one another and I told her about my travels with Ellie and of the friend I'd made in Luca.

I wanted nothing so much than to bring Ellie home, and Luca as well, for I knew she'd love them and they her. Perhaps one day my house would be filled with children's laughter. I imagined the delight etched upon my dear Mrs. Fletcher's face as she sat in her rocking chair and read nursery rhymes to them. Such a warm contrast to the reserved Halstead world I was born to, not that Grannie wasn't a dear in her own right.

Augusta Halstead was a woman of integrity who possessed a good and kind heart, but like society women of her age, Grannie put the raising of her children and only grandchild in the capable hands of governesses and servants. While she was reserved in her affections, I felt them nonetheless. She was pleased I'd returned, though she found it odd that I'd left my new bride with a friend in France. I did explain that I'd refused to put Ellie in jeopardy and insisted she not take the sea in rough weather. Being a sensible woman, my grandmother saw the wisdom in that and told me once more how happy she was that I'd settled down.

As pleased as she'd been to see me, she was absolutely devastated that her favorite coachman had been waylaid on the London docks. In sympathy, she immediately sent household help to Mrs. Fletcher and joined the entire staff in attending the simple funeral service at Stockwell Chapel. I noticed Lady Ashford's footman there. He met my eye and I saw the sadness. Thom had found love after all.

I soon learned how it infuriated Grannie that Dr. Compton was not forthcoming with the details of Thomas's injuries, injuries of such severity they'd taken a man's life. The dowager was by no means an unfeeling woman, it was simply details for her, details she felt should be explained when asked about. Knowing her questions wouldn't end until she found satisfactory answers, I did the best I could for Mrs. Fletcher's sake and my own. I explained that I'd seen the injuries for myself and none appeared to me to be so great as to cause Thom's death. From this, she reasoned the beating must have damaged his internal organs. She knew Thomas and I were friendly as boys but nothing beyond that, as our social stations in the eyes of the world were clear and unbending. To talk of him perfunctorily as though he were only my housekeeper's nephew was exceedingly difficult for me. I'd never had such a painful conversation as that.

Upon explaining the situation to Grannie, even abridged, Thom's cautionary words returned to me. Realization hit me squarely between the eyes and cold dread twisted like a knife in my belly. I thus headed to Dr. Compton's home on the end of Kennington Road. I needed to know the extent of Thom's injuries, for if it was as I suspected, his wounds would be quite particular.

The ground floor of the townhome held the doctor's office. As I was about to enter, the secretary came through the door. She assured me the good doctor was still at his desk, and would likely spare me a few minutes. Dr. Compton didn't look at all surprised to see me. He locked the door behind us and said with a genial smile, "Lord Nicolas, I knew we'd be seeing you before long."

I didn't ask why that was. Instead, I went straight to the point of my visit and asked about Thom's injuries.

"I'll say it again, as on the night you returned. Such brutality wielded on a man is not often seen outside the theater of war, and my eyes have seen much in my career."

I knew that Dr. Compton and Dr. O'Connor, his associate, shared the living space in the upstairs of the townhome. Both had fought in the same battalion in the battle of Rorke's Drift, when 139 British troops defended the South African garrison against 4,500 Zulu warriors. Yes, I had no doubt he'd seen savagery in full measure. I could only imagine again the extent of Thom's injuries. Dr. O'Connor came into the office and asked if we'd care for tea. I declined. He left and returned a short time later with two steaming cups, one of which he set on the desk. Dr. Compton said, "Thank you, Ben. Please, sit with us."

Though the doctor forwent speaking of Thom's wounds in my home the other night, he did so now. In fact, both men opened to me. They spoke at length about ruptured bowel and sepsis and the fact the body simply cannot fight an infection of that magnitude. My heart grieved and my soul ached, my stomach turned and emotion poured from me like water from a font. Only dimly aware of a comforting pat on my shoulder, at one point I discovered a brandy in my hand, which I tossed back in one flaming swallow. And in the words that remained unspoken, I heard the question. Apprehension filled my veins. They wanted to know if I was cut from the same cloth as Thom. Though I suspected as much the night Thom died, I was now certain both doctors had known about Thom's proclivity either before or after the savagery that took him. I didn't ask how. That hollow feeling returned as I pictured Thom drifting in and out of lucidity. Thom might have said anything.

I saw the thin limb I stood on for what it was and I began to sweat. Dr. Compton said, "We understand, son." With that, he reached across the desk and squeezed Dr. O'Connor's hand in a display of affection that obviously went beyond the professional. I do believe my jaw dropped to the floor. These men had attended my family's health for decades, and they were homosexual.

Both doctors had much to lose venturing forth on such a hunch. Certain my secret was safe, I nodded. The ice broken, the doctors proceeded to share the story of their lives. I learned they'd been together in secrecy for more than twenty years. I also discovered they occasionally took women to the theater and to dinner to maintain their façade as eligible bachelors too busy in their practice to settle down. Through careful living, even their housekeeper, cook, and nurses had no idea they were devoted lovers.

Taking my empty glass, Dr. O'Connor said gently, "It's obvious you and Thom loved one another, lad."

I nodded dully for indeed we had. Without reservation. I'd loved him, and my heart would ever carry his loss upon it.

"Rejoice in that, Lord Nicolas. Many people live lives bereft of love. The heart understands the gift it is, even if society sees it differently."

Dr. Compton nodded. "Loving hearts know no boundaries, son. And no matter how brief, we're all the better for whatever love we find for ourselves."

I looked from one to the other and was struck by the sadness in their eyes. I knew it for what it was. Men like us walked the edge of a knife and occasionally died by it. How could they not put themselves in my place…in Thom's place? I thanked them and took my leave.

I called for a hansom and headed home. I knew now, and the surety thudded loudly in my chest. Thom spoke of an Italian toff who had plans to hurt me. In my mind's eye, I saw the naked body lying in a heap at the bottom of a marble staircase. I saw the abnormal angle of the leg, and the hand that gripped a bleeding stump of a cock. We'd never checked for a pulse in our haste to depart. Conte Acario Bruno, sadistic sod and murderer, still lived and was bent upon revenge

The deeper the feeling, the greater the pain.
– Leonardo da Vinci

~9~

I met Ellie and Luca at the St. Katherine dock as they navigated a human sea of laborers and watermen. I waved them over. Ellie squeezed through the throng of humanity and rushed into my arms. "Oh, I've missed you so! I've been beside myself waiting on the weather."

Lord, it felt wonderful to hold her. I kissed her hard and got whoops and whistles of appreciation from the dockworkers. Luca gave me a meaningful albeit brief hug. He spoke low at my ear before pulling away, "Know I would kiss you too were we alone."

As we'd lived shrouded in gloom these last six days, Mrs. Fletcher and I had made small gestures of reassurance and forced our smiles for one another. With my two loves beside me, I found myself genuinely smiling. The sensation, and the feeling behind it, was refreshing to my weary soul. "I cannot express the ease you both bring to my aching heart."

Fingering the crape of my armband, Ellie said, "I know what

Thomas meant to you. I'm so sorry I wasn't here."

I touched her cheek. For the first time, I noticed she too wore mourning colors. I thanked her for her considerate observance, but the black churned up old pain and made me exceedingly sad to see it.

Deciding Luca would ride in a separate cart with our trunks, we headed home.

***

As soon as the door opened, Ellie immediately addressed the housekeeper. "Oh, Mrs. Fletcher, I am so terribly sorry for your loss. From what Nicolas has told me, Thomas was a fine man."

Obviously startled but not displeased by my unconventional wife's reassuring hand upon her arm, Mrs. Fletcher smiled. "Thank you, Lady Halstead. It's good to see you home safe and sound."

Ellie turned to me. "Nicolas, would you mind overmuch if Mrs. Fletcher called me Ellie? Even at home father's staff called me Miss Ellie."

Mrs. Fletcher looked at me uncomfortably. I gave her an encouraging smile and said, "She'll not rest until you do, dear. Believe me."

Mrs. Fletcher shook her head and opened her mouth to speak. I cut in, "Save the formalities for when Grannie's about. We're a family here, and we shall not stand on pretense when we're home alone."

She smiled apprehensively and turned to my wife "This old dog is likely to take a long time to learn this new trick, but I shall do my best Miss Ellie."

Unhindered by the dictates of society, Ellie gave her a hug that turned this way and that. Though obviously taken aback by such an American expression of joy, I knew Mrs. Fletcher well enough to know she found Ellie as delightful as I did. My heart warmed. Ellie had been motherless nearly the whole of her life and I knew these two would get on. I'd spent the last few days describing my feelings for Ellie because I wanted Mrs. Fletcher to have a foundation from which to know her. I hadn't quite figured out how to fully explain Luca, but I'd tiptoed around my strong feelings of friendship for him. Privy to my nature, she very well might look the other way, but how would she take my wife also loving Luca? I wasn't sure if she interpreted the depth of my meaning. I determined I'd come clean eventually. I could never lie to the old dear. When her hug ended, her eyes went to Luca, who now stood just behind me.

I said, "May I introduce our good friend, Luca Franco. Luca, may I present Merriam Fletcher, the dearest soul on earth. Without her my life would be in shambles."

Landed gentry though he was, Luca took her hand and bowed over it in deference to the regard he knew I held for her. "I am pleased to make your acquaintance, madam. Nicolas tells me you were instrumental in his rearing and would I compliment you for a job well done. He's a man to be proud of, and my very dear friend."

Luca couldn't have spoken better words. Though Mrs. Fletcher's cheeks pinkened at his compliment, she beamed. "Why how thoughtful of you to say." She looked at me with pride shining in her eyes. "And how right you are. A mother couldn't be prouder than I."

I kissed her cheek and said to her by way of my companions. "Yes, she's responsible for me being the rascal I am." The three of them laughed and on the heels of that laughter, the cart men arrived at the door with our belongings. After some direction, our belongings got settled. I paid the men and saw them out the door. Mrs. Fletcher informed us our tea was set and offered to bring the tray up to my study.

I shook my head. "I won't have you take the stairs, dear heart."

Her eyes went from me to Ellie to Luca and back. I knew it embarrassed her to be unable to work at capacity. Fifty-five years ago when she was hardly more than a girl, she started in the Halstead kitchens working alongside her mother who was the cook at the time. Through efficiency and a bright disposition, she worked her way up in service to become Grannie's lady's maid. From there she was made the Halstead housekeeper, a position held in regard by the upstairs and respected by the downstairs of the manor. Such a life of dedicated service made for a hard habit to break. Because she didn't trust anyone to keep our secrets, I indulged her insistence that our household help live off the premises.

I told my companions, "She's long-suffering of my obstinacy in this matter and believes I'm Dr. Compton's conspirator." I gave her a cajoling grin. "I merely carry out his wishes dear, and he wishes you to rest your bones for the time being."

"But your tea—"

Ellie said, "I can do that."

It was one thing for me to share tea with the housekeeper, it was quite another to do it in front of others. Seeing that obstinate stand-on-propriety glinting in Mrs. Fletcher's eyes, I spoke before she had a chance to hobble off. "Not this time, sweetheart. I'm perfectly able to wheel a tea cart and balance a tray. Why not settle yourselves in your sitting room and become better acquainted there?" I voiced it hopefully. Mrs. Fletcher knew me well enough to discern their getting to know one another was important to me. She let out a small sigh of resignation but gave me a tender smile despite herself. To sweeten the defeat, I added, "I never did mention our encounter with gypsy fortune tellers in Paris. Ellie, please start the tale while I see to our tea."

"Real gypsy fortune tellers?" Wide-eyed Mrs. Fletcher was beside herself as I knew she would be. She may have never left Britannia's shores, but her heart was that of a true adventurer.

"Oh, Mrs. Fletcher, it was a scene right out of a penny dreadful! First Nicolas had his cards read…"

I left to fetch our tea, grateful for the distraction.

***

With willow bark tea and a doctor-prescribed sleeping draught for her discomfort, Mrs. Fletcher said her good night and took herself to bed.

Upstairs, Ellie, Luca and I discussed the happenings of the last several days. After I left Paris, they'd gone to the Louvre and seen the *Virgin of the Rocks*. But as hungry as I was to learn all they'd discovered, we had other matters to discuss. Though I sincerely believed that the well had run dry, I took a deep breath — not trusting myself not to weep in the telling — as I explained the manner of Thom's injuries and my suspicion that Bruno was alive and in London. Then I lost the battle to hold back my tears.

Luca's face displayed a range of emotion, from disbelief, to pain, to rage. He caressed my cheek. "I know this pain, *il mio amore*. I would do anything to take it from you." I turned my face to kiss his palm.

"So would I." Ellie echoed. I kissed the top of her head. She clung to my arm. Feeling her fear actually made me stronger somehow and my tears dried. I covered her smaller hand with my own. I would protect this special creature with my life if necessary.

There was no need for me to say more.

Ellie said, "What do we do? That madman is here now."

"Thom said the man wants to hurt me. That's what he overheard before they beat him. If Thom was correct, Bruno held me responsible for his sorry state." Ruin lay down this path. Until an answer showed itself, I had no control. In this moment, I couldn't see anything else.

Luca sat back in his chair and tipping his head back, covered his face with both hands. His fingers curled into the midnight strands at his forehead. "Why? Why didn't I kill him? Why didn't I look to see if the monster was dead?"

"We just wanted to be gone from that place. We were fooled. After what you'd just been through, I'm the one who should have made certain he was dead, not you. And he certainly appeared dead to me."

Sitting straight, Luca looked at me, sadness deepening the blue of his eyes. "I am so sorry. I am responsible for this tragedy. Bruno would never have come if not for his obsession with me. I wish it had been me instead of your Thomas."

I shook my head.

Ellie echoed the sentiment. "Don't, Luca. How could either of you have suspected he'd survive such a fall?"

It wasn't the reunion any of us wanted. Matters were far too dire. By necessity we spent the next hour or so discussing Bruno in London. Our conversation lingered on the need for caution.

My fatigue weighing heavily, there came a point where I simply couldn't absorb any more. I rose from the settee and held my hands to them. "I've experienced such heartache this week, I can't think anymore. I'm so very tired. I haven't had a full night's sleep since before our storm at sea. My soul needs respite. Come to bed. I want nothing more than to hold you both and escape these anxious thoughts."

It didn't take long to bare ourselves and slide between the linens. I laid between them wishing like hell my mind had a valve or a key with which to shut down the specters looming within. I wished I could simply lose myself in loving. But I didn't have a means to close my mind to the ticker tape thoughts that ran endlessly. Thomas had always been my connection to the world that lay beyond titles and privilege — an enviable salt of the earth who might go where he wished and do as he pleased. Through his connections to other servants, he knew the rough side of London. Anything I'd learned about the city's seedier side I'd learned from him. If he didn't know, he'd know someone who knew someone who did. But Thom was gone. I had no such connections and I felt as helpless and vulnerable as a quail chick without a wing to hide under.

A madman was out there in a dark corner, an insidious spider weaving his web and waiting for the day I'd innocently stumble into it. Bruno wished to hurt me and how I saw it, he had several ways in which to do this. Scandal, of course. But I found it hard to believe my social ruin would be enough for the man. I loved four people alive in this world, Ellie, Mrs. Fletcher, Grannie, and Luca. Coming at me through any of these precious souls would cause me pain.

Bruno had already been responsible for my best friend's death and it chilled me to think he might have known what Thom meant to me. A small shiver ran up my spine as I had a sudden perception. A passage from the Book of Matthew flashed before my mind and I knew: An eye for an eye and a tooth for a tooth. Whatever the man proposed to do to me through any channel he found, the end would see me mutilated. I knew it as surely as I knew my own name.

Ellie's voice pulled me into the here and now, and I became aware of the small warm hand caressing my chest. I stilled it with my own. "I'm sorry love, what was it you just said?"

"I said, 'Your thoughts are miles away.'"

Luca was oddly quiet, though he too caressed me. His hand paused, perhaps waiting on my response.

I rubbed my weary eyes. "I can't seem to quiet my mind."

She kissed me softly. "Small wonder after all you've been through. Roll over."

"What?"

She gave me a little shove. "Go on, roll over."

I stretched out on my belly. Sandwiched between their warmth, they treated me to loving caresses, both soft and firm. Ellie hummed a sweet lullaby. Soothed and comforted, I drifted off to much-needed sleep.

***

I woke to thunder sometime in the wee hours to find Ellie wrapped in my arms and Luca absent. Figuring he'd simply gone to the commode, I waited. Minutes passed so I determined he went instead to fetch a drink in the kitchen. I eased myself from her side, donned my dressing gown and went to join him. I found a note tucked under the door. Taking it to the hall, I lit the lamp and read:

> *He'll not hurt either of you.*
> *I swear it.*
> *Know I'll love you always,*
> L

Steel-edged fear for Luca gripped me. I had to find him.

The mantle clock struck four times and, as if on cue, the skies opened. It was raining heavily now. I dressed quickly. Mrs. Fletcher found me in the hall searching the under-stairs cupboard for my mackintosh.

"Goodness, you can't mean to be going out in that downpour, dear."

"I do. Blast it all. I can't find my mac—"

"To the left dear, just behind your dress coat and cape."

Relieved to have direction, my blind hand found the rain coat by its rubbery texture. To my surprise, she asked, "Are you going after Luca?"

I stared at her dumbly.

She offered, "He left around midnight. I couldn't sleep and came into the hall just as he closed the door behind him."

My heart sank. He'd had hours to get to who knows where. I dragged a hand over my face, hating how helpless I felt in that moment.

She took me by the arm and led me to the kitchen. "We're both wide awake now. Come sit with me a while, dear."

To Merry Fletcher, a cup of tea was as medicinal as any potion the doctor could concoct. She had a precise and comfortingly familiar method to this simple task and I absently watched her pour. When she finished her this-and-that, I pulled a chair for her and took my seat. For the life of me, I didn't know what to say. In the end, it was my heart that spoke for me. "Do you love me?"

She blinked, obviously stunned by my question.

I knew intrinsically that she did. I'd known it for the past twenty-six years, and the fact of it was written upon her face. However I needed her to hear her own sentiment to pave the way for the truth to come. Reaching across the table, I took her hands from her steaming cup. They were very warm. "I'm serious, dear heart."

She said plainly, "I've loved you since the day your father brought you downstairs as a bundle in his arms. And then … after … after your parents…." The words trailed off as she bit back an older grief. She'd been exceedingly fond of my father, and he'd been fond of her. With Grannie's help, she'd raised me in his image.

I said, "I'm sure I loved my parents, though on the whole I have little memory of them. Whenever I think of my childhood, I remember you." With my parents and nanny dead, and my bones broken, I was naturally inconsolable. Mrs. Fletcher's tenderness saw me through pain and loss. In fact, I'd bonded so thoroughly with this loving woman that my grandmother dismissed the hastily-hired nanny and left me in Mrs. Fletcher's care. Too young to understand it at the time, I'd learned much later that Mr. Fletcher had passed just a month before I arrived in my sorry state. Widowed at thirty-three, Mrs. Fletcher had needed me as much as I'd needed her. That Grannie made this small unconventional adjustment to her household at a time when her own grief was paramount was a demonstration of her concern and affection for the both of us.

"You were such a bright and happy little boy before the accident, and so sad when Lady Augusta brought you home from France. And those nightmares of yours…"

I really wasn't surprised that she remembered. The nightmares I had as a child were so real and terrifying, I often woke screaming. She would scoop me into her comforting embrace and chase the demons away. If it were only that simple now. "You've always looked after me with a mother's love. Though Grannie did have her influence, the foundation on which I stand is your doing. Your love without condition has brought immense happiness to my life."

She gave me a tender smile and easing one hand from mine, quickly swiped the single tear that rolled down her cheek before returning it. "After Peter's passing, the good lord placed first you, and then Thomas, into my life."

Seeking lighter thoughts, I chuckled. "That couldn't have been easy with the pair of us."

The smile she gave me was sincere. "It was, and is, my joy. Thomas found his way, you know." She went on to explain how he loved a boy in the Ashford household, a footman by the name of William Trent. I knew he'd fancied Will, Thom had said as much. She told how William was the son of a baker and longed to return to a work he loved. I learned they planned to move to a small Welsh town in the countryside to open a bakeshop together as partners. Poor William had been out of town with the Ashfords when Thom passed. When I'd seen Will the other day, there was no doubt he wore his grief on his sleeve. I tucked that sad thought away.

"I've found my way as well."

She smiled. "She's a lovely girl, dear. Miss Ellie positively sparkles."

I laughed. "That she does. But there's more to her than meets the eye. To my good fortune, I've found acceptance for the man I am."

Her eyes widened slightly, as understanding came. I'd primed this pump over the last few days, and beyond that, she'd lived with Thomas and me far too long to miss such details. "You're saying you love Luca as you loved Thomas?"

I nodded.

"But…"

"She accepts me." I could see the words of caution forming in her mind and was taken back to a conversation had with Thomas the day before Ellie and I left for Gretna Green. I'd told him Ellie was accepting and he cautioned me how women often said one thing and meant another. In for a penny in for a pound, I added, "And Ellie loves Luca nearly the same as she loves me."

"Ellie loves you… both?" She pressed her fingers to her mouth.

Aside from the fact she didn't possess a judgmental or reproving bone in her body, born into the household as she was, Merriam Fletcher was loyal to the Halsteads. That didn't mean she was beyond being shocked by my declaration. I expected her to be. After all, I'd essentially admitted my wife and I took another man to our bed. I knew she was thinking about the possible scandal if the world got wind of my unorthodox love. I was a Halstead. My family held its land and peerage since before the coming of the Tudors. I sat in the House of Lords. Inheriting my father's title brought obligations to my noble family name, and especially to my grandmother.

We sat in silence. I recalled the last time we sat just so, while her mind came to terms with information she'd been given. She'd convinced me to procure this townhome so Thomas and I might share our affections away from prying eyes and potential for ruin. I could feel the old dear's mind working the situation now.

As if the empty house itself had ears to overhear us, she leaned forward and whispered, "I'm about to share something very few are aware of, and I trust you'll keep the information to yourself." When I didn't answer right away, she raised a brow. I nodded. She proceeded to tell me of the long loving commitment between Dr. Compton and Dr. O'Connor and how both men made a pretense of favoring the company of women, something Luca would be wise to do. I feigned surprise but wondered how she got the story. I had to ask.

"My Peter served with them in the war. He worked as a hospital steward. And all who worked alongside the doctors never suspected the fact of their relationship. But then Dr. Compton was seriously wounded. And Dr. O'Conner was so distraught that their nature became clear to Peter. My husband was a tender soul. He believed the Lord put people in our path to love as He saw fit. I believe that. We don't choose whom we love, love just happens to us. Peter never said a word, you know. Not a word except to me, and only because Dr. Compton was his physician through his illness."

Pieces fell into place. Her tolerance for Thomas and I loving one another very well could have come from the respect and admiration she felt for these physicians. If they might love with harm to none, then why couldn't we? Still, her next words surprised me. "Is there anyway Luca might live here, then? It would be safer for the both of you. I couldn't bear it if anything happened to you too, dear. I know what was done—" she swallowed hard to finish, "what was done to our Thomas."

Safer. I had the sudden image of Bruno standing beside poor Thom, the wicked cane in his hand raised high. She must have seen something on my face because she searched my eyes. I looked away feeling very much like a boy caught in the sugar bowl. "Nicolas, look at me."

I met those incisive eyes.

"I know you well enough to spot when you're burdened by something. Please tell me, dear. Perhaps I can help."

I began the tale with Ellie's proposal and ended with Luca leaving to find Bruno. The only thing I left out were the intimacies of our profound loving. After much consideration, I also shared what Thomas had said about the Italian toff who sought to hurt me and how I suspected Luca left to see that threat didn't happen. The range of emotion played over her features as keenly as any well-executed portrait, including wonder that such a priceless book existed, horror that a powerful Italian count could be capable of such cruelty, her anger and pain over Thomas, and of course, a mother's concern for me. I told of Luca's Cesare and the years the count relentlessly pursued him.

"My goodness. The poor lad." I could see her sympathy for the young Luca who'd been through so much pain and isolation.

I finished, "And there you have it." My thumbs absently rubbed her knobby knuckles. "As a child, whenever I was afraid, whenever I was sad, yours was the comfort I sought." I drew a deep breath and let it out slowly. "I'm afraid, dear heart. So much so it withers me inside."

She mirrored my breath. "We must find Luca."

Born into society as I was, my privileged station held me at arm's length from the rest of the world for the whole of my life. I was blind to the underbelly of London and Thomas and his contacts weren't here to help me navigate. I shook my head hopelessly and explained it all, adding, "I don't know where to search."

The rain exacerbating her rheumatism, she left her chair with no little effort. Before I could stop her, she'd retrieved for us her market tablet and pencil. "The Cooper siblings will be here at first light. I'll send 'round a note to William Trent."

Realize that everything connects to everything else.
– Leonardo da Vinci

~10~

Ellie stood at the window looking for all the world like she'd posed for Vermeer. I joined her there. Movement below in the courtyard caught my eye. With the weather finally cooperating, the Cooper maids were below hanging the laundry on the line and taking obvious care not to drag the linens in the small patch of grass. Presumably their younger brother was off to the butcher to buy Mrs. Fletcher's meats for the next few days for Ned was nowhere in sight. He'd taken our note to William Trent that morning, which had been fortuitous timing on our part. William had given his notice to Lady Ashford and planned to leave for Wales today. He replied to our note by saying he'd come.

Not turning from the window, Ellie said, "Why must you go? Why wouldn't we contact the authorities instead?"

I put my arms around her waist and, pulling her back against me, rested my chin upon her shoulder. Knowing her to be logical, I offered logic, "What could I say that wouldn't open us all to ruin?"

Turning in my arms, she picked imaginary lint off my jacket. Thom's jacket. She met my eyes. "This belonged to Thomas?"

I nodded. His everyday clothing left here would be my disguise. Smelling his scent upon them made my heart ache. I'd been compelled to hug myself when I'd donned it, in a poor facsimile of his embrace.

"Let me go with you. I might think of options along the way."

I drew her close. "We've already discussed this at length, love. While I can think of no mind sharper and more creative than yours, I'll not see you in harm's way."

"But you can't possibly be everywhere at once, Nicolas, and time is of the essence. I could—" The ringing service bell I'd rigged the other way around for Mrs. Fletcher interrupted her sentence.

I could see another salvo of well-concluded reasoning headed my way. "Please Ellie, enough. This is dangerous business."

"If I were to—"

"No. I'll not be swayed in this. William is here and I must go." Her arched brows drew together and her lips pursed pensively. When the perfect machine of her mind had worked the issue as far as it was able, she let out a deep sigh of resignation. "I love you. Please be careful."

"And I love you. I promise I'll be as careful as I can possibly be." I kissed her, savoring the warm press of our lips, a kiss that might very well be our last.

***

It didn't take much effort on my part to learn William Trent was hell bent for justice. I not only found him eager to help me find Luca, he wanted to see Bruno the murderer put down like the mad dog he was. I could certainly see what it was about him that captured Thom's heart. Stocky and plain-featured, there was a charm and wit to Will that transcended the impression made at first glance. Yes, I could see why Thomas might share the rest of his life with this fellow. I no sooner had the thought than the sad fact followed it: Thom no longer had a life to share.

I knew by his deathbed conversation that Thomas had encountered Bruno and his men at the Crested Lark down off Fleet Street. William suggested we go there on foot so he might make discreet inquiries of mollies and toms — those sexually deviant men and women who frequented the East End — of his acquaintance, along the way. Foreign deviants who hunted for like-minded partners in society's hedges might be unusual enough to be noticed among this crowd. Asking other salt-of-the-earth homosexuals if they'd heard mention made of, or seen, an Italian toff with two or three companions proved to be a valuable exercise. In relatively short order, we had a good deal of information. Two fellows confirmed Thom's initial encounter with Bruno by directing us to the Crested Lark. One man suggested we go to an oyster parlor called the Bishop's Moke. He spoke in thick Cockney, saying, "Before 'eading anywhere else, guv'na, there's somethin' at the Moke ye 'ave t' see fer yerself."

Good enough. The area bustled with shipping business during the day and business of another sort at night. The Bishop's Moke sat at the end of a rather ratty street where fishmongers dumped their cleanings on the cobblestone for the dogs, cats, and vermin. I steeled myself to the street urchins picking through the stinking refuse for their own meal. Rome wasn't the only city with the capacity to bring me low. Ahead the sound of St Mary-le-Bow's church bells rang the eighth hour. A moment later, a cloying flower-over-fish odor enveloped me. In an instant, I was accosted by a prostitute. "Cor you are a 'andsome one, what say you and I slip 'round back and wet that wick o' yours, eh dearie?"

I attempted to take her arms from me. In the gaslight I could clearly see that the rough-looking paint on her lips did little to hide the sores of syphilis. My bile rose. "Madam, I…"

"Madam? Ha!"

William stepped in and gave her a hard shove. "G'on, off with ya!"

She chortled, her voice rising as we walked away, "Back off, yer cur. Didn't ye bloody hear 'im? I'm the frigin' queen, I am!"

Some distance away, William firmly took hold of my arm to draw me close that I alone might hear his words. "Beggin' yer pardon Sir, but ye can't act the gent down here. They'll smell it on ye."

Disconcerted by the disgusting woman, for a crazed instant my mind seized upon the absurdity of anyone smelling anything down here other than unwashed bodies, excrement of all sorts, and rotting fish. I nodded. "You're right, Will. We've come too far to bugger the works now. I'll mind what I say."

He was right to caution me. Thom would have done the same. This impoverished side of London with its dark side streets was rife with crime. I didn't know if the Ripper went after men like me in addition to the prostitutes he murdered, and I didn't want to test the possibility. While he'd been inactive down here these last six years, the truth was he'd never been captured. I had the sudden urge to look behind me. The whore's ponce had just brought her a paying customer and she saw to him right there, up against the bricks. Her man had gotten more than a toss for his coin, and chances are, so would his wife. I felt my stomach flip.

We stepped aside in time to miss brawlers crashing through a doorway. The two men didn't even pause, and continued tussling on the street. A small gaggle of prostitutes convened just outside the tavern door, making bids to anyone coming in or leaving. The long-faced one took a step forward and said to me, "Ooh yer a 'ansome one." The younger of the lot stepped in front of her and in lilting Irish said, "Sure an' ye are foine. An' I can do ye better than this poxie haybag, lovie."

The others cackled, their words blending together. "Poxie! Listen t' her! Yer a foine one to talk yerself."

A half-Arab shoved her aside and took my arm, "And I can do ye both, dearie!"

Taking a page from Will, I growled, "G'on, off with ye!"

The long-faced whore said to her companions, "Don't ye see Agnes, these blokes don't like the ladies, they're bloody mollies they are!"

"Ooh that's such a shame Sally, me muff's so much tighter than an arse!" one chortled to her sniggering companions.

William pressed himself up against the younger, his hand gripping the layers of her skirt and pressing into the juncture of her thighs, "No chuckie, we're only on business t'night. Perhaps when we're done we'll take all three o' you on." Seeing the future potential for coin, they sobered.

The half-Arab tom, poorly disguised by an off-color hairpiece that partially covered her men's haircut, slid a hand inside the bodice of the Irish and cooed, "We'd like that, Johnnie, yes we would."

That possible outing squelched, we kept walking. Just ahead, we spotted the swinging shingle with a donkey wearing a bishop's miter on its head. We'd come to our first stop, the Bishop's Moke. Inside, the air was thick with the smell of buttery oysters and lemon. It might have encouraged an appetite at another location, but here it was just one more layer of stink on the damp mephitis that clung to everything along the docks. We found ourselves a corner table. When a barmaid came to take our order, William did the talking, "'Scuse me sweetheart, I'm tryin' to find an Italian bloke, a toff he is. Always has his men about him."

She looked him over, then eyeing me her eyes opened with some surprise. She stammered, "Er ... I only started workin' here last week, guv. Let me send Bertie over. He owns the Moke, if there's somethin' worth knowin', ol' Bertie's yer man."

A moment later, Bertie came up, wiping his hands on his oyster-damp apron. He too looked surprised to see me for he actually stared a moment before shaking his head. Directing his question to Will, he said, "Peg says yer askin' about the Italian toff? Sort o' a peacock with a scar on his cheek?"

Will met my eye. At my nod, he said, "Yes, that's 'im."

The barman looked at me again. It was disconcerting to say the least for I'd never before laid eyes upon him nor had I been to this establishment before. Then he turned to Will with a scowl and said, "Aye, I know of 'im but what's it to you?"

Seeing where this was headed, I discreetly slipped a £5 note into Will's hand under the table. He made as though he pulled it from his pocket, then straightened the bill crisply before setting it on the table. "Look, the toff owes me, he does. I only want what's due and I'm willin' to pay for the information."

Scowling Bertie rubbed his stubbled chin and eyed the note. I felt a sudden wave of panic. Was it too much? Would coin have been more fitting? What was the protocol for such inquiries? He made to reach for it, but Will covered the money with his hand. Drawing back, Bertie met my eyes and I saw a surprising glint of anger. His words directed at me, he repeated, "An' what's the toff to you?"

Will nudged me with his foot, and I correctly assumed he meant for me to remain silent, for he slid the note closer to Bertie. But offering no answer, he stated simply, "Our business is our own, Bertie. I know ye understand."

Bertie's mouth made a grim line. Grabbing up the note before it could be covered again, he said gruffly, "Aye. Come with me. You'll want t' speak wi' my brother."

We followed the barman through the kitchen, where an army of oyster shuckers sat beside water-filled wooden tubs of tightly closed mollusks and pried them open with knives, while others filled the orders as the maids brought them in. Up the stairs and down the narrow hall we followed until Bertie stopped by a closed door. He turned to us before entering and said, "Wait here." A moment later he led us in. There, sitting bundled in a blanket near the brazier, was a man so similar in feature and coloring to me, he might pass as my sibling if not my reflection. Will looked from Bertie's brother to me and back again. By the look of the man, he'd recently had himself quite the beating and I could only imagine what his face looked like when the injuries were new. And what injuries might be hidden by the blanket. Yellow and purple bruises were fading on his face and it looked like he had a sling tied and knotted at his shoulder. That he was nearly identical to me and had been severely beaten was quite unsettling. There was deeper meaning here than any of them realized.

The barman said, "Alfred, these men are askin' after that bleedin' Italian toff."

Alfred looked up at us, a brief glimmer of fear shown in his eyes at the mention of Bruno. A crash below called Bertie's attention. With a grunt of momentary indecision, he gave us a warning eye that clearly said that whatever our business was with his brother, we'd better tread lightly, and went downstairs.

Making an astute assumption, Will briefly laced his fingers in mine. If Alfred was the homosexual we suspected, this was a declaration that we were cut from the same cloth. Sure enough, Alfred appeared to relax upon seeing our hands.

"Don't mind Bertie. He's alright," he said. He went on to explain that his elder brother possessed a sexual appetite more conventional. Bertie did not approve of Alfred's predilections but loving him anyway; as any older brother might, he took far greater exception to his little brother being abused. He too would see the Italian toff brought to justice.

I asked, "So, the toff did this to you, Alfred? Where was this done? And why?"

He nodded. "He did, and I couldn't tell ye why. I work over at the Brimstone, ye see?" My lookalike proceeded to describe what could only be the latest iteration of the fraternal gentleman-deviant societies so popular the last century, the Hellfire Club. I'd never been to such modern-day clubs. It was something Thomas and I never needed to do. Though I'd known about them for years, I couldn't even say where these clandestine settings could be found.

Every schoolboy at Eaton tittered over the idea of such a club existing where sexual fantasy was had in full, and where a brotherhood kept one's activities secret from the world. In vogue among deviants, homosexual or otherwise, such fellowships were popular to those seeking unusual forms of sexual gratification. Drawn by the siren's call of steady pay, hefty gratuity, and perhaps driven by an insatiable nature, young men and women made themselves living playthings for the well to do. This was a nature our Alfred here seemed to possess.

Albert described for us the establishment and its location, and how one night there came an immaculately-dressed foreigner who spoke with an Italian accent. Apparently he was a handsome older fellow despite a jagged scar that ran the length of his cheek, a disfiguring scar I knew came courtesy of Cesare.

Albert said, "This toff, he asked for me, specific. Jimmy, he's the minder there. He says the toff saw me an' would have no other even though another gent wanted me first. So, I figured since he was askin', he'd pay well, if ya know what I mean. Jimmy said the toff had a mind for it rough, you know how some blokes like it rough? He wanted that an' I don't mind rough sport, as long as I have my time too. I mean, that's why I'm there, right?"

At our nods, he went on. "Sometimes rough gets noisy, ye know? There's a room below the cellar, a rum hole where the caskers stashed their spirits an' dodged the taxmen back in the day. So down I went to wait for him. It's only ever s'posed to be one-on-one unless the players agree otherwise, but this bloke brings his men down with him, an' believe me, when I heal up, Jimmy's gonna hear about it from Bertie an' me. He raised me, Bertie did. He was just fifteen when our mum died birthing me. Our da died in the spring that year, so it's just been him and me since. I've never seen my brother so angry. He's eager to find the toff or at the least t' give Jimmy a piece of his mind, let me tell ye. Bertie figures Jimmy must o' been paid extra to bend the rules.

He hates the way I live my life anyway, ye see? He was beside himself when I got back home."

The man barely drew a breath, and continued, "So anyway, I figure, alright, the man's a watcher an' he wants a show. I seen those watcher toffs before, but their coin is as good as the next man's and I'm still enjoying myself, right?"

I assumed Alfred was reliving the encounter when he drew silent a moment and stared into the grate. I followed his eye to watch the low flame flicker over the coal. He added, "So I gets ready I do, but he don't want no show. The next I know, I'm held down an' gagged. They dislocated my shoulder, they did. Hurt like a bleedin' hot poker it did, an' my arm hung useless. Still givin' me hell like somethin's wrong inside the socket."

Will and I exchanged glances. We both knew this man was lucky to be alive. I said, "Then no one heard what was happening to you?"

He shook he head. "Not for want of me tryin'! The casker's hole is a quiet place though. It's meant to be. I made my way out after, an' Jimmy helped me home, as far as I know he's kept my sorry condition a secret."

"Why would he do that?"

"He'd lose his job too if anyone found out the toff an' his men wrecked me like they had. It'll look bad for him with the Nobs that own the place if the workers get hurt, ye know? The owners would never allow one o' us gals or blokes to get hurt. Even them that likes pain in their game know they're safe. I tried explainin' this to Bertie, but he ain't havin' any of it. He wants justice against the toff and his bleedin' men, an he wants to knock ol' Jimmy's teeth out. But Jimmy did a good thing helpin' me in secret. He even found me a doctor to set my arm an' paid the man too."

Paid with his Judas's silver. I found myself angry. "Jimmy sounds a right generous bastard to me."

Alfred chuckled. "I know it looks bad fer him, but he's a good man, an' did right by me. I know if the Nobs had seen me after, they'd figure I was trouble an' wouldn't allow me back. They got rules, they do."

The disgust in Will's voice was evident when he said, "Going back seems a daft thing to do, man. By the look of ye, ye were nearly killed."

Apparently unwilling to give up his addiction to perversion, Albert shrugged like what he'd been through was akin to a walk in the park. "The tips are too good, an' with the right people, so's the rest, if ye get my meanin'."

Losing my patience for such stupidity, I asked, "So what else happened?"

He continued, "So anyway, I put up a fight as best I could hopin' to draw attention, but two on one, there's just no way to fight that for long, ya know? Not with a bloke as strong and big as an ox, an me with a useless hangin' arm." He examined a heavily bruised hand. Following his gaze I saw several likely broken knuckles. "I got buggered hard by at least two o' his men, an' the whole time this fuckin' toff comes flyin' at me hammer and tongs an' starts beatin' me bloody. At one point, he took off his frigin' shoe an' used that rather than his fists! Ye should o' seen me the next day. I had his heel marks all over my ribs and down my back. A bleedin' Marquis de Sade, he was."

I watched him reflexively cover his privates with his good hand. "Then he grabbed me, oh lord did he hurt me. An' he took out a pen knife an' made like he was gonna cut off my nob. He'd seen to it that they used me so rough, truth be told I was scared of gettin' worse. The more I pleaded through my gag, the more he seemed to be enjoyin' himself. An' I wouldn't have put it past him to lop my cock right off!"

Seething, Will asked, "And what then, the toff just stopped cold?"

Alfred shook his head, his next words contradicted by the red blush on his cheeks, "I ain't embarrassed to say it, I pissed myself. Who wouldn't, ye know? Then he starts laughin', fuckin' laughin', an him smelling like a piss pot himself. I tell ye I was scared for my life. He's a devil, a mad devil right out o' hell, he is."

More than you know.

For the first time since we stepped through the door, Alfred looked long at me. I saw his eyes widen slightly as recognition dawned. His next words came as a surprise. "You're Nicolas."

There was a second of indecision on my part, but I quickly determined I owed this man the truth for standing as my proxy, however unwittingly, and looking death in the eye. I nodded. "I am. I suspect your similarity to me was the impetus for the abuse you suffered."

"He called me Nicolas over an' over. When they first came in he called me that. I told him that wasn't my name, but he was free to play that it was. I thought it part of the game he came for, ya see. Instead he slapped me hard across the face then gagged me."

Will said, "You're fortunate to be alive, my friend."

Alfred's eyes went from mine to Will's and I could tell he clearly thought so too.

Will explained, "The fuckin' sod and his men did the same to my Thommy. For no reason at all, just on a whim." In a choked voice, he added, "And it took his precious life away from me."

Feeling my own loss, I swallowed my emotion and put an arm around Will's shoulders. "Thom was my oldest and dearest friend."

Alfred frowned. "I'm sorry for yer loss, but I can't tell ye more than I already did."

Careful of his broken fingers, I slipped a note into Alfred's hand and told him where we could be found. "If you hear of this man's whereabouts, please send me word. Discretion is imperative."

Will cast Alfred a raised eyebrow and the man's nod indicated he'd remain silent. Alfred gingerly closed his fingers around the £5 note as if he weighed whether or not to keep it.

We talked a bit longer but it was obvious that Alfred had no other information to impart. One thing had come to light in our conversation. Poor Alfred was chosen to be my surrogate. Clearly, the abuse meted out on my look-alike was symbolically meant for me.

With nothing else to go on, we said goodbye, endured the glowering Bertie in the kitchen, and headed to the Crested Lark.

***

It was half-past ten when we arrived. I knew this place well. The Crested Lark, with its unique shingle depicting a lark wearing a jauntily-angled crown, was quiet and off the beaten path situated as it was on the factory end just off Fleet Street. In a setting that could have been painted by John Maggs himself, the Lark was an old coach inn that hinted at Elizabethan origins. Even at this late hour, the place was packed tight like a box of salted cod. I felt a pang as I stepped inside. Thomas and I occasionally came here for dinner and cards.

The place had been around since Georges Fortescue, a chef for the beheaded Charlotte Corday, escaped the French Revolution and came to London. He Anglicized the tavern's name during the Napoleonic Wars and Hanley Fortescue, Georges' grandson several times removed, built upon the sterling reputation Georges and ensuing generations created. Known for being clean and discreet, not only could patrons find fresh ale, but a good French bisque and the longest-running baccarat game in the West End, with men coming and going as dictated by their winnings or losses.

I pulled the brim of my hat lower. Keeping to the wall, we headed to the corner table. From this vantage we might see who was here, and who came and went from the closed playing room. I held up two fingers to the barman and ordered our ale.

When Bonnie, the highly-freckled maid of past acquaintance, brought our mugs, I set a sovereign on the table. "Bonnie, love, we need information, and the remainder is yours if you can help us. A week ago an Italian fellow came here—"

Apparently paying little attention to my common attire, her face lit with the prospect. "We get all sorts in here, Sir. Spaniards, Frenchies, I-talians, they come off the boats, ye see, an' truth be told I have trouble tellin' them one from the other with their chatterin'."

Chuckling, Will said, "Ain't that the truth. Might ye have seen a fusty piss-smelling toffer with servants doggin' his heels?"

She covered her gap-toothed smile as she laughed. "Lord yes, I do remember him. He's been a regular here for nearly a month now. " Sobering, she added, "Gives me the all-overs, he does."

"Yes, he does the same to me. What do you remember about

him?"

"Comes for the bisque, he does. Always orders two bowls and always asks for water and lemon. The other night I asked him if he wanted the usual water and lemon with his bisque, and Lord, the look he gave me." She leaned closer and said as low as the din allowed, "I don't think he likes the ladies, if ye know my meanin' Sir."

"Have you seen him lately?" I slid the coin closer.

"Once or twice in the past week, he's come to play cards after his meal. I might have seen him earlier, but it's been such a busy night I can't rightly say. The Royal Fleet returned to port today, the girls an' I have been hoppin' tryin' to keep up."

Sailors. So that's why the West End was so bustling tonight. I was about to ask after Luca when Bonnie tipped her head. "That bloke over near the fire there, that's one o' his men. Shall I tell him you're askin' after his master?"

I looked to the fire. My heart began to pound and I pulled my cap a little lower. Sure enough, there sat one of Bruno's men devouring a bowl of bisque. I'd seen him at the garden party in Venice the night Luca informed Bruno in no uncertain terms that he and I were lovers. From here, it appeared he sported the faint yellow remains of a black eye and I wondered if Thomas had given it to him. This man was responsible for Thom's death. I could feel Will beside me seething as surely as a soon-to-erupt volcano.

When I didn't answer, Bonnie said, "Sir? Shall I—"

Coming down from the moment, stunned senseless, I quickly assured her no. I put the coin in her hand. "Please Bonnie, as far as you know I wasn't here and I wasn't asking after anyone. And do stay away from him should he come here again. That is a very dangerous fellow, and you're right. He doesn't like women."

She pocketed the coin. "Sure thing, Sir." She turned to walk away, then a thought must have come to her because she spun back again. "I don't know if it'll be any use to ye sir, but you're the second askin' after him tonight."

"Oh?"

She nodded and tipped her head to the far corner of the room. "I got asked by the two young blokes sittin' over there. I think they came in just minutes before you, but like I said, we've been hoppin'. The small one there did the askin'."

"Thank you, Bonnie."

She bobbed her head and left us. My eye sought the far corner and I blanched at what I found. There sat Ned Cooper, Mrs. Fletcher's house boy, and beside him, dressed in men's attire with her mass of curls tucked under an overlarge cap, my wife.

Will nudged me. "Who do you suppose they are?"

I turned to him, my very words sounding stupefied to my ears. "Bloody hell. Will, that impetuous creature over there is my wife dressed as a man."

"Oh Jesus, Mary, and Joseph. Pardon me for saying it sir, but whatever was she thinkin'? These men aren't out for a bleedin' tea party; they're murderers!"

I seriously doubted much thought was involved. Our man sits within our grasp and my hands were now quite tied. I told Will, "I must get her out of here. We'll have to abandon our efforts tonight."

"Sir, this may be our only chance."

I could feel how desperate he was, and he was right. I was about to tell him we'd begin again tomorrow when Bruno's man suddenly paid his tab and left. Naturally, Ellie and Ned rose from their seats. Doubtless determined to follow him, they left the far corner and slowly navigated the sea of patrons toward the door.

Will got up and looked out the window. He returned to say, "He's headed down Fleet Street. I'll run down Tudor to Whitefriars and trail him from there. Don't worry, he won't see me. Thommy always told me I was half cat." He gave me a hopeful smile despite the obvious pain of the comment.

"Be careful, Will." I left through the front door while he exited through the back. Catching my wife by the elbow the instant she stepped outside, I hissed for her ears alone, "Have you completely taken leave of your senses?"

She squeaked and whirled about. "Nico…" I quickly covered her mouth with my hand and pulled her into the doorway. Bruno's man wasn't that far down the street. He might hear my name and return. The last thing we needed was to get trapped like a fox up a tree. I cautioned rather sharply before I removed my hand, "Remain silent." Casting an exasperated eye at the anxious teen beside her, I handed him a sovereign. "Ned, for god's sake, find us a hansom. Keep this night to yourself and the rest is yours."

Just as courage imperils life, fear protects it.
– Leonardo da Vinci

~11~

We needed to talk. The house was dark when we returned and I gestured to Ellie that we should quietly take the stairs lest Mrs. Fletcher wake. We hadn't spoken a word in the coach, not with Ned sitting beside me and the driver privy to our conversation. Ellie had to have realized the moment she opened her mouth he'd know she wasn't actually a man. Considering he was driving us home, that was one potential scandal we didn't need to face.

She pulled the hat from her head and I watched her unbraid the cinnamon mass, looking like a handsome effeminate lad. Ellie's borrowed attire oddly brought to mind my drunken daydream aboard ship, when I envisioned her to be both male and female at once. The pleasant thought popped like a soap bubble as the hard truth stood before me. Effeminate lads were every bit as vulnerable to miscreants on the docks as lovely women were. Exasperated, I sighed heavily. My wife was no half-brained twit; she had to see the potential for danger. She must know I couldn't possibly keep her safe if she insisted on going off on her own. "What on earth were you thinking, Ellie?"

"I thought—"

"Stop!" I put up my hand to halt her explanation, realizing that the reason behind such a rash stunt didn't matter. The fact was that she'd deliberately put herself in harm's way. The evening had finally gotten the better of me and I poured my feelings out for her. "You know what that monster did to Thomas. You know what he did to Cesare. Do you honestly believe he'd do any less to you? He promised me he'd do worse in Venice!"

I went on to explain about Alfred and his injuries and the fact he and I looked so much alike the man could pass as my twin. Her eyes grew wide as her ready intelligence grasped the significance of a man with my face beaten to within an inch of his life. Ellie already knew how I feared for Luca and I knew she felt the same. Without mincing words, I explained what it felt like to see her there at the tavern with the murdering henchman of a misogynous madman nearby. It was obvious she hadn't known the reputation of the Crested Lark. Uninformed as she'd been, she hadn't considered the possibility that Bruno and his men might be playing cards in the next room.

That stark reality drained all the color from her face.

I added that Will went off god-knows-where to track Bruno's man alone and that was exactly what Thomas had done the night he acquired his mortal injuries. I finished, "Because I had to leave him, Will's life could very well be in danger now. I owe Thom better than this, Ellie. Much better."

Her lips quivered and tears glistened in her pale blue eyes. With her hair down around her shoulders and the sad expression on her face, she reminded me of Renoir's *Irene Cahen d'Anvers*. She said softly, "I'm sorry Nicolas, I'm so sorry. I thought it useful. I thought I might find Luca there while you and William asked about Bruno along the docks. I figured Luca would go there first because you said that's where Thomas…where Thom…" she trailed off and with a whimper and flung herself into my arms. Wrapping her arms tightly around my waist, she clung to me and sobbed.

Fearing I might have laid too much on her plate, I held her close and shushed her. It wasn't until this moment that I realized she too was wound tighter than a watch spring. When the tears had turned to hiccupping breaths and sniffles, I set her from me and handed her my handkerchief to dab her tears and nose. Looking into those eyes, I saw clearly that she felt as frustrated as I, not knowing where Luca was or in what condition. The same anxiety he and I felt when Bruno had taken her. I held her face in my hands and swept lingering tears from her cheeks with my thumbs. "We'll find him, love. I promise you, we'll find him and then put an end to this madness. I don't know how just yet, but we will."

She raised her hands to mine where I'd left them and stared into my eyes. Her breathing calmed and her sniffles abated. I felt her in my mind and realized so synchronized had our thoughts become, that Ellie's awareness was in fact an extension of my own – a clairvoyance — truth be told. Neither of us needed more words in that moment. We stood there just absorbing the fact we had each other to lean upon and this gave us the strength we needed to see us through. We'd all been helplessly tossed upon a course that wasn't of our own making, and it remained to us to survive it.

Small, nearly imperceptible changes unfolded before me as

though a beam of sunlight passed over her portrait in a mightily compressed sense of time. I watched her pupils slightly dilate as they searched from one to the other of my own. The shift of emotion showed first in her eyes. This I felt it as much as I witnessed it, for more than our minds were connected; our hearts and souls were linked. Hunting down Leonardo's book had been a lark. But what began as a lark had bloomed into companionship, commonality, and profound love between the three of us. Especially between us two. She needed me as I needed her, as we needed him.

Her face turned to my palm and I felt her kiss upon it. I swept her hair back and kissed her brow. A threshold crossed, I dropped to my knees to remove the over-large work boots and the padding of three pairs of woolen socks. When I stood, her hands pulled my shirttails free and I did the same to her borrowed shirt. We undressed as men might, with fingers deftly unbuttoning trousers, shirts, and cuffs. I was surprised to discover she'd bound her small breasts, and I half expected a cock to materialize inside her small clothes. Another time I might have found this a fantasy, but not this time. Her hand found my cock and stroked me to fullness. In the close company of men all these weeks, my wife learned to handle a cock with a maven's skill, indeed she had. But I didn't want it.

After freeing myself from her expert fondling, she redoubled her efforts and came at me again. I heard a growl that could only have come from me. Overcome by want and days of fear, I grabbed her by the upper arms and roughly pulled her against me. I kissed her hard and deep until she bent backward under the strain of punishing lips. I wanted to love her, yet truth be told I wanted to throttle her hard enough to rattle her teeth. I wanted her to feel and understand that moment of fear I'd felt when I discovered she'd deliberately put herself in harm's way. I wanted to bury myself inside her and fuck her hard and fast until we blurred and ceased to be two. She didn't fight, and though I wasn't surprised, the small lucid portion in the back of my mind wondered what path we'd take if she had. The kaleidoscope of raw emotion coalesced into passion. Mirroring the beast I was, she gave as good as she got. Our hands raked and clawed, our kisses bruised.

Taking her by her waist, I lifted her slight body high and kissed and nipped her belly and breasts. She responded by crossing her legs around my waist. When the front of her body slid down my chest, my steel had no trouble finding its way. I eased into heat as smooth and tight as an untried scabbard on a newly-forged blade. She held my shoulders to steady herself, and I grasped her cheeks to brace her weight and sunk to my cock to the root. Between my upward thrusts and her deep-seated glides, we soon had a splendid rhythm for ourselves. Seeking the speed and leverage we both craved, I walked us to the bed and fell on top of her. Tossing her slender calves over my shoulders, I gave her my all, and took all she had.

Physically spent and emotionally drained, I eased from my sheath but didn't release her, nor could I, for Ellie clung to me as well. I covered her face with loving kisses then rolled over and took her with me. She nestled comfortably in crook of my shoulder, with her slender leg tossed haphazardly over mine. I covered us with the blanket, and then pressed my lips to her tavern-smoke-scented hair. I thought of apologizing for using her like I had, but I knew I'd been used as well. Instead I whispered with all my heart, "I love you, sweetheart."

I felt the smile against my chest. "You've never called me sweetheart before."

"No?"

She shook her head.

"You're so often in my mind, I suppose I thought you already knew it."

I felt the smile again. "I know."

***

Will hadn't returned and I went to find him. Information from a mollie sent me to the West End again, but this time I knew where to go. I stayed close to the buildings as much to keep out of the driving rain as remain unnoticed. I had to be careful of the wet and moldy places where the rain dripped through the walls and made footing a slippery affair. The storm reminded me of the coach accident that so dramatically changed my life as a child, but I pushed the unwelcome thought aside. Occasional lightning showed me where to step, and I crept slowly along the hazardous stairs to follow the voices coming from somewhere above.

A door was opening just ahead, so I ducked behind a pile of broken crates. Three Italian men exited the room and left down the stairs. Seeing I was alone, I quietly opened the door whence they came and found myself in surprisingly well-appointed quarters for such a shabby building. Gaslights blazed in crystal sconces, and the inviting room gave no indication of the decay on the other side of the door. After exploring the outer rooms, I went to what I assumed was a bedroom. There I found Luca tied unconscious and naked to the four posts of the bed. I took a step toward him but a sound from the next room beckoned me.

To my horror, a battered and bloody woman lay unrecognizable in a tangle of sheets upon a narrow bed. Curled on her side, her back was to me. She too was naked, with arms tied overhead, her long matted hair covering the side of her face. Before I realized what was happening, I was set upon by two men and dragged to the other bedroom. Bruno was there, and a third man thrust a pair of rivet tongs into the blazing stove. Bruno turned to me and smiled. It was a wild, demented smile. "Ah, Lord Nicolas, so good of you to come."

With a nod to his men, they proceeded to tear the clothes from my body, my efforts to fight them three-to-one proving useless. I watched in horror as Bruno sat on the bed and ran an adoring hand along Luca's body. He fondled him with the intent to make him hard, and the way Luca's body responded, I realized he wasn't unconscious after all. He'd been drugged to senselessness. Bruno cooed, "Yes, *il mio amore*, I know this stirs you as much as I."

They roughly tied my hands behind my back and I twisted and fought again with the same result as before. Panting with exertion, I yelled, "Stop this madness!" A second later, a gag was shoved into my mouth. For a moment I thought my jaw broken.

Bruno shook his head and continued Luca's arousal. "Madness? Even the bible tells me I can have an eye for an eye, so I have been waiting to settle a score with you, Lord Nicolas. As you can see, Luca belongs to me." I watched unbelieving as he bent over Luca and licked him from navel to neck. Luca groaned and lifted his hips for more. Bruno sat up and smiled his insane smile. He gripped Luca to show me. "Look at this magnificent stallion. What more proof do you need that you mean nothing to him?"

I twisted and screamed through my gag to no avail.

"Tsk, priorities, Lord Nicolas. Priorities." He turned to his man, "You're next aren't you?" At the man's nod, Bruno said, "Show Lord Nicolas how the idea stimulates you."

I watched the man with the black eye open his trousers and free the largest cock I'd seen outside the London Zoo. The freak of nature stroked slowly. I couldn't imagine what the devil was about. Oddly, somewhere beyond us, a bell rang.

Bruno rose to stir the coals with his tongs. He said, "Before we make you a eunuch there are events you must witness." Addressing the two men who held me, he said, "Take Lord Halstead to the other room. I'm sure he'd want to see your sport with his Lady."

My eyes grew wide. The battered woman in the other room was Ellie! Bruno laughed demonically as I fought them tooth and nail. They dragged me there and I was forced to watch the man roughly set upon her. She called for me pitifully. I heard my own muffled cries, the sound drowned out by the persistent bell.

"Nicolas. Nicolas! Wake up! Mrs. Fletcher is ringing for you!" Ellie shook me hard. "Nicolas!"

"Wha...?" Roused to consciousness by a stinging slap across my cheek, I found my tousled wife straddling me and shaking me for all she was worth. Confused, I just looked at her.

"Heavens Nicolas, I couldn't wake you! And the thrashing! You nearly knocked me to the floor twice!"

Oh, my dear god, it was a nightmare. I crushed her to me and held her tight, to chase the residual horror away. The bell from my nightmare rang again and this time my mind was aware enough to comprehend it. Mrs. Fletcher was calling me and the fact the ringing didn't stop declared that whatever it was, it was urgent. I grabbed for my trousers and dressing gown and flew.

Nature never breaks her own laws.
– Leonardo da Vinci

~12~

Fearing Mrs. Fletcher might have injured herself, I hurried down the stairs calling for her as I went.

She answered from the kitchen, "I'm in here, dear."

The room smelled so strongly of vinegar, it stung my recently-opened eyes. I found the old dear holding a vinegar-soaked rag and attending smears of blood on the tabletop. "What on earth?"

"William has been injured."

My eyes darted around the room. "Where is he?"

"I'm right here, Lord Nicolas." Will painfully made his way into the kitchen from the lavatory under the service stairs. He sported bruises on his face, and his collar and cuffs were dark with blood and grime as were the front of his trousers. He said, "Pardon me, I think I've gone an' cracked a few ribs. I'll sit if ye don't mind."

"Of course. Sit." I pulled the chair.

Mrs. Fletcher checked her watch pin for the time, then

grabbed her shawl from the hook and hobbled to the door. "The dairy man will be here shortly. I'll wait out by the curb and ask him to send the doctor when he gets to the end of the row. There's still blood on the service door handle, and he doesn't need to see it. That man carries more tails than a sack full of kittens."

What would I do without her? She alone kept scandal at bay all these years. Having grown up with her euphemisms and metaphors, each as clever as the last, I quickly replaced her "tails" with "tales."

"Sorry, ma'am." Will said, starting to rise. "I made a mess, I did. I'll clean it up straightaway."

"Sit down, William Trent. You'll do no such thing!" The look she gave him brooked no refusal on his part.

Conditioned to the downstairs service class hierarchy that put the housekeeper in charge, he sheepishly lowered back into the chair. "Yes, ma'am."

Under normal circumstances, I would have stopped her and gone to fetch the doctor myself. No, I quickly amended, under normal circumstances, she'd have a live-in staff to run and fetch for her. I said nothing to stop her because I had the feeling my pending conversation with Will might be better off without her here. It pained me to watch her hobble to the door but the last thing the old dear needed to hear was anything that shone a light on what Thomas had gone through.

Ellie came rushing into the kitchen hastily dressed, pink-cheeked, and breathless. I motioned for Will to stay seated as he attempted to rise in deference to my lady.

Her hand swept to her blouse and shoes. "I came as soon as I could, blast all these buttons. Where's Mrs. Fletcher? Is she alright?" Her eyes darted around the space and lit upon the bowl of red-tinted vinegar and Will sitting with his bloody collar and cuffs and wide-eyed at hearing a lady curse. She whirled to me, and pointing there said, "What's this about?"

"Mrs. Fletcher is perfectly fine, love. She went to wait on the dairyman to ask he would deliver a note to the doctor who lives at the end of his route." I tipped my head to Will and the bowl beside him. "I'm about to hear the rest."

Ellie took a seat. She must have noticed the long rows of cuff buttons on her cream blouse were askew, because she quickly set them to rights. I turned my attention to Will. "Tell us what happened after we left you last night."

"Well, Lord Nicolas, I ran down Tudor Street to the alley and came out just ahead of him off Whitefriars. I made like to tie my shoe and he passed me. I did that to confuse him, ye see. From there I followed the bloke, with him none the wiser. After a fashion though, I think he was startin' to feel me getting closer because he suddenly stopped and turned to face me." Will stopped abruptly and looked from me to my wife. "Beggin' yer pardon Lady Halstead, but these aren't pictures a woman ought to have in her head."

"*Fiddlesticks!* William, rest assured I—"

Seeing the fact before me, I interrupted her. "Love, Will needs room to say what needs saying." After all we'd shared, I believed Ellie could hear whatever was said, but Will didn't feel comfortable. With so much at stake, the last thing we needed was for him to omit details to spare what he viewed as a Lady's sensibilities. She started to protest. I shook my head slightly. While I appreciated her stalwart desire for answers, this was not the time for it. "Please, I shall fill you in later."

Ellie knew I was sincere but it was obvious that hungry mind of hers didn't want to wait. She took that signature breath of resignation, and letting it out, said she'd keep company with Mrs. Fletcher outside. Before she turned to leave, I gave her my thanks for understanding. Her small smile told me she understood whether or not she agreed. I couldn't ask for better.

Will said, "I sure hope her Ladyship isn't vexed, Lord Nicolas. Surely ye both know better than I what's proper to say in the company of ladies, but my mum, heaven bless her, was firm on me watchin' my tongue with ladies about. And it's not a pretty thing I'm about to tell ye."

"It's alright, Will. My wife understands. So tell me."

"Like I said, the big bloke turned to face me and I stopped in my tracks. He had a thick manner of speech, he did, and I almost didn't understand him. But he says to me, 'What do you want?'"

And I says nothing to him, but I crossed the street and keeps walkin' on. I turned and saw him just standin' there for a bit watchin' me. I don't think he trusted that I wasn't after him. Right he was, the bloody sod. So I kept just abreast of him and he's walkin' faster, puttin' some distance between us now."

"Where was he headed?"

"I do believe they're holed up in Charing Cross, sir."

"And how do you know this?"

"Well, it's only a hunch, sir. I followed him to those white-bricked row houses, you know, the ones across from that statue of Charles I? Then the bloke stops walkin' and starts fiddlin' for his keys."

That was a telling piece of information. Though I understood he was reliving the details as they occurred, the pace of this conversation was beginning to grate upon my nerves. After that nightmare, the luxury of time wasn't something I felt I had. "And?"

"Then he drops his purse and keys on the pavement and bent to gather it all up. I figured he'd been drinkin' a bit at the Crested Lark, maybe just enough to make him heavy on his feet. Like I said, he's a big bloke. I saw a chance there, I did, and I took it. I come runnin' up to him and I hauled off and punched him hard. It took everythin' I had, but he heard me last minute and started to rise. My fist caught him right here, ye see?"

He pointed to my temple, showing me where he'd landed his blow. I'd d seen a boxing match once, when a man took such a blow. He fell dead just minutes later.

"I knocked him senseless, I did. He rolled over on his back grippin' his head, and I'm afraid my hackles were up so I sat on him. He came 'round a bit and fought me. Placin' his hands here. He tried to choke me. Ye see?" After his pantomime of being strangled, Will opened his collar and showed me. I could see the dark bruises, especially the thumbprints at his Adams apple, and the deep fingernail gouges that were obviously the source of the blood on his collar. He was a lucky man and I told him so.

"Aye, well he almost took my breath. I'll tell ye, my head was swimmin'. But all I could see was my Thommy under his hand, so I balled my fists and boxed his ears as hard as I could. The next thing I know, his body starts shakin' and he's pukin' all over. Then before I know it, he laid still. I killed him, Lord Nicolas. I killed him dead. I think it was that first blow. I think it addled his brain and the ear boxing just finished the job. Before I knew it, I heard the rozzers' whistles and their batons beating the bins. I didn't know if they were coming for me or not, but I skiddled out of there as fast as I could. But don't ye worry sir, no one saw me come here. I took extra care to that."

"You did fine, Will. The police would be at the door right now if you hadn't taken such care."

His eyes were troubled when they met mine. "But to tell ye honest sir, I never meant to kill him. Hurt him, yes. I wanted to hurt him for what he'd done to my Thommy and even for roughin' up poor Alfred, but I never meant to kill him."

"I understand. But know that he'd have killed you in a wink if given the chance."

Both thoughts obviously distressing, Will nodded then absently stared at his hands. I followed his gaze. The knuckles were raw and scabbed, a gash over one suggesting he'd encountered the man's teeth. It was good the doctor was coming to tend him. Through Thom, I'd heard of a man who'd fought like this and lost his life some days later to a putrid wound.

Will's next words surprised me.

"I've already got marks against me in the Lord's eyes, sir. But maybe He'll forgive me the killin' because I didn't mean to do it."

Gingerly leaning back in his chair, he peered out the doorway, presumably to see if the women were near enough to hear his next words. Satisfied, he spoke low for my ears alone, "I know Thommy loved ye, and ye loved him back. He called ye his best and dearest friend, he did. And made me swear to never tell a soul you were like us. And I won't sir. I swear it on my life."

The thought had never entered my mind. I told him that, and added, "You're a good man, Will. Thom wouldn't have loved you otherwise."

Will shook his head sadly. "No, Lord Nicolas, I'm not a good man. Reverend Bennington told me so when I was just a lad and got caught with Jack Martin, the miller's son. I was a baker's son, ye see. Jack and I were fast friends early on. The reverend found us, he did. He said we both were goin' to hell because we lie with men. He said there was no penance for such sin and everlastin' hell was a surety. So shamed by the reverend's words, Jack hung himself the very next day. I loved that boy with all my heart, almost as much as I loved Thommy. That's why I left for London. I couldn't stand to be there anymore." He took a ragged, and obviously pain-filled, breath. "Such things never bothered Thommy. He said any love was a gift from God, for God Himself was made of love. But I was raised in a different church, ye see, just like Jack was. Reverend Bennington told us about sin and hell and burning at every sermon."

Disgusted that ignorant and insensitive comments had spurred the other young man to take his life, and for this one to be tortured, I said sharply, "Reverend Bennington has no idea of what he's talking about."

My vehemence must have surprised him, for he looked at me with wide eyes. "Truly sir, ye believe that?"

I placed what I hoped was a reassuring hand on his shoulder. "I do. Believe me, Will. You surely won't go to hell."

He swallowed. "The reverend seemed so sure…"

I shook my head. "He's wrong, Will. Thom was right. Listen to me, God made you as you are and the Lord doesn't make mistakes. What's more, I'm sure the Lord knows the truth in your heart."

"My mum, heaven bless her, said that very thing, sir. But truth be told, sir, that's why I'm doomed to hell. God sees in my heart. He knows that even though I have my regrets for the bugger's death, I'd do it all over again."

My mind raced to find soothing words for his troubled soul.

"God doesn't condemn the farmer because he kills a wolf to save his sheep does he?"

Seconds passed as Will came to terms with the idea. Coming to a conclusion, the relief in his eyes transformed him. "I suppose that's right, sir. The Italian toff lost one man, one less wolf to hurt gentle folks like poor Alfred. That leaves us only the three of them bloody bastards now."

Pleased that I'd produced the right analogy, I nodded. Changing the subject, I asked, "How did you break your ribs?"

Looking rather sheepish, Will chuckled. "By my own fool clumsiness, sir. I was runnin' from the rozzers, ye see? I stayed to the streets I knew had the fewest lamps, and I thought to cut across the cemeteries because travelin' as the crow flies would get me back here the quickest with none the wiser. But I shouldn't have been runnin' blind like that because the ground was uneven. I stumbled, maybe tripped over a new grave. The next I knew, I fell headlong onto a friggin' stone lamb. It's lucky, I am. Lucky I didn't brain myself on a marble angel's wing when I fell. Knocked the wind out of me, it did. Caught me right here." He lifted his shirt, and the act inspired a sharp hiss.

"Bloody hell, Will. You look like you've been kicked by a horse."

He looked down and nodded. "Cor. I didn't have time to look at myself the two hours I was runnin'. But in the light o' day.... Right you are, sir. I caught a hoof once years ago and cracked a rib, it looked nearly the same. I'll heal this time like the last."

I was well aware broken ribs could be dangerous things. One wrongly-placed blow in a brawl could puncture a lung or the heart. Because of my love for Thom, Will's participation in all this had come to an end. I was grateful for his help but I would not jeopardize his life any longer. I asked him as many questions as I could think of, though I admit the answers did little to help me form a plan.

The sound of a man's voice twining with lighter female tones came from the courtyard. The doctor had arrived. Will said hastily, "Before I forget sir, here's the key the sod was fishin' for." He passed the blood-crusted key to me just as the service door opened and the voices drew near. He whispered, "I'm sorry I couldn't tell ye what door it goes to. And, I took his purse. I wasn't bent on thievin', mind. I thought it would appear better for us if the bastard looked to have been robbed." This too he handed me.

I nodded. "You did right, Will. And your quick thinking to take his possessions is sure to keep Bruno off his guard." I gave the purse back to him. "Keep this."

"No, sir. If ye don't mind, I'll drop it in the collection plate on Sunday."

If Bruno's man was digging for his keys when Will attacked, then it reasoned they were staying in Charing Cross and the lock that fit that key was near where the brawl took place. Will had said he was near the white-bricked townhomes across from the statue of King Charles I. To my mind, this narrowed my search immensely.

***

Acario Bruno didn't appreciate the street being blocked to his carriage, nor the walk to the lodging when he had the urge to relieve himself. The incontinence was improving as the doctor said it would, but despite this there was a warm trickle coursing down his leg. A muscle ticked in his jaw. With no other option, he turned to the shrubbery and opened his trousers just in time to piss on the ground like a peasant. Finding relief, he closed his fly and turned to his man expectantly.

Salvatore looked at Celso. Unable to speak in that moment, the man only shook his head sadly. Salvatore cleared his throat and said, "I have bad news, my Conte."

Celso started to weep.

Bruno looked from one to the other and finally demanded, "Well? What has happened here? What did the polizia say?"

Salvatore stammered, "It's Gino, my Conte. He's been set upon by bandits."

Bruno knew Gino hadn't been feeling well earlier so they'd left him to eat a light meal while the rest went to play cards. As long as his men were on hand when he called for them, he generally paid them little mind. He watched Celso pull a handkerchief and blow his nose. "And?"

It was Salvatore who answered. "Gino was robbed, my Conte. He lost his life in the struggle. Should I claim his body?"

Bruno didn't answer, but resumed walking toward his quarters.

Salvatore turned to Celso, who looked horrified. And rightfully so. He and Gino had been in love. Surely, Conte Bruno didn't mean to have Gino disposed of like a dead animal in the gutter? Salvatore ran after him. "My Conte, should I send Celso to retrieve Gino's body?"

"No."

Knowing an unmarked, or worse, a communal grave waited for Gino, Salvatore watched emotionlessly as the hearse rolled away. Beside him, a grief-stricken Celso sobbed into his handkerchief. Salvatore felt nothing.

~13~

I'd just paid the newsboy at the door for the morning paper when I met my wife coming down the stairs. I found her quite pretty, so I said, "Aren't you the feast for the eyes." The accolade gained for me a beauteous smile.

She took my arm. "That's nice of you to say, darling,"

Indeed, Ellie was a breath of fresh air, dressed as she was. Yesterday morning when I saw her laying out her mourning attire, I found I couldn't bear to see her in it another day. When my parents and nanny died all those years ago, a full two years of my young life had been black. Crape on the doors and mirrors, black livery and arm bands on the servants, black bunting on the carriage, and Grannie draped in sad stiff black from head to toe. To this day the rustle of crinoline brought about the sensation of a goose walking over my grave.

I'd watched my wife take a brush to her garment and in my mind saw endless black in the months to come and then the lavender of half-mourning would follow. Mrs. Fletcher would wear her weeds for the rest of the year, and that didn't disturb me half so much, for in reality her black was not all that different from the dark service colors she wore each day. But Ellie was young and full of life, as vivacious as Thomas had been. She should wear color. She should wear it for him and for my sake as well.

Of course Ellie argued the point, for mourning was appropriately done in stages, even in her America. With the passing of Prince Albert, Her Majesty had brought prolonged observance of death into fashion across the globe. I admit I found this bit of conventionality upon Ellie's otherwise usual unconventionality to be comparable to an odd bloom on the rose bush. When asked about it, Ellie explained that she and Luise Marie were young girls when their mother passed and their hastily-acquired governess made sure the girls observed the proper decorum in expressing the family's grief. She did, however, understand my view. After discussing my request with Mrs. Fletcher, both women agreed that my peace of mind was far more important than custom. After all, this was hardly a conventional household.

As a concession to the sedate propriety she believed necessary, Ellie's compromise was a tasseled red bolero jacket covered with embroidered silk flowers the exact shade of her mauve skirt. Mauve was a stylish new color in the drab palette of death observance but at least it was tolerable. My heart was happy to see the bolero paired with the rest. To me, color celebrated Thom's life.

Picking up a section of the London Times, Ellie read,

The body of a well-attired man in his early to mid-thirties was found in Charing Cross on Monday. This victim of robbery measured at over six feet three inches tall and weighed approximately sixteen stone. He has light brown hair and brown eyes and an auburn mustache. Any wishing to claim the body, do so by contacting Scotland Yard.

She added the next so quickly, I almost thought it part of the posting, "How heavy is a stone again?"

How it was that her country and mine shared every other unit of measure but this one? I said, "A stone weighs fourteen of your American pounds." Then I calculated. "At approximately sixteen stone, the man weighed roughly two hundred and twenty-four pounds." The thought of Thomas bending to such a brute felt like a tear in my soul. "Will is a lucky man."

She must have heard something in my tone, for she lowered the newspaper and looked at me with sad eyes. "Oh Nicolas, I'm so sorry these details bring it all to the fore. I'd do anything to take the sorrow away. I'd give anything to bring Thomas back to you and Mrs. Fletcher."

I regretted she'd never met him for she would have seen in Thom all I had. I gave her a small smile. "I know, love. Your sentiment is appreciated and brings me comfort beyond measure. I know your presence here does the same for Mrs. Fletcher." She acknowledged my words with a small smile of her own.

We sat quiet for a time, each absorbed in reading our portion of the Times, our concentration accompanied by the ticking mantle clock and the rustle of the pages. Dropping the newspaper again, Ellie said suddenly, "Don't you find it odd that Bruno hasn't claimed the body? I certainly do."

"Yes, I find it impossible to believe Bruno has no idea he'd lost a man a full two days after the fact." I wondered what he might be thinking. To my mind, his failure to retrieve his man suggested a curious lack of regard on Bruno's part. Was it possible he chose not to draw attention to himself by claiming the body? That seemed unlikely. With crime rife in some sections of the city, a body unclaimed in London was relative to a drop in the ocean. In this context, my mind briefly touched upon Luca but I quickly brushed the horrendous possibility aside.

Luca wasn't dead. He'd been gone for the better part of a week. Between us, Will and I had looked everywhere we could think to look for him. Though I didn't want to face such a thing, it had occurred to me that Luca might simply have left town. Yet, I took Bruno as my indicator. Surely if Luca was gone, Bruno would follow. The fact remained, he was still in London.

Ellie set the newspaper aside and reached for a currant-studded scone. I passed the jam pot her way and took a scone for myself. Mrs. Fletcher had proudly informed me that Will had baked them before she rose that morning, and then took himself back to bed once the Cooper siblings arrived. I smiled to myself. A baker's son, indeed. The scones were excellent fare. Thomas would have gobbled them all down in short order. The thought brought with it two distinct emotions: joy and grief.

Ellie's question was a welcome distraction.

"Do you suppose his man quit his employ? Might that have been why he was at the Crested Lark alone?"

She refilled our coffee cups and added cream to both. Both my Yank and my Venetian drank the stuff each morning. She took hers with extra cream and sugar and Luca drank his as black and robust as a sultan might take it. I still vacillated between the two fashions but either way, I admit the taste and the subsequent invigoration had grown on me. I stirred in my cream. "That's entirely possible, but knowing the establishment like I do, I'd think it more likely that the man lost at cards and left the table while Bruno and the others stayed to play."

Ellie frowned. I saw she didn't care for the possibility that her ill-conceived enterprise the other night might have gone terribly wrong for her. I didn't care for that probability either.

I absently watched her dab her scone with butter and jam, my thoughts on the last twenty-four hours. Without a doubt, Will had done me a favor by eliminating one henchman. In an ideal world, another would fall.

Having updated both Mrs. Fletcher and Ellie while Dr. Compton saw to Will's injuries, I wasn't surprised that both women held strong opinions that I too might get myself injured or worse. Both made an excellent point in the argument that followed, but there really was no need, for I was of a similar mind. If my terrible nightmare revealed anything, it was that three-against-one were not betting odds.

Ellie tsked, then laughed. "You really should tell me when you fly above the clouds. Then I won't prattle on."

As I hadn't heard laughter in days, the sound warmed me.

"I've grown accustomed to your prattling."

"Hmm."

Her dubious expression made me smile. "How do you feel about Will staying on here? He does make an excellent scone." Though Ned Cooper was a fine lad, I felt another man in the house might help keep her and Mrs. Fletcher safe. The simple fact was I loved these women and that truth put them both in danger.

Ellie brightened. "I think that's a wonderful idea. She won't let me lift a finger. Not so much as fill the kettle. I've asked Noreen, or was it Doreen? Anyway, I've asked that they send one of their younger sisters, either Colleen, or Maureen, to come help in the kitchen," Her brows drew down in concentration as she juggled the names of two sets of twins. "Fiddlesticks. I have so much trouble telling the Cooper twins apart...and they have twin brothers too. Three sets. Ned is the only non-twin in the lot!"

While I listened as Ellie related her plans that the entire Cooper horde might fill our staffing needs, my mind logistically worked the necessity of expanding the household help while maintaining our privacy. Having been reared on the responsibilities of Halstead, I was well acquainted with the intricacies of such a large estate. But my knowledge of running the household was secondhand; those details left to the very capable head butler Tamblyn and the housekeeper Mrs. Simmons. I'd never paid much mind to the workings of my household in town for our needs here were simple by comparison. Mrs. Fletcher ran a tight and efficient ship down to the smallest detail.

"Even with Ned and his sisters coming each day, she still oversees the work and insists on cooking. I can't imagine all that standing at the stove is comfortable for her."

"I can't imagine it is." I knew how Mrs. Fletcher's rheumatism pained her, but she was too stubborn by far to rest. If anyone could wear the old dear down, it was this minx beside me. It might take a little time, but she'd surrender to my Yank as surely as Bergoyne yielded to George Washington. I pictured the painting by John Trumbull and rather than a sword being handed over, I imagined a ladle. The thought made me chuckle.

Suddenly, the scone on the way to her mouth paused in mid-air and she gave me a direct eye. "It's not about William's excellent scones or extra hands to run the household. You want him here to help protect Mrs. Fletcher and me."

That's my American wife, perceptive and direct as always. That I didn't immediately reply got for me that sentient smile of hers, a nuance declaring she understood things exactly as they were.

I said, "I have several reasons, including the ones you've mentioned."

Ellie nodded, but I could see she waged a war in her mind and appreciated her conscious attempt to not argue about how safe she felt, when she knew full well I felt just the opposite. I also understood her well enough to know she was itching for deeper involvement. Pushing on, she confirmed my suspicion by asking plainly, "What are we to do now?"

"Believe me, Ellie, there's not an iota of space in my mind to worry about you more than I already do. We aren't doing anything."

My hunch proved correct as her delicate brows drew together. "Nicolas, please see reason. Together we're—"

There was no opportunity to continue with my arm twisting. Voices from the foyer declared Lady Augusta Halstead had come to call.

***

Ellie eagerly pulled Grannie close for a hug. I knew she wasn't finished with our conversation, but her greeting to my grandmother was sincere. "Lady Halstead, so good of you to visit this morning."

Ducking under her enormous hat, I kissed Grannie's cheek, which was as soft and wrinkled as worn kid gloves. "Good to see you, Grannie. Come for breakfast? I'll tell you, the scones are superb."

Grannie replied warmly, "No thank you, my dears. I'll only stay a short while. I'm playing Mahjong at the garden club luncheon today and I must arrive early to make sure everything is prepared satisfactorily." She turned slightly toward Ellie and added, "I'm glad to see you've arrived in sound condition, my dear. My grandson tells me the channel was so rough, he wouldn't allow you to cross until it calmed."

Ellie smiled brightly and put her hand on my arm. "Our Nicolas is a thoughtful husband, Lady Halstead. He is a man to be proud of."

I kissed my wife's temple. "My love, I'm sure Grannie would appreciate a less formal relationship with her new granddaughter." I raised a brow to my grandmother.

The old woman took a seat, and rested her gloved hands on the handle of her ivory-topped cane. She agreed happily, "Indeed, my dear. You're part of our family now."

Ellie beamed at the welcome. Looping her arm through mine, she said, "Then I shall call you as Nicolas does. We were in the midst of our breakfast, Grannie. If you've no time for breakfast, shall I fetch another service that you may join us for tea or perhaps coffee?"

Obviously taken aback by such an offer, Grannie cast me a disapproving eye. "Really, Nicolas."

I felt Ellie's surprise skitter up the arm she held. She might not know what was in the air, but I certainly knew where this was headed. I said, "Our maids are laundering today Grannie."

Grannie shook her head. "I know our dear Merry has had a shock, and I'm aware the shock has influenced her rheumatism. My thoughts are by no means insensitive when I say she needs help to adequately do her job. You have a wife now, young man. Ellie needs a lady's maid. You need a manservant..."

"I have Ned."

"Pish, you need a trained manservant, my boy, as well as a butler, a footman, and a coach for heaven's sake! Mrs. Fletcher needs reliable staffing here. It's unheard of, a Lord and Lady Halstead fetching and clearing like the servants. You must be mindful of what people will say, my dears. I'll send my maid to get Ellie settled in, but you simply must attend to this, Nicolas."

I found myself bristling. It was Ellie who answered. "You're quite right, Grannie. The maids and their brother have done an adequate job for Nicolas in his bachelorhood, but it's simply not enough now that we're wed. I plan to sit down with Mrs. Fletcher myself to determine exactly what is needed here. Of course Nicolas attempted to see to this immediately upon my return," she said, her hand sweeping to the black mourning bunting hanging at the mirror above the mantle, "but I insisted we be generous and give Mrs. Fletcher a little more time before we thrust new help at her. As you've said, she's had quite a shock."

That was brilliant. Following her lead, I added, "As a matter of fact, just before your arrival we were discussing our household requirements. You'll be happy to know that I've already acquired for us a footman." As an afterthought, I dropped succulent innuendo at her feet to redirect the conversation, saying, "For now with just the two of us, our needs are simple. Of course those needs will change in time. For the short term, we'll tighten our belts and make do."

Immediately grasping the intimation, as I thought she might, I could feel Grannie's mind at work. The dowager was literally awash in the idea she might soon be a great-grandmother with a Halstead heir secured. She said, "Are you certain you'd rather not have Halstead servants in the interim? Or better still, return to Halstead where you belong? Now that you've married, I've been entertaining the idea of taking up residence at the dower house."

I shook my head and chose to respond to her interim suggestion only. "Lending your servants is a generous offer Grannie, but thank you, no. I'll advertise and we'll make our choices from the applicants."

She lifted a brow at me to let me know she was well aware I'd dodged the topic of my return to Halstead.

I gave her my most engaging smile and assured her, "We'll soon have our needs sorted out." For that I got a small harrumph and an exasperated shake of her head.

***

Ellie inspected the borrowed hat. "This is a reckless thing to do alone, Nicolas. If you won't have me at your side dressed as a man, then at least take Ned Cooper with you."

I shook my head and gained in return a look of pensive consternation that silently demanded I explain. I attempted to offer reason. "Ellie, there are several reasons I'd never consider such a thing." I sat and tied my borrowed boots. Looking up, I met her eyes. "For one, Ned is hardly more than a boy. To take a lad into an establishment known for courting deviants is akin to throwing kerosene on a flame. Then too, outing myself in such a manner to a local boy negates everything I've built in my life. I imagine him confused enough by the other night."

The gears in the machine of her mind were turning as she searched for a way to get me to see reason as she saw it. I did see, god help me, I did. I saw the situation exactly the same but there was nothing else for me to do. Luca was missing and Will was injured. A madman sought my downfall and coming to know that twisted mind like I had, I knew Bruno would stop at nothing to that end, including hurting the three women I loved. In my opinion, Mrs. Fletcher was made safe by the benign nature of her profession and the fact our true relationship was hidden from society. For the most part, I considered Grannie with her entourage of friends and servants to be safe from anything but scandal, as unfortunate and as embarrassing as that would be. In truth such a scandal would likely do the old dear in. Conversely, I was certain Ellie was in danger of bodily harm.

Her next words pulled me from my thoughts. "Then how about I send word to Jean-Paul, or perhaps to my father?"

Normally her reasoning was above par. At a loss for words, I put Will's cap on my head and just looked at her. "You can't be serious. Your brother-in-law is a colleague. What's more, I've no doubt if your father had an inkling of this situation, he would see me hang for leading his daughter into this mess."

As though she couldn't believe she suggested what she had, her fingertips met at the bridge of her nose, and then immediately went to her temples. "My lord, you're right. I'm shooting in the dark, Nicolas. That was senseless of me to even suggest it." Her frustration bubbling to the surface she suddenly groaned, "Oh, *fiddlesticks*, why couldn't I have been born a man!"

Her hands went to my cheeks to caress the stubble I'd left as part of my disguise. I took those small hands in mine. "If you were a man, I'd gladly have you at my side. But don't you see, my darling? Loving you makes me a weaker man and Bruno knows this. You're my Achilles' heel, my Sampson's hair. He'd hurt you or kill you. For no other reason than to devastate me."

She searched my face. I saw my words take root when the fine tight lines around her eyes eased. "I know you're right. It's only that I'm terribly worried. I hate that you'll go out and have no one to guard your back." Resigned now, she offered what she could. "We'll lock the doors and stay inside until you return. Don't worry about us here. Focus your attentions on finding Luca and staying safe, I'll be right here waiting. I love you, Nicolas."

I kissed her knuckles and whispered, "That love keeps me stronger than I feel. I promise to be careful."

The greatest deception men suffer is from their own opinions.
– Leonardo da Vinci

~14~

Though I'd never been here before, I recognized the Brimstone Club by its easily-identifiable, though unlettered, shingle depicting six devils in the style of Hieronymus Bosch. Their forked tails tied together like spokes of a wheel reminded me of a rat king I'd once seen on display in Bavaria. Those desiccated rat corpses unluckily tied together tail-by-tail had lived and died in someone's wall in that unfortunate clump and were believed by locals to have wrought the plague in that portion of Europe. I shook the grim thought away. It wasn't wise to think about mass death right now. I had to get inside while pretending to be Alfred.

From the shabby outside, the Brimstone Club appeared to be a rambling dockside inn patronized by the usual assortment of shipyard workers, sailors, and fishermen. But the incongruent array of wealthy carriages parked at the curb suggested otherwise. Despite the care to hide emblems affixed to coach doors, I recognized several coaches among the throng. These prominent members of society didn't want to be recognized and I certainly didn't want them to see me.

With this in mind, I thought it prudent to use the service entrance in the alley as Alfred might. A large bald man let me in, and I stepped into the small crowd around him. The tattoos on his thick bare arms suggested that he'd once been a sailor who'd visited some eastern port. Given his size, I had the distinct impression his occupation in the Brimstone was bouncer. Why hadn't he come to Alfred's aid? He said, "Freddie, ye poor sod, I thought we'd seen the last o' ye."

It was exactly the welcome I'd hoped for. Nodding, I said in my best approximation of Alfred's inflection, "Yeah. Italian toff roughed me up, he did."

"Ye ever think that rough play o' yers ye fancy so much might one day get ye killed?" He leaned close and told me in a low voice, "Jimmy told me wha' happened t' ye, but not the Nobs upstairs. Jimmy's right beside 'imself fer lettin' ye use the casker's hole. If I'd o' been down here tha' night, instead of removing some soused bastard upstairs, I would ha' stopped it, ye know that's so."

That answered my question. I nodded.

"I saw them toffs in here after they did ye wrong. Bleedin' sods full o' brass. The little man pointed 'em out t' me. There was nothin' I could do that night. But I keep my eye peeled, ye know that's so." He then pulled out a knotted sailor's rope out of his trouser pocket and showed it to me. "There's justice in this world."

Seeing the deadly but innocuous-looking weapon, I nodded again. It was good Alfred had some one here to look out for him, daft as he was for returning.

A huge-breasted woman laughed with delight. "Ye know our Freddie likes 'em rough, Martin." To me, she said, "Don't ye Freddie? Ye know Madge 'n me got a wager goin'. She said ye'd never be back. I told her ye enjoyed them twisted toffs best of all, an' that ye'd be back, sure as me name is Roz O'Hurley. Gained a quid for me efforts, I did. Just with ye walkin' through that door!" She then held out a hand to a scantily-dressed blond.

I correctly deduced this was the other person in on the wager when Madge said, "Yeah yeah, here's yer bleedin' quid, now shut yer trap." She spun on her heel and left the room.

I gave Roz what I thought an appropriate Alfred grin. "Ye know me well, don't ye, Roz?"

To my surprise, she brazenly slid her hand inside my trousers and gave me a firm caress. "I do indeed, my boy-o." Her eyes got wide. "Ooh, but I don't remember yer cod being so big."

Taking a cue from Will, from the time we were on the docks, I pressed firmly into her palm before pulling her hand out of my trousers. My hand delved into her opened chemise and cupped a breast the size of a Guernsey udder. "That's what happens when I see these, Roz."

She giggled and hugged me hard against her. She whispered, "I was so worried, Freddie. I'm glad he didn't kill ye."

I chuckled, "Me too."

A voice came from the door. A tall redhead, a Scotsman by his burr, said, "I canna believe my eyes. I'm glad t' see yer brother didna come with ye, Freddie. After I brought ye home, Bertie told me if he saw me again, he'd break my farkin' knees wi' a hammer."

Based upon the information I had, I took a wild guess. "He's alright with me comin', Jimmy. Bertie's just lookin' after me, is all."

His brows drew together briefly and he looked at me in disbelief. "That's a surprise he'd agree t' such a thing."

My stomach started to knot. Had my words revealed my ruse? Apparently Bertie had said otherwise. Covering quickly, I added, "To be honest, Jimmy, Bertie doesn't know I've come to work. He thinks I've just come to be paid."

Completely disarmed, he tossed his head back and laughed heartily. "Paid! Oh lord that's rich. He thinks ye get a bleedin' pension does he?" He eyed me close and I tried not to sweat. I apparently passed inspection, because he said, "Ye healed up quicker than I expected, not so much as a bruise on ye, but it's good to see ye. Ye up fer the games tonight, or are ye just here for the chitchat?"

Not certain how to respond, I said, "I'm still sore Jimmy, but here to work."

The others laughed. Someone on the far end of the room called, "That's our Freddie, not one to miss a chance at a good buggering!"

Jimmy laughed again. "Good. Well get yerself t' the Orchard. You too Roz, a new mob of toffers just come in. I hear there's a Lord and Lady toff askin' after ye. I think it's the same as last week, wi' you an' the little man."

"Ooh, that'll pay me rent this week. An' he's not so little Jimmy, if ye gets my meanin'." Roz hooked my arm. "Come on, Freddie."

***

When we walked into the Orchard a few minutes later, I

couldn't for the life of me determine what it was. The room had naught but a Garden of Eden mural spanning the four walls and a few well-placed seat cushions. It hit me squarely between the eyes. We were to be viewed and chosen like ripe fruit. Sinful fruit. The small shuttered windows confirmed it.

I looked around the Orchard. Before me was an amazing variety of sexual potential for the well-paying patron. An assortment of at least two dozen men and women stood either costumed, or in incomplete stages of attire. Notable among them was a half-masked dwarf dressed in a leopard-skin loincloth, an enormously obese woman wearing nothing but a ballerina tutu and a tiny domino mask, a nun in full habit wielding a paddle, and a wig-wearing judge who looked to be naked under his opened robes. Others stood primping themselves in preparation for the showing. A polishing of the apple, as it were.

I thought back to our conversation with Alfred. When asked why, after he'd been beaten so severely here, that he'd even entertain the idea of returning, he'd said, "The tips are too good, an' with the right toff so's the rest, if ye get my meanin'."

I got the meaning perfectly. I admit the deviant in me was both repulsed and fascinated by this place. I thought about what he meant by "right" toff. The crests I'd seen on the coaches parked outside belonged to several families in high society. My unease magnified. I ran a hand over my chin and three days of beard stubble. In preparation for this evening, I hadn't shaved. I hoped that whoever was viewing the fruits of the orchard tonight, Will's clothing and these whiskers were disguise enough for me.

"Yer not wearing a costume tonight, Freddie?"

I shook my head. "Not tonight, Roz."

Hoisting her ample bare bosom up over the top of her corset, she said, "Got meself a gold sovereign last night with these lovies! Agnes couldn't believe it. Remember Agnes? My sister's been here but twice and didn't like it. She's looking for a position as a lady's maid now. There's a chamber maid post I read about this morning. Perhaps if they take her, she'll move up in the ranks there. I'll tell ye Freddie, tha' life's not fer me! Bad enough I take in washin'. No sir. I'm savin' me tin for New York City. An' shiny sovereigns will get me there all the faster!"

Satisfied with her appearance now, she cast me a critical eye. "If yer not dressin', ye'd better at least hang yer willie out. Ye want them well-offs, Freddie, and ye know they won't ask fer ye but unless they sees what yer peddlin'. Them's the ones who just might give ye gold after. An' besides, ye know the boss men up there don't like us hidin' the goods. They always look first before the toffers come in." She emphasized those words by plumping her massive breasts.

Taking her suggestion, I opened my fly. Her hand suddenly reached in my trousers and grabbed me. "Tsk. Yer normally ready on yer own, Freddie. Perhaps that beatin' took somethin' out o' ye? Here, I'll help ye..." The bell rang. "Och, there's no time now. Sorry lovie. But here," she pulled my cock and balls over the waistband before I could remove her hand, "this'll make ye show better. Not that ye need to primp..." She suddenly gave me an odd look that made me feel that I teetered on the edge of being found out. Fortunately, the bell rang again and everyone took their places. The sex in the air rose like fog on the moors.

Light appeared from one of the shuttered windows. I looked up to see a plushly-appointed office and, in silhouette, two men gazing down. I determined them to be the Brimstone bosses. They must have been pleased with what they saw for when they walked away, the other shutters opened in no particular order. Though I couldn't make out their features, I saw silhouettes of men and women in these viewing rooms. Next thing I knew, the leopard-skinned dwarf was called. A moment later Roz was called, as was the nun with her school paddle. I was just about to acknowledge a missed opportunity when I — or rather Alfred — was called. I tucked myself back in my trousers and felt for Will's knife in my pocket. Whatever was to come, I wasn't unarmed.

***

The male chatelaine who stood outside the orchard handed me a numbered key, and said, "There's some foreign toff asking fer you only. He sounds like a Spaniard or maybe an I-talian. E's no Frenchie. E's in room six and paid fer an hour an' a half. 'Ave yer fun an' remember t' bring the key back with ye this time."

Asking for you only. The very words told to Alfred. "Is the toff alone?"

He gave me an odd look. "'Ow the 'ell would I know that?'"

I shrugged and headed up the stairs on legs that felt like lead. I made my way down the hall and found room six but my hands were shaking so that I fumbled the key and missed the lock several times. By necessity, I planned to commit murder tonight and my nerves, at odds with my good sense, were getting the better of me.

I'd played the part so well to get this far. For the first time, I thought about poor Alfred's implication in my impending crime. Of course he'd have his wounds to show it was impossible for him to kill a man. And those at the Bishop's Moke would certainly swear he was upstairs the whole time, while others here would swear the man who'd killed the Italian toff didn't have a mark on him. Still—

So deep in thought was I, a sound behind me made me jump. It was the masked dwarf on his way down the hall.

He stopped at the door to his room, and turning to me said in perfectly-educated diction, "Don't know if anyone's said it, Freddie, but that Italian fellow who beat you so badly has been back twice asking after you."

"Thanks, that's good to know."

"I still can't believe Jimmy kept that from the bosses. I only come because it's always been safe and discreet to do so."

"I told Jimmy to keep it all a secret." Then I used Alfred's own words, "The tips are too good, an' with the right toff so's the rest, if ye get my meanin'."

He chuckled. "That, I do. Take care." He gave me a nod and went on his way.

Listening to his refined speech, it occurred to me then just who this man was. This was Stuart Braithwite, nephew of Sir Reginald Braithwite, the minister of Public Works. A moment later, a woman I recognized walked up the stairs. I turned back to the door with shoulders hunched and head down, pretending the key was stuck. Lady Philippa Winterpool followed Stuart in. I quickly turned back to the door as Sir Bertrand Winterpool came up the stairs with Roz, the latter pinching my backside as they passed.

I surreptitiously watched Roz open the door to the same room Stuart and Philippa entered, and when they closed the door behind them, I let out the breath I'd been holding. I'd never cared for Winterpool's politics in the House of Lords but found myself intrigued that he frequented this establishment. Was this fellow peer also dual-natured or were he and his wife simply voyeurs to the appetites of others? I wondered too if he knew he was about to have a go with another peer's family member.

Putting that jumble of thoughts aside, I opened the door to my assigned room. The space was bathed in darkness, save the single candle lamp that burned on the bedside table. From what little I could see in the circle of light, the room was as richly appointed in red and black as the rest of the Brimstone Club; a nod, no doubt, to the sinful décor of hell. A large plush bed dominated the center of the room. Closing the door behind me, I took off my cap and went there to wait. Opening Will's flick knife, I hid it beside me under the hat.

The seconds ticked by counted by every beat of my heart. I heard rather than saw the doorknob turn. My mouth gone dry, I swallowed hard and reached under the hat to curl my fingers around the knife's handle. The door opened and the silhouette of a man was briefly seen before the door closed behind him. He stood in the darkness just beyond the halo of candlelight. I could feel his eyes upon me and smell the scent of soap, licorice, and cigars on his skin. My heart began to pound in my chest, but not with fear. Relief washed over me.

He said, "I don't know whether to kiss you or throttle you."

Hearing the faint accent I'd come to love, I tucked the knife into my pocket and rose. "I don't know which to do either."

Luca chuckled. "Fair enough."

We fell into one another's arms to kiss hungrily. Then holding me at arm's length, he looked me over and said in a perturbed sigh, "Nicolas, why are you here?"

"I've come for Bruno."

He lightly shook my forearms, the exasperation heavy in his

tone as he said, "I left to keep the both of you safe, and yet you'd do this?"

"We're not safe. I've seen what he does, Luca. What he continues to do. I can't allow us to be hunted. I can't allow Ellie and Mrs. Fletcher to be left in harm's way, when a simple market trip leaves them vulnerable."

He sat on the bed wearily. I sat beside him and caressed his cheek. He'd left his trunk and nearly all of his belongings behind when he left us, so he hadn't shaved. His chin was dark with whiskers that made him a dashing figure for all he wore rumpled clothes. His corsair's beard was just long enough to be soft to the touch. He reminded me of a Howard Pyle pirate illustration. "Thank heavens you're all right. We've been beside ourselves with worry."

He placed his hand over mine. "I'm sorry for that, believe me. I thought it best to remove the temptation I present. If he discovered I'd been living with you, I can't even imagine what he might do." I felt a tear roll over the back of my hand when he shook his head. His words almost resigned, he said, "He's dogged my steps for a very long time, Nicolas, and this is an occurrence of my life, not yours. I won't see you and Ellie live this way, even if it breaks my heart to stay away. I've already applied at the Smithsonian Institution. Once I leave London, you will both be safe. He'll follow me there."

Bruno was responsible for years of Luca's sad self-imposed isolation. Now was not the time to argue over him leaving us. Instead, I put my arm around his shoulders and proceeded to tell him about Will taking down one of Bruno's men.

"Which man?" he asked sharply.

Momentarily surprised, I shrugged and shook my head. "I

don't know."

"What did he look like?"

"I can't rightfully say."

"Think, Nicolas. This is important."

I had small details only. I let out a slow breath and tried to picture the man as I saw him that night at the Crested Lark. "I thought him rather tall and large when I saw him rise from the table. He wasn't as dark-skinned as you, and his hair was brown, light brown and oiled back. Perhaps he was a northern Italian? I saw him across the room so can't describe his features, except for a mustache. His mustache was reddish, that much I know."

He nodded to himself, as if my description held specific meaning. I was about to ask him why he asked when exaggerated female moaning came through the wall. Roz was certainly working for her pennies tonight. I asked now.

Luca said, "Then that leaves only one to do Bruno's harm. The other is merely his manservant. As far as I know, he isn't like the rest."

I nodded. My thoughts went to the deviants below and in the next room. These people came to the Brimstone to feed their desires on both sides of the orchard wall. Perhaps the manservant worked for such a monster to appease some internal demon. "Then we shall make a point to deal with the other henchman first. Thom will have his justice, and so will Alfred."

"Alfred?"

I explained my encounter with my unfortunate double. "Bruno wants me badly enough to beat a man half to death because he resembles me. Alfred's attack is further proof of his mental instability."

Luca leaned against me and I rested my head against his. I

could feel that my words upset him. He said, "I've learned he comes regularly to these clubs, but I've missed him twice elsewhere. I'd hoped to find him here tonight to tell him I'm leaving England. The *bastardo* is elusive."

"But memorable." I relayed what Alfred had said that gained him his beating.

"Yes, his incontinence is legend. But that's all I have after days of inquiry and many sleepless nights: a cold trail and a rumor that he pisses himself." Luca chuckled pitilessly. "How that must gall him, the fastidious—" he ground out the last words in Italian, "—*figlio di troia*. Better that I would have torn out his throat." He put his head in his hands.

I couldn't quite understand the pain-riddled mumbling in Italian, but I did understand the emotion that shook his shoulders as he tried to contain it. I pulled him back on the bed and held him while our raw emotional fatigue ran its course. All those weeks ago when he spoke of Cesare, my heart wept with him as he described for us the savagery of Bruno's obsession. But empathy aside, I hadn't fully comprehended the story at the depth at which Luca experienced the ordeal. How could I? At the time, it was beyond the realm of my experience, something my mind could only imagine. But I'd recently held Thomas in my arms and witnessed the savagery of Bruno firsthand. I saw it for myself clearly painted on his and Alfred's bruised and broken bodies. I knew it now. I told Luca softly, "I understand."

He wrapped his arms around my waist and pressed his face against my neck. "I know you do, *il mi amore*, and it rends my heart in two. How I wish it weren't so."

I wished it weren't so. Residual pain welled up inside me and I held him tight. My heart held a score of wishes. I wished my dear

Thom was alive and well. I wished I could hear him laugh that good-natured laugh of his. I wished Thom were at this very moment home, holding Will wrapped in his arms like this. I drew a ragged breath and squeezed Luca to me. Thank god I'd found him. I wished we were home. I wished Ellie were with us, for only then were Luca and I truly complete. I told him so.

Rising up on his forearms, he met my eye. "Yes. You don't know how I long for those days of peace, when I thought him dead, when all the world belonged to the three of us and was ours to explore. Love came first and nothing else mattered."

I brushed the ebony strands back from his eyes. "We'll have that again. I promise you."

I knew he looked me in the eye but I could only make out the candle-lit shimmer of emotion swimming in his eyes. "I must end this, Nicolas. I must find him. Just today I learned of a place by the river called the Bishop's Moke—"

"There's nothing there; only Alfred. And he will only lead you here."

He let out a breath and pressed his forehead to my chest again. "Then I must remain here and wait for him. From what I've gathered, he's been here three times and only visited the other clubs once each." This is all I have to go on. I don't know where else to look for him."

I repeated Stuart Braithwite's words at the door, then explained my impersonation of Alfred and my newly-formed belief that his resemblance to me was the reason for Bruno's regular return to the Brimstone.

I felt Luca's reproach. "Though I understand the purpose behind it, Nicolas, your coming here was a reckless act. It might have been him at the door instead of me."

"In truth, I was hoping it was." Luca was right, of course. It was reckless but I didn't regret coming here. I wouldn't have found him otherwise. I explained Will's unwavering belief that Bruno and his men were somewhere in Charing Cross near the statue of Charles I. I could feel a new excitement in him. He said, "Then I must go there."

"Then we must go there. I'll have your word that you'll not see him alone."

He was silent.

I wished for more light in the room that I might see his eyes. Addressing his hesitation, I said, "Your Roman emperors used the fasces to signify strength in numbers. They knew a single birch rod was not as strong as a bundle of rods. Never leave us again, Luca. We're far stronger together than apart."

Again he nodded. "You're right. I've gotten so used to being alone in my dealings with him, I naturally returned to the familiar solitude that kept him at bay. Yes, *il mio amore*, I give you my word. "

I wound my arm around him to pull his face to mine. "Those days are over. You have us, and Mrs. Fletcher too. I've explained our unorthodox relationship and she accepts it." I felt his surprise. "It's true."

Once more I wished I could see his beautiful eyes, but coming to know him like I had, I could hear the slight crack of emotion in his voice. "Thank you. Let's go home where we belong."

I shook my head. "We can't leave just yet, but soon."

He couldn't fathom a reason to linger. I felt his body start and it matched his words. "I don't understand."

I sincerely wanted to leave this place but I needed to stay longer. I explained that it was necessary if Alfred was ever to return to work here.

"But the man was beaten half to death. Surely that's reason enough to stay away."

"It's beyond sensical. My short time below stairs tells me that an array of demons gets fed here." The husky groans of two men mingled with Roz's frenzied tones. Having experienced Ellie's breathy whimpers and Luca's primal growls in the throes of passion, the overblown noise from next door sounded contrived to say the least. Still, the sound of it was beginning to warm my blood. Another thought came to me. I took his hand and cupped myself with it. "I've a demon of my own. You've paid for an hour and a half with me."

"Paid for—" He laughed suddenly, then playfully added, "I was initially drawn to the judge, you know, but there was something compelling about you…"

His other finger traced my lips as his cupping hand dipped inside my trousers and freed my growing cock. I opened my mouth and he touched my tongue. There was nothing to do but close around it and suck before I left it to find his lips. Reveling in the added sensation of his stubble and fueled by my relief and longing, I kissed him.

His virtuoso's hand played me. Needless to say, a duet followed.

***

We returned to the townhouse late and to our great surprise, found Ellie curled up in a chair dozing. She'd waited for me and was beside herself that I'd brought Luca home. Our reunion had tears and kisses followed by an almost desperate loving. We were much stronger together, and together we'd find a solution.

~15~

While attending my whiskers, I caught Luca's reflection in my shaving mirror. He looked like an ebony-haired Hyperion with his damp hair a ruffled crown of uneven spikes. The towel perfunctorily wrapped around his lower half had slipped a bit, affording me a gratifying glimpse of his fine physique. William Etty would have found Luca the perfect academic model standing as he was, fresh from his bath. The towel slipped a bit more. My eyes followed the sensual line of furring that disappeared under the towel. I couldn't help myself. I paid for my daydream by nicking my chin. "Damn." The styptic pencil not only staunched the bleeding but burned like an ember out of hell; my penance for not fully paying attention to my razor.

He turned at my hiss and saw that I cut myself. I admonished him for being a distraction. He laughed and, discarding the towel completely, continued to rummage for his clothing in the travel-battered steamer trunk. Devil.

Luca hadn't unpacked as we had. All of his clothing was in need of laundering. I told his reflection, "The maids will launder tomorrow. If you're in need of fresh clothing, do help yourself to my bureau. Most should fit you comfortably."

He held a crumpled shirt to his nose and grimaced. "Thank you. I'm afraid I must."

Most of his Venetian belongings had been shipped ahead to his offices in the Ashmolean and arrangements would be made today to bring them here. For now we shared a bed, but it was clear that if Luca was to stay with us as we wished, we'd do well to heed Mrs. Fletcher's advice and follow Dr. Compton and Dr. O'Connor's example. If we were to maintain the façade of our bachelor friend living with us until he fully made England his home, a larger residence was in order.

My wife appeared like an odalisque conjured from the harem stored in the mind of Jean-Auguste-Dominique Ingres. Freshly bathed herself, she toweled off as unabashedly as a water nymph. Lest I cut my throat in their presence, I folded the straight razor in self-defense and wiped the remaining foam from my face.

On the way home from last night's surprise reunion at the Brimstone, Luca and I had exchanged our separate investigations and we now repeated it for Ellie's benefit. I knew the more we discussed the matters at hand, the greater the possibility of a solution.

Luca, on the other hand, had something on his mind, something about the situation that he had yet to speak of. I could tell by the way he held himself and the slight telltale lines around his eyes. Having singularly dealt with Bruno's obsession for so many years, it didn't come naturally for him to share without prompting. "What ace do you have tucked up your sleeve, Luca?

Some insight, perhaps? Or is it a burden you need to divest yourself of?

Ellie said, "Will you share with us? Don't keep such things to yourself."

The lines of concentration disappeared and Luca nodded. "I know Bruno's entourage. One is the manservant Salvatore Carlucci. I don't believe him to be a threat in any way. It was he who hand-delivered Bruno's love letters for the last four years, and every time, he looked as though he wished he were far away."

"Then surely he must be forced to follow that man. Perhaps he's in need of help. What reason could anyone have for serving that monster?"

"He's a meek and nervous man, but perhaps not a prisoner of anything other than perverse desires, *caro*."

"I honestly can't imagine such a thing."

"Nicolas, the man you described to me last night was named Gino." Luca hissed the name like a curse. "He was a simple-minded beast of a man, a man without conscience who gave his master an unfair advantage over others."

I looked into the glass to adjust my tie and saw the pain etched on his face. I knew, but I asked anyway, "You knew that man well?"

He drew a ragged breath and exhaled sharply. "I knew Gino very well. I am certain he murdered Carlo Posateri. He had a hand in what was done to my Cesare and to your Thomas. Bruno used Gino's size and strength against anyone Bruno wanted subdued. Of these two henchmen, only Celso remains."

I hadn't met this henchman before but I'd seen the man leave the Crested Lark. Well over six feet tall and heavy boned, and by all accounts a sadist. I was glad for his death.

***

I was the first to arrive for breakfast. Mrs. Fletcher had been successful in convincing Will to stay on as our new footman, for there he stood beside the buffet ready to serve. This was a show of course. Englishmen always served themselves breakfast.

I watched him straighten his cuffs. In that instant, I thought he wore Thom's Halstead livery. Perhaps he did. I felt a hollow in my chest. I sorely missed my Thom. Stations in life had never mattered between us, not as teenage boys and certainly not as men. The only time he addressed me formally was when there were those around us who'd come undone if he didn't defer. Thom was an astute judge of character. If Thom loved Will and desired our friendship, then so would I come to love this man as a friend in time.

"Good morning, Lord Nicolas." Will's demeanor was altered by the garments he wore. Seeing Will standing there so stiff and proper and having me addressed the same, a curious thought took me. When he and I were dressed as common workers on the docks, he was personable and far less staid.

"Yes it is, Will. I see you've decided to stay on with us after all."

"Yes, sir, and I'm glad for it. Thank you sir. It may seem queer of me to say it sir, but workin' here feels right, like I've a home at long last."

"Well, it's good to have you." His words brought a smile and with it a possible solution to the sparse servant issue my grandmother insisted I had. I could fill the house with birds of a feather and every bird in the roost would be respectful of one another's secrets. How difficult might it be? Didn't Roz mention a sister named Agnes, a maid hoping to rise in service just last night? It might be worth the effort to send Roz a note. I chuckled inwardly. How simple my life had been just a few short months ago. I tipped my head toward the breakfast chafing dishes. "Been helping. I see."

"Mrs. Fletcher's a dear old miss, she is, and Thommy always said there was no one sweeter. That's true enough. She reminds me of my Gran, lord bless." Will straightened when Ellie came in. "Good morning, Lady Halstead."

"Good morning, Will. You look much improved today. Feeling better, then?" She took a plate and picked over the chafing dishes. Then went back for her coffee.

"I am, Lady Halstead. A little sore still, but on the mend, and thank you for askin'."

"I'm glad." She poured her cream and added her lumps. "Will?"

"Yes, my lady?"

"Mr. Franco will be down shortly. Please bring another place setting for the table."

"I'll see to that right away, ma'am."

A moment later, Mrs. Fletcher joined us in the small dining room. Her eyes bright with excitement, she said, "Excuse me, dears, but William has just informed me that Luca has returned home."

The matter-of-fact way she said he returned home made me smile. "He has."

She pressed one hand to her cheek and the other to her heart, "Oh! Thank the good lord."

Luca came up behind her in the doorway and said to us all, "Good morning."

Clearly startled to hear him, Mrs. Fletcher whirled about. "It's so good to see you home safe and sound, Mr. Luca!" A flight of fancy took me as William Baird's *Poules et poussins* came to mind, for here was a hen with her chicks under her wing, if ever there was one. One chick lost, and three more found. I took an overwarm sip of coffee to swallow the lump of emotion sticking in my throat.

"Thank you, Mrs. Fletcher. It's good to be home."

She turned to us with tears brimming in those gentle smiling eyes. She didn't say a word, nor did she have to. She missed Thomas and fearing the same fate would befall Luca, she'd been worried for his safety. To her this ordeal was over. I didn't have the heart to say otherwise. Ned came to the doorway with a note in his hand. She asked, "What have you there, Ned?"

"One of the Halstead lads just brought this around back, Ma'am. It's a letter for his Lordship." He handed it to me. I thanked him and he went back to his work.

The note from Grannie reminded me of papers that needed my attention before Friday. Today was as good as any to go. We needed to send a cart to Oxford for Luca's belongings anyway. I addressed my companions, "I must to go to Halstead. My grandmother reminds me of papers that need my signature. Would you care to join me? Winter would soon drive us indoors, a ride through the countryside would be a nice change from town." I didn't add that Bruno's presence in London was wearing on me. I didn't have to.

Ellie brightened. "I would love to ride."

Luca agreed.

Mrs. Fletcher smiled. "And it's such a lovely morning for an outing. A bit cold, but bundle up and you should be fine."

I rose from my chair and indicated she should sit beside me. "Do consider taking your breakfast with us, dear heart."

Ellie nodded. "Yes, do."

She waved her hand like it was the silliest thing she'd ever heard and left the room beaming. Try as I might through the years, I was never able to get the old dear to break convention and dine with me in the presence of others, not so much as a biscuit and a cup of tea with anyone other than Thom. Our class division was such an unyielding fact in society, it necessitated the pretense she and I were forced to live under. But everyone here knew how important this woman was to me. With Ellie's encouragement and perhaps Luca's as well, she might finally acquiesce and lower the façade that declared to society she was simply my housekeeper. At least when we were home alone.

Through my good fortune and remarkable happenstance, I'd managed to build for myself a family. The thought sitting happily in my mind, I went about filling my plate at the sideboard. I turned to my new footman standing ready. I tipped my head to the doorway. "Go on, have your breakfast."

Bowing slightly, he said, "Yes, sir."

I watched him go feeling good in knowing Will was now close at hand. I found myself anticipating our ride. It was a welcome distraction to working through the issue of ridding ourselves of a madman and miraculously remaining free of scandal.

A feminine voice pulled me from my musings.

"Oh, not Luca, too. Perhaps I'll tie a kite string to both your ankles."

Not understanding to what Ellie referred, I looked at her blankly then turned to Luca with a brow raised. He shrugged in confusion.

Ellie pursed her lips and shook her head as though she carried on an internal conversation.

I set down my fork and wiped my mouth with my napkin. With my hands clasped before me like a school boy, I asked, "Alright, what are you talking about?"

"You're taking Luca on your lunar excursions now."

"My what? Oh." I chuckled. "Forgive me sweetheart, I'm afraid my mind was wandering."

She scoffed, "Above the clouds, I'd say! I'm beginning to doubt I have anything of value worth hearing."

"I highly doubt anyone could think such a thing. We certainly don't harbor such thoughts." I looked to Luca, who shook his head and grinned endearingly.

"Forgive me, *caro*. To say I have much on my mind inadequately describes it." The smile remained, but there was no light of it in those blue eyes.

We reached for her hands at the same time and once more I was reminded of our synchronized hearts and minds. Luca reached across the table and took my hand as well. Hand to hand, a current of love passed between us. In that moment, there was no need to say more.

~16~

Our hired hansom arrived to take us to Halstead. Luca asked why I chose not to stable my horse at the public stable on Teale Street. I assume he asked because he was interested in procuring a horse of his own.

"Jack Parson's stable is a first rate facility if you're looking to board there. I suppose I've just become accustomed to a hired coach. My horse, Bram, is far too old for the rigors of town. He was my father's pride and joy, just a colt when my father died, and now the old fellow is nearly forty." I added that Dilbert Brown saw to his health and keeping. The fact he was older than I lent proof to his excellent care.

Riding through the small village comprised of Halstead tenant houses and greater parsonage, I pointed out this and that as we neared the manse. My companions were both wide-eyed and chatty as we took the long drive, and for the first time I saw my ancestral home and grounds as others might. The original house had been torched under Queen Mary's Protestant burnings and later rebuilt during the glory days of Queen Elizabeth I. I hadn't thought about that in years.

One couldn't help but feel awe as the house came into view. Indeed it was an impressive Elizabethan mansion, with its expensive white stone and eighteen chimney spires. The flagrant overuse of windows and sprawling gardens were made to entice one person specifically, the good Queen Bess herself. The Queen made her rounds through her kingdom during her annual progresses. Grannie still made her rounds to visit our tenants and chaplain.

There was a touch of humor in Luca's tone. "I do believe all of my houses could sit comfortably inside this stunning home of yours, Nicolas."

Ellie said, "It certainly is a striking place with the sun shining on it like this. It was raining cats and dogs when I came with my family for our engagement luncheon."

The look on Luca's face was priceless. Apparently the absurd idiom hadn't stretched all the way to Venice. I laughed. "It is rather grand at that. It's hard to envision my living here again." Though I loved the home that came with my title and knew I'd return here one day, Halstead manor was currently far too much for my life.

We passed the great hedges and came upon the groundskeeper and his small army of sons raking the last of the leaves from the lawn. The boys had grown, but their names came to me almost instantly. From an early age, Grannie compelled me to tour our town and visit the tenants with her. I was the Earl of Halstead, after all. I needed to know them because it would fall to me to look after these people, some of whom had been tied to this place for generations. Her words came to mind on the heels of my earlier thoughts. "Privilege entails responsibility my dear, *noblesse oblige*, as they say."

I felt a sudden sinking in my chest. I had my noble obligation, as had my father before me, and his father had before him, and so forth to the very first Halstead who won the title after he fought beside Henry VII in defeat of Richard III in the battle of Bosworth Field. How could I take their livelihood away from these people because I selfishly stayed away from the responsibility of it all? Feeling guilty, I shelved the thought as we pulled to the front door.

Two footmen stood beside Tamblyn and Mrs. Simmons, the housekeeper, soon joined them. In his middle years when I was a boy, the head butler hadn't aged a day since. Tamblyn's hair only showed the barest hint of silver at the temples and his step was just as quick today as back then. Having read Oscar Wilde's *Picture of Dorian Gray*, it wouldn't surprise me if this ageless man had a portrait of his own tucked away in the attic.

As the footmen raced to see us delivered from the hansom, Tamblyn greeted us with a smile. "Good morning, your Lordship, your Ladyship. I understand you're riding today, sir." He gave a nod to the western sky. "Lovely day for it, if those clouds keep at bay."

I cast an eye skyward. I doubted they would. So engrossed in our plan to search for Bruno, I'd carelessly ignored the weather as a potential factor in our outing. "Good morning, Tamblyn. Yes. I'm hoping the weather will cooperate with my plans for the day."

The housekeeper curtsied. "Good morning, Lord Nicolas, your Ladyship, and to you sir." Ellie smiled and returned their greetings.

"Tamblyn, Mrs. Simmons, this is our dear friend, Mr. Franco."

Acknowledging my introduction, Luca tipped his head.

I asked the butler, "Is my grandmother at home?"

"She is at present, sir. But Brown is bringing her carriage 'round. Her Ladyship has an outing today."

We handed the footmen our things and went to find Grannie. Rather she found us, her lady's maid with coat, hat, and parasol in tow. "My dears, what a pleasant surprise!" Ellie and I both kissed her cheek. Her greeting turned into a slight admonishment. "I do wish you'd sent word that you were coming; I wasn't expecting you until Friday. I would have canceled my Mahjong at the Ashford's today, but there's nothing to be done at this late hour."

I said, "No need, Grannie. I've come to sign those papers, and after, we plan to take advantage of a lovely crisp autumn day. I've neglected Bram too long as it is. But first, allow me to introduce our dear friend Luca Franco. Luca, may I introduce Countess Lady Augusta Halstead, my grandmother."

Gallant and charming as ever, Luca stepped forward and lightly clicked his heels together as he took the old dear's gloved hand and bowed over it. "I am pleased to make your acquaintance, Lady Halstead."

Grannie obviously found both Luca and his manner attractive, for her weathered cheeks held a hint of a maiden's blush. "Why, thank you, and I yours, Mr. Franco. By your accent is it safe to say you're not an Englishman?"

He smiled his handsome smile. "A correct assumption, madam. I've called Italy home for the whole of my life."

I explained our chance meeting aboard ship and the odd occurrence of our association through the Ashmolean. "Fate declared we must be friends."

Her maid was in the process of adjusting her enormous hat's veil, but Grannie turned to smile anyway. "Kismet; how wonderful! Are you an art enthusiast also, Mr. Franco?"

Luca chuckled. "An admirer only, Lady Halstead. I fear I haven't your grandson's eye for detail."

I filled her in. "Luca is a historian, Grannie. His worldwide pursuits uncover historical acquisitions to fill her Majesty's museums. We've convinced him to stay with us for the time being, at least until he becomes accustomed to his new country." As predicted, I saw the dowager's albescent eyes take on that sparkle. This was the stuff that added spice to the Ashford's Mahjong table.

She put on her gloves. "How marvelous! If you were to simply move back to Halstead, there would be ample room for Mr. Franco to stay until he acquires lodgings of his own…"

Quick as always, Ellie cut in. "Grannie, Nicolas and I were discussing this very thing just the other day." She explained as Luca and I were both doing the Queen's business now, it made far more sense to find a larger townhome closer to Oxford. Sure enough, a slight frown darkened my grandmother's eyes. She turned to me. I was about to further explain, when Grannie surprised me.

"You know dear, I do understand and applaud the fact you are a boon to her Majesty's art pursuits." Those same eyes twinkling, she turned to Ellie and whispered conspiratorially, "My companions are green over my grandson's association with the Queen, and I love it, my dear. I simply love it." Back to me, she said, "But you'll have to return to Halstead sometime, my boy. Does it not make sense to do so when there is such a need?"

I hastily offered, "My townhouse is too far from my offices,

Grannie, and Halstead is further still. Ideally we'll find something closer, something in Oxford proper where Luca might have an entire floor to himself rather than simply a guest room. He has almost as many books in his collection as I." Luca chuckled.

"Oh dear, I can only imagine!" Grannie chortled, the act causing her maid to chase the veil as she whipped around to say to Ellie, "I've never seen such a hoarder of books as our Nicolas."

Ellie laughed. "Oh, so true, Grannie! But more importantly, Luca wouldn't feel the foreigner in a new country with friends at hand. Isn't that so, Luca?" Ellie raised her brow at him.

"True enough." Luca nodded and briefly cast a sparkling shadow-blue eye in my direction. The look held his unspoken sentiment.

The dowager replied, "It is difficult to put down roots in a new land, Mr. Franco." She turned to me "Why, just the other day Minerva Ashford and I heard about Constance Everstock's middle daughter Imogene. She married a missionary and settled in India, of all places. She didn't know a soul there for months, not even a single Englishman to dine with. Do you recall Imogene, dear?" Without waiting for my reply she continued on with the tale, which was fine by me, as I had no idea whom she was referring to. "The poor girl..." Grannie was off on a tear. I winked at Luca. After the entirety of Miss Everstock's plight was shared, Ellie said, "How sad for her."

Grannie nodded. "I can't think of anything worse than being friendless in a strange land. Such a lonely affair. I'm so glad you've met my grandson and our Ellie, Mr. Franco. At the very least, you'll have dinner companions until you know England well enough to set off on your own."

Luca smiled. "I am fortunate, indeed. As my work often compels me to travel, I've spent many years dining alone. It is exactly as you say Lady Halstead, a lonely affair." I felt his last words square in my chest. His self-imposed exile successfully managed to keep Bruno from those he cared for, but it came at a heartbreaking cost.

Her old eyes lit with an idea. To me Grannie said, "Mr. Bluwold has offices in Oxford, he might be able to help find suitable quarters closer to the Ashmolean. Do send him a note, dear."

That was a brilliant idea. Our solicitor just might know of properties in the area. I nodded. "I shall, Grannie. That is an excellent notion."

"Well, I must be off, my dears. We're playing pairs and it doesn't do to come late. Enjoy yourselves." She patted my cheek affectionately and kissed Ellie. To Luca, she extended her hand. "It's been a pleasure to meet you, Mr. Franco." We followed her into the foyer where she suddenly stopped at the door. The maid behind her narrowly avoided a collision. "Good heavens, where is my mind?" She turned to her maid, "Mary, do you have my grandson's letter?"

"Yes, my lady."

She dug in her pocket and pulled out an envelope which Grannie took and handed to me. "I have no time to explain now, dear, I'm late as it is. The letter says it all." She tapped a gloved finger on the envelope in my hand and said to Luca, "Do attend, Mr. Franco. I'm sure you'd appreciate dining with a fellow countryman."

The moment the door closed behind her and the servants scattered, I tore the envelope and read my grandmother's hand.

My Dears,

An Italian Count sent his man with a request yesterday. As he's on holiday in London for the next several months, the Count desires to view the art collections in several prominent houses, including the Halstead gallery. Though he'd asked for sooner audience rather than later, I sent him an invitation to dine with us after Christmas. My annual excursion to take the waters with Minerva Ashford is sacrosanct, and we'll not postpone for inopportune guests, exotic or otherwise.

We leave for Bath the Monday after Christmas and plan to return on the third Friday in January, as always. I'm sure we'll discuss it further when you're here for the holiday. The other manors have family on hand who might be hospitable to foreign personages. It falls to you to host Count Bruno, as you should. You know far more about the collections here than anyone. And do plan to stay the night, my dear. He may wish to linger over the collections another day. If nothing else, Ellie will get a feel for the place. It'll all be hers to look after one day.

Your Loving Grandmother

My mind barely registering Grannie's rote admonishment for not living on the premises, I turned to my companions. "He's finally made his first move against me."

Ellie took the letter and read it aloud, adding, "I know the old manor houses were left often open for visiting travelers, but I wasn't aware this was still a common practice." Luca followed with a low rumble of Venetian expletives that he promptly begged Ellie's forgiveness for. She waved his lapse away with her hand.

"It's not. Well, we knew he'd likely try something like this. At least Grannie will be away." I spoke the words, but the fact brought only marginal easing of my mind. Through my exposure to Thom and Mrs. Fletcher, I was well aware that manor houses were veritable beehives of speculation. Whatever the servants didn't know for certain was left to conjecture. Beyond that, Grannie was as astute as Arthur Conan Doyle's Sherlock Holmes. I harbored no doubt that she'd relentlessly badger Tamblyn, Mrs. Simmons, and the rest until she gained a complete picture of Bruno's time here. Just having Bruno at the door was a Pandora's box of potential ruin.

In a gesture I'd come to associate with his feelings of hopelessness, Luca dragged a hand through his hair before turning to stare out the window. Not one to take hopeless at face value, Ellie tapped a gloved fingertip to her lips. I knew the gears of that ingenious mind whirled away. Having grown accustomed to her logic and reasoning, I was eager to learn what she'd discerned so remained silent. Predictably, she blurted, "Do you know what I think? I think your grandmother is inconsequential to him. I think he sent a letter here because he simply doesn't know where we live."

Luca turned to us. "I believe you're right, *caro*. He was born into privilege. He would naturally assume you live here. The arrogant *bastardo* would never abandon this," he gestured with a sweep of his arm, "for the smaller home you have."

Ellie nodded. "That's exactly my thought. And he's come looking for artworks knowing your grandmother would expect you to be on hand, given your field of expertise. Nicolas, he's shooting in the dark. His arrogance tells him we live at Halstead."

A sound in the hallway warned me of a servant nearby. I put

my hand up to halt the conversation for now. I spoke lowly for their ears alone, "Let's have our ride and revisit this conversation at home where Will and Mrs. Fletcher can add their perspective. They've been victimized by this bloody sod as well." I rang for Mrs. Simmons. Then attended my papers.

"You rang, your Lordship?"

"Yes, Mrs. Simmons, please see a suitable lunch packed for our ride." I handed her the small stack of envelopes. "Please give these to Tamblyn to disperse."

She smiled. "Yes, Lord Nicolas."

Unexpectedly, Ellie asked the housekeeper, "Mrs. Simmons, who on staff delivered Grandmother's dinner invitation to the Italian Count?"

"Young Bobby, my lady. Bobby Phelps. He's one of the groundskeeper's sons." She turned to look out the window. "There he is now, the lad with the rake."

"Would you please send him in for a moment?"

"Of course, my lady."

I looked at my wife. "What's that up your sleeve?"

She smiled. "We have a key and a general location near a statue. Bobby knows the address in Charing Cross. The more information we have, the more we have to work with."

I was about to tell her she was brilliant when the freckled-face lad of fifteen came hurrying in. He swept off his hat and stood in the doorway presumably warned by the housekeeper to keep his work boots off the Aubusson carpet. "I was sent for, my lady?"

"Yes, Bobby. It's my understanding that you took a letter to Grandmother's Italian Count."

The color drained from the boy's face, leaving his freckles stark against the pale. "I — I did, ma'am." He twisted the hat in his hands worriedly. "If you would, your Ladyship, please don't send me there again."

I felt a prickling up the back of my neck. A glance at Luca showed his tight jaw. I could tell Ellie was about to ask for Bobby's reason, so I went to the boy and steered him into the hall. "We won't send you there, Bobby. I only want to know the man's address in Charing Cross." At his silent hat wringing, I assured him, "You'll not get sacked. I promise you. Now tell me what's amiss here. "

The relief of the boy was notable. He peered over my shoulder, presumably to see where my wife was. He then whispered, "I think the bloke must be some sort of deviant, sir. He held up a sovereign and told me it was mine if I undressed for him."

I tried to keep my tone level. "Did you?"

He shook his head vehemently. "Oh no, sir. I didn't. I only ran, sir. I had to shove his man hard to get past, 'cause he was makin' to keep me there, but I dashed before he closed the door behind me. I didn't … er…and I didn't tell no one either." The last came with a hopeful raise of his brow that I recognized for what it was.

"Nor will I." I attempted to appear unfazed by what I'd just heard, but I was seething inside. How dare Bruno try to accost this young man, a boy, my tenant. I added, "Stay out of London for the time being. If anyone says differently, tell them this is my directive."

"Yes, your Lordship. I will, sir. But … er … Mr. Tamblyn, sir. He usually sends me to run errands."

"My wishes should suit Mr. Tamblyn well enough. Now, tell me where our deviant Count lives."

***

I left Bram to his oats and chose a younger mount for myself. Luca knew enough about horses to be pleased with Dilbert Brown's choice for him. Ellie politely refused the stableman's choice of the calmer taffy, and chose the feisty chestnut instead. My Yank proved to be an exceptional horsewoman after all, and scandalized Dilbert further when she mounted without assistance and sat astride. To our amazement her skirt held a secret: It was actually a split skirt and surprisingly discreet. All in all, I suppose it wasn't nearly as shocking as the trousers the Manchester pit brow girls wear when they clean the coal from the screens at the mines. I could imagine her stylish utilitarian garment quickly becoming all the rage about town.

Ellie explained that women in the American west often wore men's trousers instead of the split skirt, and one had to admit a secure seat made for a safer ride. I couldn't fault her logic. Once again I was reminded of Sir Francis Galton's "nature versus nurture" philosophy. My wife's predominately male nurturing was the source of more than those abundant liberal attitudes. I found myself wondering what she could do with a pistol in her hand. I chuckled to myself; *Americans*.

As we wouldn't be returning to Halstead, I made arrangements for Dilbert to retrieve the horses at Jack Parson's stable on Teale Street the following afternoon. He'd also send the cart to Oxford in the morning.

***

The November air had a cold damp edge to it that smelled of

snow. Sure enough, by the time we rode into Parson's stable, a slushy mix of rain and snow had started to fall. I had the stable boy call us a hansom cab, and we rode the half mile home with Ellie trapped warmly between us.

William came running to help rid us of our sodden things and we waited behind Ellie while she stood at the door tapping her hat against the rail, intent on knocking the slush away before handing it over. "Thank you, Will. Oh my goodness, what a heavenly aroma."

Luca and I concurred. The house smelled like slow-roasted goose, vanilla custard, and baked plum dumplings, all of my favorites. I could hear pride in Will's voice when he said, "Mrs. Fletcher, Colleen, Maureen, and I made a fine supper with fixin's and fancies, your Ladyship." He dropped one of her wet gloves. Bending to retrieve it, Will's voice muffled through the pile of coats he held. "Uh, pardon me, my lady ..." Missing the glove, he spun around and looked behind him, the motion caused him to drop the other, and lunging for it, he dropped all three hats. I counted my lucky stars Grannie wasn't here to witness this comedy of errors. Will was by no means a lady's maid, nor a butler for that matter.

Mrs. Fletcher met us in the hall and I got two warm hands at my cheeks. "Oh, look at you all! I was afraid you'd be caught out in that weather. William has stoked the boiler, so there's more than enough hot water. Why not take yourselves up for nice warm baths?"

Ellie dabbed her rosy cold nose with her handkerchief. "That sounds perfectly wonderful; I need to thaw. Thank you both." Ellie headed up the stairs first. Over the railing she called, "Mrs. Fletcher, whatever you're cooking smells even more marvelous up here!"

The old dear laughed delightedly. I hadn't heard the sound in a while. It warmed my heart.

"It does smell delicious. You have made my stomach rumble, Mrs. Fletcher," Luca said, emphasizing his words by patting his trim belly.

She beamed. "Your homecoming is cause to celebrate, Mr. Luca. If you'd care to warm up before dinner is served, we've made sure your room has towels and whatnot." Turning to me, she said, "Mr. Luca's trunks haven't arrived, dear. Perhaps he might borrow?"

"Yes, Luca. Do help yourself.

"Thank you. If you'll excuse me." With that, Luca took the stairs.

She said, "Dinner in forty-five, dear. We were just about to set the dining table."

"Dear heart, don't bother with that tonight. We will dine from the buffet."

She waved me away. "This is your first full dinner together since Miss Ellie and Mr. Luca arrived from France. Whatever would they think of such impropriety?"

I cast her dubious eye. How could any of us take such a stand? "We have things to discuss. I want you there and Will too."

"Oh?"

I nodded. "Bruno has finally made his move against me." The worry on her face gave me a pang. I took her hands in mine and added reassuringly, "But we'll have a plan."

***

Our first dinner went off without a hitch, a testament to Mrs. Fletcher's superlative direction. Will stood on hand and bused the platters admirably, while the younger Cooper girls did whatever kitchen maids do. Knowing there wasn't a soul on earth who could stand against my Yank's power of reasoning, I set Ellie upon Mrs. Fletcher. Only then did the old dear yield the day and agree to join us. However, the yielding came with a concession. They'd join us after the maids left.

Luca dabbed his mouth with his napkin. "*Eccellente*, Mrs. Fletcher. Excellent."

"It was delicious. And perfectly timed. My father will be jealous. He's forever eating cold courses not meant to be cold," Ellie added.

I chuckled at the image. I told Mrs. Fletcher, "Yes, you've outdone yourself tonight, dear heart. My compliments for a most delicious meal. Please give my appreciation to the twins if you would."

"Yes dear, I'll tell them first thing tomorrow." Beaming, she proceeded to dish the ice cream beside a plum dumpling and covered it all with a rich purple sauce. Will served.

I tipped my head to the dish before Ellie. "Merry Fletcher's plum sauce is legend, you know."

She sparkled in anticipation. "If appearance is a part of the legend, it looks divine."

"Thank you, Miss Ellie. I've stirred more than one sauce in my lifetime."

I explained for Ellie and Luca's benefit that Mrs. Fletcher was the daughter of the old Halstead cook back in the day.

The old dear nodded. "Yes, my mother, lord bless her, worked at Halstead when the elder Lord Danby, Nicolas' great-grandfather, was lord of the manor. I was just a girl when the old master died. I might have stayed in the kitchen if I hadn't been asked for by Lady Halstead. And when her housekeeper left to care for a sick relation, her Ladyship figured as I'd grown up in the house, I'd know what needed doing. I went straight from lady's maid to housekeeper."

I chuckled, "And then I stole her for myself!" That gained for me a few smiles around the table.

***

With plates cleared and maids gone, the five of us discussed what details we had. I explained Bruno's bold request for an invitation to Halstead. Mrs. Fletcher's brows knitted in consternation.

Luca said matter-of-factly, "I'd like to see him dead."

Will nodded. "I'd like that myself, Mr. Franco. I'd like to see him put down like the mad dog he is, sir." He looked sheepishly at the women present. Though he apologized for his plain speaking, he didn't recant his sentiment.

I concurred. "Yes, I think we're all in agreement there, Will. The fact remains, we can't just go about town murdering murderers, no matter the benefit to the world." My words held the hollow ring of the hypocrite. I'd wielded the bronze figurine of Apollo with deadly accuracy once. I knew if need presented itself, I'd do it again to protect each of these dear people. Losing my appetite from the memory, I forced my dessert down. My companions chatted around me, but I found myself deeply introspective.

***

Alone upstairs, the three of us continued our conversation. As Christmas was less than three weeks hence, it was determined we'd allow the holiday to pass and see Grannie off to Bath.

I said, "That gets one person out of harm's way, but we still have thirteen others under foot."

Ellie suggested, "We could give the staff a weekend holiday with their families."

The thought had merit. Though as I saw it, the sticking point might be Tamblyn. As far as I knew, the man had no family to visit and therefore no reason to leave Halstead. I filled brandy snifters for my companions, then one for myself, and joined Luca by the fire. "Let's say we do exactly that. What then? What do we do with Bruno?"

"Can't we simply go to Charing Cross and kill him?" Luca's words, tinged with humor though they were, were obviously serious.

"In an ideal world, yes. Practically, no. I'm afraid we'll have to be more creative, love."

Then as suddenly as a bolt out of the blue, Ellie suggested we employ immersion as Leonardo da Vinci had. In other words, to come at the problem of Bruno from all sides of the equation. I thought it brilliant, as we each have our own gifts of acuity. I told her so.

Luca said, "Gino's death gives me hope."

"Hope?"

"In the past week, I'd made many inquiries at those places I was certain Bruno would frequent. From comments made, it is my understanding there was deep affection between Gino and

Celso. Perhaps this affection was love and not simply lust."

I pictured Posateri bound over his ottoman. In my mind's eye, I saw the damage inflicted upon Alfred and Thom. I didn't give a damn what their affections were for one another. I voiced it.

No sooner did I speak when Ellie's eyes brightened. She whirled to Luca to confirm whatever thought had come to her. "They were in *love*!"

A smile turned his lips. Apparently they'd understood something I hadn't. Confused, I asked, "What am I missing here?"

Ellie said, "I've scanned the newspaper every day since his death, and all say the unknown man's body was never claimed. This morning's edition says the body was sent to the City of London Cemetery and Crematorium. The cremated remains are to be deposited in a communal grave. Nicolas, don't you see? Bruno never claimed Gino's body!"

I shook my head.

Ellie took a sip of her brandy before setting her snifter down, and proceeded to discard her dinner attire. She tried again. "If the man was loved, and Bruno refused to claim his body for a proper funeral … well, I can't see a lover agreeing to that, can you? I think such disregard is bound to cause a rift in a man's loyalties."

Having companions with exceptional comprehension certainly had its benefits, for I swear there were times, by comparison, where my mind moved as slowly as an ox. I listened as they discussed the facts as we them. In that curious melding of harmonious minds, I eventually saw what they saw. Bruno had one henchman now, and that henchman had a broken heart. If Luca's collected impressions were true, then this Celso had loved Gino. And Gino had died on the street outside the house where they were staying. Logic dictated that Bruno and his remaining henchman had heard of it by now, if not seen it for themselves. Whatever Bruno's reason for not claiming his man's body for burial, the fact that he hadn't treated Gino with decency might very well mean a loss of Celso's loyalty.

Ellie said, "I feel we should somehow take advantage of the rift."

"You do have a point, but you must know there might not be a rift. Love can't be counted upon to change a rabid hound's spots."

Being the delicate gems of nature they were, Ellie carefully removed her pearls and slipped them into blue velvet bags before tucking them into her jewel box. She said, "Then we must find that out."

Deep as she was in her contemplations, her undressing was methodical tonight and appeared to be a process completely independent of her current train of thought. Ellie was very precise in her dressing and undressing. I think it was in Rome when I'd first come to realize that women, especially this one, had a set procedure to such things. They had so many garments of different purpose and shoes and ornaments to match. She sat on the edge of the bed and quickly saw to her shoe buttons with a deft twist of the button hook. My trance was momentarily broken when she said, "Luca, what do you know of Celso?"

"Nothing."

"Alright. Then what of the other man, the unfortunate manservant?"

"Salvatore has been in Bruno's employ for at least four years."

"A loyal man?"

Luca's brows drew together. "Now that I couldn't say, *caro*. It has always been my impression that it was not loyalty that held him."

"What then?"

He shrugged. "Perhaps fear."

I admitted I found that thought absurd. I thought of Alfred, and what Celso had done to him. "Some fear, that. A proverbial moth drawn to flame, no doubt."

Luca didn't comment. I followed his gaze. At last Ellie stood in her white stockings, camisole, and pantalets. She put a small foot on the ottoman and proceeded to roll her stockings down. From the side, my eye caught the flashed pink of inner thigh where the utilitarian split of her pantalets gapped open. I felt myself getting hard. I couldn't help but glance down the front of Luca's trousers. The substantial outline made me even harder. He too was moved by our nymph.

Unaware of her effect upon us, Ellie said, "Moth to flame is right. I don't quite understand how someone would stay in such a situation out of fear. If I were in that place, I'd leave in the middle of the night to get away. If that didn't work, I'd try something else."

I doubted fear was in this little Yank's vocabulary. I remembered how she'd fought Bruno's men and escaped twice. They'd taken her clothing the last time they'd caught her. I pushed the thought away in favor of the far more pleasant imagery before me. She talked on for a time and while I was certain of the logic, her words mellowed in my mind and were getting lost in the light of the picture she presented. She was Jean Francois Armand Felix Bernard's painting of *The Young Woman Undressing* come to life. The camisole came off next and revealed pert nipples as firm as her belief. Her hands went to her muslin-clad hips. "Why are you both looking at me like that? I'm making perfect sense."

Completely unabashed, she had no idea her slow stripping had affected us the way it had. I took Luca's glass and set it beside my own on the mantel, then ran a hand over the growing bulge in Luca's trousers. The sound of his deep breath filled my last inch. Gripping us both, I told her, "Have a care for our comfort, madam."

He covered my hand with his own. "Yes, *caro*. Men are helpless creatures."

A sensual smile turned her lips. She pulled the pins from her hair and the mass fell like a waterfall about her. "Is that so?"

Further prompting was unnecessary. We undressed ourselves and one another. Relishing the touch of him, I ran my hand over Luca's fire-warmed skin. Naked now, Ellie joined us by the fire. Standing between us, her small soft hands found our cocks to caress and pump slowly. When he and I kissed, she stood on tiptoes to slip her tongue amongst ours. We shared the kiss with her, and she with us, three brandied tongues sweetly exploring. Far headier than any wine.

Ellie had more on her mind. Inch by inch she moved down our bodies, her lips grazing, her hands petting, and her mouth suckling. When I felt her breath at my belly and the sweep of her luxurious hair at my balls, I knew where she'd journey next.

We broke the kiss to watch her. Kneeling before us, she was fire-lit and the cinnamon curls shimmered over her bare shoulders with the deep glow of hot coals. Ellie looked up with such a sultry expression of desire I could do naught but stare. Eyes fixed upon ours, she led the cocks to her lips. From one to the other, she painted her lips with our evident excitement, teasing us with shallow entries and broad flat-tongued licks. I could no longer tell which was hotter, the fire at my back, or this living flame before me. I held Luca's cock for her, and he held mine. Synchronized in lust as in thought, we went for her silken mane at the same instant, each of us intending to coax her closer that she might draw us inside to be consumed by her feminine fire. As foreign as the thought had been for the whole of our lives, we'd come to crave the scorching.

Lost in sensation, I nearly missed the small hand that reached for my own. I didn't miss the slight tug. She wanted me on my knees beside her. There was nothing to do but comply. Together we took turns sucking and licking the magnificent length before us while we shared our intermitted kisses. To taste him upon her lips was heady indeed and made more so by the slight hand that found me and stroked in perfect cadence. But it was his large hand that curled into my hair to pull me close. Man to man, I read the signal. No longer sharing him, I swallowed him down. Not to be left out, her tongue teased the wide O of my lips. My fingers found her slippery cleft and while she was momentarily distracted, I sucked him fast and deep. Seconds later Luca's husky groan of release filled the air.

Driven near mad by my own lust, I pulled Ellie to the carpet and there she parted the split of her pantalets and mounted my cock with her slick, lava-hot sheath. A moment later, it was Luca's warm breath at my balls and his tongue at my base. I could only imagine what magic he plied her with, for her tremor squeezed my cock tightly. I knew he'd repositioned himself to kneel behind her by the hot heat of his balls against mine, and the heavy press of his weight on my thighs. I watched the contrast of those large dark hands teasing her small breasts before they swept up and down the front of her body.

He bent his head to her shoulder and I knew he bit lightly by the gasp she gave. How often he had done the same to me, stallion he was. I thrust my hips up from the floor and reading my signal, he gripped her hips. His strong arms became the engine that drove her, and with his help she fucked me hard until her feral growl filled the room and stars exploded behind my eyes in a most glorious climax.

Somehow we took ourselves to bed, myself walking there on jelly legs. I lay between them holding both against my chest, raven and cinnamon hair scented and soft against me. Positioned like this, they reached for each other across my body and our idly-stroking fingers wordlessly conveyed the emotion behind all we'd shared. Tangled limbs snug in the linens, we returned to Bruno. I daresay doing so was an affront to the sated peace of such wondrous loving.

Ellie said, "I've looked at this through my own lens. I know what it's like to love. If someone prevented me from paying my last respects to my loved ones, my opinion of that person would sour. I know it would."

Luca said, "Agreed. I'd want my loved one to have absolution in the eyes of God."

I listened as they chatted back and forth with me between them, feeling the low rumble of Luca's deeper voice against my ribs. Gino the murderous bastard would have only the cursory last rites of an unknown pauper. In my opinion, a fine ending for a soul bound for hell.

"Well, how do we capitalize on that? If Salvatore won't abandon Bruno for whatever peculiar reasons he may have, then we must go to Celso and reinforce how cruel it was for his employer to leave his lover to a mass grave like so much ash from a dustpan. Perhaps a letter?"

"That's a thought, *caro.*"

That he didn't say more told me Luca was tired. We'd spent the day riding in the cold. Coupled with our satisfying meal and our recent loving, the curtain on our day was inevitably drawing closed. I stroked his bare back and pulled our blanket to cover his shoulders and hers, then kissed the top of Ellie's head and pulled her closer.

She snuggled to me and stifled a dainty yawn against my breast. "Was it Caesar who said, *Divide et impera?* Or was that Philip of Macedonia? I think it was King Philip…or did he say, 'divide and rule'?" She yawned again. Though her mind was still working, the telltale twitch of a relaxing leg muscle told me she wasn't long from sleep. Sure enough, their regular breathing signaled they'd both drifted off.

I lay there with a wakeful mind at war with a body desiring sleep. Divide and Conquer. Whether Caesar had coined the term in thinking of the Gauls, or Philip of Macedonia had voiced it in thinking of the Greeks, there were three men we'd face in a matter of weeks, if not before. To rid Bruno of his remaining henchman was ideal.

Beyond a doubt truth bears the same relation to falsehood as light to darkness.

– Leonardo da Vinci

~17~

Salvatore picked up the sealed envelope off the floor and read the name delicately written across the front. Celso. He looked at the door. There was no letter slot. Water droplets on the floor suggested snow had melted where it had blown in. Unless someone had had a key, he couldn't imagine how the envelope got there. Perhaps Celso himself had dropped it. No, he'd been upstairs since he took dinner in his room.

Salvatore opened the door and peered down both sides of the street in the twilight. It was cold, with only a few people walking in the snow and carriages coming and going in all directions. This was a mystery. Shivering, he quietly closed the door. He wasn't used to the heavy cold of London and longed to go home to Napoli where the sun always shined.

He turned the envelope over in his hand. He couldn't imagine who would send a letter, for as far as he knew, Celso was an orphan. There was a part of him that desired to read it. No sooner had the thought come to his mind when Celso came down the stairs. That he'd even considered opening the man's letter caused Salvatore to panic. He'd learned early on that you didn't get on the bad side of the Conte's men. That truth had severely complicated the last four years of his life. He handed the envelope over. "This came for you."

"What is this?"

Salvatore shrugged. "Of course I didn't open it. It is addressed to you."

Celso opened the seal and read silently. Salvatore watched the color drain from the man's face before he crumpled up the paper in his fist.

"What is it Celso? What does the letter say? Who is it from? Celso?"

Celso looked up, his deep-set brown eyes brimming with tears. He thrust the letter at Salvatore before turning on his heel to dash up the stairs to his room. Salvatore listened as the door closed above, then quickly smoothed the crumpled paper. The script was the same as on the envelope. His brows rose in surprise. Written in Italiano, it had a decidedly feminine quality. He read silently:

> *My Dear Celso,*
>
> *A love as complete as the love you shared with Gino is found only once in a lifetime. How terrible that he died on the street like a dog. How cruel that Conte Bruno would not allow a burial sanctified by a Catholic priest. How tragic Gino had no absolution for his many sins.*
>
> *Go home, Celso. His sins were many and so are yours. Don't allow Conte Bruno to send your soul to burn in everlasting hell. Gino would not want that for his love, for that*

is where his soul now resides.

Contemplating who the author of the letter might be, Salvatore took the match safe from his pocket. Striking a match, he held it to the corner of the paper until it ignited. The flame rose higher. Holding it by the edge, he turned the paper as it burned and watched the flame consume the words one by one: Bruno, cruel, absolution, hell...

***

"Where are you Salvatore?" Conte Bruno bellowed from the upstairs landing.

He hurried to the stairs. "Yes, my Conte?"

"Find Celso and come to me. I wish to be entertained."

Celso had gone out shortly after reading the letter. Salvatore took out his watch and checked the time. He stared at the timepiece a moment before returning it to his pocket, and then took the stairs prepared to bear the brunt of the Conte's displeasure. His heart started to pound.

What was he supposed to do? How was he to physically stop the much larger Celso from going where he wished to go? You didn't stand up to the Conte or his men. A gorge of bile rose with a memory.

~18~

Ellie suddenly sat forward and leaned over her morning newspaper with wide eyes. "What? Listen to this…" She read:

> A man in his late twenties or early thirties was found lying in the snow bound and gagged, and with his head covered in a lemon sack. He had been beaten senseless. He was discovered in the vicinity of Fleet Street and Blackfriar. Inspector Clarence Hyde-White of Scotland Yard questioned

local residents as well as patrons at the Bishop's Moke and Farley's Shoe and Stable but was unable to determine the identity of the perpetrator or perpetrators. Inspector Hyde-White is quoted as saying "What makes this case notable is the man's personal effects. The money he carried was mostly of Italian origin as were several papers found in his notecase. It was there we discovered a photograph, whereupon I immediately recognized our Richard Roe, the unknown whose body was discovered in Charing Cross not three weeks ago." Scotland Yard is hoping family or friend will come forward as he is unlikely to survive the assault...

The top half of the paper turned down and Ellie's pale blue eyes met mine. "The Bishop's Moke. Wasn't that where you and Will stopped?"

"Yes." I turned to Luca. "Dare we hope this Richard Roe is Celso?"

Luca said, "Let's assume for the moment that it is. Who would have done this?"

Ellie whirled to the footman, who stood at the buffet.

Obviously surprised, Will read her silent question and stammered, "Oh no, my Lady, I had nothin' to do with this bloke's beatin'. Mores the pity, pardon my plain speakin'." He looked to me. "Might it have been Bertie at the Bishop's Moke, sir? Alfred said his brother wanted the hides o' them that abused him. And they do serve lemons for the oysters there and would have sacks. I could find out, sir. If ye like."

"I would, Will. To my mind the article is about Celso, but we need to be sure." Pulling several £5 notes from my wallet, I handed them over. "Use this to grease whatever wheel that needs it."

***

"Your paper, my Conte." Salvatore set the freshly-pressed paper beside the steaming cup of black coffee and a plate of scones and orange slices. He said, "My Conte, Christmas is three days from today, I would like permission to attend services. There is a church not two blocks from—"

Bruno interrupted the servant with a wave of his hand. "No."

"They have a midnight service, it would not interfere with my duties, and I wouldn't be gone—"

"I told you no. Do not speak of it again. Tell Celso I want

him."

"Yes, my Conte."

Bruno went to the window. Pulling back the curtain, he looked out at the gray morning. In less than a week, he'd kill Nicolas Halstead then find Luca. Together they'd leave this cold dreary place. He pictured Luca with his beautiful eyes and imagined him unclothed and waiting. Although his wound had healed, getting hard still made him anxious. As his imagery aroused his flesh, he slid his hand inside his trousers to slow his erection. Thankfully, this time, he had no mortifying trickle of urine. The incontinence was now relegated to only those times when he had an overfull bladder.

Last night, with Luca on his mind, he was hard and firm, despite being completely headless. He felt like a man again when he realized his cock could still feel some pleasure, however slight. It wasn't the same as before Nicolas maimed him, but it was better than he'd hoped. Then again, Salvatore the *ruffiano* was a poor and reluctant substitute for Celso's talented mouth. Bruno's smile disappeared. Celso's disobedience was unacceptable. How dare he go out without a word. Bruno frowned, thinking of Celso's less-than-entertaining performances as of late. This sulking since Gino's death was starting to annoy him.

Servants were always a presence in his life. From his earliest memory they were things to be used like your horse or hunting dog. He never gave them much thought, though as of late he found himself thinking about Gino. There was a feral quality to Gino that he'd enjoyed and now missed. The man had been a beast in his appetites yet as simple as an ox. He chuckled to himself as he added, and hung like a bull.

It was exhilarating to watch Gino spear his enemies.

Remembrances brought forth Bruno's smile. He'd loved to hear their squeals nearly as much as Gino did. He imagined Nicolas in such a state. He'd had grand plans for the Englishman's slow demise, but with Gino's death, half his strength had died too. Celso would follow his orders, of course. But he lacked Gino's zeal. Bruno frowned. He'd once had a small army of men to do his bidding. They'd rejoin him once he and Luca returned to Venice. His lips turned, imagining another ox like Gino. Yes, he'd find a beast just as savage in his appetites with a *cazzo* to match. His happy imaginings were interrupted by Salvatore's return.

"Celso is gone, my Conte. His bag is gone as well."

"What do you mean, gone?" Bruno asked sharply.

Salvatore swallowed hard. "I searched the chiffonier, his clothes and shoes are gone, my Conte. Celso has left."

Annoyed, Bruno snapped and waved him away, "Leave my sight." With Gino dead and now Celso gone, he felt oddly vulnerable in this foreign place. His frown returned. He hadn't felt that way since he was a boy. Not since his nurse caught him at the candle, burning pages torn from his lesson books. She'd held his fingers over the fire until they blistered. He absently looked at his hands as if he still expected to see the blisters forty-three years later. He recalled how she'd screamed he'd kill them all, setting fires in the house like that. Not all.

Returning to the table, he dunked the end of his scone in his tepid coffee. Taking a soggy bite, he reached for the newspaper and leafed through the pages. There wasn't much that interested him about the English. He dunked again, then blinked in stunned surprise. A story froze him where he sat, and he missed the fact his scone had fallen into his coffee.

***

Rosy-cheeked from the cold and smelling strongly of oysters, Will returned late in the afternoon. It was plain to see he was excited. Rather than wait for him to clean up, we took tea in the kitchen where he blended inconspicuously with Mrs. Fletcher's simmering bouillabaisse.

"So what have you uncovered, Will?"

A born storyteller, Will proceeded to explain in minute detail. "I headed straightaway to the Bishop's Moke, sir. I had t' eat three plates of cockles t' get the girl there t' talk to me long enough to ask after Alfred." Reliving his meal, he stifled a soft belch. "Pardon me. I was glad they served cockles, never much cared for oysters."

My heart gave a tug. Every time Thom and I skipped out for cockles after cards, he'd sing me *Molly Malone*. I'd wager he'd done the same with Will. By now achingly familiar with Will's prolonged discourse, I urged, "So after many cockles...."

He grinned. "Like I was sayin', the girl there finally stops long enough so I can ask after Alfred. A moment later, he comes to the kitchen door. He looked like he's still not up t' workin', as his arm was still in a sling. I could tell he remembered me right off because he smiled and gestured I should follow him. I saw Bertie there in the kitchens, an' if I had any doubts he was the one who beat that Celso half to death, seein' him changed my mind then an' there, sir."

"Why do you say that?"

"Well, sir, remember when we saw him? He was as surly as an old badger. Today, he was all smiles. I had t' look twice t' be sure it was Bertie! He didn't even mind Alfred drawin' two pints an' takin' me upstairs. I sat down with him, an' Alfred confirmed it. Seems Celso was on the docks all set to leave by the look of him, for he had a traveling bag with him. A man by the name of Martin, a friend of Alfred's, sees him booking passage on a ship. Martin was there visiting an old mate, seems the bloke was a sailor once..."

I remembered Martin from the Brimstone, remembered too thinking the large bald man had been a sailor once, given his exotic tattoos and his pocket of rope. So Will now related third-hand that Martin recognized the man and hurried to tell Alfred. Together, Bertie and Martin, and two of Martin's chums named Samuel Snitch and Billy O'Shea, accosted Celso and gave him a taste of longshoreman justice with their slungshots.

My imagination briefly veered from the subject at hand, to recall Thom's uncle on his mother's side had been a sailor and the source of many of Thom's tales. The weapon he'd carried was the slungshot, an innocuous knotted hank of rope heavy with concealed shot. A well-placed blow could crack a skull and break a bone. Will finished his story with, "Celso was left with enough life in him as not to die at any one man's hand. The way they saw it, the rest was up to the Lord Almighty to save his life or not. By what he'd done workin' with Bruno, sir, I'd wager the Lord will send him off t' hell shortly."

Mrs. Fletcher went to her cupboard. There she retrieved a bottle of cherry cordial and proceeded to fill five small glasses. She smiled at me, her eyes swimming with sad satisfaction. Reading her thoughts, I stood. The others followed and I raised my glass. "To Thomas Fletcher."

The others raised both glass and voiced in chorus. "Thomas Fletcher."

Out of the corner of my eye, I saw Mrs. Fletcher enfold Will in her arms. His body quaked with emotion. I sent my thought aloft. One more, Thom. One more.

~19~

A fair amount of snow had fallen overnight and covered the shrubbery like French fondant on petit fours. Only now in the light of day did I notice the red bows tied to every stone urn along the drive. From the first coach light at the gate to the topmost floor, Grannie saw the manse decked out splendidly for the holiday. I suspected her goal was to put on an enticing display for my wife, who, to Grannie's thinking, would naturally want to see to this lily gilding herself as the new Lady Halstead.

We'd had our small Christmas with Vicar Stanton and his sisters Beryl and Bernadette, who recently returned from missionary work in Burma. Ellie's father and sister were in attendance as well, joined by Luise Marie's husband Jean-Paul, and his sister Pearl and their mother Maude. Luca sailed an endless sea of people wishing to know all about him and being a well-lettered charmer, he enthralled them all. My father-in-law surprised us with a letter from the merchant Pietro Ambrosini, who said he planned to make another visit to London late in the spring. He didn't mention a word about his brother-in-law, Carlo Posateri.

But the surprise of all surprises was Grannie's invitation to Colonel, Sir Robert Beaumont to join us for the holiday. After our chance meeting aboard our ship bound for Venice, it was pleasant indeed to renew our acquaintance. I couldn't help but notice the blush on my grandmother's cheeks. I surmised that I was seeing budding affection between the elders that had nothing to do with the fact he'd been chums with my grandfather.

The colonel remembered Luca and for a time, we had ourselves an energetic and animated relating of our shared travel experiences. As it had so disappointingly fallen by the wayside that evening we'd met Luca, the colonel revisited the topic of Leonardo da Vinci and other geniuses of that age. Jean-Paul was obviously beside himself to discuss the Renaissance at length, for the man barely paused to take a breath. How I wished we could have told them about the hidden messages of love from the artist to Salai, but to do so came with the potential for questions we couldn't answer truthfully. And it was certainly not the topic for mixed company, let alone the clergyman and his maiden sisters.

Later, Jean-Paul innocently let it slip that Luise Marie was expecting their first child. Everyone beamed. The way Grannie carried on over the news, you'd think her the jubilant grandmamma. Luise Marie insisted we play a round of charades and who could deny an expectant mother anything? Curiously, or not so curiously, given all we'd shared, Ellie, Luca, and I were spot on and won the most rounds. After such burden on my heart and mind, the enjoyable evening could not have gone better. Happily, yesterday's observance of Boxing Day was every bit as delightful.

I'd been surprised to find Colonel Robert was headed for Bath with the ladies. My surprise then was nothing compared to how stunned I'd been to learn he'd been tagging along for the last fifteen years! Something was afoot here. I half expected Grannie to tell me Minerva Ashford had never actually gone and that she and Sir Robert were off for their annual tryst. He joined us for our Christmas rounds through the parsonage and helped pass out packages and sweets to our tenants. It was fortunate to have him for he was jolly good company, especially that second evening when the good colonel proved himself quite the pianist for the servant's dance.

As enjoyable as our three full days were, there was no escaping the fact that our date with Bruno drew nearer. The fact of what lay beyond crept in from the sides like the unsettling imagery of Hieronymus Bosch. Though it made sense to stay and wait out the inevitable encounter with Bruno two days hence, I'd given the staff their holiday the moment Grannie and her escort left us that morning. More than half planned to leave today, while the rest would depart tomorrow. Only Mrs. Peabody, the cook, Tamblyn, and one of the new housemaids whose family lived on one of the small farms of Halstead, would remain. It was far from ideal. I wished we could clear the house. At Ellie's urging, we decided to return to London. She'd made the case that the remaining servants would appreciate their holiday with no one to see to.

I would be glad to be in our townhome and in our own bed. I was comfortable at Halstead but sorely missed my privacy. My mind knew every corner of this place, every cranny and nook. I knew the bedroom where Luca slept. I knew the colors and the furnishings and could so completely picture him alone with his thoughts. Ellie and I both missed him and we'd slept wrapped tightly together lest we roll apart and wake alone. I felt Mrs. Fletcher and Will awake in their borrowed beds on the servants' floor. We all felt Thom's absence. This was our first holiday without him and a full year of such firsts loomed on our horizon.

Ellie came up behind me and wound her slender arms around my waist. She leaned to the side and we looked out at the white perfection below. She said, "It really is a lovely place, and I've enjoyed myself. I know my father and sister did. Luise-Marie told me how happy she was that you and I wed."

"Did she now?"

"Yes, she did. So did Papa, who not only said the exact same thing, but added that he had a wonderful time. And Jean-Paul obviously enjoyed himself."

Chuckling, I wrapped my arms around hers, effectively holding her to my back. Together we watched a single rider depart down the drive. I thought him rather poorly dressed for the weather. "It was an enjoyable few days. Is Luca packed, do you suppose?"

I felt her nod against me. "Yes, Will tells me all our things have been loaded into the carriage. Mrs. Fletcher is saying her goodbyes as we speak."

A moment later, the old dear found us in the parlor. "Pardon the interruption, Lord Nicolas…" I could tell instantly by her voice something was amiss. I turned to find her holding a note, a worried expression on her face. She shook her head slightly, her eyes darting to the side. Just beyond the door, one of the remaining maids puttered in the hall. I took the note. It was addressed to Lady Halstead, I assumed meant for my grandmother. She added in a whisper, "An Italian man brought it to the door."

Addressed to my grandmother or not, I opened it and read:

> *My Dear Countess Halstead,*
> *I look forward to visiting your galleries this coming*
> *Wednesday. Indeed, I've thought of nothing else. I*
> *shall arrive at 1:00.*
> *Your Servant,*
> *Conte Acario Bruno*

This would end one way or another. I gave these two dear women what I hoped was a reassuring smile and said, "Let's go home."

***

"Well?" Bruno looked at his servant standing there in snow-wet clothing with his pink nose dripping like a spigot.

Salvatore dug into his coat with a numb hand. Pulling out his handkerchief, he dabbed the tip of his nose, then blew hard before stuffing the sodden cloth back in his pocket. "I delivered the letter, my Conte, and while I was there, I noticed a coach being loaded with luggage." He dug for his handkerchief again.

"And?"

"I — I heard the servants say the things belonged to Lord Halstead. He does not live at Halstead manor, my Conte. I thought I should follow the coach and I discovered that he lives in London, not three kilometers from here."

"I thought as much. The countess was far too eager for my visit. Nicolas never would have agreed." Bruno ran a finger over his cheek to trace the jagged scar. "Tell me about his London home."

"From what little I know, my Conte, it is a modest place that belies his title. He lives there with his wife and... and..." Salvatore paused.

Understanding lit Bruno. As quick as a striking snake, he backhanded Salvatore hard across the face. The servant staggered backward, his hand pressed to his stinging skin, his tongue tasting blood where his teeth tore the inside of his cheek.

***

Salvatore carefully refolded the letter along worn creases. He'd done so so often that the paper was partially torn in two. He tucked it back into his wallet, which he returned to his inside coat pocket. He went to the door and listened. Conte Bruno was snoring. His tongue assessed the inside of his cheek. The flesh was torn and sore but a wash of warm salt water had eased it considerably. It wasn't the first time he'd been struck. He'd dealt with far worse. His eyes welled up. Far worse.

***

The next evening Bruno called, "Salvatore, *vieni qua.*"

Conte Bruno hadn't spoken a word all day. Salvatore hurried to his master as bid. "Yes, my Conte?"

"I'm going out. Call for a coach."

"Yes, my Conte."

A half hour later, Bruno looked out the window, wondering what was taking his manservant so long to find a coach. He hated this continual inconvenience. His thoughts strayed to Venice where his own coach and gondola sat unused. Invariably, when thinking of the country of his birth and his palazzo there, his mind lit upon Luca. He'd made it an enviable showcase and filled it with innumerable pleasures in the hope that Luca would come to him. Bruno scowled. Nicolas Halstead. Luca had come to him of his own accord, and that English *figlio di troia* had insinuated himself into their long-anticipated reunion.

He looked into the night and sighed impatiently. It was snowing again. How he missed Venice for its weather. He'd been well-situated there as his highborn station demanded. In Venice he'd had adequate servants and useful men who did his every bidding. He had wonderful meals, enticing entertainment, and wealthy men of stature under his thumb. Together he and Luca would rebuild his influence there. It wouldn't be difficult. Those men with secrets feared him. He'd collected many secrets.

Above all, he desired Nicolas to fear him. He would have preferred a different outcome, something prolonged and pain-filled to match his maiming. But that would no longer come to pass, not with Gino dead, and Celso dying. A thought came to him and he pulled the small pistol from his pocket to roll the full cylinder. He'd kill Lady Halstead first and Nicolas would watch. Imagining the Englishman's anguish and pain, Bruno smiled.

~20~

Ellie returned to the library with the tea service of chamomile to facilitate sleep. She set the tray down and proceeded to pour. None of us were sleeping well as of late. She said, "I know there's a solution. We just haven't discovered it yet."

We'd meet with Bruno the day after next, and damn me if a solution existed. I, for one, couldn't see it. Truth was, Bruno coming to Halstead preceded my ruin. One word heard from Bruno about my nature, and a fuse would be lit to run through the entirety of society's servant class and the rest would follow. My reputation would be ruined, which didn't bother me half so much as imagining my grandmother's good name and social standing in tatters. I was at a loss, and I couldn't very well leave the whole bloody thing to chance. I voiced it.

Along with a reassuring caress, Ellie slid a steaming cup before me in a silent wish that I'd drink it and sleep away my headache. Seized by it these past few hours, I struggled to listen as she relayed her latest insights. We'd been endlessly discussing it. As we lay in each other's embrace after our loving last night, we'd discussed it. At first light, and through each of our meals with Mrs. Fletcher and Will adding their views after, we'd discussed it. We barely spoke of anything else. I rubbed the point between my eyes. My head throbbed with it all. It loomed so large in our lives that I felt small standing against it.

"What I don't understand is, did he just plan to launch a salvo to ruin your reputation and decided to begin there at Halstead, or did he plan to devastate Grannie to get at you? Surely he had to know the moment she invited him that you weren't involved in the decision." Ellie tapped her fingertips against her lips. I knew it as a mannerism that signaled an errant thought had popped into her mind like a genie from a lamp. Sure enough, she said, "I suppose we could send the maid, Mrs. Peabody, and Tamblyn on some long errand."

"Love, the problem is we don't know his intent." I spoke the words, but I knew. We were dealing with a man who took delight in causing pain. From the instant Alfred told of his bizarre encounter, I'd known. Bruno desired my pain. With Gino dead and Celso standing at death's door, the threat of physical danger had only lessened. Bruno didn't have the manpower to inflict torture now. But the threat of scandal persisted, and I knew even that would not be enough for him.

Ellie shook her head, obviously flummoxed. I sipped my tea, feeling impotent. For the first time in my life I wished I was completely alone, for if I were all the people I loved would be safe. It struck me then why Luca chose his isolation. I'd known it in theory, but I felt it now. This was his reason. I suddenly realized Luca was oddly quiet, that same quiet as the night he left us and walked off into the rain. I looked at him and the sadness in those snow-shadow eyes made my heart ache. I knew he felt responsible. I rested my hand on his wrist, the same wrist sporting a jagged scar gained by broken window glass, an otiose attempt to cut his bonds and help the man he loved. This was Cesare's scar. Luca saw the slow agonizing murder each and every time a stretch of his arm raised his cuff.

Ellie offered the same opinion she'd given more than once over the past week. "I know I've said it before, but why we don't just send a note to invite him here? Then the Halstead staff aren't involved."

My Yank was persistent and my headache too great in that moment to revisit all the reasons why we'd not be inviting Bruno here. I said simply, "Please sweetheart, we've discussed this at length. I have no intention of putting you or Mrs. Fletcher in harm's way."

"Yes, but that was before his henchman was beaten half to death. Bruno is alone now. Surely that makes him less of a menace?" Obviously seeking a champion for her reasoning, she turned to Luca with delicate brows raised.

He shook his head. "Nicolas is right, *caro*. Nothing makes him less of a menace. I too would see you and Mrs. Fletcher here where you're both safe. Like Nicolas, I prefer you not go to Halstead at all."

Two against one. Predictably, she set her jaw. I swear I heard the gears of her mind as they whirled, bent as she was to fortify what she saw as a perfect solution. She didn't have the opportunity for retort, for the doorbell rang below. I couldn't imagine who that would be at this late hour. I started to rise but she pressed me back into the chair. "Don't rise. Be mindful of your headache and drink your tea. I'll see who that is." She leveled us a look on her way to the door. "I'm not finished with this discussion."

Luca shook his head, "Aye. *Caparbia donna.*"

My Italian had broadened since we'd met. He made me smile. "She certainly is a stubborn woman." I laced my fingers in his and spoke from my heart, "Please don't leave us again."

Surprise flickered briefly in his eyes. He covered our clasped hands with his. "I won't, *il mio amore.* I won't."

***

Ellie opened the door to a slight man with worried eyes. "Yes, may I help you?"

The next instant, Salvatore was shoved through the doorway and Bruno stepped inside. Spinning her around, he twisted her arm painfully behind her back with one hand, and covered her mouth and nose with the other. His voice was deadly calm and quiet, "Make one sound and I shall break your neck. *Capire?*"

Unable to breathe, she ceased her struggle and nodded.

Uncovering her mouth, he reached into his pocket, then jabbed a gun barrel firmly into her ribs. "Take me to them."

Ellie didn't move. She looked to the servant with pleading eyes. As white as a sheet, he looked away.

Bruno twisted the arm higher until she whimpered. "Do not play games with me, *puttana.* I repeat, take me to them."

With no other choice, she led them up the stairs.

***

Hearing the low rumble of unrecognizable voices, Mrs. Fletcher opened the door a crack and peered down the hall to see a strange man holding a gun to Ellie. She didn't know what to do. Her first thought was Dr. Compton and Dr. O'Connor. They'd both been soldiers, they'd have their revolvers. When the hall was clear, she hurried to Will's room and shook him awake, "William, wake up."

"Wha…? Oh. Yes ma'am?"

"Listen to me. Go down the street to Dr. Compton's office and bring both men back here. Tell them I need their assistance. Tell them to bring their service revolvers."

"What?"

"Do it now, William! For heaven's sake lad, there's no time to explain."

***

I saw Ellie out of the corner of my eye and turned to see Bruno leading her through the door. I rose so quickly the chair tipped to the floor. Luca jumped to his feet.

Bruno smiled and pushed Ellie forward. He said, "Ah Nicolas, your wife was good enough to show me in. Isn't that right Lady Halstead?" He held her arm twisted behind her back. My god, how I hated him.

I ground out, "Release her, Bruno."

"I think not." He jammed the gun he held hard into her side and she whimpered.

"You sodding bastard!" I took a step toward him and stopped when Ellie cried out. He must have jerked her arm, for her face contorted from the pain of it. "Stop! You're hurting her!"

Luca grabbed me by the arm to hold me back, and growled,

"Stop or I'll kill you with my own hands."

Bruno stared at the hand gripping my arm, and I saw the tic in his jaw. He said, "You'll be rid of them tonight, Luca. Then we'll return home." His words loving, he added, "I forgive the spell this *diavolo* and his *sticchio* put on you that you injured me so grievously. I forgive you, Luca. There is enough of me to love. I remember your exquisite kiss. In it, I felt the depth of your love for me. Since the moment I set eyes upon your angel's face, all I've wanted is you, always you. *Amore a prima vista.*"

A demented Bruno spoke as if they were the only two people in the room. My mind could barely absorb the insanity of his words. I could feel Luca's trembling rage through the hand that held me back. His next words caused me to look at him in utter surprise, "*Si, amore a prima vista. Si presenterà il suo di suo marito, e io andrò con lei. TI do ciò che desiderate. Non lottare contro di essa.*"

Those words reverberated inside me. *You will release her to her husband's care, and I will go with you. I will give you what you wish. I won't fight any longer.*

Ellie cried, "No, Luca." Her back arched and she screamed in agony as her arm was cruelly twisted higher. I took another step forward. Luca pulled me back.

Bruno cocked the gun. His words were strangely distant, "Take your hand from him, Luca. You'll not touch him again. And never again will you touch this ... this... *figa.*" His last word spoken with disgust, his emotion tightening his grip upon her, Ellie rose painfully to her toes.

"I'll belong to only you. I will be yours to love, Conte. Yours. All of me in exchange for her release. I give you my word, Conte. I will return to Venice and learn to love you..."

Ellie started to sob.

Bruno's face transformed, his eyes strangely hopeful. *"Questo è vero?"*

Luca nodded. "Yes, this is true."

"I knew you'd forgive me one day, *il mio amore*. I only had to wait. Cesare D'Ovidio needed to die, Luca. You know that now, don't you? Just like they need to die now. It is the only way for you to truly leave them."

Feeling helpless, I spoke to the madman with all the calm I could muster, "Kill me if that is your goal. She's done nothing to you. Release her."

For no reason that I could fathom, Bruno's servant covered his face with both hands and began to wail. Obviously confounded by this odd behavior, Bruno turned and everything that followed became a blur as though I watched it unfold through the slits in a zoetrope.

Bruno must have relaxed his hold upon her, for Ellie suddenly kicked at his shin with her heel. A savage growl tore from his throat as she escaped his grasp. His gun fired. In a horrific illusion that slowed time, her slight body arched as she fell headlong toward me. Then in a flash, Luca threw himself upon Bruno, causing the gun to veer wildly.

"Ellie!" I rushed forward to catch her. Gathering her unconscious form to me, I frantically covered the wound in her back with my hand to keep her precious blood from spilling. Scarlet bloomed over her gown and through my fingers, the iron tang of it thick in the air.

"Ellie, oh please...dear god. Ellie..."

I heard the unmistakable click of the hammer being cocked and looked up to see the struggle for the gun that was pointed square at me. It fired again, shattering the glass panel of the bookcase behind me. A jolt of panic ran through my spine, and my body reflexively fell over Ellie to shield her. Again the gun discharged, this time striking Luca in the thigh. I watched him fall to the floor, his face twisting in a mask of agony, and hands clutching the wound.

Eyes wide and feral, Bruno whirled to me and cocked the gun. An unnatural cry of rage tore from Salvatore's mouth as he flung himself at my would-be murderer and threw the hand that held the gun upward, where it discharged in a rain of plaster before clattering across the floor. I heard a thunder of footfalls coming up the stairs. Salvatore was now a raging beast, pounding with unbridled fury. Bruno howled dementedly and fought his fervent assailant. When he caught sight of Luca dragging himself miserably across to the floor to us, he screamed, "No! Luca, stay away from them! You're mine, you're mine!"

Unbelievably, Will came bursting into the room with the two doctors hot on his heels, brandishing what looked to be Webley service revolvers. I called to them both, "Please... please help her."

Bruno struggled with a wild Salvatore on his back. Will threw himself at the pair, knocking both to the floor. I heard him rage with punishing blows, "Ye killed my Thommy, ye sodding bastard! Ye...killed...my...Thommy!" A moment later, Bruno was still.

Dr. Compton rushed to Ellie's side. He pried my hand away from her wound. My fingers were warm and sticky with her blood and seeing how much she'd lost raised a panic in my heart. I looked for Luca and found Dr. O'Connor ripping open the leg of his trousers. Blood painted my world red like a hellish nightmare. It covered the floor and her, and him and me.

Dr. Compton called out in a booming voice, "Merry, come quickly! Bring linens, towels, whatever you can find..."

From the corner of my eye, I saw Dr. O'Connor kneeling beside Luca, and beyond, a wailing Salvatore still pummeling an unconscious Bruno. Will stayed the servant's fists, and I heard him say, "Leave him, man. Ye'll kill him if ye hit him again." Salvatore rocked back on his heels and buried his face in his hands. An agonizing string of Italian spewed forth as he wept.

Mrs. Fletcher was at the door, her arms laden with towels and linens. "Oh, Mary Mother of God."

Dr. O'Connor said, "Find a rope, Merry. We need to bind that lunatic before he comes 'round."

***

Having been turned away from both bedroom doors to wait downstairs out of the way, I'd been beside myself listening to the sounds of suffering echoing down the stairway. Met with silence now, my imagination got the better of me. I took the stairs needing to know they were alright. My bedroom door was still closed, and listening there, I heard Dr. Compton and Mrs. Fletcher's voices. That I didn't hear Ellie rose a lump in my throat. Pressing my ear to the wood, I heard the doctor say Ellie would sleep for a while.

The door to Luca's room was open, and I found Dr. O'Connor assisting him to a chair. I looked him over just to be certain he was safe. His pant leg was completely cut off high above the knee, his bare thigh tightly bandaged. From the knee down he was smeared with dried blood. I had a vague recollection of Dr. O'Connor saying the bullet had gone clean through Luca's leg muscle to leave him with two wounds, the first being small and neat, while the second a torn mess that needed many stitches to close. The entire channel the bullet left through his thigh needed to be packed with sulfur. From what I'd heard, I could only imagine the agony.

Luca looked haggard and pallid from pain and blood loss. He wearily sat on the edge of the chair next to me and I squeezed his hand.

"How is she?"

I shook my head. "We don't yet know." I hadn't heard Ellie at all and though that implied she hadn't roused for the bullet's extraction, I was sick with worry nonetheless. I no sooner spoke, when Dr. Compton came into the room followed shortly by Mrs. Fletcher holding a wash basin and ewer. I jumped to my feet the instant I saw him. "Ellie?"

"Lady Halstead is fine, son. She roused for a moment, then slipped into unconsciousness again. The mind will do that if the pain is too great." He washed and dried his hands, then rolled down his shirtsleeves, then came and gave my shoulder a reassuring squeeze. From his pocket, he set a small partially-flattened piece of lead, nearly the size of a three halfpence coin, on the table. I picked it up. The slug was heavy for its size. Knowing that he'd dug it from Ellie's back made my chest feel hollow. He tipped his head toward the lead in my hand. "Thankfully, that slug was lodged against a rib bone. The rib was fractured, so we must expect her to be in a good deal of discomfort for a week or more. She's a fortunate young woman. We will have to keep infection at bay, but she'll be fine."

I tried to thank him but my relief choked me. Trying again, I met the doctors' eyes. "Thank you both."

Luca picked up the slug and turned it over in his hand. Overcome, he lay his head on his arm and wept. I stroked his head gently, and his hand came up to hold mine firmly against him. Mrs. Fletcher's hand was suddenly atop ours. Turning, I went to her. I knew my tears were safe in front of these men, and I let them fall freely.

***

I hurried through my bath to get the stink of blood and fear off my skin. I looked in on Ellie. She'd roused enough to take a draught for pain and was now sleeping soundly. After much persuasion Dr. Compton convinced Mrs. Fletcher to take a bit also, and she too slept soundly. She'd been determined to clean so we'd not revisit the horror in the light of day, but there'd be time enough to put the place to rights. I for one didn't have the stomach for more blood then and there. Mopped clean or not, I expected the image of my bloody library would linger in our minds for some time to come. Thinking on it now, I decided as soon as Will returned, I'd send a note to the Coopers telling them to take a holiday. The last thing we needed was Ned or his sisters innocently venturing upstairs.

As exhausted as he was, Luca made his way to the kitchen while I was in my bath. I felt a moment of panic when he wasn't in his room and when I found him it was all I could do not to admonish him for that foolhardy decision to take the stairs. But I understood. He'd get no sleep until Will and Salvatore returned. He needed to hear there was finally closure to this whole sodding affair. I had no doubts this time.

Alone in the kitchen, I carefully undressed him one limb at a time. Taking special care to avoid the bandage, I washed him as best I could. Though he was naturally warm-skinned, his blood loss had made him shockingly cold. His teeth chattered despite my heavy brocade dressing gown and Mrs. Fletcher's market shawl draped over his bare legs. I had to raise the flames on the stove and left the oven doors open to warm him.

***

Will came in through the service door with Salvatore in tow. One couldn't miss his smile. "We're back, sir. Ol' Bertie was beside himself at yer gift. Alfred and Bertie both say to come and eat yer fill anytime; they'll feed ye oysters and cockles, and ale for the rest o' yer life!"

I chuckled. I'll bet the brothers were pleased. With Salvatore's help, and the good doctors' carriage, Will had delivered Bruno to the doorstep of the Bishop's Moke. I knew longshoreman's justice would be served and the good Lord would decide the outcome either way. After all the man had done to Thom and Cesare, to Mrs. Fletcher, Ellie and Will, and the rest, I didn't have a crumb of compassion for him. As with any rabid creature, the world would be safer without him.

Will took Salvatore by the elbow and led him to the table then poured the man some coffee. I still didn't understand the role Bruno's manservant had played in this, but I was grateful. I thanked him. He said something in rapid Italian. As tired as I was, I didn't have a prayer of deciphering. He pulled out his wallet and from it removed a worn and tattered letter. Pulling out his pocket watch, he opened it and slid both across the table to Luca. To my surprise he then put his head in his hands and started to cry again. My god, what had this poor man gone through?

Luca carefully unfolded the letter and read. I watched him wipe his eyes and swallow hard. Whatever he was reading tore at his emotions. Setting the letter down, he looked at the pocket watch, then looked at Salvatore, and back again at the watch. His eyes grew large. He fired a question. Salvatore looked up and nodded. Luca turned to me obviously astounded by what he'd discovered. "*Gesù, Maria, e Giuseppe.* This is Fredo."

I looked at him and shook my head. I had no idea what he was talking about.

"Fredo is Cesare's younger brother!" He turned to ask Fredo a question. The man wiped his eyes with his knuckles and nodded. Luca picked up the letter and read:

> *My Dearest Brother,*
>
> *I hope my letter finds you well. It is with my deepest regret, I must tell you by the time you read it, I shall have died. I ask that you do something for me. I ask that if it is possible, you see the man who's killed me brought to justice. His name is Conte Acario Bruno. He's a dangerous man with wealth and connections that allow him to do as he wishes. I ask one more thing of you Fredo. Look after Luca. You alone in the world know my feelings for him. The Conte has set his eye upon him and I fear for his life. Please, watch this Conte from a distance only, and above all, be careful.*
>
> *I wish you were here beside me brother. I'm afraid, Fredo. The Holy Father knows love, but will He recognize mine? Will He see into my heart and know the depth of my love for Luca? If He forgives my love, then know I shall smile down on you from heaven. Until we meet again, know you hold a piece of my heart.*

Your Loving Brother,
Cesare

Luca looked at me with swimming eyes. "He wrote that letter the night after..." he swallowed, "after his attack, before he...before the fever came and he slipped away from me. I posted it the day of his funeral. He wanted to say goodbye to his brother."

I took the pocket watch and looked at the photograph trimmed to fit under glass inside the lid: two boys separated in age by perhaps as much as five years. The older of the two, Cesare, had been a handsome lad with expressive eyes. A thought struck me that the dissimilar pair may have been born to two mothers. As the man had very little English, Fredo relayed his story through Luca. Fredo was a manservant to a wealthy merchant in Napoli. Once Fredo discovered his brother was dead, he set out to find his brother's murderer, a quest that had taken three years because Bruno traveled a lot. I didn't need to be told the reason for that travel. He'd been following Luca.

When Fredo finally found Bruno in Venice, he determined the best way to watch him was from the inside. He sought employment, and what a terrible mistake it had been. For four long years, he suffered the man's abuse. After the first month, he'd given notice. He simply couldn't do it any longer. It was then he first faced punishment for daring to leave. No one left Bruno's service; the man took it as insult. The sordid details bubbled forth like water from a font, details this poor man had kept to himself for all those years. The second time he tried to leave, he was made sport of at one of Bruno's perverse soirees. He never tried again.

When he found Bruno at the bottom of the stairs broken and maimed, Fredo had been overjoyed. Then to his horror, the monster lived. He actually considered killing him for Cesare and all those years of his own abuse. But Gino was there, and sadistic Gino was extremely loyal. When Fredo discovered Bruno intended to follow Luca and kill the man Luca loved, he vowed he'd die to keep Luca and I safe. And dying would release him from hell.

He'd seen a glimmer of hope when Gino was found dead. Then Celso went missing after our letter arrived. He was surprised to hear Celso wasn't expected to survive a beating. And last night when Bruno ordered Fredo to join him, he knew at long last with the henchmen gone, he'd die, taking Bruno with him. He wanted us to know he was sorry. Sorry it took him so long to find courage. Sorry he hadn't just killed Bruno after his fall and faced Gino for whatever retaliation the brute could think of. And sorry he'd been made a coward at their hands.

Obviously touched by this tale as were we all, Will smiled encouragingly at Fredo and patted his shoulder. Fredo flinched, but smiled back. Here was a man in sore need of friends. I had Luca ask him if he planned to go back to Italy. He said though he longed to, there was nothing for him there. Four years of association with Bruno would preclude any gainful employment. Bruno had been reviled and flagrant, everyone knew his deviant appetites. He thought he might go to America.

I said to Luca. "My grandmother thinks I need manservant."

Our life is made by the death of others.
– Leonardo da Vinci

~21~

With Ellie and Luca far from able to take a lengthy journey comfortably, I'd ridden alone to Halstead for my grandmother's homecoming and was now returning home with the last rays of the sun at my back.

I'd been surprised Grannie didn't press me with questions after I told her both Ellie and Luca were under the weather. Instead she launched into a disquisition on therapeutic value of the waters at Bath. She said she'd returned "rejuvenated." I wondered briefly if the colonel had been likewise rejuvenated, and how, but I didn't ponder that too long.

Grannie reminded me that our family physician sent me to Bath after my splints were removed. I remembered. The muscle spasms would wake me as though the devil himself had dug his claws into me. Mrs. Fletcher and I soaked in the hot sulfured waters and thinking about that now, I remembered that the waters with the overbearing smell did bring me ease. I made a mental note to ask Ellie and Luca if they'd care to try it.

Grannie had been mildly disappointed the Italian Count never made his visit, but as she and Minerva Ashford spent several days with "a delightful array of companions," the mahjong table, and various luncheons would be well-stocked with conversation for many weeks to come.

At my direction, Will went to the Brimstone to find Roz and hired her sister for Ellie's Lady's maid. Agnes was bright and attentive and held her own progressive ideas. These they discussed over hairstyles. I couldn't have chosen better for my Yank. Mrs. Fletcher liked the personable girl too. Ellie was healing as anticipated. Her wound caused a full week of heart-wrenching misery that blessedly dulled as the days passed. In this, our third week since Bruno came to call, she was finally moving about with minimal discomfort

Luca, on the other hand, had a rough go of things. Early last week his painful wound abscessed, necessitating a draining and irrigation with carbolic acid. Fortunately, the doctors insisted they give him chloroform. Since then, he'd taken to using a cane. And just yesterday Dr. O'Connor vowed the leg "was healing nicely and would soon be good as gold."

By a fortuitous turn of events, the doctors heard word that one of their patients was relocating to Canada and leaving behind a splendid home. Indeed it was. Despite outmoded conveniences needing to be replaced, I signed the necessary papers that officially made it ours. It wasn't our initial plan to stay in London, but the three-story had ample room, and it was a short ride from the new house to Victoria Station. As much of what we did required travel abroad, a train to Oxford several times a week was all Luca and I needed for our work at the Ashmolean.

Our new home offered ideal amenities such as generous housekeeper's rooms and an upper floor for our live-in servants not part of the Cooper brood. The distance to the new house being nearly the same, the Cooper siblings would continue to clean and cook and run errands for Mrs. Fletcher with a slight increase to their pay to make the difference. The other selling point to this house was the ideal proximity to the Drury Lane and several fine dining establishments. With my companions healing, I found myself eagerly anticipating going out on the town as we had in Paris.

If all went well, we'd be moved into our new home by mid-February. The packing was already underway, and a crew of craftsmen was poised to modernize the house with fresh paint, electricity, plumbing, and a grand Grosvenor town gas stove for Mrs. Fletcher.

By day, our home bustled with efficiency, and by night it was often filled with laughter. The light was slowly returning to Mrs. Fletcher's eyes and to Will too. It made me happy to see it. Fredo had grown extremely close to Mrs. Fletcher, and the sentiment was returned. The dear old soul was healing him with kindness. Indeed, she was mother hen to the lot of us.

With everyone's help, Fredo's English was vast improving, though I have to say his Italian accent blended with Will's common Welsh tongue made for sentences interesting for the ear. He was an exemplary manservant with an uncanny ability to anticipate. I didn't know how long Fredo would stay with us, but as the days passed I watched his comfort grow and he was no longer flinching at every loud noise and bursting into tears afterward. I suspected the man had far more to put behind him than we knew. I had no doubt that having him here with Luca was good for the both of them. Luca was able to revisit his time with Cesare, and Fredo became a happy connection to those better memories rather than the horror of the last.

And to put our recent misery to rest, Ellie eagerly combed the Times for news of Bruno. Sure enough, not four days after our drama, she'd read:

> The body of a man in his late fifties was found bound and gagged, and stuffed into a sailor's duffle sack in the vicinity of Blackfriar near Fleet Street Saturday morning. Very recently he had been savagely beaten to death. By the cut and quality of his clothing and the coat of arms embroidered on his inner coat pocket, the victim had been a man of some standing. Inspector Clarence Hyde-White of Scotland Yard questioned local residents but was unable to determine the identity of the perpetrator or perpetrators.
>
> Inspector Hyde-White was quoted as saying, 'A coin of

Italian origin was found in the man's pocket, and brings to mind our two Italian Richard Roes: those unknowns whose bodies were discovered in Charing Cross and in the West End four and five weeks ago. It is my opinion that what we are seeing are heinous crimes against foreign-born men.' Scotland Yard assures the public this is nothing to be concerned about, but highly recommends persons of foreign origin be especially wary when out at night. Anyone with information is asked to contact Scotland Yard.

Save for the fact we'd thought him dead once before and were proved wrong, this news would greatly put our minds at ease. Needing to know once and forever, we sent Will to the Bishop's Moke. Alfred confirmed it. I had to wonder what had transpired over the four days from the time we'd dropped him off and the morning he was found. A painting by Hans von Aachen came to mind: *The Triumph of Justice*. In it Dike, Lady Justice herself, watched impassively as a lion devoured a man. Until Venice, I'd never considered myself a violent man, but in my heart I knew that I too could stand the impassive witness to that man's demise.

Bruno hadn't been beaten short of death as Celso had; rather he was served blind justice. Put in a sack like a wharf rat, Bruno was pummeled by a half-dozen men, and every man involved never knew for certain if he dealt the final blow. According to Will, this way a man's conscience was kept clear. The man who'd taken Thom from us all would never hurt another soul. Thinking of Thom, I heard his last words to me, "I love you, Nic. Do you know that? Always have."

I turned my horse around to face Halstead. The manor's white stone glowed against the backdrop of a charcoal gray sky. Eighteen chimney spires lit like a candelabra the dying light of day. I closed my eyes and pushed my last image of my dearest friend from my mind. Instead I saw Thom here at Halstead. I saw him nattily dressed in full livery, smiling at me. What a handsome, winsome fellow, my Thom. Lord, how I missed him. "I love you Thom, always have loved you. Rest easy."

***

I returned home to the window alight upstairs. I smiled seeing it, for it meant Luca and Ellie were still awake. I found Ellie in bed with Leonardo's book and her sketches. Luca was sitting beside her. I said, "Aren't you both a sight for a weary traveler?"

Ellie gave me a lovely smile. "I was beginning to think you'd stayed the night."

"As was I. Grannie insisted I stay to dine."

Luca chuckled.

"It took several hours to relay the scuttlebutt of Bath, don't you know. The place is a shameless hive of buzzing gossip. She sends her best, by the way. "

Ellie laughed, "Then I am sorry I missed it. Grannie's tales are better than any penny dreadful I've read. I've always wanted to see the temple of Aquae Sulis."

I relayed to them the tale of my experience there as a child, and told of the well-known artists who lived and worked there over the centuries, including Thomas Gainsborough, William Hogarth, and Sir Thomas Lawrence. It was settled. We'd take a short holiday as soon as Luca's wounds fully closed. I hoped that would be soon, for he was bound for Malta in March.

I quickly divested myself of my clothing and with Luca's help, my riding boots as well. Ellie winced when scooting over to make room for us. For the most part, the tenderness had abated. Now and then, she'd move the wrong way and feel it again. I joined her on the bed. She squeaked. "Ooh, Nicolas! Your feet are ice cold!"

Of course I had to press them against her. I loved that squeak and she'd warmed the bed so well. Laughing, Luca gingerly eased into bed with a slight groan, his inner discomfort no doubt met with ancillary pain from the carbolic acid burns on his skin. Together we flanked her.

In an attempt to regain our threads of insight, we'd spent the last three nights poring over Leonardo's book from the beginning. In following the mind of Leonardo and his messages intended for Salai alone, we knew we'd been given a gift. Coming at last to the winged phalluses flying to the window near a sleeping Salai, we saw the rocks of Tuscany in the distance. This was where we were when tragedy found us.

Ellie traced a finger over the sketch she'd made of their findings on *The Virgin of the Rocks* at the Louvre. "It was just there in the grotto, backward, and in Latin." She flipped through several pages in her sketch book. "*Fiddlesticks!* Oh, Nicolas, I was so worried about you, I completely forgot to write down the words."

Luca chuckled. "I remember them, *caro*."

"What did it say?"

Ellie readied her pencil.

"A marvelous thing within."

I repeated it. As if Leonardo spoke to my mind, I saw what the artist saw. Leonardo made many excursions to the caves of northern Italy. His journals contained several awe-inspired descriptions of Tuscany's geological formations. He once came upon what he referred to as a curious cave, and wrote of it,

Drawn by my eager desire I wandered some way among gloomy rocks, coming to the entrance of a great cavern, in front of which I stood for some time, stupefied and uncomprehending such a thing… Suddenly two things arose in me, fear and desire: fear of the menacing darkness of the cavern; desire to see if there was any marvelous thing within.

Metaphor appeared in my mind's eye. Love was like this. The power of it left you stupefied and uncomprehending. It left you vulnerable and fearful of heartache. But we couldn't help but venture into the cave, for we desired that marvelous thing within. These words literally described his entire life and how he loved. How well he described us.

~Fin~

AUTHOR'S NOTE

In my unusual love story, I wanted to convey how love has no boundaries. The heart really doesn't have control over who it has you fall in love with, like, dislike, or loath. We just do. The reader will see this theme repeated throughout in many different ways, both subtle and blatant. In my opinion, as someone who has been lucky in love, if consenting adults wish to commit to their love for one another, who am I or anyone to say they can't? Society needs loving commitment. Our world needs the harmonious vibration of love.

***

The main observer in this romantic tale is Nicolas Halstead, a man of means who has only recently come to discover profound truths about himself. It is through his perspective that we see and feel his Victorian world. An art historian by profession, Nicolas regularly compares life to art. Because of this, he leaves many references to artists and artworks scattered throughout the pages. These weren't artworks randomly chosen off a list when I wrote the tale. They were carefully-considered art references placed to convey Nicolas' thoughts, feelings, and impressions in a given moment. All art is emotion, and Nicolas wears his heart upon his sleeve. It isn't necessary for the reader to look up each artist or artwork, though to see what Nicolas sees will certainly add color to the tale. I hope you enjoy.

Nicolas, Ellie, and Luca may return for other adventures. If you have thoughts or ideas where they might journey next, do drop me a line at http://calliopeswritingtablet.com/

Where might an Art Historian, a Suffragette, and a Historian go? The Victorian world is wide open, and the sun never sets on the British Empire.

ABOUT ROSE

Rose loves descriptive words and chooses them as carefully as an artist might choose a color. Her active imagination compels her to write everything from children's stories to historical nonfiction. As a self-described persnickety leisure reader, she especially enjoys novels that feel like they were written just for her. "It's hard to explain, but if you have ever read one of those, then you'll know what I mean. I tend to sneak symbolism and metaphor into my writing. You might say it's a game I play with myself when I write. I so love when readers email to say they've found something." Rose likes people to feel her stories were written just for them, for that's the truth. These hidden insights are her gift to her readers.

To find out more about Rose and what she has in store, she invites you to visit her blog for updates, thoughts, and discoveries. She would love to hear from you and endeavors to answer questions and comments in turn.

http://calliopeswritingtablet.com/

Have Rose autograph your ebook.

http://www.authorgraph.com/authors/RoseAnderson

More Titles from Rose Anderson

Enchanted Skye

The Witchy Wolf and the Wendigo - Book 1: Ashkewheteasu

The Witchy Wolf and the Wendigo – Book 2: Eluwilussit

Loving Leonardo

Loving Leonardo – The Quest

Dreamscape

Hermes Online

To find these and other exciting books, please visit Indie Artist Press at http://www.indieartistpress.com.

Indie Artist Press –
Uniting Indie Authors with Discerning Readers, Every Day!

Indie Artist Press
Eagle Mountain, Utah
www.indieartistpress.com

www.ingramcontent.com/pod-product-compliance
Lightning Source LLC
Chambersburg PA
CBHW030541020726
47494CB00005B/1442